Happenstance

Carol Shields is the author of ten novels and three collections of short stories. *The Stone Diaries* won the Pulitzer Prize and was shortlisted for the Booker Prize. *Larry's Party* won the Orange Prize and *Unless* was shortlisted for the 2002 Man Booker Prize. Born and brought up in Chicago, Carol Shields has lived in Canada since 1957.

For more information on Carol Shields' *Happenstance* and to download a reading guide, visit www.4thestate.com/carolshields

'Carol Shields is an acute recorder of contemporary mores, the detail of her observations flawless, *Happenstance* resounds with a humanity and a generosity that is truly memorable.'
Daily Telegraph

'The biggest pleasure remains Shields' prose, at once dense and delicate. Her great strength is her ability to capture small moments and make them important . . . Shields displays in her careful delineation of her characters a tenderness of the ordinary which shines through the sheer cleverness of her work.'
Literary Review

'I highly recommend *Happenstance*. Both stories are funny – but compassionately so. Crucially, Carol Shields allows all the characters dignity. This is a tender, lovely book, about people who need each other. It is also superbly told.'
Marie Claire

'Working with energetic brio, Shields organises dazzling contracts of hilariousness and subtlety, high comedy and sombre complexity . . . she has constructed her work with the authentic independence of an important writer.'
Times Literary Supplement

THE WORK OF CAROL SHIELDS

POETRY

Others
Intersect
Coming to Canada

NOVELS

Larry's Party
The Stone Diaries
The Republic of Love
A Celibate Season (with Blanche Howard)
Mary Swann
A Fairly Conventional Woman
Happenstance
The Box Garden
Small Ceremonies
Unless

STORY COLLECTIONS

Dressing Up for the Carnival
The Orange Fish
Various Miracles

PLAYS

Departures and Arrivals
Thirteen Hands
Fashion, Power, Guilt and the Charity of Families (with Catherine Shields)
Anniversary (with David Williamson)

CRITICISM

Susanna Moodie: Voice and Vision

ANTHOLOGY

Dropped Threads: What We Aren't Told (Edited with Marjorie Anderson)
Dropped Threads 2: More of What We Aren't Told
(Edited with Marjorie Anderson)

BIOGRAPHY

Jane Austen: A Penguin Lives Biography

CAROL SHIELDS

Happenstance

FOURTH ESTATE • *London*

For Catherine Mary Shields

This paperback edition first published in 2003
First published in Great Britain in 1991 by
Fourth Estate
A Division of HarperCollins*Publishers*
77–85 Fulham Palace Road
London W6 8JB
www.4thestate.com

10 9 8 7 6 5 4 3 2 1

Happenstance, The Husband's Story was first published as
Happenstance in Canada by McGraw-Hill Ryerson, 1980;
Happenstance, The Wife's Story was first published as
A Fairly Conventional Woman in Canada
by Macmillan of Canada, 1982.

A catalogue record for this book is available from the
British Library

ISBN 1-84115-468-7

Printed in Great Britain by Clays Ltd, St Ives plc

The Husband's Story

Chapter One

A T THE RESTAURANT JACK WANTED TO TELL BERNIE ABOUT Harriet Post, a girl he had once been in love with. He wanted to put his head down on the table and moan aloud with rage. Instead he placed his fork into a square of ravioli and said in a moderate tone, 'History consists of endings.'

Bernie was not really listening; he was removed today, empty-eyed and vague, pulling at a dry wedge of bread and looking out the window on to the street, where a cold rain was falling. For almost a year now the topic of their Friday lunches had been the defining of history; what was it? What was it for? It occurred to Jack that perhaps Bernie had had enough of history. Enough is enough, as Brenda, his wife, would say.

'History is eschatological,' Jack said. He stabbed into his small side salad of lettuce, onions, celery, and radishes. 'History is not the mere unrolling of a story. And it's not the story itself. It's the end of the story.'

'Uhuh.' Bernie's eyes turned again toward the curtainless square of window, made doubly opaque by the streaming rainwater and by the inner coating of cooking grease. 'And when,' he asked, chewing on a wad of bread, 'did you decide all this?'

'Yesterday. Last night. About midnight. It came to me, the final meaning of history. I've finally stumbled on what it's all about. Endings.'

'Endings?'

'Yes, endings.'

'A bolt out of the blue?' Bernie said.

'You might say that. Or you could call it an empirical thrust.'

Bernie smirked openly.

'Go ahead,' Jack said. 'Laugh if you want to. I'm serious for a change.'

'For a change.'

'History is no more than the human recognition of endings. History – now listen, Bernie – history is putting a thumbprint on

1

a glass wall so you can see the wall. The conclusion of an era which defines and invents the era.'

'I get the feeling you've rehearsed this. While you were shaving this morning, maybe.'

'Let me ask you this, Bernie. What do we remember about history? No, never mind *us* – what does the man on the street remember about the past?'

'I *am* a man on the street. You tell me.'

'We remember the treaties, but not the wars. Am I right? Admit it. We remember the beheadings, but not the rebellions. It's that final cataclysmic act that we instinctively select and store away. You might say, ' he paused, 'that the ends of all stories are contained in their beginnings.'

'It's already been said, I think. Didn't Eliot – ?'

'But the ending *is* the story. Not just the signature. Take the French Revolution – '

'We've taken that. A number of times.' Bernie sat back, groggy after his veal and noodles. 'We took the French Revolution last week. And the week before that. Remember that session you gave me about the French Revolution two weeks ago? About the great libertine infusion? Rammed into Europe's flabby old buttocks?'

'Not true.' Jack pushed his plate away, belching silently; a gas pain shot across his heart. After twenty years the food at Roberto's was worse, not better – it was a miracle they'd managed to stay in business – and the old neighbourhood around the Institute, with its knocked-apart streets and boarded-up shirt laundries and hustling porn shops, was shifting from the decent shade of decay that had prevailed during the sixties to something more menacing. These days violence threatened, even in the daytime; and disease, too – someone or other had told him at a party the weekend before that you could get hepatitis from eating off cracked plates, and God knows what else. Furthermore, Jack had grown to dread the starchy monotony of Italian food; everything about it now, its wet weak uniformity of texture and its casual, moist presentation – the sight and smell of it made his heart plunge and squeeze. Was there really a time, he asked himself – of course there had been – when Italian food, even the fake Chicago variety, had seemed a passport to worldliness? Worldliness, ha! When the mere words – cannelloni, gnocchi, lasagna – had brimmed with rich, steamy eroticism? All you had to do was plunge your fork through the waiting, melting mozzarella and you were there, ah!

In 1958, Jack Bowman had eaten his first pizza at Roberto's, probably at this very table. Mushroom and green pepper. Bernie Koltz had been with him; it was the first pizza of their lives; neither of them could understand how this had happened. Jack was twenty-two years old, about to be married to Brenda Pulaski. The pizza – it was called *pizza pie* on the menu – arrived on a circle of pulpy cardboard, a glistening crimson pinwheel flecked with gold and green. Were they supposed to eat it with a fork? Neither knew. They had pondered the point, mock philosophically, until a comic courage seized them, and they had picked it up like a sandwich in young, decent, untrembling WASP fingers. The taste was a disappointment, catsup on piecrust, viscoid and undercooked, although neither of them remarked on it at the time.

In all probability, Jack thought, Bernie was fed up with Roberto's too. There was his ulcer to consider; these days Bernie automatically ordered the mildest dish on the menu and made at least a tentative effort to cut down on the wine. For some time Jack had wanted to announce, boldly, that they could both afford more than $6.25 for lunch these days; Bernie had tenure now (although Jack assumed, from Bernie's silence on the subject, that his promotion to full professor was not to be, not this year, anyway); Jack was slated to be Curator of Explorations at the Institute – it could happen any day now. They deserved better than these greasy menus and this lousy New York State wine, served in sticky glass carafes with bubbled sides; they should be kinder to themselves, move up a notch – nostalgia wasn't everything – and find a place where the tablecloths got washed and where the waiters looked less like hit men. There was food colouring, probably carcinogenic, in the spaghetti sauce – Jack could tell by the indelible pink swirls impregnated on the smooth moon surfaces of Roberto's lunch plates. On Fridays the place swarmed with wide-bottomed secretaries and sorrowing, introspective student lovers; it pained Jack to see how readily these lovers accepted the illuminated mural of the Po Valley on the back wall. It was time for a change, Jack had been on the point of saying to him. But he hadn't done it.

3

Something always stopped him. Bernie might balk; he could be difficult; he had always been somewhat prickly, and just beneath his pale, neutral, abstract freckledness lay an unpredictable populism. *So you're too good for the old proletarian hangout,* Bernie might think (but never say). *So now that you and Brenda and the kids have entrenched yourselves out there in Elm Park, you're hankering for something a little more country-clubby, huh?* Bernie's moods of grouchy unreasonableness had simmered and sputtered along for years, beginning, Jack thought, about the time Bernie's wife Sue decided to go back to medical school. But lately these moods had become more frequent – Jack wasn't the only one who'd noticed. Bernie preened his pessimism now. Brenda thought he'd behaved erratically when she saw him late in the summer; something he'd said or done, she hadn't been able to put her finger on it, but something was wrong. There didn't seem to be any single cause, although it might be any of the half-dozen phantoms that flickered at the back of Bernie's life – his stalled career, his wife Sue, his retarded daughter at Charleston Hospital. (Jack, who had his own set of free-swimming phantoms – who didn't? – could understand that.)

Whatever the root of Bernie's malaise, it was beginning to erode the old Friday spirit; the lunches – and Jack found the fact painful to face – were losing their old intensity. Sometimes, after summing up a crucial point, he had had the sick, dizzy sensation that the same point had been covered back in '75 or '68 or even '59. In mid-phrase his mouth stopped moving, frozen solid and self-conscious, stuck on a multiple memory track, gone gummy with overuse. Or worse, he heard his voice plumping up with an over-ripened, artificial passion that might have been seemly at twenty-two, but that at forty-three lacked moderation and civility and the *au point* Johnsonian balance he vaguely aspired to. And hadn't the old analytical machinery been more cleanly classical, more firmly grasped and more fruitful in the past? The year he and Bernie had discussed entropy, they'd managed to carve it up, beautifully, without all this rhetoric and false claiming of territory; it had fallen open for them with an open-throated, almost Grecian grace, slowly, mathematically, like a flower; he had *loved* entropy. *Bernie* had loved entropy, leaping in with the razzle-dazzle of a gymnast, a magician, glittering as he sprang from point to point. Democracy had prospered, too – they'd spent a year on democracy, June to June, 1965? – and the death of God, which started off slowly, but eventually led to scattered moments of near clarity – at least they'd gone into it bravely enough, unbothered by the chilly prevailing shadow of so-called experts, Tillich, Barth. But Watergate and the attendant moral compromises of America had occupied them a mere six moths, and now, with the concept of history – and Jack recalled that the topic had been Bernie's suggestion, not his – they seemed to have lost their way, making do with old arguments, retreaded, weary, occasionally corrupt. Sometimes Jack felt that they were simply reciting, and not very accurately, from under-graduate text-books: *A Survey Course in Fundamental Philosophy*. Clearly the Friday lunches had arrived at a shaky period, a critical period, and what worried Jack was that a change of venue at this moment might just signal the end – and that was one thing he didn't want to think about.

'Look,' he said to Bernie, enriching his voice with fervour, cringing to hear the squeaky tenor he struck, 'historians in the past have thought of history as a continuum. And we haven't been able to see what was patently obvious.'

'We?' Bernie knocked his head back, a cord of defence plinked.

'Universal we. Us. All of us, not just historians. It's our curse to overlook beginnings. Beginnings just don't register because we're locked into our vision of the status quo. We can't even be bothered to acknowledge the feeble stirrings – '

'You're not suggesting,' Bernie said, for a moment flashing his old Friday tone of false scorning, 'that no one acknowledged the storming of the Bastille?'

'Let's just say they didn't know what it signified.' Jack paused, shifting his legs under the table. 'It wasn't until a few heads dropped on the floor that anyone saw where it was all leading. And that,' he cut the air deftly with the side of his hand, a gesture he'd learned from long association with Dr. Middle-ton, 'that was history.'

'Hmmmm.'

'Maybe the French Revolution isn't such a good example, though. Too episodic. Take the steam engine – '

'Again?'

'When the steam engine was first demonstrated, no one

stood up and yelled out the big news that the Industrial Revolution had commenced – '

'Please, Jack. Please don't give me the Industrial Revolution today.'

'What's eating you, Bernie?'

'Didn't we agree not to call the Industrial Revolution a revolution?'

'Did we?' Jack asked.

'We agreed, remember, it was too poetic. Too cute, too much bottled-history stink to it. And it's a lousy example, anyway. It's too undefined. Just for once, give me something with edges.'

'All right,' Jack said. 'All right. I will. Remember I said this all came to me last night, about history consisting of endings?'

'So what happened last night?' Bernie asked.

'Well, let me go back a minute. Do you by any chance remember someone called Harriet Post?'

'Harriet. I haven't heard you talk about Harriet for years.'

'You *do* remember Harriet Post then?'

'Of course I remember Harriet Post. How could I forget Harriet Post?' A glutinous softening touched the sides of Bernie's face, his first smile of the day.

'It's been twenty-one years,' Jack said. 'I thought you'd have forgotten who Harriet was.'

'What about her? Isn't she in New York somewhere?'

'Rochester.'

'University of?'

'I don't think so. I don't know.'

'Well,' Bernie waited, showing impatience, 'you were saying – ?'

'She's written a book.'

'A book? I'll be damned. Good old Harriet. I'll bet there's lots of sex in it. I remember she had the thinnest little backside on any woman I've ever seen. I wonder if time's been kind to poor old Harriet's backside – '

'It's not a novel. And it isn't actually out yet. But it's been announced. In the new issue of the *Journal*. Which came in the mail yesterday.'

'*The Historical Journal*?'

'In the back. Where they have the forthcoming books section.'

'What do you know,' Bernie said with rising, almost subcutaneous excitement. 'Harriet also had very very strange tits. Very.

6

Ball bearings swinging around inside. Wasn't she in history, too?'

'I'm coming to that. The title of the book – of Harriet's book – are you listening? – is *Indian Trading Practices Prior to Colonization*.'

'Christ!' Bernie jerked upright and sucked for air. 'I don't believe it.'

There was a short silence, during which Jack drummed his fingers on the stained tablecloth and regarded Bernie's face. Outside on the street a car honked. In Roberto's back kitchen there was a minor crash of silverware.

Bernie swirled his crust of bread rapidly around his plate. 'Christ,' he moaned softly, his mouth loosening into a soft raspberry of helplessness. 'Christ.' He had a pale, witty, triangular face; there was a folded precision about his eyes, and his mouth was awkward in a sometimes touching way; women found him appealing, perhaps because of an inner ungainliness, the psychic equivalent of buck teeth or bowleggedness. A swamp of shyness dragged at him. 'All short men are like that,' Brenda once told Jack, 'especially short men with red hair.'

'You know,' Bernie said at last, working to get the words past his lips, 'it could be,' he paused again, 'that Harriet took a completely different tack than you.'

'But two books in one year, Bernie? In the same general – ' Jack stopped; a sigh sliced his breath in two.

'You never know these days, everything is so much more specialized than it used to be – '

'I did think of contacting her.' Jack fixed his eyes on Bernie. 'You know, phone her at Rochester. Out of the blue?'

'Well, why not?'

'No.' He shook his head. 'Well, maybe. But I don't think so.'

'The bitch. To tell you the truth, I never could see what you saw in Harriet Post. Those little tin tits –'

'Six hundred pages, it said in the announcement. Also maps, charts, and rare woodcuts. Rare woodcuts *never before published*.' Jack reached for the carafe and refilled Bernie's glass; pouring wine, even at Roberto's, never failed to give him stirrings of power and pleasure.

'When's it coming out?' Bernie demanded. He was alert now, intense.

'All it said was "summer publication".'

'Well, Christ, it's only January. Couldn't you, if you really stepped on it – ?'

'Not a hope. I mean, let's not kid ourselves, it's taken me years to get this far. It'll be another eight months just to get to proof stage. That's if I'm lucky. And I sure as hell don't have any rare woodcuts – '

'But it's possible.' Bernie's eyes gleamed golden under his fuzzed cinnamon halo. 'You have to admit it's within the realm of possibility.'

'Even if I could manage it – '

'We used to call her Sex Kit,' Bernie remembered. (Jack saw this diversion for what it was, a kindness.) 'After Eartha Kitt, I suppose. Though, if you want the truth, Jack,' his eyes narrowed, 'I never believed she was as sexy as she was cracked up to be.'

'She was.'

'That was before Brenda?'

'Just before.'

'It all comes back,' Bernie said.

'Like a bad dream. It wasn't, though, as a matter of fact. A bad dream, that is.'

Bernie nodded and chewed his lip; his fingers, lean but with wide pads, massaged the stem of his glass, and his eyes softened perceptively. 'About history – ' he prompted.

'Right,' Jack said, straightening, 'back to history. Where was I? When I saw that notice about Harriet's book, it came to me.'

'What?'

'That this is where it's ended. The whole thing with Harriet Post. Here she was, my first – well – lay. And now the ending.'

'Ending? I don't follow.'

'The ending is Harriet jumping me to a book twenty long years later.'

'I still don't see exactly – '

'It's an ending. A nice clean fatalistic conclusion. Lifted from the matrix – if you want to call it that – of what we can now recognize as the beginning and the middle.'

'I'm afraid I just can't see any cause-effect relationship between some ancient college screwing and the publication of a book on Indian trading practices twenty years – '

'Aha! But who said anything about cause and effect?'

'If there's no direct relationship, Jack, then what's the point?'

'There are other relationships,' he heard his voice ringing coolly, 'besides cause and effect.'

'My God, you're not going to be mystical and religious, are you, Jack?'

'Look. It's simple really. Here I've been grinding away at this Indian thing for years. And all the time she's been up to the same thing. Do you call that coincidence? Or do you call it historical destiny?'

'Destiny! Do you know something, Jack? That's a word I never thought I'd hear from you.'

' – and now the visible result. The ending. History.'

Bernie polished off his wine, licking the rim of his glass with the tip of his tongue. 'As a theory, isn't this a little on the surreal side? I mean, there are no real beginnings and endings. Mathematically speaking.'

'Maybe.' Jack eyed the drizzle of rain on the window.

'Anyway, it's lousy luck.'

'And if there's one thing I know it's that you don't pick a quarrel with history. You can't fight history.'

'Do you really believe that?' Bernie said, his head to one side and his hands spread in a lopsided Y. 'Or is that something you just this minute thought up?'

'I don't know. In a way I think I do believe it.'

'Well, do you know what I think?' Bernie said. 'I think your theory is a pile of horse shit.' But he spoke slowly, with compassion, bringing his fist down on the table so hard that the plates jumped.

Chapter Two

IT WAS JACK'S BELIEF THAT MEN SPEND WHOLE LIFETIMES preparing answers to certain questions that will never be asked of them. They long, passionately, to hear these questions, not wanting their careful preparation wasted. It was not judgment or redemption that was hoped for, but the experience of showing another human being that private and serious part of the mind that ticked away in obscurity. A wish to be *known*. And what they most desire is the moment when the stranger at the cocktail party (or the woman in the elevator or the man behind the bar) turns to them and asks, are you a happy man?

Happy? Happiness? Happiness is relative, Jack was ready to say (with an agreeable shrug); within the framework of relativity, he is a happy, or at least a fortunate, man. Pure happenstance had made him into a man without serious impairment or unspeakable losses. Evidence? There was a shelf full of evidence. He was healthy and solvent – solvency in the year 1978 was not to be despised. He was married to Brenda; how many marriages had lasted as long as theirs? He had only to look around him to see how rare that was. His children were reasonably normal. *Reasonably*: so far at least they'd remained untouched by drugs, shoplifting, truancy, and the other adolescent ills he read about every day in the paper. He loved his father and mother, who lived only a few miles away, and they loved him, although Jack acknowledged that their love, like all parental love, was composed of a number of darker feelings. He had one good friend, Bernie Koltz. His life had its particular rhythms and satisfactions. He owned his own house in Elm Park, which was now valued at an astronomical eighty thousand dollars, and worked on the staff at the Great Lakes Research Institute, the Chicago branch.

Certainly, as far as work went, there were worse lives, thousands of them. There was a neighbour of his, Bud Lewis, who worked in chemical sales and received a monthly rating from his firm. Sometimes he was number one; sometimes twenty-seven. There was his own father: forty years of standing all day in rubber-soled shoes, sorting letters into little wooden slots; retirement at sixty had been a deliverance. And occasionally when Jack was driving back and forth to the Institute he saw work gangs tearing up the streets; they worked right through the winter, these short, dark-faced, thick-chested men in their hard hats and padded jackets, hands reddened by wind, and feet heavy and inhuman in laced boots – where did such boots come from, he wondered? The bodies of these men under their stiff mud-caked workclothes seemed to Jack to be both wretched and nameless. But, of course, they weren't nameless; this was America, each of them carried a Social Security card, it was the law. Why then could he not imagine the streets and rooms where these men returned at the end of their working day? (He taunted himself with his lack of knowing.) He wondered if there would be food waiting for them, what sort of food? Would there be furniture of a familiar and accommodating sort? music of some kind? an ease of language that allowed greetings and disclosures? children? Of course – these things *must* exist. It was only some perceptual failure of his own that kept him from knowing. There must be women, too (what manner of women?) who stroked these men's bodies into forgetfulness and ecstasy before they rose to another day – 6 AM, darkness. Over and over again, Holy Christ. There would be a revolution – Jack felt sure of it – if even one of these chilled roughened workmen were to discover how he, Jack Bowman, put in his days. The softness, the security, the comfort, it was incredible, they would be goggle-eyed, they would chop him to pieces with their picks and shovels, the French Revolution all over again, and he wouldn't blame them. Sometimes, driving to work and catching glimpses of these men, he heard himself murmuring into the warm interior of the car, thank God, thank God. It had to be some kind of joke.

Here in his small corner office, the smooth walls hung with framed prints and diplomas and a photograph of Brenda and the children, he was allowed to pass entire mornings grazing on sets of footnotes or collating the latest journals, fulfilling the first commandment of the Institute, which was: Do not produce, but keep up in your field. This place was no less than a bloody sanctuary. Walk through the plate glass door downstairs and you were in another world; even Dr. Middleton, with his thickly planted, lushly growing civility, admitted it. Here there was a premium placed on lassitude, an assumption that leisure, far from being shameful, constituted the primary condition for inquiry. No five-year plans around here, and no questions asked. An occasional low-key exhibition, with the public invited; the *public* – that was another joke. Monthly meetings in the boardroom where a few items of business were disposed of. Jack could not imagine how it had happened to him – this privacy, this privilege; no clocks to punch; no timesheets to fill out – somehow, by some accident of fate, he had fallen into a job that matched almost exactly his temperament; let others scramble and scratch and change the shape of the world – all that was required of him was that he record and chart the flow of events.

Not that it was a particularly luxurious life. He'd known from the beginning that he would never be rich, not even wealthy. The low-lined sportscars he dreamed of – a particular dark red Ferrari swam into view – would in fact never materialize. Even the sixty-dollar suede vest he'd bought recently had been an extravagance. There was a ceiling now on the salaries of non-Ph.D. men. Non-Ph.D. men, in fact, were no longer considered for permanent appointments. When Jack travelled to Detroit or Milwaukee or Cleveland on behalf of the Institute to attend conferences or present papers, he was obliged to travel tourist class and, later, to hand over to Moira Burke the stapled receipts for his meals and taxis. (An endowment committee, Chicago meat-packing money mostly, examined Institute expenses twice a year.) He shared a secretary, away now on vacation in Colorado, with two other staff members, Calvin White in Geology and Brian Petrie in Cultural Anthropology. His office was small and modest, really more of a cubicle in a line of cubicles: industrial carpeting in medium grey, and a metal desk (only Dr. Middleton had a desk of distinction – mahogany, antique, immense.) The lighting at the Institute was blinding: a universalized whiteness that seemed to have no source. Jack's desk chair was standard issue, although comfortable enough; occasionally, returning from Roberto's on Friday afternoons, he had actually fallen asleep in that chair. There was only one window, curtainless, but with a neat Venetian blind; it overlooked Keeley Avenue, which was wide, ugly, and busy with traffic.

Dr. Middleton's office, which had an outer reception area for Moira Burke, was larger than Jack's or Calvin White's or Brian

Petrie's, larger and better located, positioned at the far north end of the building overlooking a tiny, soot-green park. If you craned your neck you could see a slice of Lake Michigan floating on the horizon. The grey carpeting ended at Dr. Middleton's threshold, giving way to a width of polished wood and a rich busy Indian carpet in tones of rose and blue. Jack stared down at this carpet, breathing in the cleanly filtered air, waiting for Dr. Middleton to get back from lunch.

'He should be here any minute.' Moira Burke told him. 'Why don't you sit down and wait.'

He looked at her closely, still a little wobbly from the wine. She smiled back cheerfully, and he remembered that Monday would be her last day; she and her husband were retiring to Arizona. 'The last lap,' Jack said to her conversationally. 'How does it feel?'

'Half and half,' she answered. She was polishing Dr. Middleton's oak bookshelves with an oiled cloth.

Jack looked at her quizzically. Moira had a good figure, a firm behind. Thick dark hair. In fact, she was a fairly good-looking woman. For her age. Fifty-five? In twelve years *he'd* be fifty-five.

'Half-glad, half-sad,' Moira said. 'I'm going to miss this –' she stopped and gestured comically with her cloth, 'this joint.'

'But half-glad, too?'

'Oh, sure. Bradley's ready for a change. I guess we all need a change. I've been here so long I feel like part of the furniture.'

Was this a cue? It was said by Brian Petrie and others that Moira could be touchy. 'I'm sure no one here ever thinks of you as part of the furniture,' he told her.

'Hmm.' She straightened a book, glanced at her watch. 'I don't know what's keeping him. He's usually back by two. Must've got held up. This crummy rain.'

'Well, that's one thing you won't have to worry about in Phoenix.'

'Tucson.'

'That's right. I forgot.'

'That's what I mean.' She turned to face him. 'About being a part of the furniture around here.'

Jack was shocked into silence. What exactly had he said? 'Moira. I'm sorry. I remember now it was Tucson.'

Moira's eyes filmed over, and she shook her head violently.

13

The gold chains around her throat flashed. 'Just nerves,' she told Jack apologetically, managing a smile. 'Getting Mel trained for the job. It's taken a helluva lot out of me.'

Jack nodded. Moira's job was being filled by a young man with with shoulder-length golden hair. Dr. Middleton had announced the appointment at the last staff meeting. Male secretaries were coming back, he told them, an example of history repeating itself, back to the eighteenth century.

'I've been on edge lately. Putting the house on the market, you know what it's like.'

'Of course.' He hadn't realized Moira owned a house.

'Just my nutty nervous system.' She dabbed at her eyes.

'Can I get you something, Moira? Some coffee from the machine?'

'I'm fine. Fine.' She looked at her watch. 'I'm sure he'll be along in a minute. Any minute now.'

'I could leave it for Monday morning. I've got an appointment with him for ten-thirty on Monday. About the new chapter I'm working on.'

'I can give him a message when he comes in. Was it something urgent?'

Jack had brought along the new issue of the *Journal*. He wanted to point out to Dr. Middleton the note at the back about Harriet Post's book. Have you seen this, he had intended to ask, waiting for Dr. Middleton's calm, philosophical, transforming response, longing to hear him brush this catastrophe aside, to tell him how inconsequential this Harriet Post undoubtedly was. A housewife dissertation – he had once heard Dr. Middleton use that very phrase. But Dr. Middleton was still out for lunch; he might be another hour or two. Fridays at the Institute were traditionally relaxed.

'Well?' Moira said.

'It's nothing that can't wait.'

'By the way, your wife called this morning.'

'Brenda?'

'I left a memo on your desk. I guess you missed it.'

'I was out for lunch. I just got back.'

'That's right, you go out Fridays, don't you? Your wife just wanted to remind you to pick up some tickets. She said you'd know about it.'

'The tickets, yes, well, thanks, Moira.'

'Have a good weekend.'

'You too. I mean it.'

Chapter Three

Tickets: despite Brenda's reminder, Jack had forgotten to pick up the tickets for Friday night. They were eating dinner in the dining room, halibut steaks with zucchini and mushrooms, when he remembered.

'I'm too beat to go, anyway,' Brenda said. She was expecting her period, and besides, she was going to Philadelphia in the morning; she'd spent all day packing. 'I'd just as soon skip it.'

'Are you sure?' Jack asked her, helping himself to salad. 'Tonight's the last night.'

'I'm sure.'

Thank God, Jack thought. He and Brenda went dutifully to all the Elm Park Little Theatre productions, but he wasn't in the mood for *Hamlet*. Not tonight. The seats were rock-hard – the Little Theatre had taken over the old gym at Roosevelt School – and someone had told Jack that Larry Carpenter was a lousy Hamlet: he overacted, overreached, hogged the stage, just what you'd expect.

'What if Mr. Carpenter wants to know how you liked the show?' his daughter Laurie asked him. She had just turned twelve and had a twelve-year-old's knack for spotting future embarrassments.

'That guy's a turkey, anyway,' Rob announced.

'And what do you mean by that?' Jack looked at his son sharply, took in his slovenly adolescent posture and the arch theatricality with which he tossed back his long dark hair. Jack thought: once I loved this boy.

'The guy's a jerk,' Rob said sullenly, staring at his fork.

And just who the hell do you think *you* are, Jack wanted to yell. He had no love himself for Larry Carpenter, but he hated the shallowness of his son's bombarding judgments. And he could easily imagine that he himself fared no better than Larry Carpenter in this boy's eyes – my old man's nothing but a stupid jerk, a royal prick.

'I like him,' Laurie said anxiously. 'Sort of.'

16

'He thinks he's such a dude. Hot-shot newspaper guy. Zapping around in that Porsche. Like the way he squeals into the driveway.'

Ah, jealousy; Jack might have known; Larry Carpenter next door with a brand new Porsche and he with his three-year-old Aspen. Pure jealousy. Or was Rob, in some clumsy way, being protective? Probably not.

'What'll you say when he asks you about the show?' Laurie asked again.

'We'll think of something,' Brenda said. Her eyes were cool and unclouded – tomorrow she'll have left all this far behind. Lucky Brenda.

'This crummy fish is dry,' Rob said. 'Why do we have to have fish all the time?'

'Mine's not dry,' Laurie said.

'Have some tartar sauce.' Brenda handed him a bowl.

'It's got mould on it.'

'That's parsley,' Brenda said. Such calmness; how did she do it? Couldn't she see that at fourteen Rob's behaviour had become intolerable? It's just a phase, Brenda said. He'll grow out of it. When?

The problem was, his children didn't appreciate how lucky they were. They were strong and healthy; did they ever stop to compare their health and intelligence with that of Bernie's daughter Sarah, a vegetable in the vegetable bin at Charleston Hospital? His children had three square meals a day, parents who were liberal and caring, a real roof over their heads. Whereas he and Brenda had both grown up in city apartments, Brenda and her mother – she'd been Brenda Pulaski then – in three rooms over a dry cleaner's in Cicero, and Jack's family in a six-room triplex in Austin, across the street from Columbus Park. The house in Elm Park, in fact, was the first real house Jack had ever lived in.

On the day they moved in – Rob was only a baby that summer – Jack had wandered through the empty rooms, dodging the moving men, feeling effete but triumphant. 'Domain, domain,' he'd whispered to himself, loving the sound of the word; my window ledge, my front door. Fences, hedges, shutters, gates, railings, vines – all spoke of a privacy of outlook that neither Brenda nor Jack had been schooled in. There was also a beguiling density of shrubbery and a quiet, furred rolling of twilight

17

across the damp lawns and well cared-for flower borders. The heavy General Motors cars backing out of Elm Park driveways on Sunday mornings on their way to eleven o'clock services persuaded him that post-Vietnam America was not spiritually bankrupt. There was an America that persisted despite popular notions; serious, quiet-spoken, contemplative men and women attended to their obligations and guided their children along productive paths. (A family on the next block subscribed to *Encounter*; it had once been delivered to the Bowmans by accident.)

The first thing he did when he moved in was edge the flower border in the backyard. 'If middle class means that people water their tulips,' he had told Bernie Koltz, 'then maybe middle class isn't all that bad.' Bernie had been unimpressed by this remark; deservedly, Jack had felt at the time, since he had partially lifted it, or something like it, from an article in a recent *Atlantic* – is own phoniness occasionally reared up and appalled him. Jesus!

'I'd like to live in this house for the rest of my life,' Brenda had said the summer that they moved in, lifting her bare arms to take in the varnished baseboards and the cast-iron radiators. Eight rooms of their own – his father had told him he was crazy to take on a mortgage at his age – at 576 N. Franklin, a two-storey brick house; the colour of pickled beets, Brenda had described it.

Bernie had warned Jack and Brenda when they moved to Elm Park that they might have Republicans for neighbours, but Jack had loved it from the start. Of all the Chicago suburbs it was the oldest (and the least suburban, Dr. Middleton's wife, nodding wisely, told Brenda when they bought the house). Even the street names glowed with a kind of radiant idealism. North Franklin intersected with Emerson and Horace Mann. Bud and Hap Lewis lived behind them on Oliver Wendell Holmes. Brenda bought groceries at the A & P on James Madison. Jack followed Shakespeare Boulevard to work in the morning and returned by the Eisenhower Expressway, his working day sandwiched between the poetic and the pragmatic, as he had five or six times observed at parties – a remark that he later loathed himself for having made and that he resolved never to repeat.

But did his children, especially Rob, appreciate the good

schools, the tidy green parkways, the supervised playgrounds, the well thought-of Handel Society, the reasonably accomplished amateur theatre group currently presenting *Hamlet* with Larry Carpenter in the lead role? No.

'I like Mrs. Carpenter better than Mr. Carpenter,' Laurie said, her mouth crammed with zucchini.

'She's nothing but a dumb blonde,' Rob said.

'I don't know about that,' Brenda interjected mildly.

'Doesn't anyone have anything interesting to say?' Jack tried.

'At least the Carpenters have nice dogs,' Laurie said. 'Especially Cronkite.'

'Cronkite's got fleas, the dumb mutt. They've both got fleas.'

'All dogs have fleas,' Brenda said placidly, rising, gathering plates. A section of brown hair swung across one eye.

Jack followed her into the kitchen. He put his arms around her from behind, slid his hands inside her sweater, registered warmth.

'It's only a week,' Brenda said, turning, smiling.

'I know, I know.'

Later, in the living room, they watched an old Barbra Streisand movie. Rob sprawled lewdly in a chair but kept silent, and Laurie yawned in her bathrobe. It turned out to be an unexpectedly peaceful evening. Once or twice Jack came almost to the point of telling Brenda about Harriet Post's book, but held back out of a reluctance to disturb this rare tranquillity. They ate apples, and crackers and cheese, and by midnight they were all in their beds.

Chapter Four

EARLY SATURDAY MORNING BRENDA FLEW TO PHILADELPHIA
for the National Handicrafts Exhibition. She left them a
casserole for Saturday night, Spanish rice with cheese topping.
'After that you're on your own,' she told Jack at the airport. She
said this briskly, but with a certain rising sweetness of tone she
had. She was wearing a new red raincoat with a zip-in lining,
belted and notched and top-stitched, and her short brown hair,
tinted a lighter shade than usual, had been freshly washed and
blown so that it flew out like the tipped fur of a small animal.
Ebullient, giddy, she seemed to Jack to be spangled all over with
nerves: she couldn't stop talking.

'I'll phone Tuesday night, Jack, and see how everything's
going. Listen, you've got the name of the hotel, haven't you?
The Franklin Arms. It's on the bulletin board in the kitchen.'

'Okay.'

'Damn it, damn it, damn it,' she moaned, almost, Jack
thought, like a song,' where did I put that boarding pass? I had
it right here in my hand two minutes ago and now – here it is,
I've got it. Laurie can fix pancakes one night, she'd love that, it
would give her something to do. And there's always Colonel
Sanders if you get really desperate and there's no reason Rob
can't pitch in a little. And, who knows, maybe the Lewises will
have you over one night, though I don't know, they're both so
busy at the moment. And you've got that party at the Carpenters' tonight. *If* you decide to go, that is. Anyway, you can
always get hold of me, Jack, it's not like Philadelphia's at the
end of the world. If there's an emergency, I mean, knock wood
there won't be, but if –. Anyway,' she drew her breath in
sharply and floated him a brief dazzle of a smile, 'anyway you'll
get lots of writing done with me out of your hair.'

This last remark, blithe, self-mocking, sounded to Jack like a
sop. 'Don't worry about the book,' he told her, chagrined at the
tone he struck, astringent and grudging.

'*I'm* not worried about the book,' she said. 'You're the one who worries about the book.'

'I'm the one who's writing the book.'

'I'm just saying, the world won't end if you don't finish that book.'

Was this lack of faith, he wondered? Or sixth sense? He should have told her about the announcement in the *Journal*. 'I meant to tell you yesterday – '

'Was that my flight they called, Jack? Did you hear what the girl said on the loudspeaker? I can never make out what they say on those loudspeakers, it all runs together. This is a real change, isn't it, you seeing me off instead of the other way around. I think that was it, Jack. Didn't she say Flight 452? It sounded like it. Well, then. See you Thursday. Seven o'clock. Okay?'

The kiss she gave him was nervous, close-mouthed, distracted. They were accustomed to short separations since Jack's work at the Institute often took him out of town. 'Good luck,' he called after her, aware that he was falling short of genuine heartiness and that he owed her something more in the way of a fulsome send-off. He should have brought flowers; why not? Or did you only do that at sailings? He glanced around; not a flower in sight, nothing.

Poor Brenda; it came to him suddenly that she had almost never, in her forty years, travelled alone. A few minutes earlier, when asked her seat preference, she had declared with pressing earnestness, 'Non-smoking please,' and the attendant, scanning the seating plan, had informed her that he was sorry that there were only middle seats available in the non-smoking section. Brenda, chin up, bright and amiable, had replied, 'Oh, that's okay, just so it's next to a window.'

'No, Brenda,' Jack had interrupted. 'He means that there aren't any window seats.'

'Well then,' she said with a complacent shrug, 'whatever.'

She had a way of shrugging with her voice, a kind of Slavic arching of vowels which made her appear to her friends to be a woman of great reasonableness. She could also, when she chose, suppress this same open, yawning amiability of voice, replacing it with a startled, rapid, pared-to-the-quick sensitivity – Jack had sometimes seen her switch gait in mid-sentence.

Today he had been pricked by a needle of tenderness, watching Brenda balance her leather handbag on the X-ray belt and then, carefully, tentatively, step into the walk-through metal detector. Standing there, framed by moulding, she had turned slowly around and waved uncertainly as though suddenly touched by thoughts of danger and separation. Jack had waved back, rather wildly, and for no reason that he could think of, sent her a boxer's overhead salute.

In response she lifted her arms in a wide hands-up shrug of helplessness. She was smiling. At what, he wondered – at the ludicrous idea of herself smuggling a bomb aboard – or a gun or a cylinder of heroin? Isn't this absurd, she seemed to be marvelling across the barrier, isn't this crazy to be standing here in a make-believe doorway – almost a stage setting, it's so phony – and getting riddled with rays, me, Brenda Bowman.

Departures and arrivals depressed Jack; the disturbing mixture of the significant and the trivial aroused in him a blunt sense of betrayal; why should moments of archetypal solemnity be undercut by the picayune commercial clutter of duty-free shops and mechanical scanners? Leave-taking was meant to be immensely mythical. Voyages – he thought of LaSalle's last journey on the Mississippi – should overwhelm with vast opening silences, not this noisy, amplified, greedy shuttling of human bodies. No flowers, no brass bands, no flags waving, not even an embrace worthy of the name. And especially he loathed O'Hare with its helpless public struggle to remain clean and contemporary; who were they trying to kid? If you swept the floor fifty times a day you'd never in a hundred years get the whole place free of gum wrappers. The indestructible vinyl surfaces were gouged with cigarette burns; someone had taken a razor to one of the Mies van der Rohe chairs; someone else – cretins, hoodlums – had twisted the branch of an artificial palm so that it hung grotesquely by a thread. Faint gusts of hamburger grease blew through the departure area, and a weary, blue, carnival sleaziness creased the eyelids of the girl who peddled flight insurance; *three bucks on your wife's precious body and you, Jack Bowman, could be a rich man*. Oh, yeah?

He managed, as always, to resist flight insurance; superstition kept him reluctant, and anyway, his belief in Brenda's indestructibility was complete. ('I'm going to live to be a hundred,' she'd said more than once, and she said it not with whimsy, but with powerful, persuasive certainty). Jack thought

22

of her purse, pierced by X-rays and showing up on some out-of-the-way screen as an innocent, open assembly of coins and lipstick cases, a nail file, a notebook with a spiral edge, a pen; they were all there, the lucky familiar charms that kept her safe. In his mind he saw her body spreadeagled under the sweep of the mechanical eye: skull, vertebrae, arms, legs, a luminous framework of bones spiked by a wedding band, a hair clip, a stray safety pin – well, perhaps not a safety pin.

His wife's body, Brenda's body; the thought of it pressed compellingly as he drove home through the light Saturday traffic: her familiarity, her particular resin fragrance and a frail, busy muscularity about her that made her seem both industrious and remote, so that the outlines of her body were difficult to hold in the imagination. (Harriet Post's body, paradoxically, with its slightly roughened skin and slack joints, was incised on his brain.) Did he actually perceive Brenda's body, he wondered, after all these years, or was his perception of her reduced now to touch and sensation, abstraction and memory? He had touched her body in a thousand different ways. Twenty years, in fact, of highly specific touchings. But this morning, Jack thought, suspended inside the arc of the metal detector and bombarded by busy rays, Brenda had seemed, momentarily, to lose possession of her body, as though some vital supporting fluid had leaked away flattening her, making her seem for a moment like someone else's wife wearing a red coat and waving her hand at her anonymous klutz of a husband who foolishly, pointlessly, clenched his fists in a victory salute; ah yes, a man still young enough at forty-three (though faintly, furtively balding) whose wide, unbusy face marked him as one who belonged, unmistakably, to the vague, unspecified professions; a man with a steady eye, ah yes, a man of slow reflexes. He had let his hands fall to his sides, seeing clearly as he dropped them a vision of himself, a soft-looking Saturday-morning man, husband and father, responsible, honest, a trifle bulky in a tan trenchcoat, a man defined by nothing at all except the invisible band that connected him to the woman he had just brought to the airport and waved off, the woman in the red raincoat. The husband of the woman in the red raincoat.

He gripped the steering wheel, and with a careful and deliberate effort of will – he prided himself on his fantasies, their colour and secrecy – imagined the soft inner ridges of Brenda's thighs. (He always began at the thighs.) Blue-white, tender but with a particular spongy resilience. His thumbs rotated, stroking upward into the conceived hollows of flesh, tipping toward the taut triangles of skin over softness, a giving resisting softness. Hold it, hold it still, now it was coming. Her body was taking shape again, re-establishing itself limb by limb, gleaming skin, a firm coalescence, the distinct anterior presence of – what was it – fresh lettuce, Boston lettuce? Or something.

A red light. He braked with fury. There was a splutter of rain on the windshield and a harsh-ribbed washboard wind thudding against the side of the car. Next year, he raved to himself, when the book's finished – if the book's finished – I'll turn this bitch in. Get something with guts, something that jumps when the light turns green. Zoom.

Chapter Five

IT WAS A LITTLE MORE THAN FOUR YEARS AGO WHEN BRENDA took up quilting; where had the time gone? Jack had forgotten how she got started – another case of blurred beginnings – but it must have been that out of boredom or restlessness or perhaps a frenzied half-conforming, half-angry reaction to the many women's magazines she seemed to read at that time ('How to Put the Essential You into Your Home,' 'How to Chase the Drearies from a Blah Corner') that she decided to make a bedspread for Laurie, who was then eight years old.

The design of joined squares had been cautious, primitive, almost childlike; Jack still had a memory of Brenda, a fugitive smile flickering on her face, taking him by the hand early one evening and leading him upstairs to see what she had been working on. He had been prepared to be generous. (At that time he nourished a particular belief in his own generosity, a guilty hand-me-down, no doubt, from the continuous stream of generosity pouring from Dr. Middleton, a belief that he now saw as somewhat oafish, even quaint, but that had seemed at the time humane and productive.) As it was, Brenda's quilt had surprised him. She had counterpoised the pinks and oranges and purples in such a way that they gave off a dancing, almost electronically edged vividness, and in Laurie's small dark northeast bedroom, furnished chock-a-block with Ethan Allen components – desk, dresser, bookcase – the new quilt leapt out with an insistent claiming presence. 'Very nice,' he told her. 'Terrific, in fact.'

'Brenda,' her friends said when they saw it, 'you've found your thing.'

'Brenda's an artist,' Hap Lewis told Jack at the time, as she slapped down a bridge hand in front of him. 'Not a craftsperson like the rest of us slobs, but a goddamned artist.'

From the start he had been encouraging. The children had both been in school for years and were starting to have lives of their own, at least he hoped they were; his own work at the

Institute kept him fairly busy. He'd done a number of papers on the LaSalle expeditions, some work on Indian settlement, and he had told himself that the time had finally come to get going on his book; it was now or never. He hadn't been consciously worried about Brenda at the time, but he had noted a number of small worrisome signs: her mother's death had hit her hard. And since passing her thirty-fifth birthday she had grown more compulsive and even a little demanding, though in bed she had become, each day, less ardent, less sure of herself. She pushed at her cuticles in front of the television, and seemed to spend an inordinate amount of time shopping; sometimes during that period Jack had come across lists of her errands tacked up in the kitchen – measure shoe laces, return coat, toothpaste, post office. One terrible and memorable Saturday morning, four years ago, she had gone downtown to Stevens and bought six guest towels for the downstairs bathroom, then discovered when she got home that they were the wrong shade of blue, too purple, too dark. Her response had been to weep, ferociously, helplessly, and at length. Jack had lain with her on top of the striped comforter in their bedroom, holding her in his arms, murmuring into her hair the litany of comforts that he had once chanted to Rob and Laurie: there, there; it's all right; it doesn't matter.

That Brenda should expend authentic energy on such trivia shocked him into guilt; had he done this to her? Menopause – when did that begin? Not for a few more years, please God; he couldn't bear the thought of its terrible unknown and wambly aberrations blowing his poor Brenda up like a balloon and making a loose-bosomed, boxy-jawed matron of her, pouring poisonous damaging hormones into those slender receptive veins at the backs of her girlish knees, knees which he had kissed, please not yet. (She recovered from the weeping fit; they took a long bath together, locking the door; later they took the children to McDonald's for hamburgers, which they ate in a state of giddy exhaustion.)

Jack had, in fact, been pleased when Brenda took up quilting seriously, especially when he considered the alternatives. For a while she'd talked about going back to secretarial work, and she'd even sat down at his old Remington in the den and banged away for a week or two. But in the end she decided against it; she was too rusty; she would have to learn to use an electric model; on top of that the whole thing was unbelievably tedious. And it made her back ache.

Just as well, Jack thought; he was no snob, he said, appreciating as well as the next person the value of a good secretary, but Brenda's returning to the job she'd left when Rob was born seemed to him to be dismayingly wasteful. Cycles of any kind alarmed him; he'd got that from his father, the belief that you never go back, never read the same book over again, never rent the same summer cottage two years in a row, never retrace a mile of road if you can find an alternate route. Life was too short, his father always said, and now Brenda at thirty-five was saying the same things: life was too short to spend it hunched over a typewriter, especially when making quilts was so much more rewarding.

Jack agreed. There was something he found rather pleasing about the idea of quilts, about the combination of practicality and visual satisfaction – he liked that. He could even half-way understand the satisfaction Brenda found in bringing hundreds of separate parts together to form a predetermined pattern; in this respect, he told Brenda, it was not so different from his own research on Indian trading practices. (She had smiled at this analogy – what an ass he was at times!) Quilting seemed to him more substantial, more robust than the needlepoint his mother had once done, those chair covers, those stitched birds in tiny frames; it was more than a question of fashion or scale – it amounted to a whole attitude. Quiltmaking had a built-in generosity: quilts were made to give to brides, to cover children, to wrap about the legs of the elderly and infirm. And as an art it was less deliberate, less abstract, less *artsy* than the batik and copper enamelling and abstract sculpture that some of Brenda's friends did. Hap Lewis's wall weavings with their loops and swags of wool reminded Jack of obscene bodily processes. Quilting, on the other hand, had a tradition which he as a historian could appreciate, New World in its boldness and in its blend of utility and design, in tune with the past but in harmony with the recycling psychology of the seventies, *et cetera, et cetera,* a craft, he had once told Bernie, that had powerful historical resonance. (Medieval knights wore quilted material under their armour for warmth and to prevent chafing. Mary Queen of Scots quilted in her prison to pass the time.)

For Christmas Jack bought Brenda a fairly expensive illus-

27

trated history called *Quiltmaking in America*. And it was he who had pointed out to her the quilting design course offered at the Art Institute, urging her to sign up. She had been hesitant, she hated night driving, especially downtown; it was on her bridge night, anyway. 'What have you got to lose?' Jack said – then wildly added, 'Who knows, you might even want to get into it professionally someday.'

In the end she had gone. Two of her friends registered with her, but only Brenda stuck it out until spring. A year later her design project, *Spruce Forest*, won first prize in the Chicago Craft Show and was sold for six hundred dollars.

Six hundred dollars! Jack had been astounded – though he managed to conceal his amazement from Brenda – that anyone would lay out that kind of money for a quilt; it was incredible, he told Bernie Koltz over lunch, six hundred bucks for a *quilt*. And even more amazing was the fact that the couple who bought the quilt, a fairly well-known nightclub comedian and his singer wife, planned to put it not on a bed, but on the living-room wall of their Oldtown house. 'When I look at that quilt,' the comedian told Jack over drinks at the craft show reception, 'I feel as though I'm entering a green cube of the absolutest purity.'

The nonchalance with which Brenda had parted with *Spruce Forest* ('So long, pal,' she'd said, wrapping it in tissue paper and folding it inside a Del Monte pineapple carton) forced Jack to revise his idea of her as a sentimental collector of trivia: Brenda with her wedding photos, her baby scrapbooks, her boxes of old birthday cards and theatre programmes – where had all that gone, Jack asked himself; where was the Brenda of old? Her success at the craft show, instead of weighing her down with solemnity, had seemed to loosen in her a jingle of newly minted mirth, investing her familiar daily mannerisms, her comings and goings, with a spritely cheekiness; she had tossed her first-prize certificate (with her name, Brenda Bowman, printed inside a circle of stylized oak leaves) into a desk drawer where it lay beneath a clutter of old letters. She began to work on another quilt, spending up to three or four hours a day on it, and at night, instead of being tired, she became suddenly flippant and ready in bed, chucklingly irreverent even at the peak of orgasm. She seemed newly gifted with a random knowing; ten or twelve times in the last three years they had experienced nights of extravagant sexual adventure. Something

28

had happened, something untellable. Once it had been otherwise; once she had demanded soft words, endearments, subtlety, and all the patience Jack could muster. Now she roared and bounced and moaned and then, later, in a post coital embrace, the same sort of embrace she once sought to prolong, she frequently signalled her desire for release by giving Jack's shoulder a light dismissing double pat. There was a consumed gaiety in that simple patting gesture. He had been surprised at first, then amused. Pat, pat, he waited for it now. She stopped worrying about the children, about Rob's social adjustment (all children are basically self-centred) and Laurie's weight problem (all children are either too fat or too thin). When she fried eggs in the morning she hummed *Greensleeves* or *Amazing Grace*.

Eventually, after she'd finished half a dozen quilts, she made up her mind to turn the fourth bedroom into a work space. It was on the south side of the house; the light would be just right. 'Besides,' she told Jack, 'no one has a guestroom anymore.'

'Really?' he asked, doubtful, but, at the same time ready to take her word for it; she had always had a knack for summing up. And for firmly, though off-handedly, keeping him up to date on her social readings. No one, she told him, except maybe Bernie Koltz, wears poplin windbreakers anymore; no one gives those Saturday-night dinners for eight anymore; no one goes to Bermuda nowadays, what with the political mess; no one who lives in a city keeps two cars when the world is running out of oil; no one, with the exception of Janey Carpenter next door, goes out every spring and buys a new golf skirt, a golf skirt!

Jack lacked, it seemed, Brenda's talent, the specialized sensitivity to qualify as a decoder of modern life; his conclusions were slower to ripen, and Brenda's pronouncements, though delivered with chiming friendliness, carried with them a faint whiff of custodianship. And the suggestion that he, Jack Bowman, was something of a social retardant, a woolly academic type for whom she was, nevertheless, willing to take responsibility. She was usually right – he had to admit that – and certainly it was absurd to maintain a guestroom when Brenda needed the space. He, after all, had a den where he kept his papers and research files and where he was supposed to be polishing up his book on Indian trading practices.

Her new workroom – he was grateful she had resisted calling

it a studio or, worse, an *atelier* – was hectically, openly cheerful. (Brenda is such an 'open' person, Hap Lewis was always saying.) Her quilting frame filled all of one wall with brilliant transitory colour, and a waxed pine dresser of considerable beauty (his mother's) held her sewing things, her patterns and sketches, her shears and spools; at the sunny uncurtained south window, overlooking the Carpenters' new cedar deck, hung a rapidly multiplying, immensely fertile spider plant. Yards of printed fabric – she was working her way into the yellow family, she said – swirled out of baskets and drawers. If her friends happened to drop by in the afternoon for coffee she brought them up to this room, which had become, almost overnight it seemed to Jack, the radiant core of a house that now felt timidly underfurnished and strangely formal.

Sometimes when Jack got home from work at six he would find them still there, Andrea Lord or Leah Wallberg or Hap Lewis – Hap Lewis with her wedge of ginger hair and her gift for unanswerable pronouncements – drinking out of Brenda's pottery mugs and talking the particularized politics of the craft world: guild showings, co-operative kilns, the aesthetics of mounting, the intrusion of technology, the ramifications of texture, the evils of adjudication. They would sit on the floor, these women, all of them in their late thirties or early forties, with their knees drawn up, ankles still trim for the most part, drinking their coffee in excited sips and jabbing the air with their filter-tipped cigarettes. Their voices arched soprano, searching over the mysteries of the things they made with their hands.

Things. That was what Jack could never reconcile, the fact that all their finely channelled sensitivity was spent on the creation of *things*; couldn't they see that? In their headlong rush to looms and silk screens (and in Andrea Lord's case to a spinning wheel) hadn't Brenda and her friends lost sight of the fact that all their energy led back, in the end, to things?

Because it did seem to Jack in his more clear-headed days, his wise days he called them, when the Aspen was washed and greased, his overcoat despotted, the morning coffee hot and dark and plentiful and poured by Brenda, looking thoughtful and tender in her belted robe, that this worship of *things* ran counter to the whole struggle of the race. The thought came to him, now and then, of a particular ancient earthenware bowl which had been on permanent display at the Institute since he'd started there years ago. Much mended and badly faded, it was estimated by the ceramics people to have been in continuous daily use for more than three hundred years. This particular bowl, brought from France it was thought, was of rather remarkable delicacy – considering the crude state of provincial pottery in that period – and had doubtless survived because it had been handled with the care normally given a holy object. It may even have *been* a holy object, since sanctity, as Dr. Middleton frequently reminded the staff, tends to attach to those objects which are most clearly matched with human need. That poor brown stupid bowl had done all that was asked of it, and it had done it day after day after day. Its importance was earned, and Jack could freely acknowledge its value to a pre-industrial society; if he'd been one of them he'd gladly have got down on his knees when the bowl was passed his way, gladly have lifted it to reverential lips. But haven't we – and in his brain a quizzical eyebrow went up – haven't we gone beyond all that? What about the spirit behind the bowl? What about the platonic idea of truth behind all objects? Wasn't the refining and shaping of ideas the important thing, and not filling up the world with more and more objects?

He would like to have discussed this seeming contradiction with Brenda, and he had even got as far as imagining when this discussion might take place: on a Sunday morning, the two of them waking late to the swell of music from the clock radio – he loved the comforting sound of full-bodied hymns launched clumsily into the airwaves by untidy, untrained mixed choirs; the sun from the east window would throw tipped parallelograms of light across the bed, and Brenda, languorous in the blue-printed sheets, propped sleepy and froggy-voiced on one elbow, would attend thoughtfully to his argument, nodding slowly, reflectively. Little softenings would appear around her eyes, her mouth. 'I see what you're getting at Jack. Yes. You know something, you've got a point there.'

But the time when he might have begun such a discussion had passed. For some reason – slow reflexes perhaps or simple absent-mindedness – he had failed to seize the moment when the question had possessed relevance or promise. This one small silence on his part had opened to a series of silences; acceptable silences on the whole, topics too delicate to touch upon (such as the news about Harriet Post's book) or too small to be given distinction. The name of Brenda's latest quilt, the one she hoped would win her a prize in Philadelphia, was *The Second Coming*. Was there something symbolic in that title, Jack wondered; something sexual? He hadn't asked. A soft whittling away of truth, or at least of confrontation, had placed the two of them in the safety zone: with the happily married, with the reasonably content, the spiritually intact.

Another thing: he was not altogether certain about the philosophical underpinnings of an argument about materialism; he would have to think about it, work out some of the details, discuss it with Bernie, get a few quotes from, say, Tolstoy or maybe Thoreau. Nor was he sure he could defend a life based on the abstract without sounding like a puerile hypocrite, he who last month had bought himself a sixty-dollar suede vest, he who yearned after Italian sports cars. Yeah, yeah, we know your type, some big man of ideas. Hah!

It had even occurred to him from time to time that Brenda, and not he, might be the one who was on the right track; by accident she may have stumbled ahead and laid her hands on what really mattered in the world – things, things. Historical potency and all the razzle-dazzle that went with it might reside not in amorphous systems of thought at all, but in the concrete, the measurable, the patently visible. Pots and quilts just might, in the end, lead to the final knowledge, whatever the hell that meant.

He doubted it, though.

Still, Brenda's contentment flowed from the kind of innocent vision for which one did not set traps, and her faith was too matter-of-factly assured anyway to be threatened by casual intellectual scepticism of the Sunday morning variety. Especially, he admitted to himself, especially coming from him.

Chapter Six

FOR LUNCH HE ATE A BANANA, STANDING IN THE KITCHEN, looking out the window. A grey comfortless sky pressed through the trees with the density of packed satin. It was headache weather, manic-depression weather, but at least the rain had stopped. The two backyard maples and the ornamental cherry, leafless and frenzied and wretched, snapped back and forth in a continuous tearing whorl of wind. The storm windows rattled and whined in their old wood frames, letting in, around the edges, blades of cold air.

Jack found a new package of Swiss cheese in the refrigerator, unwrapped it slowly and broke off a chunk. The garage roof was in bad shape; even from the kitchen window he could see where the shingles had blown off. Heights worried him; he secretly dreaded the twice-yearly manoeuvring of storms and screens, but the garage roof was fairly low and not too steeply pitched; he might have a crack at it himself in the spring if he got the time. Bud Lewis, after all, had put a new roof on his garage. Come to think of it, he had reroofed the whole house – had done the whole thing in a week; Jack could see the neat grey edges of the Lewis roof from here.

Quite a number of the old dark Elm Park houses with their clumsy porches and yawning hallways had been patiently restored as Hap Lewis and her husband Bud had done, the good brass hardware around the windows revealed, layers of paint scraped from the mouldings and banister, an old stone fireplace rescued from behind a sheet of wallboard. A few had gone the other direction, as Larry and Janey Carpenter had done, and gutted the house, discriminatingly exposing a brick wall here and there, painting the dining room a soft oyster, putting a skylight in the bathroom and pointing up the old bathtub with aubergine enamel; the dim awkward corners could be filled with creamy suede sofas and smoked glass tables and rough-weave cushions and primitive Inuit sculptures and healthy potted ferns until they gleamed and glittered with restraint and energy and a sense of caring

Jack was no handyman like Bud Lewis – there was no sense in fooling himself – but it might be nice, hammering away up there on the garage. Early spring maybe. A Saturday. He longed suddenly for spring: he in a light jacket, kneeling on the roof while pale fronds of sunlight fell through the branches, warming his back and shoulders; there would be birds warbling in the unfolding air; the grass would be freshly raked after the winter; there would be Brenda, a cotton scarf on her head, sweeping out the corners of the patio, and the children jumping over the flowerbed – no, that was ridiculous; they were almost grown up. Rob was fourteen and Laurie was twelve; neither of them had jumped over the flowerbed for years.

He chewed his cheese and thought how possibly destructive it might be to stand around staring out of windows; it was something to discipline yourself against. It interfered with that fine-toothed mechanism that measured and accounted for time. You lost track of reality; you could become hypnotized by electric lines and the almost imperceptible way they crossed and recrossed each other; you could go crazy counting roof shingles. After a while, if you didn't watch out, you started swaying back and forth, back and forth, in rhythm with the trees, and then you'd really had it. No doubt lots of people, thousands of them, had gone down the drain just standing around looking out of kitchen windows. Like this. Boredom had its seductive side, an allure that had to be resisted.

The house was quiet, stupefyingly quiet. Laurie had gone off to perform her Saturday-afternoon job, which was to exercise the dogs from next door. The image of his daughter Laurie filtered sadly through Jack's head; she had inherited something of his weakness, his dependence on the good will of others; it was too bad, really it was too bad. For a buck the poor kid willingly, cheerfully, stupidly kept those two mutts out all afternoon while Larry and Janey Carpenter (The Prince and the Princess, he thought of them) pleasure-mongered indoors, rolling around, no doubt, on one of their white sheepskin rugs, trying it now this way, now that, now standing on their heads. The poor kid, round and round the cold streets with Cronkite the spaniel and Brinkley the airedale; she'd cover several miles before she returned. Sheer exploitation, Brenda called it, a crime, but it kept Laurie occupied and seemed to make her happy. She looked forward to Saturdays; she'd do it even without the dollar, she once told Jack; she loved it, she really did.

Rob had gone off to the track meet at the high school. 'Who you going with?' Jack had asked him as off-handedly as he could, but Rob, bending to do up the zipper of his jacket, had mumbled something incoherent. 'See ya,' he said, making for the back door.

'Hope they get slaughtered,' Jack had called out loudly, straining for a tone of comradeship.

'Huh?'

'The other team. Hope they get slaughtered.' Did he really hope anything of the kind?

'Yeah, well . . . ' The door slammed shut.

Peace, quiet. If Brenda were here there would be coffee on the stove. Instead, in the back of the refrigerator, behind the cottage cheese, he found a can of beer lying on its side. It was only one by the kitchen clock. He would be able to work on the book until six. What he really should do, he thought, is take the phone off the hook; that would give him five full hours, a good solid afternoon's work for once, with no interruptions and no obligations. Whatsoever. On the other hand, Brenda or the children might phone, something might happen, some emergency – better leave the phone on.

He looked again at the clock, whistling sharply, almost savagely through his teeth. Five full hours; a rare event; he was in luck. Outside the window a small colourless bird of indistinguishable species perched on top of the telephone pole. When it flies away, Jack promised himself, I'll get down to work.

For a full minute the bird sat completely still; then it twisted its bobbing, round golfball of a head sharply to the right, abruptly raising and then resetting its wings. It shuddered crazily and peered straight down so that it seemed to Jack to be looking directly into the kitchen window. Maybe it's hungry, Jack thought, thinking of his mother, who put a slice of bread out for the birds every day of her life. He made a move toward the breadbox, but at the same instant the bird darted from its perch and fluttered, against a current of air, in a graceful arch down onto the Carpenters' garage.

'Tough luck, birdie-boy,' he muttered out loud, obscurely betrayed. 'No lunch for you, kiddo.'

Five minutes had passed – only five? A short sigh escaped his lips, and since he was not normally given to sighing he felt a twinge of alarm; sighing, like yawning and scratching and whining, could become habit-forming, he'd have to watch that. Four hours, fifty-five minutes to go. The span of time opened before him like a body of water; he had only to glimpse its surface and he was stricken, instantly, by a familiar rising of pain, a sharp, acid-coloured clove of pain that entered at his chest and rose with swift suddenness to his head, his arms, even the tips of his fingers. Beneath the pain, he recognized, and surrendered to, a subtext of panic, a shallow void that sucked and taunted and seemed unbearable. For the moment at least there was no escape; he could have wept. There was nothing he could do to contravene the certainty that awaited him: a whole solid clock-ticking afternoon buried alive in the dark, lonely den with that goddamned book.

Chapter Seven

ON HIS DESK JACK KEPT AN OLD WIND-UP ALARM CLOCK, more for company than for anything else; its ticking was a reproof, but at least it picked away at the silence. Today, as always before settling down to work, he wound it tightly and set it down, making it serve as an island or a kind of territorial flag in the midst of heaped notes, sliding stacks of paper, chewed pencils, chains of paper clips, odd envelopes and index cards, applecores so dehydrated they blended indistinguishably into the dry papery swirl.

From his briefcase he took the stapled manuscript copy of Chapter Six. 'Symbols and Solecism – the Concept of Ownership.' Dr. Middleton was anxious to see how this particular chapter was coming along, and Jack had promised, or nearly promised, to bring it in on Monday morning. Glancing at the title, which now seemed to border on the precious, he caught himself, for the second time in one day, sighing.

The opening paragraph – he read it over silently, nodding rhythmically at every comma – wasn't bad; not what you could call scintillating, no, certainly not scintillating, but it did seem to catch the point about the connection between ownership and status, and wasn't that what mattered in the long run? This was scholarship, after all, not Walt Disney. Keep your readership in mind, Dr. Middleton was always telling him.

But the second paragraph. No! God, no! He fished in a drawer for a pencil; paragraph two would need a little work; a lot of work. Somehow he'd wandered away from the subject and had got into the part about relative values and ritual which wasn't supposed to come in until Chapter Nine at least.

He'd have to go back again to the bloody outline, which was floating around somewhere under all these other papers. Christ, what had he been thinking of? A real digression, unforgivable, but then the mind worked like that sometimes, which was one of the problems with scholarship, the way it flattened and confined the speculative impulse. Should he leave it or cross it out? If he did leave it in he would need an elaborately detailed justification, and the thought of organizing a footnote on that scale was too oppressive to think about; it would have to be removed.

In a drawer he found a fresh sheet of paper and rolled it carefully, evenly, into the typewriter. Margins set. Page number. Indent. Now –

The little clock ticked. Ten minutes went by. Jack wrote a sentence, which was: 'The Indian concept of trade was vastly more sophisticated than previously thought for at least three reasons.'

The room was quiet. Through the walls he could hear the grim blue gnawing of wind. Brenda would be in Philadelphia now. Odd, how he'd never been to Philadelphia; all the places he'd been, but never once there. She would have checked into the hotel and registered at the exhibition centre. Probably she'd been given one of those little plastic name cards to pin to her shoulder – Brenda Bowman: Chicago Craft Guild. She'd be standing somewhere, a little to one side, but still well within the swelling flow of delegates who would be greeting one another, sizing each other up, smiling, making facile but cheerful connections – 'Well, I don't know him personally, but I certainly know his work.' Or 'You say you're from the Windy City, I have a brother out there in electronics.'

Painfully he rewrote paragraph two: the syntax wobbled, but the essence was there as long as he remembered, when he came to the final draft, to refer to the Iroquois in a note. He'd have to look up the exact reference, but he was sure he had it somewhere on an index card. It didn't seem to be on the desk, though; he'd have to leave it for the moment, get back to it later.

He wondered at times if his writing might go better if he had the advantage of more agreeable surroundings. These porous walls seemed to exhale the deadly gas of inertia. There was a chilly cramped look of underachievement about the den; instead of built-in bookshelves that would have warmed and settled the room, he and Brenda had made do with a pair of tentative unpainted bookcases from their student apartment. The file cabinet of painted metal was utilitarian and non-threatening.

Jack's desk was the same blocky, reproachful oak office desk of his childhood; his father had bought it for five dollars in a second-hand store in Austin when he was twelve, and it was somehow too solid to throw away. ('The wood alone is worth twice what the old man paid,' he told Brenda.) Jack had wanted to paint the walls the same apple green as the living room, and Brenda had wanted a sunny yellow, since the north side of the house was dark. They'd settled on a bargain gallon of eggshell latex which rapidly darkened to a streaky cream. It was a gloomy room, anyway; the windows were narrow and leaded, insistently serious, and the radiator, which was small and corroded, never felt more than faintly warm to the hand. At this time of year, January, the room was both cold and damp.

Their house, though he loved it, especially in summer, lacked style; it was one of Jack's mild regrets that he and Brenda hadn't quite managed to pull it off. The house – except for Brenda's workroom, which was a mutation from a much later era, had never really fulfilled its promise. What was missing was a vividness and direction that was the essence of style. Could it be, Jack sometimes wondered, that he and Brenda were people who had no real style of their own? It seemed to come more easily to others. The Carpenters with their cedar planking and pottery planters. Even the Lewis house across the way had a kind of style. It annoyed Jack a little to think that Bud Lewis had, by dint of his joyless versatility, his expert home carpentry, and his knack for landscaping, brought a glow to the narrow old house he and Hap had bought on Holmes Avenue. There must be *something* in Bud Lewis, a smouldering of imagination, barely visible, which he himself lacked. Once, at the Institute, he had chanced upon a copy of a letter of reference addressed to Dr. Middleton in which he, Jack Bowman, was described as a 'hard-working young man but rather colourless.' Colourless; the wound had lingered for months; the injustice of it stung him to the heart. Did Brenda, he wondered, perceive this terrible colourlessness? (Later the pain subsided, became a memory, a portion of suffering concluded and filed away.)

'What we really should do is start from scratch and do the whole house over,' Brenda said from time to time, eyeing the beige grasscloth in the hall and the apple-green living room with its darker green open-weave curtains and chocolate-brown corduroy sofa (if in doubt, choose chocolate brown, someone had advised them). But so far they hadn't managed to get around to it. They were busy with other things. Or else it cost too much. It might be best, they said, to wait until Rob and Laurie were older.

There might, Jack sensed, be another reason: an unspoken wish not to interfere overly much with the substance of the house, with its still obstinate purity. He and Brenda wanted, half consciously, it seemed, with their neutral colours and sheer curtains, to do the house the minimal amount of harm. 'Your trouble,' Brenda said once, nudged by a flash of insight, 'is that the historian in you resists corruption.' In the early days of their marriage she had frequently mentioned his historian's calling, deliberately, proudly, interjecting it into conversation as one does the name of a loved one.

There was some truth in it; he was, in fact, hesitant about imposing the vernacularism of decoration on what had once, in another time, existed as an idea. This house – he could see it clearly in his imagination – had once, briefly, stood as a skeleton of fresh lumber, and before that it had stretched, two-dimensionally, on a sheet of blueprints. But first it had been someone's idea, someone anonymous and long-dead, but nevertheless someone by whose leave he and Brenda held their occupancy. They should have bought a new house, he sometimes thought, and written their own history. As it was he could never shake off completely an uneasy sense of tenancy, especially sitting here in this chilly, depressing den.

Brenda thrived in her sunny workroom upstairs; *she* never complained of feeling lonely and shut off; she liked nothing better, it seemed, than to shut herself up with her quilts for hours at a time – in these last weeks before the exhibition she had sometimes spent up to five or six hours at a stretch. There were thousands of stitches in *The Second Coming*. Of course, hers was a different kind of work, less demanding in some ways, less intense, but still it wouldn't hurt to think about redoing the den, putting in a larger window as the Carpenters had done, opening the place up a bit, painting this gloomy woodwork, at the very least have something done about the heating system.

Harriet Post. He wondered what kind of room she sat down in when she began to write her book. Had all those maps and rare woodcuts been assembled in a trim modern university office? At her kitchen table? – it was difficult to picture Harriet at a kitchen table. In a basement study panelled in knotty pine with an electric heater sparking away in a corner? He knew nothing of her life after she left Chicago except that she was living in Rochester; he had seen her address year after year on the alumni list, Rochester, New York, the same street, the same number. And he knew little about Rochester except that it was said to be ugly and have bad winters, but perhaps Harriet lived in a good part of the city; every city had at least one decent section. Probably she was married. (He thought of the springiness of her oddly shaped breasts, the narrow blue-tipped nipples, the colour of washable ink.) It would have been typical of Harriet to keep her maiden name. Perhaps, like Brenda, she had taken over the family guestroom for her work, hung plants in the window, hummed *Greensleeves* while she pored over her notes. God, the afternoon was slipping away; he'd better get going.

Paragraph three. He read it slowly, unwilling to believe he'd really set down these words. Could he actually have written this parsley-strewn clutch of sentiments about the purity of the Indian mind ('Trade approached the gracefulness of giving'), committing to paper what Dr. Middleton – chin stroking, lip licking – would call a romantic indulgence? It would have to go. Zap. Wham. Out.

But he paused, reading it over; could he afford to take it out? He needed every word; as it was, Chapter Six was fairly thin, thinner even than Chapter Five had been.

Concentrating, shoulders back, eyes level, he read it once more. Christ! Then, because he felt a desire to pierce the unmoving air in the room, he tried reading it out loud. His voice caught, a strangled squawking; he could hear a distinct Boy Scout earnestness. Jesus.

He cleared his throat, tipped back his chair, and read it again – much louder this time – in stage British, clutching himself at the throat, squeezing in the vowels, plunging from phrase to phrase, from curdled outrage to wet sobbing sweetness. He should have been an actor, he thought, brightening; he should try out for the Elm Park Little Theatre, must make a point to speak to Larry Carpenter about that one of these days. If a solemn prick like Larry Carpenter could be an actor – of course, he'd bombed out on the Hamlet thing – then why couldn't he, Jack Bowman, take to the stage?

No. Absolutely no. There was no question about it, the paragraph would have to be completely redone. He grasped the pencil, feeling stiff waves of refrigeration settle around him. The whole thing would have to go; tears stood in his eyes. 'I have no faith in this,' he thought, sighing.

And this time his sigh took in the deskful of papers, the cold room, the emptied house.

'I'm a man who has lost his faith.'

He said this aloud, knowing he was giving way to the cheapest kind of self-dramatizing, but recognizing at the same time that what he uttered was perfectly true. His previous and frequent – especially lately – midnight encounters with the spare unlovely belly of truth were nothing compared to the heft of this announcement. He was, had chosen to be, powerless. Avoidance had led him to a dead end; a gigantic spiritual pratfall awaited him. He repeated: 'I am a man who has lost his faith.'

As he spoke he listened to the curious lifting tendrils of his voice; the tone was bleak but unmistakably decent, and the words, let loose in the air, carried with them a certain richness of decision. Well, it was established then, his loss of faith. Officially.

Then, far away, he heard the doorbell ringing. It rang only twice, long enough, though, to send him stumbling, joyfully reprieved, out of the room to answer.

Chapter Eight

'B ERNIE!'
'Hi.'

'What're you doing out this way? On a Saturday?'

'Just thought I'd drop by. You busy?'

'No. Not at all. Well, I was working on the book, but I was just thinking of taking a break anyway. C'mon in, come in.'

'You're sure you're not – '

'No, absolutely, I mean it. Come on in out of the cold.' Jack held the door open, dizzy with hospitality.

'Christ, it's cold.' Bernie, in a light navy windbreaker, was shivering. Bareheaded, his ears a bright pink – Jack had heard him boast that he didn't own a hat – he moved into the hall and set a suitcase down on the floor.

'Winter's really here,' Jack said with inane, florid, furious good cheer. Thank God, thank God for Bernie, the afternoon was saved, *he* was saved.

Bernie's round nose glowed red from the cold. 'When winter comes,' he said, rubbing his hands together, 'it comes with a vengeance.'

'And you're the one,' Jack challenged, happy now, though puzzled – weather was something they never discussed, 'who's always giving me the bull about the Windy City myth being an exaggeration.'

'Why is it we stay here in this city and live with all this grit?' Bernie produced a Kleenex and blew his nose loudly. 'Tell me, is there any material in the universe that is as hard and compacted and flinty as a piece of Chicago grit? God, you know something, I've got grit in my bloodstream, grit in the joints, grit in the groin, give me a few years and I'll have grit lodged in that little spot in the back of the brain, what do you call it – the seat of the involuntary nervous system?'

'The medulla.'

'The medulla! How'd you remember that Jack?'

'God knows.'

'That little black thing shaped like a cigar. It all comes back. First-year Psych. Actually, that's why I'm here. My medulla is acting up again.'

'You need a beer. How about a beer? If you don't mind a warm one, that is. I was just going to get one myself.'

Bernie stood silent and unmoving in the hall.

'Well, what about it?' Jack pressed. 'It's Saturday afternoon. Surely you've got a little time.'

'I've got time,' Bernie said, coming to life and slowly unzipping his jacket. 'Time, if you want to know the truth, is what I've got. I've even got time, in case you're interested, to deliver a lecture on the nature of time, *kairos* and *chronos*, extemporaneous, without notes even. I could go on and on. There's the human concept of time, the dimension of time, the incumbency of time, the sovereignty of time, the incursions of Chicago grit into the manifold layers of time – '

'Time to sit down?'

'But have *you* got time? You've got that woozie out-of-joint look. You're in the middle of writing. I see you haven't thrown in the towel after all. And I'd hate to interrupt when you – '

'Since when did you start being deferential about – ?'

'Since this morning. When Sue – you remember my wife Sue – when Sue informed me I was insensitive to the feelings of others. I tried, God knows, to tell her it was the grit in my medulla but – '

'Where are you off to anyway?'

'Me?'

'With the suitcase?'

'That, as they say, is a long story. A longish story. With many and manifold layers of meaning.'

'You're drunk,' Jack said appraisingly, stepping back.

'You're absolutely wrong.'

'Weren't you and Sue going to Fox Lake today?'

'She had to work. She got a call from the hospital this morning, could she come in and relieve somebody or other.'

'Again? Didn't that happen last time?'

'And the time before that. And here we are back on the subject of time. Remember the year we did time? When was that? 1969?'

'You may not be drunk but there's something wrong.'

44

'It's probably the tranquillizers. They take off the old sardonic edges. Give me this nice, easy-going, adagio style.'

'Tranquillizers? You? What do you mean, tranquillizers?'

'Sue gets them at the hospital. Freebies. Every profession has its perks, and hers are those little blue-and-yellow pills. They keep the libido trimmed down a bit too. Sublimation, you know. It's the thing now. Sublimation is sublime – it's the same word, you know.'

'I'm going to make you some coffee.'

'You're going to sober me up. Ah, the good host. You're wrong though. I'm not even slightly high.'

'Stay here. I'll be right back. You don't mind instant, do you. I'll make us both some coffee.'

'Did Brenda get away?' Bernie asked bleakly, lowering himself onto the brown sofa and pulling at his eyebrows mutinously.

'I put her on the plane this morning.'

'*You* put *her* on the plane? Now there are those who would see a hint of chauvinism in the way you put that.'

'Oh?'

'So here we are,' Bernie paused. 'You and me.'

'Just make yourself at home.' Jack called from the kitchen, running water into a pan.

'And the kids?' Bernie called, more feebly now.

'Out for the afternoon. Rob's at the track meet and Laurie's out walking the dogs next door. This place is a morgue. I'm really glad you came by, in fact.'

'Good,' Bernie said with a flatness of tone that Jack found curious and alarming. 'That's good.'

The water came slowly to a boil. From the living room there was silence. Jack found mugs – Brenda must have twenty odd coffee mugs, most of them in earth tones with rough unglazed edges that made his tongue curl back. He measured Nescafé and stirred in water. Cream? He'd known Bernie all his life but couldn't remember how he took his coffee. Anyway, there wasn't any cream. And black coffee was what he really needed at the moment.

Taking a cup in each hand, spilling a little on the hall rug, he came back into the living room.

Bernie had stretched himself out on the sofa. His Adidas, mud-spattered, had been removed. His eyes were closed.

'You asleep?' Jack asked, hesitant.

'No.' The voice sounded plugged and dangerous.

'Look, do you want your coffee? I made you a cup.'

'No.' Bernie turned his face away. 'Thanks anyway.'

'What then? How about a salami sandwich? Have you had lunch?'

'Sue's left me. For good. This morning.'

'Sue? I can't believe – '

'For good.'

'Let me get you a drink, Bernie.'

'No. Christ, no.'

Softly, solicitously, Jack asked, 'What do you want then?'

'Actually,' Bernie said, his face pressed into the soft brown cushions, 'actually, I want to cry.'

Which he did, to Jack's horror and disbelief.

Chapter Nine

WITH JACK'S ARM ACROSS HIS SHOULDERS, BERNIE FELL asleep at last, and Jack went upstairs to find him a blanket; the living room with its new storm window was several degrees warmer than the den, but still decency seemed to demand that Bernie's sleeping body be covered. He was adequately enough dressed in his jeans and sweater (a maroon acrylic, stretched at the wrists, pulled thin at the elbows) but the position in which he lay – his legs pressed together and drawn up slightly at the knees, an arm thrown awkwardly (grievingly, it seemed to Jack) over his shoulder – gave the impression of helpless nude exposure. In fact, at the back, where Bernie's sweater had pulled away from his belt, there was a curved, tallow-coloured moon of hairless flesh. Jack, arranging the blanket over the sleeping form, felt a shock of love. This man, this person, Bernie Koltz, was his oldest friend. Almost, in fact, his only friend.

Only one friend? There must be a measure of failure, Jack supposed, in the admission that he had gone this far in his life, forty-three years, and achieved only one friendship.

For Brenda it was different; it had always been different for Brenda. To begin with she seemed to have no instinct for discarding; Jack had always felt amazement at the way she managed to carry her friends like floating troops in and out of the openings of her life. It puzzled him that she was still in touch, after all these years, with her girlhood friends from the old Cicero neighbourhood, with Betty Schumacher and Willa Reilly and Patsy Kleinhart and even Rita Simard. And at least twice a year she got together for lunch in the Fountain Room at Field's with friends from Katherine Gibbs, where she'd taken the two-year course in Secretarial Science, as it was called then. Furthermore she frequently saw the three girls – these girls in their forties now, married and with children – from the typing-pool days at the Great Lakes Institute; Jack had once known these women too, but for him they had faded to the faintest of images – he heard their names, Rosemary, Glenda, Gussie, and their faces rose up briefly from a white mist, then immediately receded. Brenda got phone calls, fairly frequently, from couples they'd both known when they lived in the Married Student Complex; it was usually Brenda, and not Jack, whom these nostalgic couples, passing through town, asked for. Not that he minded; Brenda was the one with the patience for friendship; he admitted it; she remembered names; she kept in touch; she had the impulse – or was it imagination? – to invest in people a clear corporeal sense of intimacy. So-and-So, she was forever saying, was one of her closest friends.

Close. A troubling word; it mystified Jack, and occasionally caused him a degree of disquiet – could it be that he was missing a piece of sensory equipment? Or was it a question of definitions? It might be, he reasoned, that Brenda's concept of the word close was altogether different from his, more inno-cent, or a little uncomprehending. Did closeness mean, as Brenda seemed to think, remembering birthdays and keeping the names of people's children straight and murmuring over and over those difficult healing phrases, *I know how you feel, it's not half as bad as you think, it'll look better in the morning*. It occurred to him at times that Brenda's friends with their confidences and instructions might be simply slicing the fat off each other's backsides. There was something inherently selfish about the idea of closeness when he thought about it; the long drawn-out confidentialities, damp and demanding, the giddy, wilful let-ting down of hair. Let my grief be yours. Let my anxiety rest on your head tonight, old pal, take my weakness, give me your strength in return.

And secrecy, always secrecy, the abrupt, theatrical, almost literal running down of a curtain. When Brenda talked to one of her 'close' friends on the phone – to the braying, wild-haired Hap Lewis in particular – she invariably cupped her hand over the receiver and spoke in a shallow, anxious, breath-wedged voice. Whispers, subterfuge, weighty suggestions, meaningful pauses. Once or twice Jack had chanced upon a roomful of Brenda's friends, and the conversation, warmly flowing before he entered, had lapsed awkwardly into a secretive, bitten off, embarrassed silence.

'What do you talk about all the time?' he'd asked her.

'Everything,' she'd answered. And then, seeing his expression, smiled cannily and added, 'well, almost everything.'

'Such as?'

'It's hard to say.'

'Why?'

She looked at him. 'Well, for one thing, we don't assign topics the way you and Bernie do.'

Her tone was reasonable but pointed. Her eyes watched his. He knew, of course, and had always known, that she lacked faith in his friendship with Bernie. 'Is Bernie really a *close* friend?' she'd asked him not long ago.

'Of course he's a close friend. Jesus.'

'How can he be if you never really talk?'

'We talk. You know we talk.'

'But you never . . . you never reminisce.'

'Maybe not, but we talk.'

'Do you talk about Sue, for example? About her, what do you call them – her adventures?'

'Affairs, you mean?'

'Yes.'

'Once or twice. Obliquely.'

'Obliquely! And I suppose he never mentions Sarah.'

'Good God, Brenda, it's a somewhat painful subject, for both of them. Can you really blame Bernie if he doesn't – '

'Pain is supposed to be shared.'

Jack stared at her. 'Isn't that a little pious?'

'Is it?'

'Well, here you sit with two normal, healthy, intelligent kids – '

Brenda was unmoved. 'Sarah's his child. Regardless. And here you are, Jack, his so-called friend, and he never mentions her to you.'

'What I said was he doesn't talk about her directly, but he mentions sometimes when they've been out to Charleston to see her – '

'It's really incredible.' Brenda shook her head. 'Incredible! And this is your closest friend.'

Jack had tried to explain, but it wasn't easy. He'd grown up on the same block with Bernie Koltz. Once, an impossibly long time ago, their parents had played euchre together. Jack and Bernie had gone through Austin High School, both non-ath letes, both non-joiners, and after graduation they'd taken the 'El' downtown every day to Illinois Extension at Navy Pier and later to De Paul where Bernie eventually did a Ph.D. and where he now taught in the Math department. (He had never lost his busy, meticulous sense of prodigy.) Bernie had been best man at Jack's wedding – treating the occasion with enormous seriousness – and Jack, several years later, when Bernie met Sue, had done the same for him.

For a while the four of them got together fairly often in each other's apartments for dinner, but Brenda and Sue had not, even in the beginning, taken to each other. 'I can tell she thinks I'm a complete moron,' Brenda complained. 'She's always asking me what I think about disarmament or something.'

'You're projecting,' Jack said.

'I'm too dumb for her,' Brenda said.

'You're not dumb,' Jack said, 'you're oversensitive.'

'I'm sorry, Jack,' Brenda said. 'I really am sorry.'

They persisted for three or four years, and then the dinners gradually became less frequent. Sue was qualifying for medical school and, at the same time, was getting heavily into gourmet cooking. Several times in one year she served them strange, small, bony birds: pheasant, Cornish hen, quail, flamed in different kinds of brandy. Once, at one of these dinners, Brenda extracted a wishbone the size of her thumbnail; she slipped it into her pocket and showed it to Jack when she got home. 'This is crazy,' she whispered, 'this has to stop.'

Jack saw the hopelessness of it, but was nevertheless disappointed. He had no brothers or sisters of his own, and it had given him an odd thump of pleasure to hear Rob and Laurie, babies then, talk about going to see Uncle Bernie and Aunt Sue. In fact, though the children saw Bernie only occasionally now, they still spoke of him as Uncle Bernie; *Aunt* Sue had been dropped – Sue was nervous with children, once, years ago, asking the two-year-old Laurie, 'What did you do today?' After Sarah was born, Sue and Bernie decided to forget about having a family. (Sarah, five now, had never achieved consciousness. She was better off, Sue said, at Charleston, where they knew how to look after her; life was such a waste; Sarah probably wouldn't live long, Sue said; there was a pattern in these cases.) Sue and Bernie stayed on in the apartment near Lincoln Park, an apartment that had triple locks on the doors and smelled of cats and frizzled garlic, and Sue started back to medical school. Abruptly, to Brenda's relief, the invitations stopped completely. Bernie and Sue had a different group of friends – Jack scarcely knew them, but they seemed to be lean, energetic couples immersed in unpronounceable specialities, branches of Psychiatry or Demographic Studies or East European languages. Except for the Friday lunches and one or two evenings a year, he and Bernie had gone their separate ways. But despite this, Jack had never for a minute stopped thinking of Bernie as his closest friend.

A close friendship. Ever year at Christmas he gave Bernie a bottle of rye, and Bernie gave him a bottle of scotch; it was a tradition, aside from Friday lunches at Roberto's, their only tradition, the outgrowth of a private and dimly remembered joke. The annual whisky exchange never failed to send Brenda into one of her rare hand-waving fits of atavism, full of Slavic inversions and lamentations. 'And this you call a gift. Between friends! A brown bottle for him and a brown bottle for you, this is a gift? This is caring? Jack, you amaze me, you really amaze me.'

Perhaps it was really true that men seldom make close male friends after the age of twenty; Jack had read something along that line recently. Was it in one of Brenda's magazines? Or a *Time* essay? Maybe in a *Reader's Digest* – he sometimes glanced through them when he stopped in to see his parents. Men were failures at friendship, the article said. The drive to compete and conquer or something like that was what did it. It froze the spontaneous bonds of affection that eased the friendships between women. (He had observed Brenda closeted with her friends; even on the telephone she leaned, sympathetic and nodding, into what seemed a sealed, privileged bathysphere.) Men, it appeared, were forced to make do with uncertain professional associations or with old, imperfect friendships formed in youth, unwieldy friendships that required constant efforts at resuscitations – the visiting of old haunts, or conjuring through the circuitry of alcohol, ancient, riotous adventures, staying up until two or three or four in the morning trying to remember what happened to old What's-his-name who grabbed them in a back alley one Halloween night back in 1944 and shook the living shit out of them; Jack's friendship with Bernie was the only friendship he had that transcended this.

Brenda seemed to have the idea that close friendships had something to do with the baring of souls; somehow she'd never grasped the fact that something else was involved in his friendship with Bernie. And, having this single and unique friendship, he realized that he was more fortunate than many of the people he knew. His father, for instance; most of his father's friends had died – not that he'd ever had that many – and as far as Jack knew he hadn't made any new friends in years. His father read paperbacks now and watched television and waited for Jack's visits. When Jack's mother went shopping, he tagged along with her and carried the bags; he never used to do that; it was something to do, he said. It was the same with other men Jack knew. Calvin White at the Institute was a man of single-ply emotions who had the soft look of a loner; he spent his weekends working on his model railway. Even Dr. Middleton seemed to have no real friends. Jack had heard him refer often to certain associates or colleagues or co-workers, and though he spoke of them with warmth, Jack couldn't recall that he had ever mentioned anyone as being a friend.

He, at least, had Bernie – and how many friends did one person need? There were the Lewises, of course, Hap and Bud. He and Brenda had known them for more than ten years now, and for the last six they'd played bridge with them twice a month, relaxed Sunday evenings in the Lewis living room, 1950-ish evenings, Jack thought: a cardtable and chairs, a bottle of Spanish wine, a dish of cashews. But he had difficulty thinking of them as friends. Hap Lewis had hairy legs and a coarse slamming way with a deck of cards and a rollicking aptitude for opinion-letting – she made a hobby of vivacity – and Jack came away from these evenings sick with pity for Bud, who was obliged, he imagined, after the cards were put away and the cardtable folded, to mount the stairs and take the braying, gesticulating, cursing Hap into his arms. (Though Brenda confided to Jack that Bud and Hap actually had a good sexual relationship and that Hap was basically very vulnerable. 'Really?' Jack had said, unwilling to think how this information had been transmitted and at what cost.)

As for Bud Lewis, he was a lean man with a dark wolfish face, a year or two older than Jack. He worked in the sales department at a chemical firm. His hair was heavy and cut in bangs like a stage Roman and his face was blank as an athlete's. He moved slowly, abstractedly, with a density of patience. An expert bridge player, he arrived at his trumps with a menacing, laconic bending of the final card. He also grew tomatoes from seed under glass and, on Saturday mornings, soberly tuned and adjusted the motor of his 1976 Pontiac. He coached his son's soccer team – Jack had never got over thinking of soccer as an exotic sport – and played a fair game himself. When he spoke it was in flat grammatical English, ploughed with mid-western half-tones; but also with nimble transpositions of phrase that Jack supposed came from his early immersion in the Chicago Lab School. Hap and Bud. Their closest friends. Or so Brenda described them.

Jack had doubts. How could it be true when, after all these years, the bridge nights still commenced with a good quarter-hour of heavy ice breaking? There sat Brenda, stiffly centred on the Lewises' American Provincial sofa with her hands in a worried knot, Hap flying back and forth across the room looking for her cigarettes, and Jack and Bud Lewis facing each other over the coffee table and saying: Have a good week? Not bad. What's new at work? Same old thing more or less, what's up at your place? Same old headaches with the additives, lobby group after us all the time, political thing, we think. Speaking of politics, what do you think of Carter hoisting the dollar? He'd better or we'll go smash, never mind the so-called line of defence. Nothing's going to save us but our own efforts in the end, I don't know.

At last, at last, Bud, with a look of chilly eagerness in his eyes, carried in the bridge table and snapped open its legs. Ready? He positioned the cards on the table. Then Brenda relaxed, Jack pulled his chair forward, Hap lit up, and Bud said, fanning the cards into a semi-circle, 'Here we go.'

The evenings always ended better than they began, and Jack, at times, almost believed Brenda when she referred to the Lewises as their best friends. Bud wasn't half bad, he'd think to himself at the end of a rubber, at least he didn't gloat over his slams, at least he didn't bore hell out of them with office politics. He seldom, in fact, referred to the office, though he did drop occasional clues about what went on in the strange world of sales, confiding to Jack a week ago that since business was slow at the moment, he had been concentrating on cold calling. Cold calling? Bud explained: cold calling was when you initiated a new contact, when you call unannounced on a potential client. Jack had nodded, *Of course, of course*, but imagined curt refusals, doors slamming. Christ, how had *he* been so lucky? His small comfortable office at the Institute. Dr. Middleton, ease, courtesy, open schedules, plenty of time, tea served in china cups at staff meetings. Tea! While Bud Lewis was out making his cold calls, the poor sap.

And who else could he call a friend? There weren't many. Brian Petrie at the Institute, Brian with his egg-rich aura of expertise? Brian had once confided to Jack that he spent ten minutes a day under a sun lamp; that had been years ago, but Jack had remembered, and the small confession of vanity on Brian's part had put a curse on any possible friendship. Who else? Larry Carpenter? He hardly knew him after two years, and had the suspicion anyway that Larry felt for him the same kind of condescension that he felt for Bud Lewis. To Larry *he* was the dull plodder, the man who performed inconsequential and unimaginable daily acts. The thought struck him that everyone might be a Bud Lewis to someone else, tolerated, examined for 'good points.' No, he could never be a friend of Larry's. Certainly he could never talk to Larry Carpenter in the same way he did to Bernie at Roberto's on Friday afternoons.

The Friday lunches: they were in a low period now, of course. And occasionally Jack saw himself and Bernie as they really were, absurd and a little pitiful in their scrambling for the big T Truth, a couple of self-conscious, third-rate, midwestern pseudo-intellectuals, tongues loosened on cheap wine and cliché nihilism, playing a game in which there was more than a suggestion of posing. Much more.

But, on the other hand, the Fridays, at their best, had given him some of the most profoundly happy moments of his life. There had been Fridays when he'd struggled around the corner to Roberto's through sleet storms. He'd turned down invitations from Dr. Middleton to lunch at the Gentleman's Cycle Room. At Roberto's he'd suffered bad service and cold food, and twice his coat had been stolen. But the pleasure, the sweet, reassuring pleasure of it!

Even the regularity of the meetings was preserving. Once a week. It made a time frame of easy proportions, effortlessly adhered to, having the grace of continuity without the weight of appointed occasion. On good days, on lucky days, the antiphonic reverberations heightened like sex his sense of being alive in the world, of being, perhaps, a serious man, even a good man. He felt strange pricklings at the backs of his hands, and a pressure in his chest of something being satisfied and answered. Not that the satisfaction was actually sexual; it was something else, something different but akin to the kind of ecstasy he felt lying in bed with Brenda, holding her in his arms or pressing his face in her shadowy thighs; then his body was invaded by the kind of joy that leaks around the edges of music or from certain kinds of scenery, the singular and untellable sense of arrival.

On Fridays, talking to Bernie, there had been moments when he'd felt a similar kind of arriving, times when he and Bernie had reached out and touched, at exactly the same moment, the identical fragile, inchoate extension of an idea. Of course these moments were rare. They always came as a surprise. You had to get through hours of cold groping; a certain amount of luck was required. But when it happened, Jack felt himself transported to a clean, cool chamber of pure happiness, his heart stopped, his body stilled. The experience – he wondered if Bernie felt it too; they had never discussed it – was something he hadn't attempted to describe to anyone. Why should it be described? It seemed enough that during those rare moments the rest of his life appeared worthy. And possible.

And always, though Jack had never given the thought expression, he had known that the other kind of friendship was there too. Brenda's kind of friendship, caring, dependence, support, consolation. It had always been there, the knowledge that, should he need help, Bernie would supply it. Bernie would stand by him. He had never doubted it. This afternoon, shut up in the den with his lost faith, hadn't the image of Bernie's solace – the possibility of it anyway, brushed past him, lightly promising a form of release? It was there, waiting in reserve. And yesterday at Roberto's he had come close to drawing on it. Harriet Post; rising out of the past with her damned book, the unreasoned treachery of it; he had wanted to weep and beat the table and cry out for deliverance. But he'd held back. He was not one to confide easily in others, having, he supposed, a selfish desire to possess for himself his imperfections. He had grave doubts about the wisdom of casual sharing. Still, there were times when it was hard to hang on alone.

But he had held back, and he was glad now. He'd managed to contain it all, to smooth it over, incorporate the news about Harriet into the formal argument. It would be a mistake to demand too much and too often of his friendship with Bernie; something inevitably was risked, something sacrificed. It was enough anyway to know that the possibility of help existed.

What he had never imagined in his wildest dreams – why was it he was a man with so little imagination? – what he had never imagined was that it would be Bernie who would turn to him. Christ!

It was getting dark. A pool of light from the street lamp outside fell into the room, a faint stippling, bluish-white through the curtains. Jack's hands trembled as he felt for the light switch; the sight of Bernie's flowing tears had shaken and exhilarated him.

It was almost six o'clock. Evening. Time to put Brenda's casserole in the oven.

Chapter Ten

'D^{AD?'}
          'Laurie! My God, you scared me. I didn't hear you come in.'

'I came in the front door.'

'I didn't hear you.'

'What are you doing, Dad?' she said, peering at him across the kitchen. Her face glowed a roughened vegetable-like red from the cold, and her dark curly hair stood straight up.

He held up his hands. 'What does it look like? I'm making a salad.'

'Oh.' She stepped back.

He was always offending her, always speaking with unnecessary sharpness. 'Look, Laurie,' he said. He took a breath. 'Why don't you take off your coat and come give me a hand.'

'Okay,' she said in a larger voice, brightening at once. She was, Jack saw, too easily placated, too easily won back. Watching her unwind her long scarf, he felt his heart clutched with love. There was something soft, something surrendered in this strenuous amiability of hers.

'I wonder,' he said, 'if you happen to know where your mother keeps the salad oil and stuff?'

Laurie's round face with its large, very dark brown eyes beamed confidently at him. There was a suggestion of Brenda in that face, a sleekness about the cheeks that hinted at good nature, and the same wide cleanliness between the eyes. 'Sure,' she said, almost jaunty now, sliding out of her ski jacket and letting it fall on the back of a chair.

'Hang it up,' Jack said automatically, but he made an effort to keep his voice level, 'and by the way, do you know it's after six? I thought you were supposed to get home before it got dark.'

'I was only next door. I couldn't very well get attacked just cutting through the bushes, could I?'

'Hmmm.' He drove a knife through a crisp new head of lettuce.

'Dad?'

'What?'

'Dad. Uncle Bernie's sleeping on the couch. In the living room.'

'I know.'

'Why is he?' She was standing on a stool, rummaging in the cupboard. With sorrow Jack observed the awkward roundness of her body; the soft heft of pre-adolescent thighs and trunk; baby fat, Brenda called it.

'Why is he what?' Jack asked.

'Why's he here? On the couch?'

Her tone, easy, musical, pleased him for some reason. He liked the busy, surprising way her hands were moving across the shelves, and there was something agreeable about her matter-of-factness, as though Bernie's unusual presence on the living-room sofa was no more than an interesting puzzle whose solution she would gladly see solved. She waited, her face ready.

Outside the sky was black and filled with wind; Jack could hear bare branches cracking against the drainpipe at the back of the house. The kitchen felt warm, dry, a cube of light on the dark street, and across the illuminated safety of the table he watched Laurie turn and break an egg into a small glass bowl. 'What are you doing now?' he asked her.

'It's for the salad dressing.'

'An egg?'

'Caesar salad,' she said. Then, entreatingly, 'Is that okay?'

'Good,' he said. 'Great. You know I love Caesar salad.'

'Uncle Bernie –'

'Uncle Bernie's staying overnight tonight,' Jack told her, placing a feather-edge of enthusiasm on his voice.

'Oh.' She turned to him happily and her shoulders contracted with pleasure. 'He's sleeping here? Tonight? On the couch, you mean?'

'I don't know about the couch,' Jack said. 'I haven't thought that far ahead.'

'Because he could have my room,' Laurie said. 'If he wanted to.'

'Well, okay. Maybe. Why don't we ask him when he wakes up, where he wants to sleep.'

'I mean, I could sleep in the quilt room. On that folding bed.'

'Okay. We'll see.'

'Or you know what, Dad?' she said, excited. 'Mother's away, so he could sleep on her half of the bed.'

She spoke urgently, delighted with herself. She had stopped stirring the oil and vinegar around and was waving the fork back and forth in the air, dazed by her own good sense.

'I don't think so, Laurie.'

'Oh.' She began to stir the dressing again, slowly now, absorbing this unexpected 'no.' 'Okay,' she said at last.

Then the back door slammed, letting in a burst of icy air. Rob was home. His blue and white satin jacket radiated with its own cloud of cold. He had grown two inches in the last year, and the kitchen seemed cluttered with his arms and legs. 'I'm starved,' he said, glancing suspiciously around the room.

'How was the track meet?' Jack asked with hollow heartiness, and as he spoke he could feel the question drifting off into the air, apparently unanswerable.

'Not bad. What's to eat?'

'Spanish rice,' Laurie said. 'Who won? Did Elm Park win?'

'When're we eating anyway?'

'Soon,' Jack said shortly.

Rob was opening the oven door and lifting the lid from the pyrex casserole. He grunted, made a face, and gave a ripe snort of disgust. 'Do we have to eat this crap?' he said.

Jack felt the room rock. For a fraction of a second – it couldn't have been more – he was sure he was going to kill Rob. His right hand jerked upward and with horror he saw that he was still holding on to the paring knife. So this was how it happened, kitchen murders, blood on the floor, bodies falling, blind unreasoned passionate rage.

The word crap? It wasn't that; the kids used that word all the time; he used it himself, TV was crap, Nixon was crap, the newspapers were full of crap. It wasn't just today; today's explosion was months overdue. But today, finally moved, he had wanted to smash Rob's face in, to bring his fist up against Rob's nose; he wanted to knock those teeth right out of his head. He made himself take a deep breath and then, trembling, he brought his arm down, carefully placing the knife on the counter, parallel to the edge of the cutting board. The room seemed overbright, blazing. He stared at his son.

Rob stared back, a little frightened now. He was almost as tall as Jack, but a good twenty pounds lighter. 'I hate Spanish rice,' he said weakly.

'You can damn well go hungry then,' Jack said, breathing out sharply. Lout. Insolent lout. Barbarian. Stomping in, as though he owned the place. He could feel his heart pumping blood; there were kids in the world who were starving to death.

For half a minute or more no one spoke. Rob stood, fixed to the floor, his face, with its roughened acne mask, gone suddenly formless, uncertain, and Jack could feel like a physical force his son's instant contrition. He could also sense, and was frightened by, his own inability to let the matter drop.

'Just who in hell do you think you are, stalking in here like this, demanding – '

'Okay, okay,' Rob said, backing off.

'There's salad,' Laurie croaked tearfully from the corner, 'Caesar salad.'

'He goes without dinner tonight,' Jack said stiffly, taking up the knife again and hacking off another wedge of lettuce.

'I said okay, didn't I,' Rob shot back as he dashed from the room and up the stairs.

Silence. The kitchen was stilled. Jack stared unbelievingly at his daughter, who had stopped stirring; her poor mouth sagged open; her hands hung dead in her lap. What in God's name had happened, he asked himself. The bubble of gaiety that had contained the two of them a minute ago, only a minute ago – where had it gone? What in hell – he surveyed the silent kitchen – what in hell had happened, anyway?

The oven was set at four hundred degrees, and the smell of Spanish rice rose in the room. He remembered, with something like anger, that he didn't like Spanish rice. It was one of those budget dishes Brenda used to make when they were first married, hamburger stroganoff, tuna-noodle pot, corned beef pie. Brenda was a good cook, more than a good cook; why, when she was away for a meal, did she leave them bowls of pallid, insipid, impossible food? Was it a punishment of some kind, a way of reminding them of the enormity of her absence?

Upstairs he could hear Rob stomping about, slamming doors. Laurie sniffed in her corner.

'Never mind, kiddo,' Jack said, patting her soft round shoulder. 'All the more for the rest of us, as your Grandpa would say.'

Then, briskly, he made himself a gin and tonic, finding in the dining-room cabinet, the tall frosted glass he liked, shaking ice cubes out of a tray, measuring out a good double ounce of gin. Outside the wind whistled and blew. Usually about this time of day he could see the moon rising over the garage roof. There it was, behind a bank of dark marbled cloud, a scattered, impressionistic luminosity. Maybe it'll snow, he thought idly.

He was about to carry his glass into the living-room; he was halfway there when he heard the soft breezing sound of someone snoring.

He'd forgotten. Bernie was here.

Chapter Eleven

As it happened Bernie loved Spanish rice. He hadn't had it in years, he said, not since he and Sue were first married. 'Glad you woke me up,' he told Jack. His eyes were dull and rimmed with a watery line of red, but his voice was steady enough. To Laurie he said, with sturdy, dutiful blandishment, 'You know something – I think this is the best salad I've had since I don't know when.'

Laurie had set the table in the kitchen. 'It's cozier in here,' she explained. She closed the red denim curtains at the window over the sink so that the room seemed warmly sealed and softened. She put three woven placemats on the kitchen table, and then she folded paper napkins into fans, weaving them in and out of the tines of the forks. She carried an African violet in a clay pot from the window sill and positioned it in the middle of the table.

'Hey,' Bernie said to her, 'you didn't tell me this was going to be a party.'

Gravely ceremonial, she placed Bernie at one end of the table, Jack at the other, and herself in the middle, collapsing into her chair with a noisy hostessy flounce. 'There,' she puffed, surveying the table, her face open and expectant, her dark curls shining.

Rob stayed upstairs in his room; they could hear his radio playing loudly. The Rolling Stones. A driving beat. Jack cleared his throat – he felt compelled to explain. 'Rob's not eating tonight,' but Bernie only nodded and reached across the table for the salt.

It was then that a numbing gel of self-consciousness came over Jack; he could actually feel the cold, slow tensing of his skin and outer muscles. It reminded him of being at the dentist and having an injection of novacaine and then losing, by degrees, control over his face. His hands, clumsy as boxing gloves, gripped the fork, and his knees, suddenly bulbous, knocked against the table leg. A calm disbelief seized him – this embarrassment of intimacy had come too quickly; how had he arrived at this motionless disarray, this unjointed unreality?

His relationship with Bernie, with its limits and rules of procedure and orderly, trudging self-restraint – had all that been so quickly overturned? It was Saturday night; he had suffered the spectacle of Bernie's tears; he had put an arm across his heaving shoulders; now he was sentenced, it seemed, to total disorientation. Here sat his oldest friend, yet it was impossible to meet his eyes. Should he, he wondered wildly, attempt to restore the old sense of balance by picking up the threads of yesterday's discussion, go on with his idea about history being a matter of endings? No, the idea seemed suddenly childish. It would be too obvious a diversion. It would be insensitive. Why would a man, abandoned by his wife, want to dwell on a chilly abstraction like history? Better just keep quiet and eat.

He chewed on, engulfed by his own lumbering silence. He had always had, he knew, a disabling lack of nerve for new situations, and now, almost unconsciously, he cursed Brenda for abandoning him on this day of all days. For leaving him with Bernie's tears and with their two puzzling and difficult children and this sticky bowl of pink rice. What had irked him, he realized now, was the assertiveness, the greed, with which Rob had plunged into the house, demanding as his right, food, warmth, clothes on his back.

Bernie's presence – his firm occupancy of the kitchen chair and the rigorous plying of his fork – nudged at Jack. And so did the suitcase still standing in a corner of the hall. What was the matter with him? Was he so uncharitable? And did Bernie perhaps detect a subtle failure of welcome – was that why he was ploughing through a second helping of rice, knocking back a glass of beer, attempting jollity?

This was the kind of silence that could be ruinous, and he was grateful to Laurie who, as she ate, recited for them her recipe for Caesar salad. Oil, lemon, parsley, garlic. She seemed intent on her newly created role, eating with elaborate delicacy and taking masterful, cheerful charge of the conversation. Bernie, blinking, eating, smiling, listened in a daze.

'Have some more rice, Dad,' Laurie urged. Although she had perfect teeth, she had in the last year devised a new way of smiling, a curious closed smile with a demented sweetness about it.

'Doesn't anyone want any more?' she demanded, and Jack could hear disappointment in her voice.

'What about you?' Bernie asked. 'Cooks should get their fair share.'

'I'm stuffed. All that junk I ate over at the Carpenters.'

'I thought you were out walking the dogs,' Jack said.

'I was. Brinkley doesn't heel anymore. Mrs Carpenter says they're sending him to obedience school, and do you know what Mr. Carpenter said?'

'What?'

'He said "in a pig's eye." I thought people only said that in the movies.'

'Uhuh.'

'He's in a bad mood. Mrs. Carpenter said I could open the dog food when I got back, but he said he thought I'd better get a move on. And then Mrs. Carpenter said I could stay and help her with the party food. And do you know what else? She said I could call her Janey. She said because there weren't all that many years between us.'

'She did, did she.' Jack sipped at his beer.

To Bernie she explained, 'They're having an enormous party tonight. Huge. Shrimp and stuff. Lobster salad with guess what in it? Pecans. And these little pastry things with curled up ends and chicken inside. I've been helping her poke the chicken in.'

'And she let you have a taste?'

'A taste!' Laurie rubbed her stomach with enthusiasm and rolled her eyes. 'I've eaten tons. *Tons*. She – Mrs. Carpenter – Janey – kept asking me to taste everything for her. Like she wanted to know if there was enough salt in the dip or too much curry in those chicken things I told you about and stuff like that. She made this neat dip out of sour cream and grated turnip. She said last time they had the caterers do everything, but they always brought the same old stuff and it was kind of soggy. Do you remember, Dad? If the food was soggy at their last party? You were there.'

'Actually,' Jack paused, wishing he could say something that would make her laugh, something that would compensate for the ugly scene with Rob before dinner, 'actually, as I remember that last party, it was the people who were soggy.'

Laurie didn't laugh; she looked puzzled. 'The people?'

'It's only a joke.'

'What do you mean they were soggy?'

'Nothing. I didn't mean anything. To tell you the truth, hon, I can't remember what the food was like. Or the people.'

The Carpenters' last party, and Jack reflected with a mild wave of belligerence that it had been only six weeks ago, seemed little more than a blur. He had been on edge for some reason that night; he had wanted to go to a movie, something trashy and softly coloured with tap dancers, where he could drift off holding on to Brenda's hand, but instead they had got dressed and gone to the party, where he had drunk too many scotches in too short a time, and to complicate matters he and Brenda hadn't known anyone there. Larry and Janey Carpenter had moved out to Elm Park less than two years ago. They had made a few friends, the Lewises and the Wallbergs and the Bowmans. They'd joined the Little Theatre and the tennis club, but most of their friends seemed to live downtown. There were, as Jack remembered, quite a few journalists and theatre people at the party (Larry wrote on theatre and, sometimes, wine, for Chicago *Today*); there were at least two psychiatrists and a handsomely dressed, articulate group of people who seemed to have something to do with raising money for a ballet committee. No one had sat down. Jack, who had spent the afternoon cleaning out the basement, was weary, but it hadn't been the kind of party where he felt he could ease himself into an armchair and fade away. After a while he found a doorway in the dining room to lean against, and he dimly remembered having a long conversation with a young, sharply made-up girl in a dark green corduroy suit who told him she was a troubleshooter for a uranium company. Troubleshooter? It sounded bizarre; he wanted to ask exactly what that meant in terms of the uranium industry, but he hadn't. At the time he suspected she might be pulling his leg; now, six weeks later, he was sure of it. He had felt middle-aged and dull. The backs of his knees hurt. He remembered remarking to her that he was engaged at the moment in writing a book, and she said, shifting into a mock southern tone, 'Ain't everyone?' What was that? He'd opened his mouth, about to ask what she meant, but she had wandered away toward the bar. There was a great deal of food, but it seemed to be hours before it appeared. Then, finally, later still, there was some coffee and a tray of French pastries; he especially remembered the chocolate eclairs because he had been talking in a corner to a political columnist from Chicago *Today* – an older man with a crude knobbled profile and a reputation for having once held hawkish views on Vietnam – who stuffed his eclair into his mouth, and then, carefully, meticulously, licked each of his fingers in turn, first the little finger, then the second finger, and arriving, finally, at his thumb, which he twisted and smacked between thick pink lips. Jack watched him, fascinated. He should start reading this man's column again, he thought to himself, to see if he's softened up on communism. There would be something affirming about such a softening up. He was about to confide the fact that he too was a writer of sorts, in the midst of writing a book on Indian trading practices; but he stopped himself; enough of that for one night. About the rest of the evening he recalled nothing.

Except for one thing. He remembered, in perfect, reprintable, film-like memory, the moment when he and Brenda arrived, a little late, at the Carpenters' front door. (He had put on his new vest; then, at the last minute decided against it.) Janey Carpenter in a calf-length calico dress had flung open the door and astonished them both by dipping all the way to the floor in a strange, slightly tipsy curtsy. She had very pale blonde hair, longer than most women were wearing this year, especially women in their late thirties.

'Enter, neighbours,' she cried over the hubbub. 'Greetings.'

Jack had always thought her a little cool, and the warmth of the greeting had surprised him. From nowhere Larry appeared, steadying Janey with one hand and taking charge. He was wearing a deep brown Norwegian sweater with dropped shoulders and suede patches at the elbow. His softly shining sandy-beige hair lay neat as a wig. 'Jack! Brenda!!' He pronounced their names with the heat of exclamation but not the force. 'Let me introduce you around.' Larry's voice was smoothly elegant, but with a tremulous lack of substance about it, like yogurt packed into a carton. 'This,' Larry said, his hand on Jack's shoulder, 'is our next door neighbour Jack Bowman, an expert on Great Lakes Indians. And *this* is Brenda,' he smiled, paused, slid an arm around her waist, 'who is a quiltmaker in her own right.'

Brenda never blinked, and at the time Jack thought she might have missed it; she had drifted off after that, found someone interesting to talk to, a man who travelled around the world photographing beaches for a tourist agency. Jack had caught a glimpse of her later over the buffet table, had heard the word Madagascar float in the air, but it wasn't until they got home that he had a chance to talk to her.

It was two-thirty in the morning. She had fallen backwards onto their bed, still in her dress, shrieking with laughter. 'A quiltmaker in her own right! Oh, Jack, I thought I was going to burst. Didn't you want to howl? All night long I kept thinking about it, didn't you? Every time I saw Larry going by in that woolly sweater of his I just wanted to die laughing.'

They had held on to each other; their rhythmic laughing made the bed shake. They rolled over and over, and Jack, unzipping her dress, had felt almost mad with gratitude: she had seen how funny it all had been. (She didn't always laugh at the same things; only a week before, early one morning, he had been sitting on the edge of the bed putting on a new pair of socks when he simultaneously found himself in a state of erection. Impulsively he had peeled the sticker off the socks, a little round gold and black sticker which said 'New Executive Length.' He glanced down; it was really quite a presentable erection, and he had stuck the label on its swollen tip. Then, wrapped in a towel, he had caught Brenda off guard in the bathroom and, flicking the towel aside, he'd shaken his hips and cried, 'Ta da.' He had been so sure she would laugh, but instead she'd gazed mildly at him from behind her face cloth and said, 'Oh, Jack honestly.')

But she had laughed at Larry Carpenter's introduction – *a quiltmaker in her own right* – and for that he loved her. He adored her for that. As late as it was, in spite of all the scotch he had drunk, they made slow, languorous love, more attentive than usual. Thank you, thank you, thank you, he had thought, clamping his mouth onto her breast, while the memory of the preposterous Larry Carpenter kept breaking through their embraces like a prized bubble of craziness.

The joke had lasted for days. 'Here's an egg in its own right,' Brenda said, handing him his breakfast the next morning. 'Here I am,' Jack called, arriving home early from work, 'your husband in his own right.'

Larry Carpenter, with his English raincoat and his won-

67

drously shaped head of hair, dissolved before them, an absurd scurrying grasshopper of a man, deserving every nuance of ridicule they could devise. They watched from the window in the mornings as he climbed in his yellow Porsche and backed out of the driveway. 'A sportscar in its own right,' Brenda announced, making a face.

Within a week the joke had worn thin, all its comic possibilities exhausted. It had seemed, somehow, mean-spirited to go on with it any longer. When Larry phoned on the next Sunday afternoon asking them to come in for a drink, Jack had insisted that it was their turn. Larry accepted quickly, almost with gratitude. 'We'll be right over,' he'd said.

They had sat in the living room in the last of the afternoon light. Jack made screwdrivers, and Brenda passed cheese and crackers. Larry, relaxed, talked mockingly but with good humour about the state of the theatre in Chicago, about the renaissance of amateur local theatre. He had been touched, he told them, to be given the role of Hamlet, he who had joined the group only a year and a half ago. His modesty, so unexpected, was becoming. 'There's something,' he said, 'almost heroic about an amateur group taking on a production of *Hamlet*. They almost know in advance that they're going to fail, but they plod on nevertheless. Amateurism may save us in the end, keep us from washing down the drain on our silver-plated fannies.' Janey had nodded, agreeing; she had been particularly sweet that day, Jack remembered.

And now, already, they were having another party. 'Very informal,' Janey had told them when she phoned. 'More of an open house sort of thing. The whole cast from *Hamlet* and some other people I know you'll enjoy.'

'Here we go again,' Brenda sighed, banging the side of her head with her fist, but then she remembered, gleefully, that she would be in Philadelphia that night.

Jack – thinking of the girl in corduroy and the midnight blur of alcohol – had decided not to go. He would spend a quiet evening at home; they would never miss him in all that crowd.

But here it was, Saturday night. His son was sulking upstairs. His daughter was chattering and humming and washing dishes and driving him crazy with her bottomless fund of good will. Bernie Koltz sat morosely, like a depleted monk, at his kitchen table, puffing air into his cheeks and staring at the curtains.

'Bernie,' Jack said at last, 'do you know what you need?'

'What?'

'You need to meet some new people. Have a drink or two. Three even.'

'Like a hole in the head.'

'Why not? We wouldn't have to stay more than half an hour. It's just a drop-in party, no big deal.'

'I don't know,' Bernie said.

Suddenly Jack knew he couldn't bear the thought of sitting home all evening. 'Bernie,' he said, 'you really should go. I mean it. Sitting around at a time like this is crazy. It's the worst thing you can do at a time like this. People can get seriously depressed. Remember what's-his-name, that guy who used to work in your department? What you need is to get your mind on something else.'

'I've brought a book.'

'Listen,' Jack told him, 'I'll lend you a clean shirt. I'll phone over to the Carpenters' and tell them I'm bringing a friend along. They're not all that bad, and the food'll be good. You might enjoy it. It's Saturday night, you need to get out of yourself, you need to forget for a few hours, you need to get some kicks out of life, or what's it for? Hell, Bernie, we can't sit around like this. Come on.'

And to himself he was saying: a better man would resist, a better man would remain at home tonight. He would carry a ham sandwich and a glass of milk upstairs and enact a reconciliation with his son, who is sensitive, who could never bear to be scolded when he was little, who is suffering, who is hungry. A better man would stay home, play Scrabble with his daughter, make her laugh, thank her for doing the dishes, tell her stories, tell her he remembered being her age and what it was like. A better man – where was he? – would give his full attention and sympathy to his oldest friend, his friend who has today suffered a major catastrophe in his life, who is feeling lost and alone and frightened and even tearful. A better man would carry armfuls of seasoned logs up from the basement, lay a fire in the living room, call the children to watch a ceremonial match being lit – they used to love that once. A better man refused invitations from those for whom he felt a casual aversion, he had better things to do than squander his life on social trivia. A man's time on Earth is limited, it has to be carefully, seriously, spent. There was his manuscript awaiting his patient attention; this day might still be turned to profit, he could still, if he wanted, salvage something.

'Well,' Bernie said, 'maybe – '

'Great.' Jack moved toward the telephone. 'I'll give them a call right away.'

Chapter Twelve

B ERNIE ASKED: 'WHAT'S LARRY CARPENTER LIKE, ANYWAY?'
What was he like? Jack hesitated, thinking of Larry's
successful, intelligent face and narrow late-thirties body. He
liked Larry well enough when they were talking together at an
Elm Park party or over the back hedge. At these times, talking
one-to-one, he found Larry engaging and even generous in his
judgments. But at other times, if he happened to think of Larry
at all, his mind conjured up images of distrust; there was an
empty field of *ennui* about Larry, an insouciant fending off of
inquiry; the truth was that Jack thought of Larry Carpenter as a
bit of an ass, something of a prick, in fact. Even Brenda thought
so. How could this be, this seeming paradox?

Perhaps because the Carpenters managed to convert their
state of childlessness into an intellectual refinement. Janey, it
seemed to Jack, was sulky and coy, with her pale hair and vivid
Vogue magazine mouth; but at times she showed a fleeting
prettiness. Larry treated her tenderly, as though she were a
child. He was not an easy man to figure out, and Jack's feelings
about him consisted mostly of a vague wariness.

He offered Bernie a version of his first meeting with Larry,
which occurred on the weekend the Carpenters moved in. It
was late fall, the end of November, in the middle of a Saturday
afternoon. Jack had been standing in his backyard with his
hands jammed into the back pockets of his pants, breathing in
the blackish smell of decayed leaves and woodsmoke.

A young man's voice, buoyant and carrying the unmistakable
stamp of the eastern seaboard, floated across the hedge – Larry
Carpenter in person, *the* Larry Carpenter. Jack had read his
column in Chicago *Today* on and off for the last two years –
often, he admitted, with amusement; this was a man who
would say anything for a laugh.

Hey, Larry had called to Jack across the lawn that first day, hey, neighbour, anytime you want to uproot this jungle, I'll go halves with you on the demolition cost.

Jack had been immediately thrown on the defensive; he loved the wild bank of nameless, shapeless bushes that bordered and protected his yard, and it was his intention to keep them forever; on the other hand, it had seemed only decent to go over and introduce himself.

So you're a historian, Larry Carpenter had exclaimed in a light, waltz-time voice, well, well, maybe you can tell me, then, something about the history of this crumbling wreck of a house my wife and I've just bought. Lord, lord, Larry had said, we must have been crazy to take this on, it's going to take us forever just to get the place cleaned up.

Carefully, knowing he was meeting Larry's suave resonance with unfelt heartiness, Jack explained to this boyish stranger in the grey mohair sweater – Larry was partly hidden by leafless branches – about old Miss Anderson the former owner, about how many years she'd lived in the old house, it was something of a legend, to tell the truth; about her two cats, Aristotle and Plato, about how her sight had been failing for years, how she tried year after year to find high school boys to look after the yard and wash her windows but they always let her down, how she was forced to live on a teacher's pension granted back in the days when pensions had been peanuts. Christ, she bought meat only once a week, she had told Brenda; she was really quite a terrific old gal, actually, Jack said to Larry Carpenter. He said *this*, he who had loathed Miss Anderson and had found the ridges and sexless elongations of her face appalling and terrifying, he who cringed at the asthmatic whine with which she assailed those – like himself – who called on behalf of the Heritage Committee. Old Cactus Cunt, they called her in the neighbourhood, and now, Christ, here he was, standing in his own backyard, his own turf, his own territory, leaning on a bent branch of maple and creating, involuntarily, a tawdry fiction, a melodrama about this marvellous old crone, this real life stoic and neighbourhood character, this heroine, in fact – the old darling herself, bless her.

Larry Carpenter, listening, nodding, had rummaged in the roots of his neat beige hair; he had fixed Jack with a sharp look of incredulity; a smile started to break on his lips, although all he said was, yes, well, about this jungle, if you ever do decide –

Later, upstairs, Jack found Bernie a shirt. 'I think this'll fit,' he said.

They were dressing together. Bernie, Jack saw, wore orange jockey shorts. They hadn't dressed together for at least twenty-five years, not since the old summer days in the locker room at the Forest Park Swimming Pool.

'Unless you'd rather have that blue shirt. Doesn't matter to me.'

'Anything,' Bernie said shortly.

'Well, at least that one fits.'

'Thanks.'

'You don't want a tie, do you?'

'Just the shirt's fine,' Bernie's voice pulled down firmly.

'Okay.' Jack buttoned a cuff and regarded himself in the mirror.

'What's that?' Bernie asked. 'On the hanger? By the blue shirt.'

'That? A vest.'

'I never saw you wear that.'

'Well, I haven't exactly worn it. Not yet anyway, it's still new. But – '

'It looks like suede.'

'I don't know why I bought it,' Jack heard himself say. 'Impulse or something.'

'Well, look, if you're not going to be wearing it tonight, maybe I could wear it. To go over the shirt.'

'Well – '

'Unless you were going to. It doesn't really matter to me.'

'Well – '

'I don't really – '

'Sure. Go ahead. Someone might as well wear it.'

'We're delighted you came.'

The Carpenters seemed to be genuinely pleased that Jack had brought Bernie along, and why shouldn't they be? Jack thought. Bernie Koltz was more than presentable, possessing as he did the bodily compactness of the true, tensely tuned intellectual. His face, at middle-age, had come into fashion: a quizzing ironic muzzle, handsomely grotesque, with pinkish thoughtful eyes that projected liveliness and rascality. Tonight he looked especially modish and jaunty.

'Come, come,' Larry said, 'let me introduce you around.'

He ferried them around the living room, through the study, into the dining room. To all the people standing in casually formed groups with drinks in hand, he said, 'I want you guys to meet Jack Bowman, our local expert on Great Lakes Indians. Trade customs, beads, and blankets. And this – this is Bernie Koltz, have I got that right? Good. Who teaches at De Paul. Math, you said, Bernie? Would you believe I did my Math with matchsticks, right through fourth-year Economics? I still get out the old matchsticks at tax time, ask Janey. Look, I haven't even offered you two a drink. This is old-wine night, I don't know if Janey explained on the phone. We've got some hard stuff if you'd rather, scotch, vodka, some terrific rum, whatever. But we thought you might like to try some of this stuff Janey and I got in Beaune last summer. You've got to have a taste, anyway, after all the trials and tribulations of getting it into the country. Not to mention a measure of criminality. It's not great wine – we got stuck with a few roughs, but this bottle here happens to be a smoothie, at least my palate says it is, try a little. By the way, have you met Hy Saltzer? He does bricks, come on over and let me do the honours.'

'He's darling, Jack,' Janey Carpenter whispered in the kitchen.

Jack had wandered in looking for ice for his scotch and found Janey taking a tray of cheese puffs out of the oven. She was looking flushed and pretty; he'd never seen her look this pretty. A queer cinnamon perfume rose from the region of her throat.

'I like his eyes,' she told Jack. 'I noticed them right away.'

'His eyes?'

'And that terrific suede vest. That toast colour. Sort of muted. I love it.'

'Uhuh.'

'Is he, well, married? Or what?'

Jack helped himself to ice and nodded vaguely. 'Separated.'

'Aha.' She threw Jack a small shrug that said: sad, but that's how it is these days.

'His wife, Sue, is a doctor,' Jack explained, sipping scotch, 'psychiatric medicine.'

'Have they been separated long?'

The question, or perhaps the way she posed it, seemed indecently curious; Jack hedged. 'It's fairly recent,' he told her.

'I thought so,' she nodded knowingly. 'Something about his eyes. You can usually tell. Have a cheese puff.'

'I will. Thanks.'

'Anyway,' she paused an instant on her way into the dining room, 'I think he's sweet. Sweet.'

This party *was* different from the last one. Jack saw here and there neighbours, faces he recognized. Some of them he knew well. Irving and Leah Wallberg, Robin Fairweather and his new wife – Christ, she couldn't be more than twenty-five. The Sandersons, Bill Block. And Hap Lewis, who asked him about Brenda. 'Did she decide to take all three quilts, Jack? Or just the two?'

'Three. I think that's what she said. The box was heavy enough, anyway. We sent it air-freight.'

'Brenda showed them to me yesterday. All three. But my favourite, my absolute favourite was *Second Coming*. Those colours! And what she did around the edges! Have you ever seen anything like that kind of feathering effect on the edges of a quilt before? It's things like that that Brenda excels at. Jesus, I mean she's got that folk thing down solid, and then there's that Van Goghish vitality spilling out, and all the time it is so goddamned restrained. Like a kind of quietness that's all her own, like a trademark. Unique, kind of. I suppose you could call it energy contained. This feeling of, you know, wildness, but it's a tongue-in-cheek wildness. There's sex in those forms, but order. Like you can sense a pattern in the universe if you know what I mean, an underlying order. That's what I was telling Brenda. Discipline within chaos. But strength, a really tremendous flow of calculated strength, do you know what I mean, Jack? I can never put these things in words, it's all so fucking abstract, but that's what I felt, I really did.'

Jack listened. He nodded and sipped. 'Yes,' he said. 'I think so, too.'

'I work for a Chicago-based mining company,' a woman in a velvet skirt the colour of blue plums told Jack. She was standing by the fireplace smoking a small cigar. My God, he thought. Her again.

'Oh?' Jack said. 'Sounds interesting.'

'Uranium. It's shitty work if you want the truth. I have to take nothing but shit.'

75

'Doesn't everyone?' What did he mean?

'It's a PR kind of thing. A troubleshooter, they call me. Ha.'

'Why do you do it?'

'I have to do something. Jesus, I've got a kid to support. A boy. Eleven years old. I'm the sole support.'

'I have a daughter who's eleven,' Jack said, remembering as he spoke that Laurie had turned twelve.

'You do? Really? What did you say you do?'

'I'm writing a book. About Indian trade practices.'

'My God, that sounds fabulous, I mean it. Tell me about it.'

Did you and Brenda see the play?' Leah Wallberg asked him.

Of all Brenda's friends he liked Leah best. She had a wide pink apple-shiny face and a plump body filled with soft slopes. When she talked she had a trick of lifting her hands into small shapely gestures, the gestures of a much younger and more slender woman, exquisite, precise, as though she were inscribing words on sheets of air. By profession she was a designer, and it was she who had designed the stage setting for the Little Theatre production of *Hamlet*.

'No,' Jack told her, 'we missed it, I'm afraid. Brenda's been so busy this week getting ready for the exhibition. She worked up to the last minute. And then I forgot to pick up the tickets – '

'Don't apologize, Jack. Really. You haven't missed a thing. Not a thing.'

'We heard it was a little slow in spots.'

'That's putting it kindly. Kindly! It was,' her wrists made double hoops in the air, 'it was a qualified disaster. But please don't tell anyone I said so. Especially You Know Who.'

'A qualified disaster?' Jack asked. 'What do you mean, qualified?'

'Well, you know, you can't wreck *Hamlet* completely. Something comes through. Peggy Giles was a pretty good Ophelia, especially when you think she's only nineteen. Robin was good too, but then he always is. But, ahem, Hamlet – '

'How exactly did he get the part?'

'Do you know,' she shrugged prettily, 'I'm not sure. We just sort of gave way to him. He seemed so anxious. He just wanted it so much.'

'You were mesmerized.'

'I guess so. Really, Jack, it serves us right. I guess we just

76

thought, here is this theatre critic, he's just got to be a great Hamlet. I don't think anyone else even auditioned once they knew he wanted the role. But when you think about it, it's crazy. It's like saying *you're* an Indian because you know all about them.'

'But I don't – '

'The only lucky thing was that there were only four performances. Because he kept getting worse each time. Louder, stagier. It was almost dangerous to sit in the front row, Irv said – you could get knocked over by that swirling cloak of his. Lord! And I don't think he realized how really lousy he was either. That's the funny thing about it. But I don't know, it's not all that serious, I suppose. At least he had the nerve to try. I guess you have to give him some credit. It takes nerve to find out you can't do something, what do you think, Jack?'

'I agree. Absolutely.'

The Carpenters' glass and rosewood table was covered with plates of food. Jack helped himself to a sliver of smoked trout and winked at Bernie across the room. Bernie was lifting a wine glass to his lips and seemed to be listening with great attentiveness to a sharply gesticulating young man in a purple shirt and small black beard who was quizzing him with the sucking ferocity of a plunger. He had a damp mouth and smiled like an actor. Bernie was concentrating so hard that he didn't see Jack winking at him. Why was he winking, anyway? He never winked. It wasn't his style; it wasn't in his canon.

What he needed, he decided, was a drink.

In the kitchen the Carpenters were quarrelling. Jack found them facing each other over a tray of dirty wine glasses.

'You can still phone the bloody office and have it killed,' Janey was saying to Larry in a low voice.

'I can't do anything of the kind,' Larry said. 'Even if I were inclined to do it, it would still be too late.'

'It's not too late. I happen to know it isn't. Remember that time when they took out your review and put in the Russian ballet thing? That was right at the last minute.'

'Janey, listen. For one thing it's too late and for another thing it's unprofessional.'

'Unprofessional! You make me laugh. You're the drama critic. You're supposed to give the assignments.'

'It can't be done, and that's all there is to it.'

Jack stood awkwardly in the doorway. They turned and saw him, and Larry, for the first time since Jack had known him, seemed embarrassed.

Janey sprang forward and took Jack's arm. She was breathing rapidly and was flushed with wine. 'Jack, what do you think? Larry, why don't you ask Jack what he thinks?'

'I can come back,' Jack said. 'I was just looking for some ice.'

Janey wouldn't let go of his arm. 'Listen, Jack, Gordon Tripp – do you know Gordon Tripp? – the movie critic for *Chicago Today*? – well, he's doing a write-up of Larry's performance as Hamlet. It's supposed to be in the morning paper.'

'Forget it, Janey,' Larry said.

'Now do you think that's fair?' Janey asked Jack. 'You know they never cover amateur performances. Never. And now, just because Larry happens to be – '

'I don't think Jack's particularly interested in whether or not *Hamlet* gets a review in the paper.' Larry said this in a voice that was reasonable and good tempered, but Jack noticed that his hands were trembling in mid-air.

'You could have it killed,' Janey said, louder now. Her eyes had the mica brightness of real tears. 'You can just pick up the crummy phone and tell them at the office that you won't stand for it. That you want it out. You don't have to take that kind of crap from Gordon Tripp. You've got seniority. You can just tell him to shove it. He's no theatre critic, anyway. Who does he think he is?'

'There is no way I can stop a review, Janey, so let's just forget it.' Larry pulled open the giant door of the refrigerator. 'And now, Jack,' his voice was solemn, even though his eyes were oddly locked into dazed focuslessness, 'you were saying something about ice. Let me see if I can find some for you.'

Jack carried his drink into the living room. There were soft lamps lit all around the room, creating a white silk patrician ambience. He sat on the arm of a velvet chair and talked to a woman in a paisley blouse. He had never been able to see the point of paisley. She was an agreeable woman, however, with a dull silver chain around her throat, and she told Jack that although she wrote fashion features she would really like to do a book someday.

'Really?' And Jack told her a little about his own book.

She was fascinated by the idea of history, she said; the Indians of the southwest had been nuanced to death, but she thought the Great Lakes Indians had been neglected, especially their attitude toward property and trade. Jack sipped his drink, cheered by her observations. She was quite a bright woman, really. After a while she told Jack a long story about her graduate thesis on John Donne, which was rejected at the last minute because she refused her professor at South Carolina certain bizarre sexual favours. Jack nodded and commiserated; he didn't believe a word she was saying. Christ, Christ, Christ, Christ, Christ.

'What's the matter, Jack?' Janey asked him, smiling. She seemed to have recovered her good spirits.

'I can't find Bernie. I wonder if he went home. I've been looking everywhere for him. I just realized how late it was.'

'He's asleep,' Janey said, open-mouthed with tenderness.

'What do you mean, asleep?'

'I was upstairs a minute ago,' Janey said, 'to powder my nose. And when I peeked into the guest room, there he was. Sleeping like a baby.'

'Passed out?'

'Like a baby.' She smiled wonderfully.

'My God, how am I going to get him home?'

Larry joined them. He was rather drunk but pleasant. (Larry Carpenter is a charmer, the paisley woman had told Jack.) He gave Janey's shoulder an affectionate squeeze and said to Jack, 'Why don't you just leave him here until morning? He's okay, I think. I checked on him half an hour ago, and he was breathing like a generator.'

'It would be a dirty trick to wake him up,' Janey murmured.

'My God,' Jack said, shaking his head.

Larry spread his hands, grinning boyishly. 'Really. I mean it. Leave him. We'd love an overnight guest, wouldn't we Janey?'

'We'd love it. We've just had that room papered and we'd love –'

'If you're sure.' He longed, inexplicably, to please them.

'No problem at all, Jack, no problem at all.'

It was 4 A.M. when Jack went home, scrambling through a break in the bushes, catching a leg of his pants and muttering shit, shit, shit. In the east the city lights had turned the sky into a pale dome of hammered aluminum. The air was ringing with frost. He found the back door unlocked; he should have told the kids to lock the doors; they should have known better than to leave it open.

Inside it was quiet and dark. There were shoes on the stairs, a strong sense of habitation. He ought to check on Rob and Laurie, push open their bedroom doors, make sure they were all right, but he was already in bed before he thought of this. Medium-drunk, he was rapidly on the way to unconsciousness, but he took note of the unusual coolness of the bed sheets: Brenda was in Philadelphia; what was she doing at this moment? He pictured her in a narrow bed, weighed down by a mountain of quilts, *The Second Coming* folded on top.

The room receded dangerously. Exhausted as he was, he made an effort to take bearings: Bernie Koltz was flat out next door, and Bernie's wife Sue was sighing in the arms of her lover – somewhere in this city her sighing was contained and answered. Harriet Post was smugly sleeping the night away in a dim Rochester bedroom, her manuscript stacked and stapled and ready in a cardboard carton. His own children were asleep; children can always sleep; it was one of the compensations of childhood, the ability to transform pain overnight into the abstraction of history.

Sleep was coming to Jack, too; he stretched and let it invade his body. Words and deeds rained down silently on his dying consciousness; dreams rose, an interlacing of forms printed on the inside of his eyelids. He was suspended in snow, growing lighter and lighter, but something was asking to be remembered, something singular and plaintive – what was it? Then it came to him: his lost faith. Today, sitting at his desk, he had discovered himself to be a man without substance. The remembrance closed the day. There was a simplicity about it like the evenness of church music. Amen.

The room grew darker, but he hung on for another minute to the thought of his absent faith, holding it safe in the failing transparent vessel of his brain, partly warmed by the anguish it created, partly comforted by its decency.

Chapter Thirteen

O N SUNDAY MORNING JACK WOKE AND FOUND THAT THE
void left by his shattered faith had inexplicably grown; it
had spread alarmingly in all directions, a living thing, kicking
and groaning, animated like a breathy conga line, involving not
only himself now, but others. Perhaps it was the emptiness of
the queensize bed; he wasn't used to waking and seeing
Brenda's side of the bed so severely undisturbed. The quilted
bedspread, with its blues and greens in overlapping spears of
colour, lay in smooth contrast to his hot rumpled sheets, and
this smoothness posed a question: why? Why, after twelve
years, had Sue and Bernie ended their marriage? Had they lost
faith, too? Faith in what? Jack didn't know. Why did people
insist on making for themselves, and for others, pools of loneliness and suffering? No, suffering was too strong a word, too
noisy with literary echoes, too Protestant. How had he arrived
at this point of immobility, self-insulated, sealed off?

Jack pulled himself out of bed, pushing the thought of
suffering aside. What he needed was hot coffee.

His pain, like a stubbed toe, had a rapid countdown; ease and
forgetfulness came always; it could be depended upon.

The faith Jack had lost wasn't a religious faith. He had never
been a church-goer, nor had his parents been church-goers.
'Only sinners have to go to church,' his father used to say with a
waggish snort, gulping his Sunday-morning coffee. Jack's
mother had fretted now and then about it, saying in her small
sinus-muffled way, 'I don't know, we really should go, at least
at Easter we really should go.' But they never did.

In spite of this fact, Jack had grown up in the belief that
Sundays were days of particularized ritual. There was a difference in the pacing of time: a slowing of speech, a grave
attention paid to newspapers, armchairs, the temperature of
the living room, the view from the apartment, the quality of
sunshine coming through the cloud cover. Certain things were
expected; Jack's mother, who cherished regularity, attended to

that. Even now, at seventy, she seemed uneasy if the day's special observations were somehow interrupted or disturbed. Her long-ago response to the invasion of Pearl Harbour had passed into family legend – 'But it's Sunday,' she had protested.

On Sundays she rose at seven, drank a cup of instant coffee and began to clean the apartment. Wednesday was her regular cleaning day, but on Sunday she 'straightened up,' beginning by shaking out the rug in the hallway of the apartment, then working her way through the living room, the small, seldom-used dining room with its ring of dark varnished furniture, and then the kitchen. After that she began on the three bedrooms, first the spare room, formerly Jack's bedroom, and then the small, dark pink bedroom at the back where she slept now. Because Jack's father liked to sleep late on Sunday – late meant nine o'clock – she did his room last, humming fitfully as she worked, sometimes talking to herself a little. She damp-mopped all the floors and dusted the table tops, reaching inside the lampshades to dust the tops of the lightbulbs – she had read somewhere that large amounts of electricity were lost because of dusty lightbulbs. In the winter she filled the pans of water on top of the radiators. She watered the wandering Jew, which sat on a low table by the front window, and then she opened the back door and put a slice of bread on the fire escape for the birds. What kind of birds were they? Jack had asked her once. Surprised, she had shaken her head; she didn't know, she'd never learned the names of birds, and except for robins and bluejays, they all looked alike to her. Jack and Brenda bought her Belding's *American Guide to City Birds* for her birthday, and she had sat down with it at once; for an hour she leafed through the more than two hundred pages, then closed the covers with a snuffling of pleasure, a smile of ease. But she'd never opened it again, though she kept it importantly on a shelf under the magazine rack. Someday, she told Jack, when she had more time, she'd study it carefully.

After she set the bread out for the birds, she took a package of sweetrolls from the freezer, opened them and arranged them on a blackened baking sheet and put them on the bottom rack of the oven. (Before arthritis attacked the joints of her fingers, she had made her own banana loaf and cinnamon rolls for Sunday morning; now they made do with Pepperidge Farm or Sara Lee.) She put on a large glass pot of perked coffee and then she set the kitchen table with plastic placemats, plates, and knives. By this time Jack's father was dressed and shaved, and the two of them sat in the kitchen, sipping coffee, watching the clock over the Frigidaire and waiting for Jack and Brenda and the children to come.

They normally arrived a little after ten.

When Brenda's mother Elsa was alive they used to bring her along with them. Jack's parents had loved Elsa; the fact that Elsa wasn't married, that she had never been married, made her especially loved. 'That poor woman,' Jack's mother used to say, 'it's not easy for a woman, a life like that.' Elsa's unmarriedness – a fact known but never referred to – gave her a certain mythic enlargement, and she had been a large woman anyway, in the literal sense, both tall and fat, with a flamboyance of style that was also out-sized; in another age she would have worn peacock feathers in her hair. Her breasts – she called them bosoms, emphasizing the plural as a kind of joke – had been huge and heavily weighted with costume jewellery; she loved copper chains and had had a number of turquoise pieces. The dresses she wore were of nylon jersey. 'I like a nice print,' she used to say, 'so the dirt doesn't show.' These dresses, size twenty-two, swung around her compacted bulk with a warm-breathing coquettish rhythm, sensuous and powdery. She loved cologne, all kinds of cologne. Her eyes were round and bright, and she had a florid face, puffed and spread out like a peony. She was always laughing.

'That Elsa's the limit,' Jack's father used to say, shaking his head, 'a carload of laughs.' Jack's mother said often that Elsa was a real goer, a humdinger, and that it was just a joy to sit and listen to her go on. Elsa's voice had been exceptionally heavy for a woman; at the same time it was very low in pitch with a light Polish accent, thin as gilt, which kept it from sounding mannish. She especially liked to argue politics with Jack's father, ancient politics from the thirties and forties, slapping the edge of the table with the flat of her hand as she talked. Roosevelt had been a goddamned saint, she claimed, one of God's own marching angles. A bastard, Jack's father pounded back, and a goddamned blight on the country. 'You got to be kidding,' Elsa slapped away. 'Why he was a millionaire, he didn't have to butter his own pockets like that bum Daley.' (She had a gift for mixed metaphor; Brenda was her heir.) 'You know something,'

Jack's father told her, 'it's the rich crooks like Roosevelt you got to watch out for, they want to give everyone else's money away.' 'He was a saviour,' Elsa panted, 'but the poor sob with that ugly Eleanor of his.' Then she laughed, her dentures flashing iridescent in the sunlight – she laughed to show she didn't mean any harm.

Jack's mother always wrapped up the extra slices of banana bread in waxed paper for her to take back to the dinky little apartment in Cicero – 'for a snack later on' – and Elsa, who was a spectacularly demonstrative woman – that must have been her downfall, Jack's father once said with a wink – hugged and kissed them all, even Jack's father, whom she kissed square on the mouth – a wet smack – all the time declaring loudly. 'This sure is better than sitting in that old church listening to the priest, eh, having a good laugh, a good laugh is what keeps you greased up.' Sometimes she said, her eyes squeezed and glistening, 'My God, what would I do without youse?' (She always said youse; it was her only imperfection, her daughter Brenda maintained.)

She died four years ago September at fifty-six, from complications following a routine gall bladder operation. There was a funeral in a grey cement Catholic church in Cicero on a Monday morning. Afterwards, standing on the steps of the church, Jack had looked across at his father and saw him crying, a sight he had never seen before. His forehead appeared red and wrecked, the nose bulbous and glistening. He had wiped at his eyes with a handkerchief and in a choked voice muttered, 'Well, I'll say this, she was one hell of a good girl.' There were people standing all over the cold steps listening to him. Elsa had worked for thirty years selling men's socks and underpants at Wards, and a great many of her friends from work had come to the final mass. One of them, a girl of twenty or so, came over to where Jack's father was standing; she flung her arms around his neck, heaving with grief, causing him to utter what he believed to be a stinking lie: 'Now, now, she's happier where she's gone to, it's all for the best, you know that, don't you now?'

After Elsa died Jack's mother fell into a brief depression and her arthritis flared up so that she could hardly sleep. For a while she kept seeing women on buses and in stores who looked like Elsa. That was normal, said Brenda, who was coping with her own grief; that was what often happened after a sudden death.

'You know something else,' Jack's mother went on, her eyes pink, 'whenever I make banana bread I start to bawl.'

'You've still got us,' Jack told her. 'And the kids.'

But in the last year Rob had started staying home on Sunday mornings. He liked to sleep in, he said. If he went at all, he went grudgingly.

And so Jack was surprised on the Sunday morning after the Carpenters' party to find him up and dressed and ready to go. He stood at the back door, zipping his jacket, stamping into his boots. He didn't mention the argument of the night before, nor did Jack. The whole uproar over the Spanish rice seemed shockingly absurd, shameful, trivial, the kind of meaningless explosion that occurs between very young children, the kind of thing best forgotten, especially today on this most glittering of mornings.

It had snowed during the night, the first real snow of the year, a soft, thin, watery layer of Chicago snow, barely enough to cover the spikey backyard grass and leave a flattering loaf of whiteness on the garage roof, but it pleased Jack to see the clutter of back fences reduced and simplified by so neat a covering. The Carpenters' new cedar deck was levelled to mere surface; over the roof of his own garage Jack could see the steep Victorian angles of the Lewises' house, the way in which the damp snow clung to the sloping dormers and topped the chimney. The louvered shutters of the upstairs bedrooms were closed; they were probably still asleep. Poor Bud, Jack said to himself, cold calling all week. But his sympathy was fleeting, unfocused, dislodged from any genuine feeling. The sun, after all, was shining. This morning's snow seemed a gift, coming as it had so early in the new year and arriving with secret absolving power while he slept. 'Deep and crisp and even,' he sang to Rob and Laurie as he backed the car out of the garage.

'Ha,' Rob said, but in a friendly way.

From the backseat Laurie let out a scream. 'Daddy!'

Jack jammed on the brakes. 'Christ. What now?'

'Uncle Bernie,' she screamed. 'You forgot about Uncle Bernie.'

The engine died, Jack started it again, trying to be patient, taking it easy, remembering the choke, speaking softly to the ignition key, saying calmly, 'Bernie's still at the Carpenters'.'

'What?' Laurie shrieked, leaning over into the front seat and pounding his shoulder. 'Is the Carpenters' party still going on? Now? In broad daylight?'

The car shuddered, then slid into gear. 'He slept over there last night,' Jack said, increasing his speed, turning carefully and heading down James Madison Street.

Even Rob looked surprised at this. 'Huh? I thought he didn't even know them before last night.'

'True, true,' Jack said, his tone lightly philosophical, phony even to him. The tyres spun on the wet street; the snow was melting already.

'Why'd he sleep over there, anyway?'

'Well,' Jack paused, 'they've got all those extra beds, I guess that's why.'

'But he'll wake up and he won't know where we've gone,' Laurie said. 'He won't know where we are.'

'I left him a note. I left the back door open for him and a note saying where we are. Okay?'

'I guess so,' Laurie said.

'Weird,' Rob said. 'Weird.'

'He could've had my bed,' Laurie said.

'He could've slept on the couch,' Rob said.

'I offered my bed,' Laurie said. 'Remember? I offered it yesterday.'

'I know you did, sweetie. Now please don't yell in my ear like that. Daddy's got a headache.'

'Ha,' Rob said softly.

'What'd you say?' Jack came to a stop sign and jammed on the brakes, but the car skidded on the wet snow and travelled several feet into the intersection before coming to a stop. 'What'd you say?'

'Nothing.'

'Nothing?'

'Nothing.'

They arrived at ten-thirty, later than usual.

Chapter Fourteen

'WELL,' JACK'S FATHER SAID, EASING HIMSELF INTO HIS
Lazy Boy and lighting his first cigarette of the day, 'what's
new?'

He was a tall, sparely built, nervous man with standing
plumes of fine white hair and large, clean, pink ears. He was
sitting with his back to the window, and his ears seemed to Jack
to be flamed with light. Now that he had retired from the post
office he wore old white dress shirts at home, the sleeves rolled
up, the collar unbuttoned. He had a thin knobbed neck, reddish
in colour and a trifle distended, and small bright blue eyes that
blinked behind sparkling lenses; he'd put off his first cigarette
until 11:45 this morning, and – Jack found this even more
unusual – he'd put off his first question until this moment.

'What's new?'

Jack loved his father and mother and knew how much they
relied on him to bring them the news, whatever that meant –
the news that didn't come in the morning *Trib* or winking
through their TV screen, the real news. His mother was in the
kitchen now, washing the breakfast dishes and listening to
Laurie. He could hear Laurie describing the curried chicken
rolls she helped make at the Carpenters' yesterday, and his
mother was saying, 'Well, well,' in a slow, contemplative,
spiral-like way that indicated her mild amazement and total
rejection of such things.

'Really nothing new,' Jack said. For a moment he considered
telling his father about the party last night, and then decided
against it. He seldom told his father about the parties he and
Brenda went to; his parents didn't go to parties; they thought
parties were for small children on their birthdays. He might tell
him about Bernie and Sue splitting up and how Bernie had
temporarily moved in with him. His parents knew Bernie well
after all these years; before Bernie's parents, Beanie and Sally,
retired to their mobile home in Clearwater (Bernie called it
Blearwater) they had known them, too. They knew Sue slightly.

87

Jack's father thought Sue was 'stuck on herself' and his mother thought she was a little 'high and mighty.' Nevertheless Jack knew that news of a separation would alarm them needlessly. Better save it for another day. What else was new? His loss of faith? Impossible. His malaise by now had formed a cool alluring surface; he felt oddly protective toward it, reluctant to see it reduced to January blues or male menopause. And he made it a point never to alarm his parents.

'You say Brenda got away okay?' his father prompted.

'No problem at all.'

'Philadelphia. Why're they having this thing in Philadelphia, anyway? City of brotherly love.'

'Search me.'

'Take Chicago. It's a helluva lot more central, if you know what I mean.'

'I suppose.'

'Chicago's a good convention town, a great convention town. Always has been. American Legion, your Shriners, Lions, and so on.'

'Hmmm.'

'Speaking of that, I was saying to Ma, I'm glad Brenda isn't staying at that hotel where they had the – what do you call it, a few years back? The Legionnaires' disease.'

'I thought they finally proved that – '

'What would she have to pay for a hotel room in Philadelphia? Per night, I mean.'

'I don't know, Dad, maybe thirty, thirty-five.'

'Whew!'

Jack knew his parents found it puzzling, the fact that Brenda had left for a week to attend a craft exhibition. A craft exhibition! They'd never been as far as Philadelphia; they'd never been east of Columbus, Ohio, where his mother's sister once lived. Nor had they ever spent a night apart except for the times when one or the other of them had to go to the hospital, the time Jack's father had his appendix out and the time his mother had the tests for arthritis. Jack suspected that they had exaggerated notions about the importance and prestige of jet travel and that they were mystified about the rites that surrounded it. A week ago, sitting at the Sunday breakfast table, his mother had solemnly passed Brenda a square white envelope. Inside was a *bon voyage* card, bluebirds flying across a sparkled sky, and inside the card was a ten-dollar bill folded in two. The card had been signed – in his father's strange rocking hand – 'love and kisses from Ma and Dad Bowman.'

'You shouldn't have done that,' Brenda had said, her eyes suddenly swimming with tears. 'They shouldn't have done that,' she told Jack again on the way home; but her tone had changed; it seemed to Jack that she sounded inexplicably defensive – even, for some reason, a little angry.

Now Jack's father was saying something else; he was saying with a wink, 'I guess you won't have any trouble getting along for a week on your own. That there Laurie's getting to be a big girl.'

'It was really my idea, Dad, Brenda going to the exhibition. She didn't see how she could get away for a whole week, but when she got the invitation I told her, why not, you only live once.'

'Listen,' his father said, leaning over and lowering his voice. 'What's got into Rob this morning?'

'Rob?' Jack glanced into the dining room where Rob was sitting at the table, reading the Sunday papers. 'Rob?'

'He sick or something?'

'I don't think so. Why?'

'Because,' he leaned closer, 'because he didn't eat a thing this morning, not a damn thing. You notice that?'

Jack shrugged. 'Kids – '

'God, the way that kid used to eat. Like a horse. Oh boy, remember the time he poked all the raisins out of his cinnamon roll and I said, what's the matter, Rob, don't you like the raisins? And he said, yeah Grandpa, i like the raisins a lot, that's why I was saving them for the last.'

'Some more coffee?' Jack asked, rising; he'd heard the cinnamon roll story before.

'Ma's making another pot, be ready in two shakes. You were going to tell me something, before we got off on the subject of Philadelphia. What was it?'

'Nothing. You asked what was new and I said nothing much.'

'What about at work? What's new at work these days? You been busy?'

'Same old thing more or less. We're setting up this new display. I told you about that last week, I think. This Pattern of

Settlement show. Great Lakes settlement. Kind of a statistical thing. I'm not all that involved in it.'

'You know, I was thinking about that one night this week. In the middle of the night I woke up thinking about that. What's it going to cost, an exhibition like that? I was wondering.'

Jack hedged. 'Well, this is one of the smaller exhibits, as exhibits go, not like that thing we did last March on the History of the Chicago River.'

'Well, approximately then, what's it worth?'

'Three thousand? Something like that. I'm not sure, to tell you the truth.'

'Three thousand bucks!'

'It's partly the labour. They have to install a lighting system –'

'Three thousand bucks. Whew! Anything else new?'

Jack thought hard. 'Moira Burke is leaving this week. Tuesday. Her husband's retiring. They're going to Arizona.'

'The sunbelt, eh?'

'Uhuh.'

'Who's Moira Burke?'

'You met her, Dad. Last March. At the Chicago River reception, you and Ma. She's Dr. Middleton's secretary. She's been with him twenty-five years. At least.'

'If she's the woman I'm thinking of, she's a good looker. Brunette?'

Jack nodded. 'Not so bad. They're having a farewell lunch for her on Tuesday. The whole staff, I think.'

'Hard to find a good secretary nowdays. I read an article about that. Too bad Brenda didn't keep up –'

'They've already found a replacement for Moira. They've had someone training.'

'I'm thinking of giving up smoking.'

Jack started to laugh.

'What's so funny?'

'You're smoking a cigarette. Right now. I guess it just struck me as kind of funny.'

'I've been reading this book. You seen this book here? Called *You Are Your Own Keeper*.'

'No. But I think I've heard –'

'Written by a doctor. An MD. He starts off explaining how people get hooked on things. Slavery, he calls it. Like we're all like that, slaves, pure and simple. It's not weakness though, he says, it's human nature. But he maintains no one has to be a slave. You can make a decision and break the cycle. At any minute of any day you can sit down and make a decision, this man says. He says habits are only habits if we think they're habits. You have to write it down though. He thinks that's the crux. If you don't put your decision in writing it doesn't mean a damn thing, it just evaporates like air. You've got to put your John Hancock on it. He calls it reinforcement. It makes it concrete.'

'Reinforced concrete?' Jack felt a surge of warmth toward his father.

'Something like that.'

'So you're giving up smoking?'

'Not altogether, not altogether. But what I went and did this week was write down on a piece of paper: I, John Bowman, will smoke only five cigarettes each day for the next week.'

'And?'

'Then you're supposed to take that piece of paper and hide it away. You're not supposed to discuss it with anyone. Like I'm not supposed to be sitting here talking to you about it. He sees it as a contract, see. A written contract with yourself, is what he calls it.'

'What if you break it?'

'Well, so far I haven't. This doctor maintains that by putting it in writing, you've got like a guarantee. You put a date on it and even the time of day. This here now is my first cigarette today. I've got four to go, it's part of the contract. That's how it works.'

The books Jack's father had read – all of them paperbacks – were stacked on the bottom shelf of his smoker's stand. *Take Charge of Your Life, Achieving Inner Peace and Better Health, Twenty-Two Days to Increased Effectiveness, Life Crises and How to Make Them Work for You, Living with Passion, Memory: Your Secret Weapon against Age, Imaginative Marriage and How It Operates, A Psychologist's Guide to Inner Fulfilment, Yes You Can, Goodbye to Lower Back Pain, The Undreamed-of Power of Friendship, Striking Back and Winning, The ABC's of Loving Yourself.*

Jack's attitude toward these books was basically sceptical. He clearly saw the transparencies of the self-improvement vision, the simplistic assumption that the human will can be snapped back and forth like a rubber band. It infuriated him, when he stopped to think about it, that greedy popularizers were allowed to exploit basic human insecurities. From time to time he'd tried to press other books into his father's hands: novels, history, travel; but his father, at least in recent years, seemed to be interested only in these endless self-help bibles.

Occasionally Jack had glanced through his father's books, catching a glimpse of what he felt might be the well of his father's most private longings. He'd even felt himself faintly drawn in by the seductive power of the chapter headings: 'Begin Today,' 'Taking Stock,' 'Overcoming Obstacles.' The anecdotes used in these books to illustrate the various human dilemmas had sometimes caught his imagination; yes, he'd thought, I know how that feels, I've been there. He'd even felt the miniature scattered fires begin to turn, saying: yes, we can survive if we only acknowledge our own courage; yes, there is a final knitting up of meaning, a universal means to truth; brotherhood, goodness, purity, and action are more than the loose abstractions Bernie and I have reduced them to. Looking through his father's books, Jack could guess what it was that made them so popular.

What he couldn't understand was why his own father had taken to reading them. His father was sixty-eight years old, in good health, but nevertheless a year away from that well-advertised statistic on death and the American male. The shape of his life had already been drawn; he was a married man, father, grandfather, Republican, retired mail sorter. He lived in Austin, a part of Chicago that in the last ten years had become mainly black; nevertheless he refused to budge; they'll have to carry me out, he said. He was a subscriber to the Chicago *Tribune* and Chicago *Today*, an American citizen, a disbeliever, a smoker of Winstons, a payer of taxes, a lover of Schlitz, owner of a two-toned grey Pontiac in fair condition, an inactive Mason, a recipient of Social Security cheques – what was his father doing reading these books that advocated new systems of thought, new lifestyles and modes of behaviour, new freedoms and possibilities that he could not possibly achieve or even entertain at this time in his life? He was sixty-eight. Did his father – his father! – really want to find a new creativity in his marriage? Did he really give a fuck about reconciling his goals with his self-image? It was crazy, crazy; it was a new American form of masochism, the new perversion of the old American dream. For the life of him Jack couldn't understand what his father was doing reading all those books.

Nevertheless he lifted his feet onto the hassock, settled back and, calmly enough, told his father that he would be interested to hear how the five-cigarettes-a-day campaign was going. 'Sounds like an intriguing idea,' he said, at the same time reflecting to himself that he had somehow managed to become better at being a son than he was at being a father.

His mother came in then, with a pot of coffee and two mugs hooked on her finger. 'Here you go,' she said; her face was composed, almost merry. She had straight grey hair, combed back behind her ears and anchored with combs. Her earlobes were white and plumply innocent; she'd never worn earrings in all her life because she was sure they must hurt. She regarded her husband and son with love. Although she adored her daughter-in-law and thought of her as her own daughter, still Jack sensed that today her joyousness had something to do with the fact that Brenda was absent.

His mother amazed him. Once she had lived in the world, another world, marrying at seventeen a man she met at a dance, someone called Raymond R. Raymond, a shoe salesman. They lived in two rooms on North Avenue, and after a year Raymond R. Raymond lost his job and disappeared. She never heard from him again, although it was believed he went back to Upper Michigan where he came from. All this happened before Jack was born, before Jack's parents met each other. His mother, it seems, survived this blow, and went back to work in the sausage plant. Jack's father told him the whole story one afternoon, one Sunday afternoon in the park, when Jack was eleven or twelve. 'You ought to know, just in case,' he said. In case of what? Jack couldn't imagine. Just in case, his father had said, and with those words he placed a *de facto* censure on the story of his wife's first marriage; it was never again discussed. But never forgotten, either. Raymond R. Raymond – the man who broke Jack's mother's heart. No, Raymond R. Raymond didn't break it; for the extraordinary thing as far as Jack could see was the fact that his frail, nervous and shy mother had managed to absorb this short marriage and desertion and put it behind her. What courage she must have had to go back to work and to be led after a few months to still another dance, this one at the Old Windmill where she met Jack's father who had also, by chance, been taken there by friends. They had danced together twice that night and her new life had begun. His mother amazed him.

She handed him a mug of coffee. Out of the blue, Jack asked her a question. 'Ma, do you by any chance remember someone called Harriet Post?'

'Harriet Post.' She filled the second mug to the brim. 'Harriet Post? That sure rings a bell. But you know my memory for names, Jack, it never was any good. Faces, now. But Harriet Post, you say. Wasn't that your old piano teacher, Jack? Remember she used to come here Wednesdays that year you were learning piano.'

'No, no, Ma,' Jack's father said, reaching for his coffee. 'You remember Harriet Post. I know you do. We met her at that fancy do at the Institute last spring. The Chicago River thing. End of March, wasn't it? She's Dr. Middleton's secretary. Been with him twenty-five years and now she's retiring, Jack's been telling me. Going down to Arizona.' He slapped his shirt pocket for his cigarettes, tapped one out. 'Arizona, that's the place. Everyone's going down there.'

Chapter Fifteen

AFTER A WHILE ROB GREW RESTLESS AND TOOK A BUS HOME, muttering something about homework to be done, about an algebra quiz Monday morning. Laurie settled herself down with the new *Reader's Digest*. Whenever she visited her grandparent's apartment she liked to line up the couch cushions on top of the long, low radiator in the front room and stretch out there on her stomach with a book. She had been doing this for years, since she was a very small girl, three or four. Jack, eyeing her sprawled form – the whiteness of the solid legs, the roundness of rump – speculated that in another year she wouldn't be able to fit herself on the radiator anymore; even now her feet dangled off one end, one foot kicking idly at the hot water pipe.

Jack and his father decided to go for a walk through Columbus Park. They often did this on a Sunday, just the two of them. Jack's mother never came along, although Brenda was always saying to Jack that he should urge her to get out more, that it would do her good to walk a little. And it *would* do her good. Her face, especially around the eyes, was pale as plaster; there was a flakiness about her mouth and chin, a dry talcum-enriched spoilage about her throat and neck. The crisp air would undoubtedly refresh her. But Jack was reluctant to press the point; she had always been a woman relieved to be left alone indoors, where she could do what she was good at doing: straightening a scatter rug with the toe of her bedroom slipper, fluffing up a cushion, folding the newspapers in neat piles. How was she to occupy herself out in the wide freshness of the park? There was nothing but public grass and the huge simpleness of space; what was she to do? And there was her arthritis. The cold crept into her bones; even with heavy lined gloves on, the cold still got in.

Jack and his father, taking their time, their *sweet* time as Jack's father called it, walked in a long leisurely diagonal through the entire park, past the lagoon and the chilly baseball diamonds and the fountains. The water was shut off now, and the fountains were splotched with rust and mildew, and dead leaves were stuck to the rounded iron edges. After that was the area known as 'The Gardens,' and then the damp expanse of the golf course.

It was early afternoon, and at the end of the grass some people were gathering. There must have been forty or fifty of them, Jack estimated, mostly young people, students probably, even a few children. One woman had a baby strapped to her back. Some of them carried signs.

'Now what in Christ – ?' Jack's father yelped softly.

'Looks like a meeting of some kind.'

'Christ, I know what it is. I saw that in the paper this morning, that same bunch. It's those crazy hunger strikers. They won't eat. Did you read about them, what they're up to?'

'I haven't seen today's paper yet.'

'It's about those two scientists. The ones the Russians are keeping in jail. These hunger-strike people want to get them out of jail and send them to Israel or something.'

'I think I heard someone talking about that last night – ' Jack had a vague, jumbled memory, something someone had mentioned at the party, another crisis shaping up, the authorities cracking down again in Moscow.

The people with the signs were standing in a rough circle, some of them hunched over and shivering. This seemed a peaceful demonstration, unlike those Jack had witnessed in the Loop in the late sixties. Once, on a Friday, he and Bernie had come out of Roberto's and found themselves in a thicket of hurling bodies and thwacking police clubs. He had been frightened; for a minute he had thought anything could happen. Then a cool voice in his head took over, saying: here you are in the midst of a riot, here you are viewing a phenomenon of the times. But times had changed. The post-Vietnam, post-Watergate demonstrations seemed to him to have a degree of futility and bedragglement about them.

One of the demonstrators in the park was lifting his arms – a calm Old Testament gesture – and speaking. He was a large, boyish, white-haired man wearing a plaid poncho that reached to his knees. His voice was so low that it was impossible to hear what he said, but Jack could make out the lettering on some of the signs. *Freedom to Dissent – Freedom to Breathe. America Next –*

Hold Fast for Freedom. Another sign revolving, bobbing up and down, proclaimed *Americans Do Care*. Jack and his father stood watching as the circle broke abruptly and reformed into a long staggered line. Jack could hear singing – what was it? – 'The Battle Hymn of the Republic'? It seemed a quaint choice, an echo from the sixties. *Glory, glory Hallelujah* floated unevenly through the nearly empty park as the marchers filed toward the west gate and made for Austin Boulevard. Jack and his father watched until the last one was out of sight.

'A helluva lot of good it does for them to go and starve themselves,' Jack's father said. 'I mean, who the hell cares?'

'I suppose it's just a way of getting people to take notice. A tactic of sorts.'

'You'd think we didn't have plenty of problems right here, crime in the streets and what have you, inflation, bunch of small-time bums in City Hall, welfare, and these guys get all steamed up about a couple of Russians who probably can't even speak English.'

'I suppose you have to start somewhere,' Jack said with a feebleness that dismayed him.

'I say, let the bums starve if that's what the hell they want.'

They cut through the tennis courts and then through the children's playground, heading for the extreme southwest corner of the park, the dark, sober, wooded corner that Jack liked best. Except for this one corner, Columbus Park seemed to him to be exactly like the other big city parks, dusty, littered, prescribed, a facility rather than a piece of creation, all the areas designated and apportioned, utilized and maintained and knowable – all but this one corner. How had it come into being? It was a mystery. Jack could only imagine that years ago someone at City Hall had decided that what the west side of Chicago needed – what Columbus Park needed – was a microcosmic wilderness. A chunk of nature at the city's edge, a wilderness the size of a handkerchief. The whole area couldn't have been more than an acre in size, perhaps an acre and a half, but its minuteness had been cunningly camouflaged by thickly planted pines and spruce and by an intricate system of rustic paths weaving back and forth. Here and there the ground had been artificially elevated; there was an impression of harsh rocky out-cropping, a raw unbidden underground force. There was a stream and even a small waterfall that rested, if you looked carefully, on concrete piles. The water rushed over these falls with surprising speed, crashing into a foamy pond, yellow-ish in colour and smelling of urine. The pond itself drained magically, steadily, into a culvert, artfully concealed by plant-ings. Despite the rankness of the water, the air in this part of the park had a scrubbed, Wisconsin-like scent of pine pitch and earth-rot. Jack never came here without the phrase 'sylvan glade' popping into his head.

Sylvan glade – but when he'd first discovered this place years ago, the phrase sylvan glade hadn't been part of his vocabulary; then he had called it simply 'the woods.' That was when he was ten or eleven years old, when he and Bernie Koltz came here almost every day. In those days there had been a slatted wood and wire fence around this section of the park and a stern sign warning that trespassers would be prosecuted. It hadn't stopped them, of course, since it had been ridiculously easy to lift the fence and scramble under. In those days he and Bernie brought sandwiches and apples and stayed all day long in the woods. The stream, the pond, the waterfall, the secret boreal foliage and the still, ferny undergrowth had seemed to them to comprise their own planet; Jack felt about the woods not so much a sense of possession, but a feeling of refuge, of safe enclosure – hardly anyone else was ever there, although once they had seen a tramp kneeling in the bushes, his pants down, poking at something with a stick. The sound of rushing water shut out the traffic noises from Austin Boulevard, and the tops of the red brick apartment buildings could barely be seen over the heights of the trees.

It was summer; once under the fence, they were free to be anything. He and Bernie explored the woods, climbed all the trees that were climbable. At first they built forts and dams out of branches. Later on they played other games, games that had little to do with the actual wilderness setting – the protecting woods merely offered a sanctuary in which they might act out their preposterous daydreams of adventure. Mostly these daydreams had to do with the war, with the exploits of a particular crack commando squad – The Blue Jays? – the bomb-ing of enemy bridges, the hurling of grenades, the complicated, theatrical one-man missions in pursuit of Tojo or Mussolini or Adolf Hitler himself. Between them they shared and shifted the hero's role, accomplishing the impossible and unthinkable, crawling on their stomachs through the thorny underbrush, clawing their way into enemy foxholes, attacking with bare hands, gouging out eyes, plunging bayonets directly into warmly beating Nazi hearts. In these games recognition, gratitude, and fierce manly modesty all had a part. Some of the games were as long and as complicated as movies, requiring voice changes and shifting sets of characters; sometimes they took on the part of the enemy, sometimes the terse military commanding roles of Admiral Halsey or General MacArthur. They expertly imitated the sound of whining bullets, the rattle of machine guns, and the whistling and exploding of bombs. Their stories – dramas – turned over with spontaneity, with an easy, instant, willing adaptation; the scenes bled together, firming, fading, recurring, and reaching peaks of near tearful splendour. Wounded, they fell to the earth, released groans of agony into the leafy trees, uttered fearful tense messages moments before death came – *can you get through the lines . . . MacArthur's waiting . . . tell him I did all I could . . . . aaaaahhhh.*

At midday they stopped and ate their sandwiches by the side of the waterfall. Once they brought potatoes and made a bonfire, then quickly snuffed it out before the smoke gave them away. They took off their shoes and walked in the shallow creek water, and once Jack spotted a large toad, squat and brown, quivering on a flattened stone. He had been astonished at the sight. He couldn't believe that a toad could live and grow to such a size in the city of Chicago; it occurred to him that the brown toad might have no idea about the size of the park; probably he thought this was a jungle he was living in, immense and eternal.

Why exactly had this corner of the park been locked up during that time? Jack didn't know. He had never known. It might have been that the pond was considered dangerous for small children. He had never asked or even wondered very much about it. The encircling fence and the padlocked gate had not seemed particularly mysterious to him when he was a boy. The warning sign with its threat of prosecution – a word Jack confused with execution, imagining a mean-mouthed, squint-eyed firing squad – had seemed no more than a part of the larger universal prohibition that existed everywhere: certain things were not allowed, certain acts were not permitted, certain places were off limits; this section of Columbus Park was closed, it was as simple as that. The fact was immutable, and required no explanation – it was like the dark forbidden forests encountered in certain old folk tales, phenomena unassailable at the level of logic.

But today, entering the woods, he asked his father if he knew why the woods had once been closed.

At first Jack's father couldn't recall that the woods had ever been shut off. Then, pausing to think a minute, he remembered. Yes. This part of the park *had* been closed once, he said. Back in the forties. During a polio epidemic. Closed for a month.

'A month? Only a month? Are you sure? I'm sure it was longer than that. It *seemed* longer. More like years.'

'A month. Two months maybe, July and August it would have been. That's when the polio always was. We used to call it infantile paralysis. The infantile. Every summer here in Chicago we had the infantile. You'd be too young to remember or know what was going on – '

'I remember.'

'One year – I forget just when it was – it was real bad. Hundreds of cases. It was always in the paper every night, in the headlines. Ma and I always looked quick at the headlines for the number of new cases. They closed this part of the park then, for a month or so.'

'It was hard to believe; at last Jack felt a great reluctance to believe. His father's memory, God knows, was unreliable, especially lately, but at the same time the explanation had a simple, locked-together rationality about it. It was, he had to admit, undoubtedly true – it all fit together except for the period of time, the one or two months. It seemed impossible to Jack that what stretched so luxuriously long in his memory could be so foreshortened in reality. But on the other hand he knew – he was a reasonably observant father – that children have a way of distorting the size of events and the quality and measurement of time that surrounds them. His memory could easily have been tripped up – it wouldn't have been the first time. It may even have been a deliberate tripping up; he may, unconsciously, have wanted to remember the woods as being perpetually forbidden and dangerous, a kind of private wilderness positioned in a pure, unmarked cosmic zone of timelessness. Children did such things. He could imagine that he and Bernie might have wanted to create at the edge of Chicago, within walking distance of home, a private illusion of impossible continuing adventure. It made him smile to think of it.

Even with adults it happened, of course; all kinds of fantasies bumped along through history, half the time obliterating the facts, half the time contributing something human, a pleasing transposition of logic, a way of balancing the seeming precision of clocks and calendars. He would have to discuss that with Bernie, the place of illusion in history. The *value* of illusion. Dragons, for example, and unicorns: imagined creatures, but still a part of the human past, viable and accountable and more important in their way than real creatures like wolves and bears. How treacherous it was then, all these massed, tentative notations, illuminations, recordings; simmered down, what did it come to but mere vagaries of wishful thinking? History was no more in the end than what we wanted it to be. Like the woods in Columbus Park. The fence around the woods had been down for years, twenty-some years, yet Jack persisted in thinking of the place as being sequestered; mentally he had never really stripped away the aura of prohibition, and nowadays when he came here with his father on Sundays, although his younger self was only obscurely recalled, he still experienced a small jolt of surprise and disappointment to find he could enter freely.

The main paths of the park now led directly into the wooded area, and there seemed to be more space between the trees. The light was differently coloured, brighter. Some of the walks had been surfaced with asphalt; a certain amount of seasonal pruning took place. Despite this, it was never crowded. Today there were only three small boys, skinny, black, wearing jeans and identical blue velvety sweaters; brothers, it looked like, dangling fishing lines into the stream. 'Ha,' Jack's father said, 'they'll be lucky, getting anything live and kicking out of this sewer.'

Last night's snow had gone. All of it had melted, leaving the ground soggy underfoot. The upturned branches of the evergreens shone splendidly green, and the sky was tree-blurred and glassed over with a cover of cloud. The sun, watery, orange, fuzzed at the edges like a Nerf ball, seemed more of a moon than a sun. It's going to rain, Jack thought.

His father had already asked the question Jack knew he would ask: how was the book coming?

Every week he tensed for the moment when his father asked this question; yet, when the moment finally arrived, when the question came sailing through the air at him, he was unfailingly surprised at how easily he found the words to make a reply. And always the words were both true and not true. 'It's coming,' he'd say, or 'It's slow, but it's shaping up, I think.' He felt amazement and guilt at how easily his father's curiosity was satisfied; his father asked so little really, never questioning Jack on particulars, merely nodding, smiling widely, saying something spirited and affirmative, something fatherly. 'Slow but sure is what I always say,' or, 'Well, well, just so you keep plugging, so long as you don't get bogged down on a plateau,' or 'Rome wasn't built in a day, you know that, we all know that.'

These offerings of his father – if offerings was the word – seemed to Jack to be so innocently, willingly, delivered that he had sometimes found himself rising to the incandescence of the moment, seeking, for his father's sake, to extend its duration. He exaggerated his progress, showed unreasonable optimism. 'Should be there by spring,' he'd told his father a few months earlier, standing in this very spot next to the big feathery Norwegian spruce. 'Dr. Middleton says he has at least two publishers who've shown interest.'

'Wow!' His father received these progress reports with headshaking pleasure. 'Boy, oh boy, that'll be something all right, a book writer in the family, I can just see it. Sort of raises your status quo, if you get what I mean.'

Today the ground at the bend of the creek was slippery. 'Watch your step, Dad,' Jack said.

'I'm fine, I'm fine.'

'It's the melted snow, it's made it muddy here.'

'I can see it, for Pete's sake, that's what I've got glasses for.'

'Just warning you – '

'Anyway, you were saying, about the book – '

'I was just saying that Chapter Six's almost finished. I'm taking it in to the office tomorrow so it can be typed up. Dr. Middleton wants a look at it.'

'How many pages would that be?' his father asked, turning to Jack, his face alight.

'Thirty or so. I'm not quite done, but I'm going to go over it again tonight.'

'Your mother's going to be real happy to hear that. Did you tell Ma?'

'No, I didn't. Of course, it's still pretty rough, lots of finishing touches, lots of work to go – '

'Let me ask you this, do you think it'll be in the library? When it's all done?'

'The public library? My book? Oh, I don't know about that, Dad. It's sort of specialized for the public library.'

'Well, for Crissakes they've got books on all kinds of strange things. Crazy damn things like collecting bottle tops and what have you. And here you are, a Chicago boy, born and bred – '

'I don't know, Dad.'

'Let me tell you what I was thinking. I woke up the other night. I don't sleep that well anymore, that's why Ma thought she'd be better off in the other room – '

'You told me that.'

' – she's better off without me waking up at night all the time and bumping around. As a matter of fact I read an article about that very thing, and you know something? It's perfectly normal, they say, at my age. The human being, when it gets older, doesn't require the same hours of sleep, it's absolutely normal. Where was I? I woke up the other night and I had this idea. I said to myself, when Jack's book's done, all finished with the cover on and everything, I'm going to go out to the store and buy a copy and give it to the Austin Library. A donation like. And, and, I thought I could stick one of those little stickers in it, you know, donated by John and Selma Bowman and – '

'Dad, I don't think they do that anymore – '

' – John and Selma Bowman, the parents of the author. Now how do you like the sound of that? This was in the middle of the night when I thought this up, so I got out of bed and wrote it down. I didn't want to forget about it. The parents of the author. Well? How do you think that sounds? Not so bad?'

A pause. Then Jack said, 'It's a long, long way from being finished. And, Dad, as a matter of fact, I may be in for some competition. It turns out that someone else has written a book on exactly the same subject.'

'Someone else?'

'This happens all the time, of course. It's nothing unusual. I found out about it the other day. Out of the blue. It's kind of a bad break, I guess you could say.'

His father had stopped walking. 'This other book, is it any good?'

'I honestly can't say, Dad.' Jack thought he saw the corners of his father's mouth tuck in. His thin whittled face seemed to shrink, a frail wedge between the wide ears.

'Well,' the voice held a tremor, 'do you *think* it's any good, Jack? The other book?'

'Actually, it's probably going to be – chances are it's going to be . . . pretty good.'

'*Going* to be?'

'It's not out yet. Not until summer.'

'Well, hell,' his father said slowly, his mouth puffed like a wreath, 'well, hell, Jack, you'll be finished before this other guy. I mean you've got the edge on him, haven't you? Spring, you said, wasn't it?'

'I'm not all that sure about spring – '

'Anyway, what the hell difference does it make? So there's two books about Indians. Everyone likes to read about the Indians.'

'It's starting to rain, Dad. Maybe we'd better head back.'

'Just a few measly drops, that's what they said on the news, scattered showers.'

'I'd better be getting back, Dad – '

'It's early, we just got here. Why don't we walk up there on the other side of the bridge?'

'I really should get home. The kids – Rob – and I've got that chapter to go over. For tomorrow.'

'Jesus, yes. I forgot about that. You've got to get that ready by tomorrow morning. Let's take the short cut, we don't want to meet up with those hungry hippies. Ha. Be home in a lamb's tail. You know something? It's going to really rain, by Christ.'

Chapter Sixteen

JACK HAD LEFT THE BACK DOOR UNLOCKED FOR BERNIE, BUT when he and Laurie got home late in the afternoon, the house was empty. Laurie dropped her coat on the floor, wandered into the living room, and switched on the TV set. On the kitchen table Jack found a note from Rob.

> Gone with Bernie K. to Charleston. Back around 7. Sue K. phoned, wants you to phone her back at hospital 366 4556. Mrs. Carpenter phoned and said Mr. Carpenter would live.
> Rob

He read the note twice. The words were clearly enough written in Rob's neat hand, the capital letters a trifle flamboyant, but the smaller letters tidy, economical, with finishing strokes that were definitive and strong. A good aggressive hand, Jack thought, pleased. Rob was generally efficient about taking down phone messages; all in all, Jack mused, he wasn't such a bad kid. Surly. Greedy at times. But surprisingly respectful, the way, for example, he always remembered to say *Mr.* Carpenter and *Mrs.* Carpenter. As kids go these days, he could be worse. He could be into drugs or shoplifting or flunking out of school. He was fairly reliable when it came right down to it, fairly responsible. But this note made no sense at all.

'Mr. Carpenter would live.' Jack said it out loud to the kitchen wall, testing the words for meaning: 'Mr. Carpenter would live.' Damn Rob anyway, why was he always so vague? That time he sent the post card from Cub camp when he was eight: one sentence – 'It's okay about the snake.' Now this – 'Mr. Carpenter would live' – he should know better. Perhaps it had something to do with last night's party. Maybe Larry'd really tied one on; come to think of it, he *had* looked pretty well oiled when Jack last saw him. Probably woke up with a hangover. But he *would* live – Jack supposed he was to take that ironically; he would survive his hangover; was that what this note meant?

No, too far-fetched; ridiculous. Might be a good idea to give the Carpenters a call. Just in case.

He dialled the number, listened for an answer, but there was no one at home. He counted to ten and tried again; no one.

Next, gritting his teeth, he phoned Sue at the Austin General. Dr. Koltz had gone for the day, he was told. No, she hadn't left a number. Jack put down the phone, breathed out a low whistle of relief; the last thing he felt like doing was talking to Sue Koltz.

The sense of being reprieved always came sweetly to him. He was tired. Last night's party, that swirl of faces, all that booze, how many scotches had he had? Bernie weeping, Brenda away, the damned Indians and their bloody trading practices. And Rob leaving meaningless notes on the kitchen table. Now Laurie had turned the television up full blast; the football game, the post-season special, the Bears and the Packers, already into the third quarter. Damn it, he'd meant to watch the game. His head hurt, his eyes felt sore. He'd forgotten to pick up a carton of milk. There didn't seem to be any food – he'd never seen the kitchen stove so cold and clean. Outside, the rain was pouring down.

Once again he read the note, line for line this time, word for word. What was Bernie thinking of, taking a kid Rob's age out to Charleston? Rob had never been near an institution like Charleston. Of his two children, Rob was the sensitive one. Once, years ago, Jack had seen him weeping as he watched the dispatches from Vietnam on television – children, horribly burned, wrapped in blankets by wailing mothers. Charleston would be shocking; he himself had never been to a place like Charleston. (Fortunately there had been no need. He shrank from the thought.) It was plain crazy, all of it was crazy. But the craziness, he noted with something like calm, was indecipherable, out of reach. And what could he do? He had already done what was required of him, returned the call to Sue, tried to get hold of the Carpenters, pondered Rob's presence at Charleston – he'd done what he could and, for the moment, was absolved. He could now fold this note, put it in his back pocket, push the contents outside his consciousness, and wait for the moment of enlightenment that would come, that would certainly come, to explain its meaning.

Most probably the explanation was something laughably simple; probably Rob had written this note quickly; Bernie would be anxious to get going; it was forty miles to Charleston Hospital where Bernie's daughter was, and there was always lots of traffic. In his haste Rob must have made some minor ellipsis or some curious small error of syntax, enough though to throw the whole message into question.

Jack mistrusted paper, anyway. Words, ink, paper, the limitations of language and expression, human incompetence; it was absurd, the importance that was put on mere paper. For a historian he had always had a peculiar lack of faith in the written word, and furthermore, he had never been fully persuaded that history was, by definition, what it claimed to be, a written record. More often, it seemed to him, history was exactly the reverse – what *wasn't* written down. A written text only hints, suggests, outlines, speculates. A marriage licence wasn't the history of a marriage; he had given this example to Bernie not two weeks ago. A written law, set down on a sheet of papyrus or a clay tablet, wasn't a statement of fact, but only a way of pointing to a condition that didn't exist. Everything had to be read backwards in a kind of mirror language.

Then there was the further problem about the reliability of the recorder, the one who performed the actual task of writing. Take diaries, for instance, he had said to Bernie. For every diarist there were ten thousand non-diarists. So who was to be trusted? The singular exception, with his poised compulsive quill, or the thousands of thronging cheerful non-recorders who make up the bulk of society? To record was to announce yourself as a human aberration, a kind of pointing, squealing witness who by the act of inscribing invites suspicion.

But this was only the beginning: there was an even greater fallacy, as Jack saw it: the fact that most of life fell through the mesh of what was considered to be worthy of recording. Jack had gone into this very argument with Bernie only a few weeks earlier, presenting the case of the English barmaid, a story he had invented on the spot and for which he had since developed a certain fondness. The English barmaid, he told Bernie over lunch, lived in the town of Birkenhead in the year 1740.

'Why Birkenhead?' Bernie had been alert and obliging that day. 'Why 1740?'

'Well, Birkenhead because records were less reliable in the provinces. And 1740 because that puts her fairly safely in the camp of the illiterate. To continue – '

'Okay.'

'One day this illiterate provincial barmaid was working down at the local pub. It happened that it was late afternoon, May the fifteenth, say. Business was a little slow that day, so she had a chance to polish the brasses, set up the tankards for the evening trade, give the old floor a push with the old broom – '

'Then what?'

'Then, about dusk, wham, the door opened, and in came an unemployed agricultural worker.'

'Illiterate?'

'Absolutely. To the toes. Also itinerant, a stranger to the Birkenhead region. Hailed from the south, so he said, speaking in his soft unfamiliar accent. Well, he plunked himself down on a bench, tossed a threepence on the table, and announced that he was thirsty.'

'Go on. You're taking too long.'

'It soon became apparent that he thirsted for more than brown ale. He eyed the barmaid up and down, took in her flashing black eyes and her . . . generous, country-sized pro- portions, her air of ease – '

'I can tell it's been a while since you've seen any English barmaids – '

'This stranger leaned over and managed to grab the wench's wrist – '

'The wench? Jesus.'

'He pulled her close. And whispered into her ear. Would you, he said, care to go for a walk when you've finished work? Down by the river, he said.'

'Is there a river in Birkenhead? What river?'

'Any river. Make it a pond then. As I said before, it was May, the month of May, the blossoms were out, there were daffodils.'

'Not by any chance a *host* of golden daffodils?'

'And, what's more important, lots of tall grass. Take note of that, tall grass is crucial to this story.'

'I can imagine,' Bernie said.

'Take my word for it. The two of them, the strapping young stranger, the lovely young lass, walked through the tall sweet grass. Eventually they decided to sit down in the tall sweet grass, rest themselves a while.'

'Ye – es.'

'The stars were starting to come out – '

'One by one.'

'And the stranger, this unemployed illiterate agricultural worker leaned over and slowly unbuttoned the barmaid's blouse. He was breathing very rapidly by this time, at least so it seemed to her.'

'This is one of your better stories, Jack.'

'After that there was a loosening of petticoats, a fumbling of knickers.'

'Aha! I think I see where this may be headed.'

'And there, under the silent stars and the blank stare of the moon, the barmaid of Birkenhead was ceremoniously deflowered.'

'Penetrated. Through and through?'

'Completely.'

'And?'

'That's it. The end.'

'The end of the story? No punchline?'

'No punchline. Well, there *is* a little postscript. Really a non-postscript since, literally, it was not written down. It's just this – that the deflowering by the river remained a secret. Each went his own way after this magic evening. But in the heart of each, this evening lived on. And on and on. Now do you see the point?'

'To tell the truth – '

'This moment was historical. It happened. But in no way did it enter into written record.'

'It might have.'

'How?'

Bernie thought a minute. 'What if she got pregnant? You could hie yourself over to England, go to the parish church of Birkenhead, look up the year 1740 in the records, and you'd find a registration of a birth, nine months after the event. Then you could call your story a historical event.'

'It so happened that on this night the stars were benevolent. Conception did not take place, there was no pregnancy and no registration of birth. But can you deny it? That this wasn't history?'

'What if the barmaid got old and forgetful and happened to mention the encounter to a passing minstrel who was really a novelist in disguise and who later wrote a book called *The Tall*

Grasses of Birkenhead? Then you might be justified in calling it history, though of a very doubtful sort.'

'But this was not the case,' Jack said. 'The barmaid converted to Methodism, quit her job, married a very up-tight shoemaker and lived the rest of her life as a god-fearing woman. She never told a soul, though doubtless her thoughts occasionally stole back to that moment of passion. But there was absolutely no written record of this event, you'll have to take my word for it. Her body is a poor, unmarked skeleton now, under the chapel floor. Even the skeleton is slowly – '

'No, it's no go, Jack. I won't buy it. You've got to write off the whole episode, picturesque as you may find it. There is no way you can possibly call this a historical event, and you know it.'

'But isn't that completely absurd when you and I both know it's true?'

'You want to go outside the definitions,' Bernie said, 'but you can't. This story of yours has no more weight than a dream would have.'

'Maybe dreams are historical happenings, too.'

'If they're recorded, yes, I'd agree to that much. Your problem is you want history to be more than it can possibly be. You want it to contain everything. All the grains of sand in the universe. Christ, you think history's a magic bulldozer, sweeping it all up as we go along. When all it is is a human invention – rather a presumptuous one, too – and, my God, it's got all the human limitations. Plus time limitations, technical limitations, the whole thing. It's never going to be more than the dimmest kind of story telling.'

Bernie was right, of course; Jack knew he was right. Even if the English barmaid had left a written record, he would never be able to bring himself to trust it. She had a soul of permafrost, despite her willing nature. If, for instance, she had somehow been taught to write in her old age – Jack pictured her bent over a rough table, a small leaded window furnishing light – what she would put down would be something altogether different from her actual experience in the tall grass; the minute her pen touched ink, a second self would begin to flow, conditioned, guarded, forgetful, ecstatic, vain, lyric, discursive, the words becoming what all recorded history becomes eventually, a false image, bannered and expository as a public freize, a mixture of the known and the unknowable. The shapely distances of the past were emblematic and no more.

Even something as brief and as nearly accidental a notation as his son Rob's message sagged under the weight of particular assumptions. Mr. Carpenter would live. Mr. Carpenter would live? The assumption would have to be – Jack turned it over in his mind as he opened a can of chicken noodle soup – the assumption would have to be that Mr. Carpenter's – Larry's – ability to live was somehow thrown into jeopardy; a calamity of some kind had overtaken Larry Carpenter. And no ordinary calamity, either; it would have to be something extraordinary and serious.

He dumped the soup into a saucepan, added water, heated it briefly over a bright flame, then poured it into two cereal bowls.

Laurie was lying on the rug in the living room, watching the last sixty seconds of the game. Green Bay was within inches of the goal line as Jack handed her a bowl of soup and slumped into a chair. He loved the Green Bay Packers, and he waited, expectantly, as the front line was whistled into motion and they let loose with their invisible ball.

It looked so simple on the tube; Green Bay was so close, only a yard away, and yet they failed. Jack leaned forward, spilling a stream of soup on the rug, but he couldn't make out exactly what was going wrong. Arms, legs, a close-up of shoulders and bullet-heads and dancing buttocks, sliding and collapsing; where was the ball? A referee stepped in, raised burly hands above his head; the game was suddenly over.

Laurie pulled herself up, stretching. Jack scooped at the last of his soup, thinking he was still hungry, then thinking that he really should phone the Carpenters again.

He could see the corner of their house from the window; there was a light burning; someone was home. He should do something. Yes, he would phone. Right away. Before he changed his mind.

Chapter Seventeen

MONDAY MORNING. JACK WAS WAITING FOR DR. MIDDLETON to arrive; he was early, it was just 10:25. For some reason he was trembling slightly; high on his left cheek, just beneath the eye, a nerve twittered. His throat rasped with dryness. Of course he'd hardly slept last night; it was midnight before things calmed down, and after three before sleep finally came – he'd dreamed, amazingly enough under the circumstances, of Brenda, a lush, burrowing, sexual dream. The alarm had gone off at seven sharp.

It was only natural, Jack reasoned, to feel a little on edge after a night like that, and his edginess was sharpened now by the sight of Dr. Middleton's desk, broad, heavy, calmed by neat piles of papers that were weighed down by small flashing specimens of Michigan ore. An antique desk lamp with an amber glass shade spread a circle of warmth on the fine-grained surface. A framed photograph of Mrs. Middleton – smiling, her Nordic lips relaxed – stood in one corner; next to her the telephone gleamed with a gentlemanly lustre. 'Dr. Middleton should be here in a sec,' Moira Burke told Jack.

She was looking jaunty on her second last day at work, almost military in a navy blazer and yellow silk scarf, thickly knotted under her chin. Twin arcs of blue eyeshadow made her look tough and quizzing.

'So,' Jack said in what he recognized as his phony good-cheer voice, the one he dredged up for hangover mornings, 'so, at last, D Day's finally arrived.'

'Ha!' Moira said.

He had more or less decided what he would say to Dr. Middleton about Chapter Six. That was one good thing about driving in from Elm Park; those early morning traffic jams provided an opportunity to get your thoughts together. Not that there should be any real difficulty, he reflected, since confrontations with Dr. Middleton required no explanation beyond the simple truth. There was about Dr. Middleton a square, straightforward frontality, unusual in a man of his particular discipline. Jack saw him as a kind of boulevard historian with an intellect both spry and elastic, and a rare willingness to deal with actuality so that there was no need for elaborate excuses or face-saving alibis. Delays, distractions, detours were all acceptable in this civilized environment. Jack could relax, take a deep breath. So he hadn't managed to get Chapter Six rounded off as promised; Dr. Middleton certainly wasn't going to fire him for that, or clap him over the head with a ruler; the worst that would happen would be a mild, sympathetic indication of disappointment, an almost imperceptible shaking of the head, a tapping of his pen upon the desk blotter, an instant's brief silence. Why then this turmoil?

Moira gestured toward a chair. 'Why don't you sit down. Might as well take a load off your feet while you're waiting.'

'Maybe I will.' There was something coarse about Moira – 'Take a load off' – a broad, snapping brassiere-strap bravado – would Mel, her replacement, be any different? Jack turned and gave Moira a companionable, low-energy smile, uttering a soft moan. 'Monday morning,' he explained, his fingers moving painfully to his temples.

'You really don't look all that perky.'

'What a weekend!'

'Oh?' She looked interested.

'Fellow next door tried to kill himself.'

Why had he said that? Why had he spoken at all? He hadn't intended to, not to Moira. Christ! At least he hadn't mentioned any names.

'Really?' A rewarding gasp.

Jack felt himself growing calm; Ah, the insidious pleasure of passing on bad news. 'Early Sunday morning, about eight. They found him just in time.'

'How – ?'

'The old garage trick, carbon monoxide. Had the car running, the door shut. But he's going to be all right, they think. No brain damage, at least nothing that can be detected at this point.'

'Old? Young?' Moira eased herself into a chair. Her brow split into a half a dozen evenly spaced furrows. Attractive.

'Middle,' Jack said. 'Thirty-something. Late thirties.'

'That can be a bad time,' Moira said. 'I remember that period. Thirty, early forties – '

113

Stop. Jack cringed; he didn't want to know about Moira's early forties. Or anyone's early forties. 'Another neighbour found him. Lucky, really. This other man, Bud Lewis, is a jogger. Three miles every morning before breakfast, even Sundays, if you can believe it. He does laps around Van Buren Park, thirty, forty laps every day. Well,' he paused, 'fortunately he starts his run down the alley behind us, and he was just going by the garage next door when he happened to notice some exhaust leaking out under the door. Lucky it was a cold day.'

'I'll say – '

'He broke the window and got in somehow. It was just a little window. He had to hoist himself up and then crawl through to get inside. They said at the hospital that if it had been another five minutes – '

He paused. *Five minutes*; he watched Moira absorb the implications beyond that five minutes.

'Men,' Moira remarked with energy, 'are under a lot of pressure these days. In their work. It never lets up, it's a jungle. My husband, Bradley, he's had his rough times.'

'Yes,' Jack said, 'these things happen.'

'Or family pressures, too,' Moira said. 'They can be just as bad.'

'Yes.'

'I nearly went to pieces when our daughter Sandra quit high school. She was on the honour roll and then she got in with the wrong crowd. Drugs. I know what it can be like. You get over it but it takes a toll.'

Jack nodded. He had met the daughter once. She had come with Moira and her husband to one of the exhibits, but that had been years ago. She'd been about eight then, with long beautiful brown braids. What could have happened to that little girl? Poor Moira. Poor little girl.

'Do they know *why* he did it? Like did he leave a note? They usually do.'

'No, no note. But they figure it was depression.'

'Depression can be bad.'

'It sounds crazy, to me anyway, but he was in a play, this man. A local thing, strictly an amateur deal. But someone went and did a review of it for the papers, called it a real bomb, and zeroed in on him in particular.'

114

'I've seen some of those play reviews. In Chicago *Today*. And in the *Trib*. They can be pretty biting. Downright cruel.'

Jack stopped, caught himself. Should he be telling Moira all this? Janey had been emphatic: she didn't want the whole world knowing about Larry, at least no one who didn't absolutely have to know. She'd even gone around, she said, to all the nurses on the floor and begged them to keep the thing quiet. Larry would die if this gets around, Janey said. 'You know what they'd say, Jack. That Larry Carpenter can dish it out, but he can't take it. That's what they'd say, I can just hear it.'

It was true the review had been rough; late last night Jack finally got around to reading it, and as he read, his heart froze. A royal hatchet job, unsparing. But at the same time it occurred to him that if he hadn't lived next door to Larry Carpenter, if he hadn't known where it would end, he might have read the same piece with a certain amount of – what? – glee? Here was a drama critic drowned in his own brand of vitriol. Rough justice. Just desserts. A chunk of irony to chew on. There was no doubt about it; Larry had on occasion been equally vituperative. He had a short, sharp way with the second-rate, although he normally muted his blows with the special Carpenter cleverness – perhaps that made the difference. Gordon Tripp – and Jack had always considered his movie reviews to be stylish and distanced – seemed out for blood; every word fell with malice. (Or did it? The year he and Bernie had discussed modern morality, Jack had argued that evil was the result of simple carelessness.) Larry must have got on the wrong side of Gordon Tripp. Either that or Larry really was the 'most pompous, self-congratulatory Hamlet, amateur or professional, ever to disgrace the Chicago stage.' (Something of an overkill, a statement like that, the kind of thing Larry himself would have avoided.) Had Larry really stood at centre stage and 'declaimed in the manner of a wet owl on the make, horny with ego, pop-eyed with importance'? Christ! Was it true he had 'scratched at his crotch behind the canvas trees'? (If he did, Janey said, it was because the polyester armour itched.) 'This too, too arrogant flesh isn't solid enough to play Mickey Mouse, let alone Hamlet,' Gordon Tripp had railed. 'Could it be that the Elm Park Little Theatre forgot about the shoes of the cobbler's children? Or were they simply bowled over by a case of downtown puffery?' (Leah Wallberg would burn at that, probably already was burning.) 'At least,' the review concluded, 'theatrical history has been made. Hamlet, as played in the venerable old suburbs by Chicago's own Larry Carpenter, is no longer the tragic hero Shakespeare envisioned. He has been remodelled out of all recognition into a kind of Clark Kent unable to locate a phone booth.'

It was too bad. It was ill-natured and uncharitable. But suicide? Janey said Gordon Tripp, once a friend of Larry's, had been miffed when Larry's column was picked up for syndication and his wasn't. A case of jealousy, clear and simple. She also suggested that it hadn't been the review alone that had set Larry off. She'd told Jack and Bernie late last night, sitting in Jack's kitchen, eating chicken wings, that there had been other factors involved, *numerous* other factors. Larry had had a good deal to drink that night; certain kinds of red wine, Janey told them, were scientifically known to have a negative effect on the psyche. (Jack remembered how Larry had looked late Saturday night, strangely calmed and amicable; but according to Janey, he was sailing, by that time – fully rigged for disaster.) The play itself had worn him to a frazzle, late-night rehearsals, the demanding four-hour performances. And once, years ago, Janey confided, at Princeton, just before mid-terms, Larry had had a sort of breakdown. Nothing serious, but he'd had to drop one or two courses. He's really, Janey said, whispering, sort of a *lonely* man. So –

Janey, leaning on the kitchen table, had been close to hysteria, her green eyes glassy, feverish. She was ravenously hungry, grabbing the chicken wings out of the sauce with her fingers and stripping off the meat. Her blonde hair fell greasy and lank, the clumped strands separating over her ears. There were fearful, sodden elongations around her mouth, but her lips were soft and sensuous, with a look, Jack thought, of summer fruit. She had phoned Larry's parents in Connecticut; his father was coming on an early-morning flight and planned to go directly to the hospital.

Sitting there, the three of them, they seemed to Jack to be swimming in the heightened, ardent immediacy of other, earlier lives. Hospitals; whispers; heroism; the gorging of food; manic celebration, dangerous and cautionary and somewhat reverent. On impulse Jack had opened a bottle of wine.

Bernie tipped back his glass. The high red frizz of his hair caught the light; separate threads sprang up, bluish and electric. Tonight he looked exceptionally young; he looked twenty years old tonight. Earlier in the evening he had been fiercely apologetic about dragging Rob out to Charleston in the afternoon to visit his daughter Sarah. Rob, he said, had been sitting around the house, looking dejected, and on impulse Bernie had asked if he wanted to come along for the ride. (Rob came home from Charleston sick with shock, his stomach upset. Bernie had had to stop the car twice for him on the way.) It was all right, Jack said. He'll forget about it in a day or two, Bernie said. Of course, Jack said – weren't people always saying that kids were overprotected these days from the realities of death and deformity? He'd said it himself more than once. Well, Rob had made up for it today; he'd gone straight to bed when he got home and had fallen asleep in minutes.

'I can't get over Bud Lewis,' Janey went on, her mouth full, a bead of sauce jiggling on her lip. 'If it hadn't been for Bud jogging by at that very minute – I'll just never be able to thank him if I live a hundred years. Neither of us will.'

'It really was a – ' Bernie hesitated, and Jack hoped he wouldn't say the word blessing or, worse, miracle, 'it really was incredibly lucky.'

'And if Bernie hadn't been staying here in our guest room last night – ' Janey had inhaled sharply, gazed at Bernie with sober regard – a near brush with tragedy had cleared away her sulkiness, 'if he hadn't been in the house I don't know what I'd have done. It must have been fate. I'd have gone to pieces, probably. I was shaking like a leaf when Bud brought him in. He carried him in. Actually *carried* Larry into the house.'

'You were a lot more collected than you realize,' Bernie assured her. His tone was intimate. 'You were the one who just picked up the phone and asked for emergency. While we were arguing about who to call first.'

'And they got that oxygen unit here so fast,' Janey's voice shrilled, ecstatic. She reached across for another chicken wing. 'How long would you say, Bernie? Ten minutes?'

'No more than that. Fairly swift anyway for that hour in the morning. And they sure knew just what to do when they got here.'

Janey turned to Jack. 'I guess you heard,' she said quietly, 'what Bernie did?'

'What?' Jack said, hating himself for not knowing.

'While the ambulance was coming? That ten minutes when Larry was lying there on the couch with his eyes shut? Bernie gave him mouth-to-mouth resuscitation. While I was tearing out my hair and running around screeching, he gave him mouth-to-mouth.'

'Well, I – ' Bernie said.

'The doctor, the man in Emergency, said it probably kept the brain cells alive for that critical – '

'I took this course a couple years ago,' Bernie apologized. 'First aid.' His voice cracked.

'And he stayed with me all morning. At the hospital.'

'I hated like hell to leave you alone in the afternoon. If I hadn't had to go to Charleston – '

Jack looked at him closely. When had he last seen Bernie's face as luminously tender as it looked at this moment? He and Janey had been awake since eight; and both of them looked radiant.

And *he* had slept through it all, all of it. Bud Lewis breaking the glass on the garage window – with his bare hands, Janey said; he had had to have stitches. *He* had slept while Bud Lewis carried Larry into the house. And how exactly had this feat been accomplished? Had Bud carried him in his arms the way a child would be carried? over his shoulder? how? *He* had slept through the arrival of the ambulance and the valiant oxygen unit. Probably there had been a siren. Bernie breathing into Larry's unconscious mouth. Jack had slept through that, too. Asleep, dreaming, always asleep, that's where he had spent his life, asleep; that's where he always ended up, in a state of semi-consciousness, just outside the crowding of real events. Shut out. Cut off. As though a partition existed in the world, a heavy wall of plate glass, unassailable, where on one side people moved through immense self-generating dramas, conquests, feats of courage and knowing. Brenda was on that side; so was Larry Carpenter and Janey and Bernie and so, incredibly, was Bud Lewis. *Bud Lewis*. While he – and a few others like him, he supposed – stood immobilized on the other side; all they could do was watch it happen; there was no way through for people like him. They were condemned, something predetermined perhaps, something faulty in the genes, a primal failing, an unlucky star. He was going to be, would always be, a man who

118

listened to the accounts of others, a man who comprehended the history of events but not the events themselves. He was a secondary-source man; he hadn't even gone to see *Hamlet*; even a simple thing like that had slipped past him. And here, at his own kitchen table, he was an incidental witness, a grotesque and fatal second step behind. Bernie and Janey seemed scarcely aware of his presence.

Nevertheless they appeared reluctant to leave. It grew later and later, but still they stayed. After a while Janey became exhausted and tearful. She began rambling, somewhat incoherently, about how she and Larry, a couple of years ago, feeling rootless, toying – she might as well come out with it, she said – toying with the idea of a divorce, had moved out here to Elm Park as a sort of last-ditch experiment. But they couldn't seem to fit in; hardly anyone ever invited them back after their parties; they couldn't understand why this was, but knew it must be, in some way, their own fault. 'And now look,' Janey was saying, 'Bud Lewis stepping in and saving Larry's life. And Hap Lewis sending over these chicken wings tonight, sweet and sour. And Bernie – even if he isn't really a neighbour – and you, Jack, phoning and asking me over here – ' Tears fell out of her eyes, spilled onto her hand. Her face melted, collapsed, reminding Jack of Laurie when she blubbered. He had wanted to put his arms around her.

'Look,' he insisted, 'you can't possibly stay in that house alone tonight. I can easily make up a bed for you here. There's Brenda's workroom – it's got this folding bed thing – '

'Bernie's offered to stay over again tonight,' Janey said. 'But, thank you, Jack, it's really wonderful of you to think of it, everyone's been so wonderful.'

'After all,' Bernie cut in, 'I've already broken in the sheets.' He spoke with resonant logic, almost merriment.

'And the hospital might call,' Janey said. 'They promised to call if anything came up, anything at all. They said I could see him first thing in the morning.'

'At least,' Jack said, 'let me drop you at the hospital in the morning.'

'Oh, I can do that,' Bernie said quickly. 'I'll be right there, it's no trouble. Actually, it's right on my way to work.'

They had left it at that. And when Jack drove off the next

morning, Bernie's car was already gone. He decided he would phone the hospital at noon to see how things were going. For the moment, there seemed little else he could do.

'Sometimes,' Moira Burke was saying into Jack's ear, 'sometimes I actually think women are stronger than men. That neighbour of yours, for instance – I don't think a woman would kill herself over a little bitty thing like that in the newspapers.'

'You could be right,' Jack said.

'Do you think so? What I've always thought is that men have more sensitive egos than women. Too sensitive for their own good. A few years ago – '

Where was Dr. Middleton? Where was he? When was he coming? It was already 10:45.

Ah, there he was. Jack could hear his soft cough, his footsteps in the corridor, the swish-swish of his black umbrella.

Chapter Eighteen

ON MONDAY MORNING ROB STAYED HOME FROM SCHOOL. He was still feeling under the weather, he said. His legs felt like water. Under the weather – one of Brenda's expressions, part of the cheerful propitiating vocabulary she attached to minor disasters and ailments. Down in the dumps. Off your mettle. On the fritz. Out of whack. She was good with the children when they were sick, positive and brisk, a swift, willing creator of eggnogs, cream soups, scrambled eggs. She had a way with a thermometer, holding it up to the level light of the window, absorbing the calm numbered reading, then shaking it down cleanly, reassuringly; when it came to disease, she had a core of optimism. Jack wondered if Rob might possibly have a fever.

At noon he phoned home from the office. Rob's voice, when he finally answered, sounded indistinct.

'Were you asleep?' Jack asked sharply.

'Sort of. Half.'

'What do you think it is? Flu?'

'I don't know. Just sick. I'll be okay tomorrow.'

'Didn't you have an algebra test today?'

'I can make it up. It was just a quiz.'

Jack could hear weariness in Rob's voice. Maybe he was just worn out, sick of school, fed up with the dark glooms of January mornings. 'I hope you fixed yourself some breakfast.'

'Yeah. I had some tea. That stuff of Mom's, the Chinese stuff.'

'Tea? That's all?'

'I'm not hungry.'

'You need some food in you.' He was sounding like Brenda, like Brenda's mother.

'Dad?'

'Yes.'

'How come there are bones all over the kitchen table?'

'They're chicken bones. We had some chicken late last night, after you were asleep. Bernie and Mrs. Carpenter came over for a while – '

'There are hundreds of bones.'

'Hardly hundreds,' Jack said. Rob had an annoying tendency to exaggerate.

'It makes me feel sick, looking at all those bones.'

'Don't look, then.'

'How can I help it? They're all over the table.'

It was true that the kitchen was in a mess; in the morning, getting breakfast, Jack had moved gingerly around the edges of the room, finally carrying his corn flakes and orange juice into the dining room. There *had* been an impressive heap of gnawed bones on the table. Nice of Hap Lewis to think of sending something over. (Jack wondered if there wasn't something rather funeral-baked-meats about it – probably not; Hap Lewis came from downstate, Danville; leaving casseroles at back doors was probably second nature to her.) He'd have to clean up the kitchen tonight when he got home. There were wine glasses standing among the bones, and two empty bottles. Paper napkins wadded into balls. Beer bottles on the counter – from Saturday? A jar of instant coffee on the windowsill, the lid lost. An empty soup can, a casserole soaking in the sink – joined now no doubt, by a shower of tea leaves. Laurie's ski jacket was on the floor; he'd almost tripped over it on his way out the back door.

Years ago, he used to phone Brenda at lunch time. The children had been babies then. It always amazed him to hear people talk about the tumult of the sixties. *His* sixties had been passed in a daydream: work at the Institute, Brenda and the children, golf on Sundays when he could afford it. In those days, to save money, he'd carried sandwiches to work to eat at his desk. When he'd spoken to her on the phone, sipping coffee from a paper cup, he liked to close his eyes and call into his mind the image of Brenda, how she must look standing in the kitchen by the wall telephone. He had been young, barely thirty. Domesticity had been more precarious and precious. Mere objects had moved him to euphoria; cans of vegetables standing in cupboards, blankets folded on a closet shelf, his socks knotted in pairs in his top drawer – the thought of these things, their arrangement and persistence, had filled him then with amazement. Brenda, in those years, still slender, had worn

122

blue jeans around the house. (Recently she'd gone back to blue jeans after long phases of pedal pushers, plaid slacks, double knits.) Then, she used to answer the phone in a voice that was exasperated, amused, tender, put upon. The kids were driving her crazy. They were pulling over lamps and chairs, crawling into cupboards, smearing jam on the walls, fingerprints everywhere. They never spent an hour without spilling milk on the floor. They were beautiful, though, intelligent, responsive, alert, agile, inventive, self-confident. When they grew up, the world would be theirs for the asking; there would be nothing they wouldn't be able to accomplish.

Jack had joined instinctively in these dazzling visions of the future, visions that were freshened each night as he helped Brenda button their perfect, rounded, sweet-smelling bodies into pyjamas. His children, his progeny. (He loved the word progeny, loved himself in the role of progenitor.) How could he and Brenda have divined what was to happen? They had been taken in; the early vision had been false. It wasn't that the children had disappointed them, were no longer beautiful. But grace, which they'd thought was imperishable, had fallen away; the childish ease had been somehow damaged; difficulty and nightmare had crept in. Well, that was the way it was.

'Hey, Dad,' Rob said into the phone. 'Guess what? It's snowing out here. Is it snowing downtown?'

Jack looked out his office window and felt a jump of happiness. 'Hey, it *is* snowing. What do you know.'

'How long's Bernie going to stay with us?' Rob had decided to be conversational.

'I'm not sure. I'll ask him tonight what his plans are. Actually, he's sort of staying next door at the Carpenters'.'

'I know. Weird.'

'Well – ' Jack began, hovering on the brink of some kind of explanation, then deciding against it. What was there to be explained, anyway?

'Maybe he'll get back together with Sue,' Rob said, filling in a silence.

'Maybe.'

'She phoned this morning. She wants you to phone her at the hospital.'

'Shit.'

'What?'

'Nothing. It's just that I've got so much to do. Okay, I'll phone her later.'

'What's up with Mr. Carpenter? How's he doing?'

'No real news.'

'He's going to be okay though?'

'They think so. I just phoned the hospital a few minutes ago, but all I got was the switchboard. He's stable, she said. In a stable condition.'

'I guess that means he's going to be okay.'

'Probably. It's hard to tell. Apparently it takes forty-eight hours until they can really tell.'

'Is he nuts or what? Why'd he do it?'

Jack hesitated. With Rob he had to be careful to weigh his words – Rob tended to dramatize things. 'I think,' Jack said cautiously, 'that he just hit a low moment. Depression.'

'Was it that thing in the paper? About the play being such a bummer?'

'Partly. They – Mrs. Carpenter thinks that that's what might have triggered it off. But these things,' he hesitated again, 'are usually more complex than they seem.'

'Why would a guy like that want to do himself in? A guy with a car like that.'

Jack decided to ignore the mention of the car; Rob wasn't that simple; he was just fishing for something else. 'Everyone gets depressed now and then,' Jack told him. 'Everyone.'

' Yeah.'

'Now listen, let's get back to you for a minute. I phoned to see how you were feeling.'

'I already told you, not too bad.'

'What exactly does that mean?'

'Huh?' Rob sounded belligerent.

'What I mean is, when did you start feeling sick? Was it yesterday morning or was it later, in the afternoon?'

'Both. I don't know, all day I guess.'

'You didn't mention feeling sick in the morning. Remember? You were okay when we went over to Grandma's and Grandpa's.'

'Uhuh.'

'Was it when you got out to Charleston?'

'I don't know. I can't remember.'

'Well, try to remember. Because if you've got something,

some bug, I can phone the doctor and get you on to some medication.'

'Let's drop it, okay? I'm fine. I'll be fine tomorrow. I already feel better.'

'What I'm trying to say is, you've never been to Charleston before. Or any place remotely like it. For that matter, I haven't either. It would be only natural if you – '

'You mean you want to know if I'm really sick or is it just psychosomatic.'

'Well,' Jack hedged, 'yes, I guess that is more or less what I was wondering.'

'I dunno. Maybe. Sort of.'

'You can't be a little more specific than that?'

'Well, it was kind of – '

'Upsetting?'

'Weird. Creepy, unreal. There was this one guy – Bernie said he was eighteen. With webbed feet and no nose. He just sat there on the floor in this big room and made these sounds. He . . . he had to wear diapers.'

'I know,' Jack said, not knowing.

'We had to walk through this long room full of these creeps to get to the room where Sarah was.'

Jack waited.

'She was in a bed. A crib, with sides on it. She didn't look like five years old. She looked like a baby. She weighs thirty pounds, that's all. She didn't even look like a girl. She didn't have any hair, not very much anyway. You could see the bones through her head, right through, the skin was so thin. She was sort of grey-looking and her eyes were shut and she's got these tubes in her nose.'

'Rob – '

'Even if she opened her eyes she wouldn't be able to see anything. And Bernie – '

'What?'

'He goes out there every Sunday. I guess Sue does, too, most of the time. They just go out there and stare at it. Just stand by the bed, I guess, and stare at it.'

'I know these things must seem tragic – '

'Then, before we left, do you know what he did, what Bernie did?'

'What?'

125

'He leaned over and kissed her. On the face. Just above where the tube went in, on the bone part. I guess that's when I started to feel – '

'Sick?'

There was no reply.

'You still there?' Jack asked.

'I better go, Dad. I'm going back to bed, I think.'

'Good idea. I'll see you around six. Okay?'

Jack put the phone back. He sat at his desk for a few minutes and watched the snow come down, large wet flakes drifting past his window and falling out of sight into the invisible street below. He felt panic, a shortness of breath, a sharp pain that was not his but that belonged to his son. Couldn't he, with a doubling of will, keep Rob safe a little longer? Spare him terrible sights? Deter him from absurd sacrifices? There must be a way, if only he had the imagination to find it.

As an emergency distraction he browsed through the new *Journal*, and as a self-imposed piece of torture read once again the announcement of Harriet Post's book. There was a clean cutting edge to the pain it brought today, not entirely disagreeable. He opened his briefcase and got out the manuscript for Chapter Six. He should have gone out for lunch; or ordered a sandwich; he felt hollowed out. There was a push of pressure in his chest.

Everyone else on the floor was out for lunch. When had the place ever been this quiet? For once even the noise of the traffic seemed muffled and distant. All the sky was filling with whiteness. Amazing how the corrupt, old downtown sky could be so quickly transformed and widened.

Chapter Nineteen

FROM A MACHINE IN THE CORRIDOR HE BOUGHT HIMSELF a cup of coffee and something called a Leisure-Snak, made of pressed sesame seeds and honey, which he chewed while he browsed through the newspaper. He lingered over it, feeling obscurely that he owed himself half an hour's escape. There was a new play at the Apollo and a review of it by Gordon Tripp. Jack skimmed it quickly, taking in the mildness of tone, the straining toward fairness, a certain surprising humility: 'This young playwright has things to teach all of us.' Of course, Gordon Tripp must know about Larry by now – some sort of chastening must have taken place. At the bottom of the review was a brief note in italics from the editor: *Our regular reviewer, Larry Carpenter, is on vacation.*

On vacation! So much for history. So much for the reliability of the printed word. Wait until Bernie sees this.

And what was this on the back page? A newsphoto of the hunger marchers in Columbus Park. Jack recognized the man with the poncho and the white hair. The picture was over-exposed and crudely flecked with white, but he could make out the placards and, yes, there was the woman with the baby on her back. He and his father had been standing just off to the left. If the photo had been half an inch wider, they would have landed in Chicago *Today* – his father would have liked that. Perhaps they *had* been in the picture; these pictures were always being cropped to make them fit on the page; it could be that he and his father ended up in a wastebasket at the Chicago *Today* office. The caption read: *Hunger strikers demonstrate on behalf of Russian dissidents Sunday in Humboldt Park.*

Humboldt Park!

But this was Columbus Park. He'd been there, And besides, he recognized the corner of the wrought-iron fence. Someone – the photographer? the person who wrote the captions? – someone had made a mistake.

A mistake, and yet hardly anyone in the whole city of

Chicago would know a mistake had been made. The people in the photo would know, of course. And he and his father. But no one would bother writing to the newspaper asking for a correction. Why should they? It was too trivial: Columbus Park, Humboldt Park, it was all the same.

Nevertheless – and Jack felt perversely pleased by the fact, almost triumphant – it represented a false recording, similar in a way to Larry Carpenter's 'vacation.' It was this false form which would undoubtedly survive; this moment of history would have taken place in Humboldt Park. The picture would be filed away forever, and what was written underneath would become the truth.

The historical knot is hard to untie; unlocking one moment of history can be a life's work. So said Dr. Gerald Middleton, appearing as Guest Lecturer at North-western a year or so ago. A particular kind of persistence is required, he said. A temperament that is rigid but at the same time capable of settling for less than perfection. There must be a willingness to stop and rest from time to time on certain boggy suppositions. Hardness and brilliance were desired but seldom attained. The task was heartbreaking. The men who choose to be witnesses and recorders of the historical process must partially remove themselves from society. What was needed was a steady but disinterested hand, groping and feeling its way – no wonder, he said, historians were generally considered to be dullards (appreciative laughter). There must exist, he went on, an instinct for melding particular but seemingly unrelated facts, and this instinct, which required a leap of imagination, was accessible only to those fortunate few – he eyed his audience warmly – who possess that vital element, a historical sense.

A historical sense; a sense of history, a relatively rare thing. Brenda, for instance, had no sense of history. It had taken Jack years and years, first to discover this, and second, to comprehend the fact that she was able to function in the world without it.

She had no father, either, had never had a father; this and the missing historical sense seemed to Jack to be inextricably linked.

'But you must have had a father once,' Jack remembered saying to her the first time they met. She had been working then as a junior typist at the Institute, and Jack, beginning his

128

research project on LaSalle, had stopped in at the Institute library to look at some old maps. She had been helpful in an awkward way. And remarkably friendly. He'd asked her out for lunch, inviting her around the corner to Roberto's. They sat in a corner booth and talked about where they'd grown up, the schools they'd gone to, their families, and that was how Brenda happened to tell him she had no father.

'Well, of course there was *someone*.' She'd smiled beguilingly at him over her bowl of vegetable soup. Her teeth were good. 'A biological father, but that's all.'

Why was she telling him this? They'd just met. 'But you're so off-hand about it,' he told her.

'You'd have to meet my mother,' she said to Jack, laughing, 'to understand.'

You'd have to meet my mother – the words, lightly uttered – carried carloads of predetermination – yes, he would have to meet this girl's mother. He *would* meet her mother. For once he grasped the fact that something was happening.

'But didn't you mind?' he asked her, 'not having a father?'

'Isn't it funny, everyone asks me that. I just say it's like being born with one toe missing. You never miss it if you've never had it.'

'But surely you had to explain it somehow. Wasn't it hard, when you had to fill out forms, at school for instance, asking for your father's name, date of birth, occupation and all that?'

'I just left a blank. That's how I always think of him, as a matter of fact. A blank. Like one of those metal slugs people put in juke boxes. Origin unknown.'

'You mean you really don't know? You never asked?'

'No.' The smile again. Teeth on the small side. 'Not really.'

'But you must have been curious – '

'No. You'd think so, but I've liked the old blank. I'm used to it. I just sort of inherited it, so to speak.' She shrugged, a gesture which would bind him to her forever, a miniature lifting of the shoulders, a sway of breasts under her soft sweater.

'Most people would want to know,' Jack said. 'The circumstances, anyway.'

'Probably,' Brenda said. 'But I'm lucky. I guess I just don't have much curiosity or something.'

She's sublimating, thought Jack at the time; he had taken the required course in basic psychology.

129

But when he knew her better, when he'd been married to her for several years, he realized she had been truthful. She was not curious. She lacked all sense of historical curiosity.

Her imagination, it seemed to Jack, was confined to a thin slice of present time. Confinement, in fact, was the word that came to mind when he tried to picture Brenda's concept of time. 'Tell me what comes into your head,' he'd asked her once, 'when I say George Washington, the Battle of Tippicanoe, Dunkirk, and, let's see, the Magna Carta.'

They had been lying in bed, a weekend morning in the Elm Park house. 'Just tell me,' he said, 'what kind of image comes to you?'

She lay back, her eyes shut. 'Coloured slides,' she said at last. 'A handful of coloured slides.'

'But are they in any particular order?' he'd persisted. 'Are some further back than others?'

She'd taken her time answering, cushioning him, no doubt, from possible disappointment. 'No special order,' she said. 'They're just, you know, lying in the same old box.'

He couldn't believe it.

'Well, maybe some are further back than others,' she'd said. 'I mean, I know perfectly well there's an order to it all. Magna Carta first, then George, but as far as I'm concerned, it's all back there together.'

He was amazed. What she had revealed, it seemed to him, was a kind of spacial blindness; she could see backward in time, but not with the perspective and shading that Jack had long taken for granted. And she didn't *care*. He would have pitied her if pity hadn't seemed so ludicrous.

He *had* taken it for granted, his vision of time, assuming that everyone perceived events as he did, through a multiple lens, a dense superimposed image composed of layers and layers of time. The image was always with him. Driving home from work, he was never entirely unconscious of the fact that he and the Aspen were skimming across the surface of a great alluvial basin; under the concrete of the expressway, just at the rim of consciousness, was the old glacial lake, Lake Chicago. For him the lake was still there, would always be there, a sub-image that a thousand layers of concrete couldn't obliterate. He could, if he wanted to, keep going, driving straight through Elm Park, out into the country, past small country towns and the sad rural frosts of the Illinois farmland, following the path of the old glacier to its westernmost limit, populating the spaces as he went with overlapping generations. Place names along the way would call into being events and genealogies, chanting soberly in an off-stage colloquy, all of it profiled and indexed on an inner landscape, enough room for everything, everything in its turn.

The time line in his head curved and circled – each century with a colour, an aura, of its own – a complex grillwork placed over the transparency of the past, winking with patterns and riddles and curious, random, heroic happenings. He couldn't remember a time when it hadn't existed. Except for this one luminous structure, his head seemed to him to be no more than a ragbag stuffed with half-truths, faulty resolutions, phoniness, evasions. But when he scratched for authenticity he never failed to find, securely in place, the wide-screen full-colour panorama of time. Once, when he was about fifteen, he and his father had taken the El downtown. General MacArthur, discharged by President Truman, was making a triumphal tour of the country. There was a motorcade down State Street, and through the crowd Jack had glimpsed the blurred redness that was General MacArthur's face. An abstraction made suddenly, vividly real. The time line had touched him them, connecting him directly to all possible events and creatures. Past and present flowed together. At the time he had supposed it must be the same for everyone.

It wasn't only Brenda; he'd talked to other people, felt them out. And was finally convinced that he had *it*, what Dr. Middleton called a sense of history. It was more rare than he had thought, and its rarity made him doubt, in his case, its truth. Perhaps it was an affectation, an intellectual adornment; no, he tested it, imagined living without it, and watched the structures on his mental horizon collapse. It was his!

That *it* was overly expanded and lacking in details, he admitted; he was, in a sense, no scholar, but only someone who was able to feel out the surfaces of time. Trade practices, the whole Indian thing – his interest in these things was simulated, not even, in fact, part of his area of specialization, belonging more truly to anthropologists, sociologists, economists. But it had been open, available, as Dr. Middleton explained. No real work had been done in the area. There was no point in going on with

131

LaSalle; LaSalle had been done down to the last hangnail; it was time for Jack to move into a new and potentially rewarding area. He might lack expertise in this new area; there were certain books he would have to look at, theses to consult, but it was virgin territory. It was his if he wanted it, and he did have what mattered most, the feeling for history.

How simple, how accessible the world must look to Brenda – but how flat, how lacking in colour. She would probably shrug and compare it to the missing of a toe – you didn't miss what you never had. This though, he knew, must be a larger loss, a leg gone or an eye put out.

She had been wearing an angora sweater the first day he met her and took her for lunch. Some shade of blue. After the soup she had had a toasted cheese sandwich and coffee. She only had an hour for lunch, she said; she had to get back.

'Couldn't you, just this once, be late?' he had pleaded.

'I just started working there a month ago,' she told him. 'I wouldn't have the nerve.'

'We could order a bottle of wine,' he said, feeling daring.

She was already pulling her coat on. It was late March, a cold spring day. 'Wine for lunch isn't my cup of tea,' she'd said without a trace of irony, and he had felt a small expansion of joy.

'Please?'

'I'd love to but I've got to get back. Honestly.'

He'd walked her down Keeley Avenue to the Institute. The sidewalks were covered with a gauze-like frost. At the entrance she turned and shook hands with him. She was wearing mittens; it must have been the fashion then. The mittened hand in his, the soft wool touch of it, sprang a lever of love in his heart, a flare of happiness that left him dazed for weeks.

All that winter he'd been going out with Harriet Post, a professor's daughter from Madison, Wisconsin, whom he'd met in his American Civilization seminar. Harriet of the springy nylon sweaters and straight A's. The first time he took her out they'd gone to a movie called *Wages of Fear*. He'd walked her home to the apartment where she was living, and kissed her chapped lips in the shadow of the front door. She had reached down, unzipped his pants and slipped her hands inside – an event that had filled him with astonishment and joy, but that

132

for sheer power was equalled by the weight of Brenda's mittened hand in his.

He would have to choose.

And he had chosen the prized and possible safety of his desire for Brenda. The ease of it had made it seem right. All around him, flickering at the edge of his vision, were storms of passion, strife, risks, and dangerous and unproductive longings, but he had made his choice.

The historical underpinnings of that choice had occasionally tormented him. Had it been a choice conditioned by the tenor of the times, those curious mid-fifties, the sunny optionless Eisenhower days? Had he, slumbering in the faint radiance of Hollywood – June Allyson, good teeth – made the cliché American choice, purity over corruption? No. He hadn't chosen Brenda for any of those reasons. She, for reasons that he had never fully understood, had chosen him.

Chapter Twenty

'THIS IS THE LOUSIEST MOVIE I EVER SAW,' ROB WAS SAYING, an arc of wonder in his voice.

'There's nothing else on,' Laurie said happily.

'Shh,' from Jack.

It was eight o'clock, still snowing. Tonight it had taken Jack two hours to drive home; for the first time that he could remember, the Expressway had been closed to traffic. Now the three of them were watching an old Betty Grable movie on television. They were eating the hamburgers and french fries he'd brought home – except for Rob, who was gulping China tea and looking pale.

'Can I have yours?' Laurie asked him.

'I don't care.'

'I'll split it with you,' Laurie offered.

'Take it all.'

They were sprawled in the living room, at peace with each other, relaxed. A slice of pickle slid out of Laurie's hamburger and landed in her lap; she retrieved it distractedly, eyes on the screen, glued to Betty Grable's face. 'She *is sort* of good looking,' she said, 'except for that hair. And the way her eyes kind of pop.'

'And that weird hat.'

'That's what they wore,' Jack said.

Betty was playing a sweet young thing kicking her way to stardom. A place in the chorus line was more than she'd ever dreamed of. But she knew she had to be tough if she was going to make it to the top.

'Is this for real?' Rob asked. He was looking somewhat brighter, Jack thought; at least he's not moping in bed. Maybe Bernie's right – kids forget quickly.

Now Betty was dancing on the sidewalk in front of the theatre. She had just seen her name up in lights, and happiness had overtaken her. Passers-by were stopping to watch her. They began to tap their umbrellas on the pavement. Then they

134

too started to dance. They hoisted Betty up on top of a mailbox, where she tapped and sang with insane, open-mouthed joy. Her arms sliced crazy, brave windmills over her head, and her legs stretched out, inhumanly long.

'Hilarious,' Laurie said, chewing.

Then Betty was back in her dressing room, sombre now, rebuffed, injured, baffled. Her voice was stiff and courageous. She couldn't help being decent, she said. That was the way she was.

Jack put his feet up on the coffee table. He had hours of work to do for Tuesday, all of Chapter Six promised – again – for the next morning. But first he owed himself a little relaxation, a little time with his children.

He regarded them with love; what had he and Brenda done to deserve these two good, intelligent children? The innocent, rapt attention with which they gave themselves to this improbable and dreadful movie touched him. Tonight, watching Betty's sequin-splashed resilience, he felt his despair resting lightly on him. He would like this moment to stretch out forever, an eternity of Betty, her hair ribbons bobbing on blonde curls, her short pleated patriotic skirt flashing red, white, blue. Beautiful.

And then the sweet spot of the evening: when Laurie, watching Betty hook up her diamond-mesh stockings, cried out, 'Look, Daddy, she's wearing those one-legged stockings.' Even Rob laughed.

It seemed that Larry Carpenter was making good progress.

Tonight news of him came from all quarters. First Hap Lewis phoned to tell Jack that she had got through the hospital switchboard at last and had actually spoken to the floor nurse, the bitch. 'She isn't allowed to give reports on patients,' Hap said, 'but she did say that there's absolutely no cause for concern.'

'Well,' said Jack, 'that's certainly good news.'

'Who would ever have thought it,' Hap said. 'Larry Carpenter. Of all people. It makes you wonder.'

'You're right,' Jack said, wishing Hap would say goodbye and let him get down to work. But she hung on; she seemed to be waiting for something. Then it came to him – of course.

'You must be proud of Bud,' he told her. 'If it hadn't been for Bud – '

'I know,' was all Hap said, but she said it with immense solemnity. And Jack had a sudden flashing image of a future in which both Bud and Hap would be transformed into other, nobler people. Bud would emerge from his lean, shadowy stillness, shed some of his easy dexterity. Hap would move by imperceptible degrees toward a new softening, a kindly, embracing awe for life's darker complexities. It seemed to Jack that he could hear the beginnings in her duskily withheld voice tonight. 'I know,' she said once again.

Bernie himself brought news from the hospital. He had dropped by there earlier in the evening to see if he could do anything. He looked burly and cold in his snow-covered windbreaker, the very image of the loyal family friend standing by in the moment of crisis. Larry was allowed no visitors, Bernie said, except for Janey and his father. (The father had arrived in the morning, had seen Larry briefly, conferred with the doctor, and had taken the afternoon plane east – just missing the storm; his short visit was a sure sign, Bernie said, that everything was going well.) Larry would have to be under observation for a week. He'd be seeing a psychiatrist, of course. Janey was calm. Bernie had arranged to pick her up later at the hospital and bring her home. He should be on his way now, he told Jack; he only came back to let Cronkite and Brinkley out for a run. Janey would be waiting. And what about tonight: where would he stay? Bernie didn't say. Jack didn't ask.

Sue Koltz phoned. 'Don't panic now,' she told Jack briskly, 'I'm not after Bernie. I'm after you.'

'Oh?' Jack could tell she was calling from the hospital; she was using her doctor voice, crisp, acerbic; he pictured the cropped colourless hair above the white coat, the slight red blotchiness of her neck.

'I know he's there, all right. At least I'm pretty darn sure he is.'

'Actually – '

'But to tell the truth I'd prefer not to see him at the moment. Not until I've settled a few things. Thought a few things through. You might just mention that to him, that I don't want him hounding me.'

'Hounding?'

'I saw him tonight, in the waiting room here at the hospital. I just managed to duck out of sight in time. I don't,' she spoke with icy deliberation, 'like being spied on.'

'I'll tell him.'

'Well, is he or not? Staying with you and Brenda?'

'Look, Sue, I don't really think it's my place – '

'I know he hasn't been back to the apartment. I was there this afternoon picking up some things and feeding the cat. God, all this snow, we're getting buried. And Bernie doesn't have his overcoat with him. I saw it hanging in the closet.'

'I imagine he'll survive.'

'Or his boots.'

'I'll lend him mine.'

'Actually, Jack, I've called you a number of times. Then it gradually sank through my thick skull that you weren't going to phone me back. That you had no intention of phoning me back.'

'I have tried. A couple of times, but you're never – '

'I can understand you might be reluctant to get involved – '

'Sue. It isn't a question of reluctance, exactly. I've been up to my ears with other things, swamped. And I've got hours of work ahead of me tonight. So – '

'By the way, one of your neighbours has been admitted to my floor, not that I'm supposed to mention this kind of thing. Carpenter. Larry Carpenter. Did you know?'

'Yes, I know.'

'I had a look at him this morning. He's in pretty good shape, considering.'

'That's good news,' Jack said.

'He's lucky to be alive,' Sue said. And added, with surprising kindness, 'the poor bastard.'

Poor bastard, poor Larry Carpenter. For the first time Jack thought about Larry. A shadowy double image came to him: Larry's hands shaky as he reached for ice cubes; and his eyes fixed in space.

Amazingly enough he had hardly thought of him at all, only of the blare of circumstances, the Saturday-night party and the tense, triumphant Sunday-morning rescue. He had not thought at all about the actual moment when Larry entered the dark garage, shut the door, got into the car, and turned on the engine.

Someone whom he and Brenda knew – not well, but moderately well, as well as they know many people – decided to terminate his life, and almost succeeded.

And then later at the hospital – Jack tried to picture how it must have been: Larry surfacing to consciousness in a strange bed surrounded by screens and the unglinting whiteness of faces and walls. Movements of air and sounds. The clinking of hospital apparatus, footsteps, the stirred breath of voices, all of it testifying to failure. Would this knowledge of failure come to Larry gradually as in a dream or would he open his eyes and immediately perceive what had happened? And would he come back to life with anger or gratitude? All suicides are victims of the moment – where had he heard that? One of his father's books, probably. Those who survived were supposed to welcome their reclaimed lives and be thankful to those who intervened. Really?

And then what? How was the new post-suicidal life to be lived? Everything back to normal, clickity-click? All the old routines taken up again? Hi-ya, Larry, how you doing? Larry backing his car out of the drive, setting off to work. Would the day come when he would again invite people to his house for parties, press introductions upon them, uncork bottles of bur-gundy – Jack could not imagine any of these things happening. Nor could he imagine what he would say to Larry when they met – as they surely would – over the shrubbery. Sorry to hear you've been sick. Sick, ha! Hope you're feeling your old self again. What old self, for crissake? Sorry about what? Welcome back to the land of the living, you poor bastard.

Should he send flowers? No. A note? Brenda would know. A short note, something sympathetic and encouraging. Why were people so afraid of words these days?

He rummaged in a drawer for writing paper; he should send it tomorrow – hadn't Bernie said he'd be in the hospital only a week? He found Brenda's notepaper. 'Hasty Notes' it said on the box, and on each sheet a picture of a deer, Bambi-style, nibbling grass. No! There was always his typing paper, ordinary bond, fair quality. Dear Larry, he might write, all best wishes for a speedy recovery. That sounded fairly neutral, but more the kind of thing for after an operation. Dear Larry, my thoughts are with you? Too social, too dishonest, although true in a way. Dear Larry, so you couldn't take it when the chips were down, eh? Dear Larry, I know how you feel. I know exactly how you must feel. I can understand . . . .

By midnight Jack had made the decision not to send a note, but to send a plant instead. Cut flowers, nice at this time of year, would be overly suggestive of celebration. Or severance. A small green plant with broad healthy leaves; he didn't know the name of the plant he had in mind, but he could visualize perfectly its shape and colour. He could phone the florist near the hospital in the morning and have it delivered. And tell them to include one of those tiny florist's cards. *From the Bowmans*; that would do it. The decision spread a tent of calm over him.

The house was quiet. Both Rob and Laurie slept well. Rob, in fact, had gone to bed before ten; maybe, Jack thought, he did have some kind of bug. If he's not better tomorrow, well, we'll face that when it comes.

It was too late to phone Brenda in Philadelphia, although the thought had come to him earlier in the evening. What would Brenda be doing? a banquet? the mayor's reception? She would be phoning anyway on Tuesday, she said – tomorrow night. And it was too late, too, to phone Harriet Post, but he would, he decided, try to reach her tomorrow. The thought of speaking to Harriet over the telephone – an alarming thought earlier in the day – now seemed ripely possible and even rational. He should have phoned days ago, when he'd first seen the announcement of her book. (Had he feared she might answer his call with a puzzled, irritated 'Jack who?')

It was Dr. Middleton's idea that he contact Harriet. Dr. Middleton had received the news of Harriet's book with gravity and alarm, more alarm than Jack had been prepared for. 'This is most worrying,' he had said, his hands travelling across the width of his chin. 'This bears looking into.'

On the other hand, Dr. Middleton had never heard of Harriet Post. 'De Paul graduate, you say?' She was certainly not a recognized scholar in the field; her name was not in the least familiar to him. At the same time, he went on, areas of expertise were changing all the time. Lately amateurs – he pronounced the word with some harshness – had started crowding in, some of them not easily dismissed or despised. The best policy, Dr. Middleton felt, was cautious inquiry. And since Jack was acquainted with Miss Post – *Miss Post* – it would be relatively simple and quite professional to approach her and attempt to ascertain the scope of her monograph. If it turned out that too many similarities existed – these things did happen from time to time – it was sometimes wiser to cut one's losses, to shift the focus perhaps, or even – here Dr. Middleton hesitated – even to abandon the project if absolutely necessary. Meanwhile, he looked forward to seeing Chapter Six on Tuesday morning. Ten o'clock. He had been surprisingly firm about Chapter Six.

In the empty kitchen Jack made himself a cup of instant coffee and a slice of toast, which he spread with raspberry jam. He kept his eyes averted from the chicken bones still heaped on the kitchen table. And from the kitchen sink, which appeared to be clogged with tea leaves. The den was bitterly cold, and for a minute he considered carrying the typewriter into the living room. But the coffee table was covered with debris from dinner. And soup bowls? Of course, he and Laurie had had soup last night. Tomorrow he would have to organize the kids and clean the house up. He was running out of rooms. For tonight, there was no choice but to put up with the cold den. On the living-room floor he found a blanket – could this be the same blanket he covered Bernie with last – when was it? – last Saturday afternoon? He wrapped the blanket around his shoulders and settled into his desk chair. The old gooseneck lamp ground its harsh oval of light onto the typewriter. He tapped out a sentence.

> The patterning of trading goods in the lower Great Lakes Region suggests a number of ways of interpreting the relationships and communication level between various tribal communities.

In the middle of the word 'communities' the typewriter ribbon jammed, rucking up between the little steel teeth that held it in place. He attempted, gently at first, to pull it down. It refused to slip back. He pulled harder. The ribbon, an old one, tore in two. Oh, fuck it, shit.

By extraordinary good fortune there was a new ribbon in the desk drawer. He pulled it out, hardly able to believe his luck; Brenda must have bought it, ah Brenda. He took it from its box and examined it, his elation dying. He had no idea how to put it into the typewriter.

Brenda had always changed the ribbons for him: Lesson One at Katherine Gibbs. Besides, she was good with her hands, while he – how had he reached this age, forty-three, without knowing how to change a typewriter ribbon? Fuck. He'd watched Brenda do it dozens of times; she did it in a trice, in a wink of the eye, whipping it out of its box, snapping it in place, trying it out by typing a few words on a scrap of paper. She was always leaving these little scraps of paper in the typewriter for him: 'The lazy brown Brenda jumped over the quick foxy Jack' or 'Now is the time for all good Jacks to come to the side of their Brendas.' And once, in their first apartment, a winter night like this, 'I love you love you love you love you.'

Between 12:30 and one o'clock he tried to insert the new ribbon. What he couldn't understand was what made it so difficult. It couldn't be as complicated as this – thousands of ribbons, exactly like this one, were changed every day all over Chicago, all over America. Why were there no instructions on the box? What was the matter with him? His fingers were black from inked ribbon. His coffee was cold in the cup and he had started to sweat. The clock ticked maddeningly; the house seemed lurid and frightening and his stomach contracted; he would never get the cock-sucking thing in.

Then, like a spark catching in his brain, he thought of Laurie asleep upstairs. Laurie: she had inherited something of Brenda's knack for mechanical things. Once, when he'd taken the lawnmower apart, it had been Laurie who had managed to get it back together – he had put a nut on backwards. She knew some surprising facts, such as how to turn off the water main that time they'd had the broken pipe in the bathroom. Once, when the windshield wiper was sticking, she had freed it by bending the blade a fraction of an inch.

He tiptoed up to her bedroom and pushed the door open.

The room was filled with reflected whiteness. Behind the swags of white net curtains, snow was falling. A streetlight held the snow in a lacework suspension; snow was falling on Elm Park roofs, windowledges, hedges, every object made double-edged and newly created, transformed under its load of brightness.

Laurie, asleep on her back, lay with her hands flung open, looking braver now than she did awake. Her breathing came evenly and with exquisite calm. Jack sat for a minute on the edge of the bed, regarding her.

'Laurie,' he whispered.

'Yes.' Her answering voice was husky.

'Sweetie, open your eyes.'

The eyes opened at once, stared at him blankly.

'Laurie, listen. Do you know how to change the typewriter ribbon?'

'Yes.' Her eyes shut again; she was drifting back to sleep.

'Laurie. Dear? Daddy wants you to get up. For five minutes, okay? Just to put the ribbon in. Can you do that for me?'

She was on her feet, lurching toward the lighted hall, hitching up her pyjamas as she went. At the stairs he took her elbow so she wouldn't fall, but she glided steadily now, with a sleepwalker's numb radar. Downstairs in the den she stood, swaying slightly, in front of the desk, and Jack placed the ribbon into the palm of her hand. It took her ten seconds to put it in. He could hear it snap into position. She had done it, it seemed to Jack, with her eyes shut.

'Okay, baby. Go back to sleep.' Then, 'You're a doll.'

She started back up the stairs; her hands stretched ahead of her, feeling the way, and Jack rushed to her, swooped her up in his arms and carried her up to her bed. She was amazingly heavy; he couldn't remember when he had last picked her up. Would she remember in the morning, being carried upstairs in his arms and tucked into bed? Probably not. She was asleep already.

He was so grateful. His gratitude was extreme, absurd. Already he was seeing this moment with the gauzy brightness of nostalgia; the night it snowed, the night his daughter came to his rescue. Laurie.

Chapter Twenty-One

WHEN HE WOKE IT WAS NOT TO THE GREY DULLNESS OF a January dawn, but to sunlight entering the bedroom as a long rod of translucence lying across the top edge of the curtain. Morning? Something was wrong; this sun was wrong; he must have slept in. The clock on the bedside table said eight-thirty.

Impossible. Unless he had forgotten to set the alarm. And the appointment with Dr. Middleton was at ten o'clock. The spectre of Dr. Middleton sprang into view, a Torquemadian fury. No, that was unlikely, impossible in fact, completely out of character – yet, when Jack pictured Dr. Middleton as he really was, full of calm, reliable expectancy, he felt a surge of rage.

And no time this morning for a shower; he chafed at the sacrifice – he was not the same man without the daily galvanizing thrust of hot water thumping between his shoulder blades; the stickiness of genital flesh and night sweat slowed him down, reduced his powers. Well, it couldn't be helped. He dressed quickly, T-shirt, boxer shorts. The new suit – it was Moira Burke's farewell lunch; a certain formality was in order – with the faint pinstripes, cream on chocolate. The pinstripes had been Brenda's idea; pinstripes were back, she said; everyone was wearing pinstripes this year. Nevertheless Jack felt uneasy in the new suit – there was something period and flashy about it.

At least the children were up, their rooms empty, Rob's room a dust jumble of heaped clothes, coffee mugs, magazines, and records, but in the centre his bed stood, neatly, quaintly made up, topped by one of Brenda's early quilts, a blocky bright collage of navy sailboats, spritely green sea waves, and a primitive orange-coloured sun with long arms of light travelling all the way to the scalloped borders. It had been meant for a younger boy, a different kind of boy.

Laurie's room, neater, paler, was ablaze with sun, and from her window Jack surveyed the brilliant new Siberian landscape. Franklin Boulevard was buried. This was *real* snow; he hadn't seen snow like this for years. Well over a foot it looked like, and the drifted peaks around the sides of the houses and trees had the Dream Whip perfection of snow that he remembered, probably falsely, from childhood. Forts, tunnels, towers, miracles of possibility. Once in Columbus Park by the fountain, in the the light of the moon, he and Bernie had made a snowman with a thrusting torso and an immense icy erection; the next day penis had been knocked off; the following day the whole snowman had melted to a soft lump; Chicago snow had no keeping power. Even a full day's deluge like this would be gone in a matter of days.

Laurie stood at the kitchen counter crumbling Shredded Wheat into a bowl. 'You're going to be late,' she said, her mouth full; her eyes watchful.

'You don't say.' Why did this child of his always seem to have her mouth full? 'You could have called me,' he said in a somewhat kinder voice.

'I'm late too. Rob got me up. Did you see the snow?'

'Where is Rob, anyway?'

'School.' That jarring cheerful tone! At this hour of the morning!

'He's feeling better then?'

'I dunno.' Why didn't she know?

'Did he eat breakfast?'

'I dunno.' Again? 'But he made some coffee. A whole pot. You want some, Dad?'

He brightened. 'Real coffee?'

It was good coffee. Perfect, in fact, fresh and dark as chocolate. He would have liked a second cup, a third; he wanted – he longed – to linger over the papers this morning, to huddle in a corner of the dining room with his coffee cup and paper, burying himself in the steamy fumes and the stern crises of inflation and unemployment and hunger strikes. The decisions of the auto industry, the arrests of murderers, the marriages of movie stars – it kept him sane and safe to read that the world was going forward despitethe complicated meddling of human beings. What had Carter said about the Russian dissidents? What was happening to the ceasefire in Lebanon? He knew Carter would say something cautionary and self-serving: Americans stood for individual freedom but would not, ahem, interfere; he knew too that one Middle-East ceasefire would blend inevitably with another, and all so far away; the world would endure as long as the *Trib* was able to boil columns of print from human catastrophe. It was comforting and preserving, a pleasing drug to feel one's self at times of little consequence. But today he was already running late. Christ, it was nine o'clock. Laurie streaked past him to the front door, shrieking, 'I'm late, I'm going to be late.' A cry of anguish.

His briefcase stood ready by the kitchen table. He had placed it there last night, early this morning really, at 4 A.M., after tapping out the concluding sentence of Chapter Six.

> Thus it can be seen from the foregoing that the extent of ritual exchange between the different families and communal groups was less pronounced than previous evidence has led us to believe.

Firm but speculative, the right touch, or so he had thought at 4 A.M.. He really should look it over again.

He put on his overcoat and a pair of warm gloves. In the back of the hall closet, behind the vacuum cleaner, he found his old rubber boots, shiny and floppy, with cheap looking buckles, ten years old if they were a day. These boots seemed at least two sizes too large, incredible.

Stepping onto the back porch he found himself suddenly up to his knees in snow. It was deeper than he'd thought, fifteen inches at least and twice that where it had drifted. The sun sparkled on its wet surface; the temperature must be exactly at the freezing point. He should have turned on the weather report. From the back steps the whole world acres – of it, it seemed – looked deserted. Where was everyone?

The width of snow beckoned With enormous difficulty, holding his briefcase high in the air, Jack waded through the yard to the garage. A ring of numbness instantly gripped his calves; the snow had fallen inside his boots, wet caked chunks of it plugging the flapping boot tops. Already the neat hems of his pinstriped pants were soaked through. Goodbye, knife-edged press, goodbye, trim, tailored hem. Christ!

Behind the garage the back alley, normally a narrow and scraggly-edged passage, had become a newly created meadow, filled from end to end with glittering, sun-topped snow. Jack saw at once that he would have to give up the idea of driving downtown. It was ludicrous, taking a car out in this weather. It would take him hours to shovel his way out to the street.

Impossible even to open the garage doors. He must have been crazy to think he could drive; it was absurd. Thank God for the El.

It was just eight short blocks to the station, a four-minute walk usually, but today he was walking through fresh heavy snow. He was aware suddenly of the weight and sloshiness of his socks; the snow with its wet, collapsing, counterfeit solidity was breaking under his feet to instant iced greyness, a level sherbet of slush. It had been a mistake to take the alley; he would have made better time going down the street. Luckily, though, someone had gone before him, and he took pains to walk carefully, easing his boots into the deep regular holes of footprints; in and out, in and out. Whose footprints? Rob maybe on his way to school? Or Bud Lewis? Where was everyone? he wondered.

As he ploughed along, the bottom of his woollen overcoat collected a weighty border of crusted snow; he shifted the briefcase high under his arm, pinching it in place with his elbow, and hoisted his coat tails as high as he could. Immediately a coat button snapped off, sprang into the snow and disappeared. At the same instant the briefcase slid sideways from under his arm, landing upside down in a drift. God! He tore off his muffler and mopped at it furiously, hoping the zippered closing was waterproof. A chill struck the back of his neck; his teeth were suddenly chattering.

Twenty-five feet and he'd be out of the alley. He lifted the briefcase, balanced it with one hand on top of his head, and with the other hand gathered his coat, skirtlike, womanlike, in front of him. It must be 9:30. It had taken him half an hour to get to the end of the alley; this was insanity.

Once in the street, walking became somewhat easier. He kept to the middle of the road, stepping carefully along a tyre track. There was little traffic to be seen – Elm Park was a desert. Even the station was close to being deserted – just three people on the platform. He set down his briefcase with relief, feeling light-headed and slightly sick.

'Don't know if the trains are running,' said a woman with a shopping bag and a voice like a door buzzer. 'I've been waiting twenty minutes already.'

'I've been here for twenty-five,' a slim girl in a knitted hat said.

146

'They're running all right,' counselled a grey-headed, square-nosed man in a yellow ski jacket. 'I heard it on the radio. They're slow, but they're getting through.'

'I've got to be downtown by ten,' Jack told them all.

'Fat chance,' cheered the slim girl.

'No way you're gonna make that,' the man in the parka said. Smartass!

And at that moment, the train, almost silent in the sparkling air, pulled into the station. A quarter to ten. Jack felt a kick of joy. He could still –with luck – make it.

The city flashed past, familiar but strange under its quiet village-like covering. Chicago seemed innocent, intact, becalmed. The man in the yellow parka, rank with whisky-breath, wanted to talk weather records – the ice storm of 1949, the blizzard of '53, but Jack kept his eyes on the window. The Merchandise Mart, immense and antique, the quick one-second leap across the white band of river and into the Loop. Ten o'clock. He was late. But nearly there.

He ran the eight blocks to the Institute. The downtown streets, deserted, seemed nevertheless miraculously cleared of snow, an empty, almost nuclear blank. There was scarcely a car on Keeley Boulevard; Jack skittered down the middle of the street, his black boots flopping. At the corner of Keeley and Archer the stop light had gone blind. A power failure? He stopped for a second or two in the centre of the intersection and whirled around in the white glare; the streets stretched wide and empty, a circumference of stripped light, opening to clean-liness and a clear sky. He felt like yelling.

The elevator at the Institute was dead, too. He pounded up the stairs, down the corridor. It was 10:30. He was half an hour late. The tiled floor was slippery underfoot. His breath was coming hard. Outside Dr. Middleton's door, he knocked. No answer. He banged. Nothing. He took off his boots and shoes and, sighing, padded down the hall to his own office.

Why this jubilance? He couldn't imagine where it had come from. He peeled off his coat and hung it on a hanger, letting it drip on the closet floor. He spread his soaked gloves on the heating duct, turned his boots upside down in a corner, removed his socks. And then, kicking the door shut, he took off his drenched pants. Poor old pinstripes – they'd never recover from this. He squeezed as much water as he could from the legs, wringing them out over his philodendron, then pressed the material flat on his desk with the heel of his hand. There was an extra hanger in the little closet, and Jack hung up the pants carefully, running his hand along where the crease had once been.

An extraordinary surge of energy seized him. He considered doing push-ups on the office floor. Knee-bends? Too bad he didn't have a chinning bar in the office like Brian Petrie. Smiling foolishly to himself, he sank into his desk chair and clutchedat his hair. His bare legs were beginning to warm up; his thighs tingled. He had made it, he had beat Dr. Middleton to the office. He had, in fact, beat everyone. He was the only one here.

No. Someone was knocking on his door. 'Come in,' he bellowed happily.

It was Moira Burke. She was wearing a soft blue skirt, velvet. And a silk blouse with large loose sleeves. Her hair had been done in a new way, something vaguely Grecian, Jack thought, the way it looped grandly over her ears. Her smile was crooked, perplexed, tentative, hard.

'Moira! You made it through the snow.' He was shouting.

She answered shortly. 'I took a taxi. All the way from Evergreen Park. Fourteen bucks.'

'What about Dr. Middleton? We had an appointment for ten.'

'Ha! He phoned. Can't get in, he says. All the roads in Highland Park are closed.'

'Christ. I stayed up half the night finishing Chapter Six.'

'Hmmm.'

'Moira! Your lunch. What about the farewell lunch?'

'Cancelled.'

'What?' He whirled his chair around.

'Cancelled.'

'You mean postponed. They'll reschedule it. Tomorrow or something.'

'Tomorrow. Don't make me laugh. Tomorrow I'll be in Arizona.'

'Oh, Moira.' He stood up abruptly. Moira's tense locked eyes reminded Jack sharply of Larry Carpenter standing in his kitchen. He opened his mouth to speak.

She crashed against his chest, beating on his shoulder with her fist, wailing.

Chapter Twenty-Two

'THESE THINGS HAPPEN,' JACK WAS SAYING TO MOIRA.
'You're telling me,' she said.

They were eating spaghetti at Roberto's. The mood was one of emergency celebration. Back at the Institute Moira had produced from her desk drawer a small plastic hair dryer that she applied first to Jack's pants and then to his socks and boots. In an hour the pants had dried stiff as construction paper, and their heat against his calves had been unexpectedly pleasurable, the flushed sensual pleasure he remembered feeling on rainy days when he was at school, baking by the radiator after recess.

At Roberto's he and Moira were the only customers. And for some reason the spaghetti was passable today, the sauce plentiful and spicy. There were no waiters in sight; instead the meal was served by the cook, a short man with a heavy neck and shadowless slits for eyes. His jowls danced, dark and friendly. 'I just about stayed in the sack this morning,' he told them, coming out of the kitchen. 'At first I thought, what's the use, no one'll turn up for lunch on a lousy day like this anyways. Then I thought, hell, I better see what's what, check the refrigerator, what with the electricity conking out all over the place. You know something, I've never closed this place down yet, except for Christmas Day and New Year's. That's a record, twenty-five years, and all that time I've never closed, rain or shine. Not a bad record, so today I said to myself, what's a little snow?'

Jack straightened. 'Then are you,' he paused 'the owner?'
'Right on. Owner, proprietor, founder, and cook.'
'I've been coming here twenty years,' Jack said.
'Is that right? Waddya know.'
'And I've never seen you.'
'I keep to the back. I like to keep an eye on things.'
Jack had to know: 'Are you Roberto?'
'You guessed it. Hey, you folks want some wine to warm you up?'

149

'Absolutely,' Jack said, taken aback by the hideous ring of zeal in his voice.

'Tell you what, the wine's on me today. You and the wife want the cheap stuff or the good stuff? Have the good stuff. I've got a double bottle here, a magnum, they call it. Bet you didn't know I had some good stuff around. It's not on the menu on account of the kind of clientele we get here, they don't know wine from bananas, present company excluded. Only I can't drink the crap we serve, so I keep a few bottles locked up. I gotta lock up everything, or you know what'll happen. That's why I make it my business to stick to the back. Keep my mouth shut and my eyes open. Wide open. Well, enjoy your meal, folks.'

Jack, his feet warm under the table, gratified by the glow of the soft red wine, tried to divert Moira. He spoke rapidly, almost compulsively, filled with a sombre excitement, wanting to commit for her a pure act of kindness, to fill the emptiness of her disappointment with his own misery; the whole world was plagued with disappointment, he wanted to say, a series of disappointments. She was not alone, she was in good company, no one had a monopoly on suffering, we all have setbacks. In his case – he leaned forwared on his elbows – in his case it was Harriet Post; after all these years of work, he told Moira, he was going to be stomped upon by a woman in Rochester, New York, called Harriet Post.

'Lord,' Moira said. 'Of all the rotten breaks.' She shook her head sadly, making Jack feel, guiltily, that he had earned her sentiment falsely; something lavish and accidental about Moira's face made it shine with too-easy a sympathy.

Tonight, Jack told her, he was going to phone Harriet Post and find out the scope and nature of her book. But regardless of what she said, he had decided, almost definitely, that he would abandon the book. What was the use? 'As Dr. Middleton says –'

'That old eunuch,' Moira muttered under her breath.

'It's better sometimes,' he drew a sharp breath, 'to cut your losses.'

'Hmmm.'

'These things happen,' he told Moira, astonished at the firmness in his voice.

It seemed to him that he'd been hearing that phrase a lot lately – *these things happen*. Wasn't that what someone said about Larry Carpenter's suicide attempt? He'd said it himself to Rob when they were talking about the visit to Charleston – *these things happen*. The words had a seductive ring of magic about them – say them fast enough and they expelled blame and responsibility. They had the power to defuse all kinds and shades of disappointment. You have to acknowledge the realities, roll with them, *et cetera*. Men and women do conceive monstrous children, do dissolve their marriages, do commit suicide; they win a few, lose a few, they suffer absurd humiliations. His own children, despite the fact that they lived in a century characterized by alienation and in a city famed for violence, would undoubtedly survive. The world wouldn't end because Harriet Post had cut him out – what was the use crying over spilt milk, as Brenda would have said.

'You really don't mind, then?' Moira said, her eyes, to Jack's surprise, brimming with tears, 'after all the work you've put into it?'

'What can I do?' He shrugged. And wondered if he should confess to her that the thought – the mere thought – of abandoning the book had come as a release. Since Dr. Middleton first implanted the idea in his head – 'these things happen, Jack' – he had at last, this week, found space to breathe. It was true. The small spark of possibility had burst into flame – he could, he saw, with a measure of dignity, walk away; he could put away his notes forever.

'Uhuh,' Moira nodded. She had always appeared a heavy-featured woman to Jack; today her lips had a frilled swelling, a wobbly near-tearfulness that was oddly attractive, reminding Jack of his curious demi-excitement as he stood in the office and experienced the pressure of Moira's thighs through the thin material of his undershorts. He reached across the table and refilled her wine glass.

He grew boisterous and told Moira that he never should have started the Indian thing. It wasn't his kind of research; he did better on short papers, on specific problems. Some people liked long, in-depth studies, but for him the Indians and their trade practices – so abstruse and difficult to document – had been frustrating and wearing. A bore. One long nightmare.

Why was he telling Moira this? It must be the wine going to his head. She was nodding now, smiling at the floor, looking revived. She let loose a bark of harsh public laughter that Jack found cheering.

'The trouble is,' he told her, 'everyone keeps asking me how the book is coming along. My parents, they can't wait to see me in print. *Their son*. It's what they've lived for. Even my kids ask me when the book's finally going to be done. *The book*. And this guy next door –'

'The one who tried to kill himself? In the garage?'

'That's the one. He invites me to parties – he's always having parties, the kind of parties you don't get invited to unless you do something, and he introduces me to people as this guy next door who's an expert on Indian trade practices.'

'You could tell them all to fuck off.'

Jack regarded her over the empty plates. Her face was flushed. The wine bottle was empty. Empty! And Moira was drunk.

'Would you like some coffee?' he said. He heard his voice, buoyant and chivalrous; his stomach turned. The checks on the tablecloth hurt his eyes. 'We could order a pot of –'

'Would you like to make love to me?' Moira asked.

'I'm sorry, I didn't mean –'

She said it again, easily, as though the nozzle of her hair dryer aimed up his wet pant-leg had given her the right to say anything. 'Would you like to make love to me this afternoon?'

'I really think we should have some coffee,' Jack said.

'No, that isn't what –'

'Wouldn't you rather –'

'I'm going home,' she said, suddenly demure. 'I'm going to get a taxi.' One of her silk sleeves shot crazily into the air. 'What's another fourteen bucks? Tomorrow I'll be free. Broiling in the good old sun.'

'I'm sorry if –'

'Would you mind,' she spoke with deliberation, 'calling me a taxi?'

He moved to his feet. There was a pay phone by the door, and Jack staggered over. The inside of his head had loosened to plaster, a buzzing whiteness, long, lined chalky arches stretching as far as he could see, Catholic-looking and pure. He wanted to tiptoe through them lighting candles as he went. Salvador Dali. He managed to dial a taxi.

'Ah,' he said to Moira, coming back to the table. 'You're the lucky one. Arizona, lots of years ahead –'

'I love you.' She was speaking quietly and with a quavering

unevenness of tone. 'I'll never see you again after today so I can say what I want for a change. I love you. You don't know anything about me. All the time I've been at the Institute. How do you think I've stood it, typing all those reports on glacial remains and fur traders with French names – I had to put in the goddamned French accents by hand, did you know that? Not the most thrilling job in the world, let me tell you. And Dr. Middleton oozing all that Old World stuff, begging my pardon six times a day, it hasn't been a bed of roses. I had to keep myself going somehow. I had to keep sane. Sexual fantasies, it's called. And you – you're my partner, my steady, so to speak. Bet you never suspected a thing.'

'Moira – '

'When it first started, me thinking up these fantasies, I thought for sure I was going nuts. Oh, Moira, I said, you're ready for the nut house. The men in the white coats. Ha. Then I read a couple books from the library, by this New York lady, who writes about sexual fantasies and who says even people who are normal and love their husbands and so on, even people like that have these weird ideas at times. Like with men they work with, you know.'

'I think – ' He gave his awful laugh.

'The things I've done to you. Oh. The things you've done to me.'

'Christ, Moira.'

'Don't be embarrassed. It's not something to be embarrassed about, its normal. You should read this book. And you'll never see me again, so why be embarrassed? What does it matter? I'm not crazy. I hope you don't think I'm crazy.'

'Of course not – '

'Sometimes you tie me to the bed with my pantyhose. Some-times I suck your fingers, one by one. You nuzzle the backs of my knees – '

'Don't you think – '

'This morning? When you stood up in the office? with those boxer shorts on? To tell you the truth, I'd always thought you'd be the type to wear jockey shorts. That's how I've always pictured you, all this time – '

'I'm sorry if – ' He held his mouth stiff.

'Sorry? Don't be sorry for crying out loud, it doesn't matter to me. Underwear, what's underwear? It's what's underneath in a person that matters to me.'

'I'm glad if – '

'I could have picked someone else. Brian Petrie. I tried him for a while. But the thing about you that really got me was, now don't laugh, was those little hairs on the tops of your hands. Even on the fingers. You don't see that too often, the hair growing that far down on a man's hands, all the way to the nails, almost. I noticed it the first time Dr. Middleton introduced you. Way back when. Happy to meet you, you said, and I was thinking, my God, those beautiful hairs standing like that on the backs of his hands.'

Jack couldn't speak, although he wanted to. Moira's hands lay on the table, palms up – *I've told you everything*, she seemed to be saying. And he, in return, had told her nothing, nothing that mattered. Nor would he ever. A sudden perception of human secretiveness came to him, the depth of it, the useless-ness of it, the waste.

Unburdened, Moira seemed to grow sober. She seemed younger now, in a state of repose. 'You did come,' she said with this new calm voice. 'You were the only one to come through the snow today. That says something, doesn't it?'

He wanted to say yes, but feared the entrapment of words; instead he covered her hand with his; it was soft as a young girl's. What had he expected? Roberto called from the kitchen, 'Hey, there's a cab sitting out front. You call a cab?'

'Yes.' Moira spoke distinctly.

Jack helped her into her coat.

'Don't you ever have fantasies?' she said, clutching the bone buttons.

'Yes. Of course. Everyone does.'

'I'm drunk. God, am I ever soused.'

'So am I.'

'I love you.' She bumped against him on her way out the door. 'I love you, too,' he called after her. What did he mean by this? He didn't know. He hoped she wouldn't turn around and ask.

Chapter Twenty-Three

FOR A NUMBER OF REASONS, NONE OF THEM VERY CLEAR, Jack decided to walk home to Elm Park. Moira's outburst had left him giddy; a shaky euphoria filled his head; his teeth were chattering; he felt overwhelmed and dizzy. He needed to think, to descend. There was no use going back to the Institute – today was plainly going to be an unofficial holiday. And it appeared from the look of the vacant snow-blasted downtown streets that there were no buses running. He supposed he could get the train, but what was the rush? It was only two o'clock; he had all afternoon to walk home.

It was something he'd never done, although now that he thought about it, he couldn't imagine why not. Ten miles wasn't considered such a spectacular distance, nowadays; for a marathon runner, for a jogger like Bud Lewis even, ten miles might be thought of as little more than a warm- up. It would do him good to walk ten miles, it would sober him up, it would use up the afternoon – for the afternoon suddenly yawned before him, a maw of time that he must somehow fill. A long solitary walk was what he needed. He could even say later, should people ask him, or even if they didn't, that on the day after the big storm he had walked from the Loop out to Elm Park. 'Is it true you walked all the way from . . . ?' 'Are you the guy who actually . . . ?' (He often wished he could shut them off, these buzzing thoughts – why was it he could never do anything, never even think of doing something, without playing at doing it; there was something despicable in his small rehearsals and considered responses; was he the only one in the world who suffered these echoes?)

Strange that he could have lived in Chicago all his life without ever once entertaining the idea of such a walk. Why was that? No, it wasn't the distance itself; there was something prohibiting about this particular distance, the sprawl of it, the seeming impermeability and unyieldingness of its layers, its tough urban clutter. It stretched, a wide alien terrain, a dry basin, which could be safely traversed only from within a closed vehicle.

And walking ten miles out in the country was one thing, but walking one's way out of the hub of a large city was plainly eccentric, cheaply romantic in fact, troubadourish. And furthermore, there was no easy way out to the west side, no channel of softened parkland to scurry along. Just the whole harsh, seedy nexus of city blocks and masonry and traffic – and now all this buried in snow. And danger of course: gangs on corners, knives, strange tongues and taunts, hucksters, pickpockets, drunks, pimps. Today, though, it was easier to believe that these dangers might be quelled. The snow was less a hindrance than a form of mitigation. It was whiteness that made the idea of walking home seem possible. Snow and purity: a symbolism effortlessly grasped; snow was capable of making strange instant conversions, offering as it did a casual coat of simplicity atop Chicago's jumble-heap. One snow-plugged city block would look like all the others; one trafficless city street like the next; neighbourhoods would meld together, one after another, a blurring of postal districts, precincts, schools. It pleased Jack, and made him feel oddly safe, to think of this new nameless-ness, and the way in which the snow had obliterated geographical boundaries, stretching even beyond the city limits to bind this rusty downtown sprawl to the stillness of forest preserves, small farms, villages, lakes. He breathed deeply. The wine was wearing off, replaced now by a quirky mushrooming of faith in his own feet and in the huge white light of the sky. He decided to take Washington Boulevard all the way.

He had a liking for Washington; in the summer its surface was smooth and bland with asphalt; it seemed to him the most civilized of the east-west streets, straight as an arrow, but with certain continental softenings here and there; further out there would be Garfield Park, the golden dome of the Conservatory, trees and apartment buildings whose substantial brown facades glowed in good weather like trustworthy faces. Even downtown Washington purred with a different, richer tune. There was something better-behaved about it, something cooler, more mannerly. The snowploughs had partially cleared the road, leaving long mounds of snow on either side. He walked in the middle of the street, facing the white glare. A few drivers on the roads, seeing him plod along, slowed so as not to splash him with the rapidly accumulating slush.

One car pulled up beside him, a small rusted Ford with a melting crust of snow on its roof. A man leaned out the window and offered Jack a lift. 'Hop in if you're going west.' He had a crazy mop of hair, student hair, and a fine face.

'I'm out for a walk,' Jack said, then called after him, 'but thanks anyway.' It had been years since he'd been offered a ride by anyone.

By the time he reached Halsted the flapping of his boot tops had become intolerable. He noticed a cigar store near the corner and went in and asked if he could buy a ball of string. 'String?' A short, stout, immensely wrinkled old woman in a grey cardigan sat on a stool by the cash register, looking as though she had never heard of string. Her voice was purest Chicago growl. 'We don't handle string here. We don't get much call for string.'

'I just need a couple feet. To tie the tops of my boots. The snow – '

'Well, if that's all you need – ' The mouth smacked shut; was this thick, moist drawing back of lips a kind of smile? 'I guess I could let you have some of our own string.'

She cut a length, divided it in two and handed it to Jack. Her earrings clacked against humped shoulders. 'Here,' she said. 'You can sit down over there and tie up your galoshes.' A command.

He sat on a wooden box and laced the string through the boot buckles, then wound it twice around each leg, stuffing the bottoms of his pants down inside so that they formed a fairly comfortable cushion between his ankles and the sliding rubber. Then he stood up; ah, much better, much more secure; he felt he could walk miles now.

'Thank you so much,' he said. God, he sounded elegant – awful. A gentleman out of a costume romance.

She was reading a newspaper, but looked up. 'Holy Jesus, what's a little string on a day like this.'

'I'm surprised you've stayed open on a day like this.' Jack lingered by the door; only at Halsted and already dying for conversation.

'Yeah, well,' she shrugged, 'the choice we got is do we open or do we leave the dump wide open for looters. Kids out looking for cigarettes, up to no good – '

Realities, Jack thought, walking between Halsted and Damen toward the dark shape of Chicago Stadium, the continual facing up to realities; was that any way to live a life? – always on the lookout for muggers, looters, loiterers, always assuming the worst would happen if you let down your guard for a minute? Did it ever let up for the people who run cigar stores? Did it, for that matter, ever let up for anyone, this daily dealing with actualities? This cautious daily round, this sameness? Something unexpected had to happen to break the cycle; a special set of circumstances was required.

In the last hour a man had offered him a lift; a woman had given him a piece of string. It wasn't enough. Ah, but a woman had told him she loved him. She had loved him for years. It was incredible. The more he thought about it the more incredible it seemed. He felt dizzy, but fortified; a muscle twitched in his face. And what else? It was January and Chicago was buried in snow. It had to be a record of some kind. And here he was, walking down Washington Boulevard at three o'clock on a Tuesday afternoon. Surely that was enough to blow the whistle on ordinariness. Or at least call a temporary suspension. Another thing: no one in the world knew where he was. He could not be reached. Nothing at this moment was demanded of him; he could not be held accountable. He had, right in his two hands, a whole afternoon, wide open. It might be an illusion – it *was* an illusion – but for the next three hours, which was what he estimated it would take him to get from Damen to Elm Park Avenue, he was, temporarily, set free, an invisible man gliding down a ghosted street in an unfamiliar city.

A few cars passed. Willa Cather School sat darkly vacant; a few children played in the snow outside – the schools must be closed – and threw snowballs. He felt himself impervious to danger and catastrophe. The lunch with Moira had left him curiously anaesthetized, but at the same time liberated. Certain answers had been given him, but the answers themselves were mysteries that couldn't be named. Washington Boulevard was a country road and he was walking into the dull, metal-coloured sun toward a not unpleasant net of connections and possibilities. Tonight he would phone Harriet Post. Tonight Brenda would be phoning home from Philadelphia, the clear lightness of her voice breaking through the receiver. His children would be waiting at home. He would speak to them wisely. He would talk to Bernie, sit down with him, ask him what he intended to do, and offer, if asked, advice or consolation. Order could yet be made of his life.

He passed a locked store that had a hand-printed sign in the window: Catfish. An intense sobriety overcame him. He should reach out, dispense his calm awareness to others. If some poor guy came along asking him for a buck, he would give him ten. If he got mugged, he would say, take my wallet, take my hat and gloves, take everything. He was a man, a historian, walking home; a certain seriousness had been called into his life today, a levelness of vision, considered and selfless. Discontent, he reflected, was caused only by a reluctance to look at life soberly – we cannot always be escaping into easy exits.

'Of course,' he had told Moira Burke, standing drunkenly in the open door of Roberto's, 'of course, I've had sexual fantasies.'

But what he had withheld from her was the fact that his fantasies invariably circled around Brenda, his wife; and always they were played out in the safety of familiar surroundings, the house in Elm Park, the blue and white bedroom with the pictures of the children on the dresser. Moira would have been astonished and possibly saddened to hear this, after the books she'd read. Even he was somewhat astonished and saddened; either he had no imagination or he was possessed of a dull nature, doggedly monogamous and domestic. (Someone he'd met at a party recently, a psychologist with the school board, had told him that the average male thinks of sex once every twenty minutes – he had wondered, and doubted, how average he was.)

The sweet swelling of Brenda's hips – Jack could not imagine a time, although he knew human flesh inevitably sagged and aged, when he would not be stirred by the sensation of his open hand resting on Brenda's hip. Or her fingertips, easy and familiar, brushing the side of his face.

Twenty years ago Harriet Post had invited him up to her one-room apartment and had, with a single gesture, elbows over-head, whipped off her sweater. She had yanked open the studio couch with a thump that banged thrillingly on his heart, and said, 'Well?'

The first time she had had to help him, but he learned fast. Winter evenings, lying on the black corduroy cover of Harriet's studio couch, he practised the intricacies of timing and intensity, feeling his slow body coming to life. Beneath him Harriet moaned and gasped realistically; her thin pelvis had the weight of wood framing securely nailed. He swam over her body, almost drowning, almost melting into her, but called back always by something dry and careful at the back of his head, a shameful prickling speaking to him in a voice oddly akin to radio static, saying, 'But what is this for? What is this for?'

After he married Brenda the voice went away. It disappeared without a trace. He hadn't thought of it for years. Nor had he ever told Brenda about it; he wouldn't know how to tell her. He was merely grateful to be rid of it. And amazed. He had, he sensed, just narrowly escaped, although from what he wasn't sure.

On Washington Boulevard it was growing cooler. Crossing Kedzie, the string around his left boot snapped. Shit, just when he was starting to make good time. Next to a liquor store, locked and chained, was a café, miraculously open, 'Margie's lunch,' and he stopped to buy coffee and to retie his boots. The place was deserted. He sank onto a counter stool and felt the jarring weariness of back and legs; he flexed his knees, testing the alternate shocks of pain and relief, and it occurred to him for the first time that he might not be able to make it after all. Kedzie was less than half way home – Christ. He eased off his boots and through his sock he could feel, on his right foot, a small blister starting on the top of one toe.

'Ya wanna doughnut with that coffee?' The boy behind the counter looked about Rob's age. White teeth in a black face, tentative and sick with melancholy.

'Just coffee. Black. You wouldn't have a piece of string by any chance? For my boot?'

'Naw. We don't have string.'

'I guess maybe I could tie this back together, only it's a bit short.'

'Jeez, where'd you get those boots, man?'

'I've had them for a while.'

'You're kiddin' me. How you move around in boots like that, man?'

'If I just had a little piece of string –'

'Hey, gimme that. Lemme see that.'

Jack handed the pieces of string over the counter and

watched as the boy grasped them, whirled them between pinkish-brown fingers, made a thick-looking knot that he tested with a sharp tug and a meow of satisfaction. 'Hey, man, that oughta do.'

'Well thanks.'

'If I was you, I'd get me some new boots.' He looked at the ceiling and gave a sharp, mysterious cackle.

'Yes, that feels a lot better,' Jack said. The coffee had warmed him through, and he felt ready to go again. 'Well, so long.' He smiled hard across the counter, trying to force this young boy to smile back; he had laughed – why couldn't he smile?

The sun was going down as Jack crossed Garfield Park and arrived at Pulaski. The buildings on the corner – a grill, a gas station, the Temple of Deliverance – seemed to catch fire. A good Chicago name, Pulaski, Brenda's maiden name. You know, 'Pulaski, like the street,' Brenda had told him when she had introduced herself. And afterwards, whenever he saw a sign with the word Pulaski on it, he was able to recall exactly the way she had said it: lightly, but with a meaningful intensity, as though it were a very old joke, but with some juice left in it. She had held her head slightly to one side, her lips parted, the start of a smile.

How easily he was able to retrieve these images. It was as though he carried a film strip around with him, a whole history of Brenda Pulaski Bowman that was altogether separate and different from her history of herself. No doubt she had a film strip on him, too – he could not imagine what it would consist of, but its details would be puzzling and foreign. Certainly he had never dreamed that he had lived another life all these years inside Moira Burke's head. (He thought of tying her up with pantyhose and felt a painful piercing pressure rise at the back of his throat, a hillock of pleasure – should he laugh or weep?) The number of histories one person might have locked in his head was infinite. The most sophisticated tracking device in the world couldn't collect them all and consolidate them (something he must discuss with Bernie on Friday). Some source would be forgotten or some fact left unexamined.

He remembered one night years ago telling his mother he was bringing home a girl called Brenda Pulaski. 'A polack girl?' his mother had asked, alerted. 'Polish,' Jack had corrected her pompously. His mother would never remember now that she

161

had uttered those words – 'a polack girl' – and would never recall the variety of expectations that word aroused. Once, only once, he had brought Harriet Post home. A Sunday; his mother had fixed a pork roast; and now she couldn't even remember who Harriet was.

In all probability, Jack thought, Harriet had forgotten his mother too, forgotten the pork roast and apple sauce, possibly even forgotten about him and their long nights of groping on the narrow studio couch. When he phoned her tonight, he would have to start from the assumption that she had forgotten; he'd have to work his way back slowly. 'Hello? Harriet? This (ahem) is a voice from the past, I don't suppose you remember me, but . . .' Or boldly, 'This is Jack Bowman, Harriet. From Chicago? 1956?'

Cicero Avenue. At last. A furniture store on the corner advertised a four-room special. A medical clinic sat in gloomy darkness. It got dark fast this time of year. At least Washington Boulevard was fairly well lit. If he saw a taxi he might give in and ride the rest of the way. The blister on his toe was getting worse, and he was starting to feel shaky with cold. It was five o'clock.

He passed a florist's shop, 'Flower City,' and was surprised to see that a shop selling such nonessentials was open. A tidy balanced arrangement of gladioli filled the window, and there was a sign: *Sale. Today Only* – which struck Jack as hilarious. Who would rush out to buy sale flowers on a day like this? Was today someone's wedding day? Or funeral? Then the idea came to him that *he* ought to buy some flowers. He should – and the idea lit him up with happiness – he should send Moira Burke a bouquet of flowers.

Here he was, outside a lighted flower shop. And Moira Burke was at home, packing her suitcase, sobering up, arriving, no doubt, at dread realizations. His heart flared with genuine warmth. He would send her some flowers. But not gladioli. What would a lover send? Roses. 'Do you have any roses?' he asked the woman behind the counter. She looked at him suspiciously. She had her coat on, her keys in her hand, and seemed anxious to lock up.

'We've got anything you want,' she told him. 'In the back.'

'A dozen roses?'

'You want to take them with you or send them?'

'Send them. Evergreen Park. Do you deliver out there?'

'I can arrange it, but it'll cost plenty.'

'Can you guarantee them for tonight?'

'I don't know. With all this snow? Maybe. I can try.'

'It has to get there tonight.'

'What d'you want on the card?'

'What card?'

'The card that says who the flowers are from.' She was faintly mocking, tapping her pencil.

'No card,' Jack decided. 'Just the flowers.'

'Suit yourself.' She gave him a level look.

'Can you take a cheque?' he asked.

'Hmmm. I don't usually.'

'Please.'

He pulled off his gloves and reached for his cheque-book, and under the bright lights the hair on the back of his hand danced. He spread his fingers, observing the play of light; he was a man who was sending roses to a woman who said she loved the hair on his hands. He shook his head, dazed, happy. What was to be done with knowledge like this?

'Thank you, Mr. Bowman. If you'll just sign here – ' The way she said Mr. Bowman, the way she handed him the pen, told him he was getting close to home. Another hour, if he walked fast.

It was actually a little more than an hour before he stood by his front door. The sky overhead looked matted and close, and the snow in Elm Park was thicker and firmer than the city snow, banked everywhere around the lighted houses, beautiful. Small shrubs swayed with the weight of it; his own house was delicately lined with narrow shelves of blue-whiteness. No one had bothered to close the curtains, and light poured out the living-room windows, sending golden squares across the front yard. He pushed open the front door and inhaled warmth and the smell of meat cooking. Laurie met him with a ferocious, head-on embrace. 'Bernie's here. He's fixing us steak. T-bones.'

Rob appeared in the doorway to the kitchen, dreamy-eyed, looking surprisingly tall. 'Mom just phoned from Philly. Ten minutes ago.'

'Five minutes ago,' Laurie corrected him.

'She's called?' Jack felt dizzy with fatigue. 'Already?'

'We all talked to her.'

'What did she say?' He should take off his coat, sit down, get out of these boots.

'Just that she's having a great time.'

'A great time?'

'*The Second Coming* got honourable mention,' Laurie said.

'What else?'

'Besides the honourable mention?'

'Did she say anything else? Any messages?'

'She said to give you her love,' Rob said.

'Is that all?' Jack said. He was so tired he thought he might faint. 'Is that all?'

Chapter Twenty-Four

Bernie, whistling, stomping, served the steaks at the kitchen table, plunking them onto plates with a meat fork. There was something bewildering in this domestic scene – Bernie performing kitchen duty like a lodger who had been pressed into service – but Jack, who was sick with hunger, felt too grateful to ponder the point. Looking around he saw, too, that the kitchen had been cleaned up. The dishes had been put in the dishwasher. A large green garbage bag, neatly tied, waited by the back door. Even the floor looked as though it had been swept.

Bernie, chomping into red meat, was cheerful but agitated; his amber bush of hair rose steeply off his forehead, and there were ridges of whiteness over his eyes. Jack would have liked to have told him about going to Roberto's today, not about Moira Burke, but about coming face to face with the real-life Roberto, but Bernie was preoccupied with other things; tonight he was going to the Austin General to visit Larry Carpenter. He glanced at his watch; visiting hours started at eight.

Larry was feeling much better, Bernie reported, at least that was the latest news according to Janey, who had spent all day at the hospital. He was feeling ready to have visitors, Janey said, and the psychiatrist thought that it was probably a good idea. One at a time of course. Janey had asked him to go with her tonight for an hour. 'Oh, and by the way, Janey says to thank Laurie for feeding the dogs.'

'I meant to send a plant,' Jack said.

'Larry's actually cheerful, Janey says. It's amazing. Anxious to get home, get back to the paper and all that.'

'So soon?'

'She says he might even be able to come home tomorrow. Of course he'll have to be on tranquillizers for a while.'

'I suppose.'

Bernie jumped up, grabbed for his jacket. 'Sorry to eat and run like this, but I'd better get going.'

Silence. Then Rob, eyeing Bernie's windbreaker, said, 'You want to borrow my ski jacket?'

'This'll be fine. It's not that cold.'

'What about boots?' Jack asked.

Bernie shrugged, a dipping vaudeville shrug, and a strange neighing laugh came out of his mouth. 'My shoes are already soaked, so why worry now . . . . '

'About tonight – ' Jack began.

'Don't worry about me,' Bernie smiled, giving off an almost bridegroom aura, 'I'll just bunk in next door.'

He left by the back door; they could hear the slipping of his shoes as he stepped onto the wooden porch. Under the kitchen light Rob and Laurie sat silent as statues; without looking up, Jack could feel their eyes on him, accusing. Damn it, why on him? Laurie sawed at her steak and said, 'I still don't understand why.'

'Why what?'

'Why you didn't come home on the El instead of walking.'

'Why?' This quizzing wasn't what he had expected. Not that he expected congratulations or a round of applause for something that now seemed whimsical as well as foolhardy; but on the other hand, he hadn't anticipated this kind of challenge, either. 'I don't know,' he told her.

'You never did it before.' She was genuinely puzzled – Jack recognized the tone. It was the puzzlement of a very young child threatened by change. Twelve is not very old, he thought.

'Maybe that's why I did it,' Jack said. 'Just because I'd never done it before.'

'That doesn't sound like a very good reason – '

But Rob cut in. 'You don't have to have a reason for everything you do, stupid.' There was a clink of comradeship in the way he pronounced the word 'stupid' that took the edge off.

Jack regarded him across the table, solemnly approving.

Rob was on his third cup of tea. He wasn't in the mood for steak tonight, he said. No one was surprised at this; no one even questioned him. He'd been like this for days now.

But his loss of appetite had yet to assume the weight of fact. Jack had not begun to worry about it. Or even, for that matter, to acknowledge it. On the other hand, it had been noticed. And absorbed. And for the moment, at least, accepted.

166

The long-distance operator was wonderfully kind. 'I'm really, really sorry about this,' she said.

'What are my chances if I try again in an hour?'

'I don't know.' She was letting him down gently. 'They tell us we won't be able to get through to Rochester tonight, or Buffalo either, for that matter.'

'Are you sure?' He had already rehearsed exactly what he would say to Harriet. 'What I mean is, it doesn't seem possible that Bell Telephone can't – '

'It *is* unusual, but they tell us,' – who were they? – 'that our storm has moved that way.'

Jack loved the way she said 'our storm.' He pictured her as a slightly older, slightly greyer version of Moira Burke, and was reluctant to hang up. 'We received a long-distance call from Philadelphia this evening,' he told her. 'If you can get through from Philadelphia, wouldn't it make sense that you could get through to Rochester?'

'What time was this Philadelphia call, sir?' Why did she have to spoil it by calling him 'sir'?

'About six, I think it was.'

'Well, all I can tell you is that things have got a lot worse since then. Apparently there are lots of lines down, and we've been told that the east is getting hit a lot harder than Chicago.'

'Incredible,' Jack said sociably. 'Hard to believe that anything could be worse than what we had.'

'Isn't it,' she commiserated. 'It's been unbelievable.'

'It looks as though I'll have to try tomorrow night.'

'You shouldn't have any trouble tomorrow night. I'm sure the lines will be in order by then. I can practically guarantee it.'

'Who were you trying to phone?' Laurie asked as he hung up. The three of them were sitting in the living room, reading.

'A woman who lives in Rochester.' *A woman who lives in Rochester* – as though she were someone mythical, the Lady of the Lake.

'Who?' Laurie asked directly.

'Her name is Harriet Post.'

'Harriet Post?' Rob came out from behind the newspaper. For an hour he'd been reading news stories about the storm. 'Who's Harriet Post?'

Jack sat back, sipping at his coffee, happy to have an audience tonight. 'As a matter of fact, Harriet Post is someone I used to know back when I was a student.'

'So why are you phoning her?' Laurie seemed more than usually intent.

'Well, I just discovered that she's written a book. And it so happens that it's the same kind of book I've been working on.'

'Indians you mean?' From Rob.

'You mean you've both written the exact same book?'

'Well, more or less. What happened was she didn't know I was writing it, and I didn't know she was writing it. It's not unusual, this kind of thing. These things happen.' Useful phrase.

'So why're you phoning her?'

'Well,' Jack paused, 'I have to find out exactly what material her book covers. What I have to do, at this point, is decide whether it's worth finishing my book or not.'

Rob put the paper down. 'You mean you might not finish it?'

'Well, it would be a bit absurd to have two books on the same subject. Coming out in the same year. If you see what I mean.'

'Yeah,' Laurie said, 'that would be dumb.'

'That's for sure,' Rob said, going back to his newspaper.

Jack listened to the wind rattling on the storm window. He felt peace drifting over him; he could fall asleep right in this chair.

At midnight the telephone rang.

'Hello,' he said in a daze.

'It's me, Jack. Dad.'

'Dad. For Christ's sake, what's wrong?'

'Nothing wrong. Nothing at all. You sound as though you were asleep.'

'Just dozing. Not really asleep.'

'Just thought I'd phone.'

'Is Ma all right?'

'She's fine, just fine. Been sound asleep for hours.'

'And you're okay? Weathering the storm?'

'Fine, fine, no problem for us. No sidewalks to shovel here.'

'Dad?'

'Yes.'

'Why are you phoning? You never phone in the middle of the night. Something's got to be the matter.'

168

'Nothing, Jack, nothing – '

'You can't sleep. Is that it?'

'Well, that's nothing new with me.'

'Then do you mind telling me – '

'Well, I bought this new book the other day. I've been reading it all day.'

'What book?'

'It's called *Living Adventurously*.'

'Go on.'

'It's by this California real estate man. Or at least he used to be a real estate man. A smart man, it sounds like to me. At least he's got a lot of good ideas.'

'Such as – '

'On how to put adventure into your life. You know what I mean, Jack. Getting out of the old rut.'

'Uhuh.'

'Like all kinds of things you can do without rocking the boat completely.'

'Such as?'

'Well, this is just an example, you can eat your dessert before your dinner. That's one thing, he says.'

'Oh yeah? Did you try that?'

'Tomorrow. Another thing he says is write someone a thank-you letter, like some cousin maybe or your congressman. Out of the blue, you know.'

'Did you do that?'

'I'm thinking about it.'

'What else?'

'Well he says, phone someone up in the middle of the night. On impulse, like.'

'And you did.'

'He says if you're going to put adventure into your life you've got to start with something small. So I start thinking, why not?'

'Great, Dad.'

'Glad you weren't in bed. I'd have hated to wake you up.'

'I'm just going now.'

'Well, then, I'll say goodnight.'

'I'll see you tomorrow, Dad.'

'Tomorrow? Tomorrow's Wednesday.'

'I thought I'd stop by on my way home from work.'

'Are you sure? On a Wednesday.'

'I'm sure.'
'Well – '
'Goodnight, Dad.'
'Goodnight, Jack. Sleep well.'

Chapter Twenty-Five

O N WEDNESDAY MORNING JACK'S DAUGHTER LAURIE WAS
going to be killed. Or so she said.

She was going to be killed, slaughtered, by her seventh grade
Home Economics teacher because she hadn't bought the pattern and material for the skirt she was supposed to be making.
'Don't be silly,' Jack told her. 'It's not the end of the world, not
having a pattern.'

'It is, it is,' she wailed miserably. Her head rolled back and
forth with the rhythm of suffering, and her fists thrashed at the
air.

'You'll just have to bring it tomorrow,' Jack said firmly.

She began to cry wildly, not bothering to cover her face with
her hands. Laurie's tears, so different from Brenda's rare slow
tears, boiled out in steamy sheets. 'She'll kill me. You don't
know her.'

It was eight o'clock. He had been sipping a cup of coffee
quietly when Laurie had come howling into the kitchen. 'Why
didn't you mention all this yesterday?'

She let loose a long cry of grief. 'I forgot.' Her face was
swelling before his eyes; the amoeba softness of her body
always moved him to pity.

'You've probably had weeks to get it.'

'Mom was going to get it for me last week.' She was holding
on to the back of a chair, blubbering more quietly now.

'Your mother was busy last week.' Here he was, making
excuses for Brenda – he felt a spurt of anger, *Damn it, Brenda,
what's going to become of this kid, with you* – the phrase *gallivanting
across the country* occurred to him, but he rejected it as unfair.

'Okay, okay, Laurie, what time do you have Home Ec?'

She slammed her fists into her eyes and stopped crying. 'At
9:30. Right after Home Room.'

'Look, honey, I can't promise. I've got an appointment with
Dr. Middleton for ten. But I'll try, okay?'

171

'Oh, Daddy!' The force of her gratitude was annihilating; her soft face shone wonderfully.

'Just write down exactly what you need and I'll try to drop it off at school. I'll have to leave it at the main office. Do you know what you need?'

'I've got the pattern number right here. It's Butterick. They've got it at Zimmerman's.'

'And the cloth?'

'It has to be part polyester. But not plain. It's got to be a print.'

'A print? Okay.'

'But Daddy, it's got to be a small print, okay? Mrs. Frost said a large print would just make me look like an elephant.'

'Did she, sweetie?'

'And a dark colour. She said I have to have a dark colour. It would be more flattering, she said.'

'Whose skirt is this, anyway? You can have what you want, for Pete's sake.'

'I'd better get what she says to or she'll kill me. Oh, and Dad, a zipper. A seven-inch zipper, okay?' She grabbed his hand, kneaded it violently.

'God, Laurie!'

'Do you really think you can get it there by 9:30?'

'Sure,' he told her. 'We'll give it the old try, anyway.

Rob, waking late, yawning, gathering his books together, putting on his snow boots, was – in contrast – infuriatingly calm. Almost in a trance. 'Hey, Dad, do you think you can drop me at school? I slept through my alarm.'

'I've got to pick up something for Laurie. Can you be ready in five minutes?'

'I'm ready now.'

'What about breakfast?'

'I had some coffee.'

'How about some toast or something?'

'I'm not all that hungry.'

'Why not?'

'What do you mean, why not?'

'Okay, Rob. That's enough beating around the bush. What's going on with you?'

'Me?'

'As far as I can make out, you haven't eaten anything since last Saturday.'

'I don't know what you're talking about.'

'Oh yes you do.'

'So?' he said 'So I'm not hungry. Is that supposed to be some kind of crime?'

'It happens to be Wednesday. Saturday to Wednesday – figure it out. That's a fairly long time for someone who's supposed to be healthy.'

Rob examined the backs of his hands, brooding.

'Just tell me this much, Rob,' Jack sucked for breath. 'Are you ever planning to eat again?'

'Sure.'

'When?'

'Saturday.'

'Saturday? Why Saturday?'

Rob made a face at the floor. 'That makes seven days.'

'I see,' Jack said. Amazingly, he did see. There was no explosion of light inside his head; instead the truth struck him with a clear, approaching ringing noise, rather like a bicycle bell. 'This is a kind of starvation thing you're on, then? A fast?'

'Sort of, yeah.'

'I see.' Couldn't he think of anything better to say to this boy than *I see*! 'Well, look, do you mind telling me if there's any particular reason?'

'No reason, not exactly. I just want to see if I can do it.'

'You're not doing penance for anything?'

'No.'

'And it doesn't have anything to do with going out to Charleston last week?'

'No. It's not that, I'm over that. In fact I told Bernie I'd go out with him again on Sunday.'

'To see if you can do it.'

'Sort of.'

'I see. I think I see.'

'It probably sounds crazy.'

'No. Well, it may sound crazy but it's probably not.'

'Now that really does sound crazy.' From Rob's throat came a dry croaking sound.

'Look, Rob, we'd better get going. I don't even know if I'll be able to get the car out of the garage.'

173

'A lot of snow's melted. And Bernie shovelled out most of the alleyway yesterday. De Paul was closed so he was here all day.'

'Good old Bernie. He cooks us steaks and shovels our alley. What did we ever do without him?'

'About Bernie,' Rob began, 'do you think, I mean does it seem sort of odd to you, Bernie staying next door?'

'Sort of.'

'I was wondering if they . . . do you think they? . . . Bernie and Mrs. Carpenter . . . do you think they, well – '

'Probably. Yes. Chances are good. Human nature being what it is.' Jack searched through his coat pockets for his car keys. How calm he sounded, how surprisingly moderate and detached.

Rob rubbed at his chin with the back of his glove. 'Well, doesn't that seem kind of . . . I mean, here's Mr. Carpenter in the hospital. I mean the guy tried to do himself in. And Bernie's, well, you know, screwing around . . . with his wife.'

'Have you seen my car keys?'

'On the hall table.'

'Thanks. Lots of things probably don't make a whole lot of sense. Sometimes people don't react the way we think they're going to.' He waved his arms in the air. 'Like when Grandma Elsa died. The funeral was on a Monday, remember? You were only, lets see, ten – '

'I remember the funeral.'

'Well, do you remember after the funeral? What we did?'

'Not exactly.'

'We went back to Grandma's and Grandpa's apartment and played canasta all afternoon.'

'Canasta?'

'I know it's not the same thing, but what I'm saying is – '

'I know what you're saying.'

'I'm sure when Mr. Carpenter gets home everything will be back to normal.'

'Have you ever – ? I mean after you married Mom did you ever . . . you know . . . with someone else?'

'Never.' The force of declaration in his voice almost took his breath away; so many small dishonesties in his life, so much false posing and faithlessness, but now and then an exhilarating chance to tell the truth. 'Never. I can't tell you why. But to make a long story short, I never wanted to. It's too complicated, but never.'

'We better go.'

'What's the first thing you're going to have when you break your fast?'

'A kingburger. With the works. And a double order of fries and either a banana milkshake or a large root beer. I haven't decided for sure yet, but probably it'll be the root beer.'

Chapter Twenty-Six

THE OFFICE WASN'T THE SAME ON WEDNESDAY WITHOUT Moira.

Calvin White, Geology, who had the office next to Jack's, leaned against the coffee machine just after lunch, lamenting the fact that now that Moira had left and been replaced by the golden-haired Melvin Zaddo, the Institute had become an all-male bastion. 'Moira kept us on our toes,' Calvin said, somewhat ambiguously, swirling coffee in a styrofoam cup.

Brian Petrie, Cultural Anthropology, agreed. Moira Burke was going to be sorely missed around here. 'The hours that woman put in! *Unpaid* hours. It was Moira, if you remember, who put up the Christmas decorations in the board room. Year after year, for crying out loud.'

'Mel Zaddo looks like a loser,' Milton McInnis, Restoration, said. 'And he can't spell.'

'Poor Mel – can't spell. Ha!'

'His typing's not too bad,' Calvin White said with a squeezing frown. 'Amazingly good, in fact.'

'He's got that look of temperament,' Brian Petrie said. 'The way he slinks around. Up one day, down the next.'

'He did all right condensing those minutes,' Jack said. 'A surprisingly good job, to tell the truth.'

'I've a feeling he won't be around all that long.'

'The amazing thing is that Dr. Middleton ever – '

'Bizarre's the word.'

'It's going to be interesting to see how long he manages to hang on to that hair of his – '

'Just so he gets the cataloguing done – '

'And mans the phone the way Moira used to – '

'That cologne,' Brian Petrie said, 'or whatever it is he wears, is getting to my allergies.'

'Moody as a rooster, but – '

'Time will tell.'

'Apparently; he's already negotiating for one of those new typewriters. With the ball?'

'Christ, those have been around for years.'

'Not here, they haven't.'

'Here he comes, speak of the devil. My God, purple pants.'

'Hi, Mel, how's it going?'

'Not bad.'

'Well, you're on your own, starting today.'

'Yeah, it looks that way.'

'Coffee?' Jack asked.

'No, thanks. I just wanted to tell you, Mr. Bowman, that there's someone waiting for you in your office.'

'For me?'

'She says her name's Dr. Koltz.'

'Dr. Koltz?'

'So she says.'

'Well, well.'

'Hello, Jack.'

'Sue.'

'Surprised?'

'A little. Sit down. Let me take your coat.'

'You know, I've never been here. To your office.' Her tone was peremptory, but sensuous too.

'It isn't much. Sit down. Please.'

'Look, I don't want to keep you.'

'Don't worry. I'm not all that busy this afternoon.'

'You sure?'

'Sure. Sit down, really. You're looking . . . very well.'

'Thanks. It's the hair.'

'Nice.'

'They call me Fuzzball at the hospital.' She smiled abruptly, shyly grateful, pleased with herself. 'Dr. Fuzzball.'

'I like it,' he told her truthfully. Sue's cheeks, with short fringes of hair against them, had always seemed aggressively bony to him. Like sinuses turned inside out. The curls were an improvement. Her face looked out, intelligent and lively; he could imagine that such a face might excite ardour.

'So how's the great book coming?' she said, sinking into a chair.

'Not so great, as a matter of act. It seems' – here I go again, he

177

thought – 'it seems someone else is coming out with a similar book. Dr. Middleton – maybe you remember meeting Dr. Middleton at our place once – '

'How could I forget.'

'We had a long talk this morning, and he thinks . . . he agrees with me that maybe I'm flogging a dead horse.'

'The book you mean?'

'I haven't decided definitely, but it looks as though I might dump it.'

Sue's small eyes blinked once. 'Dump it?'

'Chuck it. Give it up.'

She filled her cheeks with air and let it out with a pop. 'Well, sometimes, Jack, I think maybe there are too damn many books in the world. I ask myself sometimes, who's going to read all those books?'

'That's the question, all right.'

'Jack, listen to me.' Her voice plunged an octave, going suddenly splintery. 'I know Bernie's at your house. I mean, he's got to be there. Right? It's the only place he could be. You know how I know? Because you're the only real friend he's got. So I brought a few things I thought he might need. His overcoat and some sweaters and socks and stuff like that. I thought I'd drop them off here and maybe you'd see that he gets them.'

'Sure. I'd be glad to.'

'And the apartment keys. My set.'

'You don't need them?'

'I moved my stuff out this morning. My clothes I mean. And the cat. I left everything else. Maybe you could tell him that, okay? Would you do that?'

'Okay.'

'You sound kind of dubious, Jack.'

'No. I was just thinking – of course it isn't my business – '

'*Tell* me what you're thinking, Jack.' She put her small elbows on his desk; her bare elbows reminded Jack of new potatoes, brown and cunning. 'You never say what you think. You never have. At least not to me. I suppose when you and Bernie get together, it's different.'

This struck Jack as an accusation. 'I was just thinking that this seems a little final. The handing over of the keys and all.'

'I know. Final and sad. Don't think I don't feel it, too.'

'It's just that I can't help thinking that, here you are – you've packed up Bernie's overcoat and lugged it way over to the Institute, up the elevator, into my office, just because you thought he might be cold. Doesn't that sort of suggest, well – what I mean is – doesn't that say something? That you must still love him a little.'

'Don't – '

'Doesn't it – ?'

'But I don't.' Tears filled her eyes. Her mouth was faintly blue. 'I don't want him to be cold, I don't want him to catch cold and get pneumonia. But I don't – love him anymore.'

'How can you be so sure of a thing like – '

'About a year ago Bernie and I went to a movie.' She took a breath. 'Woody Allen. One of the old ones. You know, we never go to movies. Hardly ever. In the middle of this movie I turned and looked at Bernie. He was eating popcorn. I looked at the side of his face, and I knew I didn't love him anymore.'

'Just like that.'

'More or less. I wish it wasn't like this, believe me. But it's gone. Part of it was Sarah, of course, but it's gone.'

'And you don't think it could come back?'

'No. It's all history now, as you and Bernie would probably say, something metaphysical like that. Isn't history your topic this year?'

'Yes,' Jack said, feeling obscurely foolish.

'Twenty years you've been at it, you and Bernie. Every Friday! Amazing.'

'Yes.' Jack couldn't tell whether she was taunting him or not. 'Not all that amazing – '

'I suppose you'll go on forever.'

'It's hard to say – ' He felt a flutter of panic.

'You'll be grey-haired, the two of you. Or bald. It'll be interesting to see if you become more abstract or less.'

'I'd think – '

'I'll put my money on less.'

'I'll let you know.'

'I'd appreciate that. Seriously, I would.' Her head swayed, willow-like. 'I suppose I'll worry about Bernie for quite a while. Do you think he'll be okay, Jack? Or not?'

Jack paused. Happiness was only a useful abstraction, Bernie had said to him once, the year they did Kierkegaard, 1972.

'Well, Jack, what do you think?'

'I think he'll be fine. Really. Of course I have to admit we haven't really talked about – '

'Of course not.' She was only slightly mocking.

'But, who knows, maybe our next topic will be – '

'Love? Now that would be interesting. I wouldn't mind eavesdropping on that.'

Jack smiled, and said nothing.

'You and Brenda,' Sue went on, 'you've been lucky. You've got a kind of context or something with the kids. How are the kids, anyway? I haven't seen them for ages.'

'Not bad. Growing up. Half the time they drive us crazy but – they're okay.'

'Great.' A chilly smile, determinedly bright. The question had been merely a polite inquiry.

'At the moment Rob's on a kind of strange kick. Maybe . . . well . . . maybe I should ask your advice. It's a sort of medical question.'

'Masturbation?'

'He's not eating.'

'Really. Why not?'

'He's fasting. For a week he says.'

Her face softened. 'Part of the hunger strike group?'

'No. He's on his own. A solitary fast.'

'Testing himself,' she nodded. Jack had never seen her so solicitous. 'Lots of kids do that. I wish I could do it. I've gained ten pounds this last year.'

'It suits you.'

'Thanks. Anyway, a week shouldn't hurt him.'

'He won't collapse or anything?'

'As long as he drinks plenty of fluids he could go for weeks. They even say it's good for people in small doses. Makes them feel like they've got control of their lives.'

'Maybe I'll go on a fast.' He was only half joking.

'You, Jack?' Her mouth pulled sideways. 'You make me laugh.'

'Really? Do I really?'

Chapter Twenty-Seven

'YOU SOUND LIKE YOU'RE SERIOUS, JACK,' HIS FATHER SAID. 'I can tell.'

'Yes.'

'But you haven't completely one hundred per cent made up your mind?'

'Not a hundred per cent. But almost.'

His father drummed on the table, thinking hard. His mother nodded in a kind of agreement, or was it sympathy? Jack could see the familiar pink spot at the top of her scalp where the hair parted. She worked her jaw soundlessly; her face was long and narrow. They were sitting solemnly around the kitchen table, the three of them, drinking coffee.

Jack had stopped by on his way from the Institute, something he seldom did. He had arrived at 5:30 to a strange scene.

'The door's unlocked,' his mother's voice had quavered, and he had come in to find his mother and father sitting side by side on the old red couch. His parents' living room was in semi-darkness; there was only a small table lamp on in one corner and the purplish flicker of light from the television. It took Jack a minute to make out what it was they were doing.

His mother's hand lay on his father's lap atop a white hand towel. His father held in his hand a small pair of scissors, manicure scissors, and with it he was cutting her fingernails. 'You want to turn down that volume, Jack?' his father directed.

'Sit down,' his mother sang, 'We're almost done here.'

Jack sat and watched. His father finished with the cutting, and then he filed her nails with an emery board, grasping each of her fingers in turn. And last, finally, he painted each nail with a coat of clear polish. The air in the small room filled briefly with varnish fumes; speechless, Jack watched his father holding the delicate Cutex brush and making deft feminine little strokes. It took him less than a minute – he must have been doing this for years, Jack thought – and then he screwed the top back on and set the tiny bottle on the coffee table, offering no explanation at all.

And why should he? Jack asked himself. His mother had suffered arthritis in her hands for several years now. It had been a long time since she'd been able to knit or even hold a pen in her hand. It stood to reason that she could not look after her own nails, although, oddly, this was something that had never occurred to him.

Later, in the kitchen, Jack explained about the book, and his parents listened silently.

'I can sure see what the problem is, Jack,' his father said. 'I certainly see what you're driving at.'

'It's not so much the work,' Jack explained. 'It's a question of needless duplication. And is it worth it in the end?'

'It's not like you *have* to finish it,' his mother said, pouring more coffee. 'Like there's no rule that says you have to.'

'That's for sure,' his father said. 'After all, you've got a good job, book or no book.'

'And, as you said, Jack, these things sometimes – '

'So what's to worry about?'

'I guess I was just afraid the two of you might be disappointed.'

'Jesus, Jack, you can always write a book later on. Pick some other subject, what the hell.'

'Plenty of time for that,' his mother said. 'You're still young.'

'Not that young.'

'The important thing,' she said, 'is to do what you want to do.'

'How d'you like this coffee your mother bought?' His father's face had a steamed, exuberant look of contentment.

'Good,' Jack said. 'Nice and strong.'

'Turkish coffee. Ever had Turkish coffee? Your ma bought it today at the deli. Remember that book I told you about? *Living Adventurously*? Try Turkish coffee, he says. For a change. Just one of his many ideas.'

'Have some more, Jack. I made lots.'

'Sure, help yourself, it'll put hair on your chest, as the saying goes.'

He hadn't thought them capable of this – this kind of diversion and easy forgiveness; and their concern for that crazy thing, that illogical and shapeless thing – his happiness.

He listened to their voices; first his father, then his mother, back and forth, back and forth, a kind of weaving. His mother's polished nails caught the light; she saw it too, held up her hands, spread her fingers, appraised them with mild approval.

Jack watched them; between them, it seemed, they'd made and kept countless bargains. And he had imagined them powerless in his absence.

Chapter Twenty-Eight

HISTORIANS, JACK THOUGHT, TEND TO SEE TIME ARCHI-tecturally, as something structured and measurable, something precise and non-transferable. A hundred years is a hundred years. Five days is five days is one hundred and twenty hours. The fact that five days can be sometimes short and sometimes long is immaterial and romantic. Which had always seemed to Jack to be one of the failings of the historical perspective. There was, he knew, such a thing as slow time and fast time. History was a double-souled art, a yardstick and a telescope.

It seemed to him by ten o'clock on Wednesday night, after Rob and Laurie had both gone upstairs to bed, that Brenda had been away for a hundred years, not five days. He remembered what she looked like, but he couldn't remember the sort of thing they talked about on midweek evenings like this. Public affairs? No, seldom anyway. His day? Her day? Children? Odds and ends? Gossip and resolution? Weather? What?

A little after ten there came tapping at the front door. It was Bernie, shivering with cold; Jack had wondered what had become of him.

'Here,' Bernie said, coming in, 'with my apologies.'

'What's this?'

'Your vest. Remember? You lent it to me last Saturday.'

'What's it doing all wrapped up?'

'Dry cleaners. Somehow – it must have been toward the end of the evening – I seem to have dumped about a gallon of wine on it. Red wine. Anyway, I think they got it all out.'

'I've got something for you, too. Here, in the closet.'

'My coat! How'd you get that?'

'Sue brought it to my office this afternoon.'

'Sue?'

'She thought you'd be cold.'

'She was always big on gestures.'

'And,' Jack paused, blinked, 'she sent the apartment keys, too.'

'Keys?'

'Her keys. She said it was all yours. The apartment, that is.'

'I figured it would work out that way.'

'I'm sorry, Bernie –'

'Don't be. It was inevitable.'

'Would you like a drink or something?'

'No. I'm heading back to the apartment tonight. Might as well start in on the new life.'

'Why don't you stay here tonight? You can have the sofa. There's no rush.'

'I think I'd rather get back. And actually I appreciate your letting me hang around here all week.'

'Why don't you stay just –'

Bernie sank into a chair. 'I've got something to tell you.'

'What?'

'Larry Carpenter came home today.'

'You said he might. Last night you said –'

'The story they're giving out is this. That last Saturday night he had too much to drink. After everyone went home he decided he'd drive down to the lake and see the sunrise, but passed out in the car, right after he turned on the engine.'

'Before he opened the door?'

'Right. You've got it.'

'What did I tell you about history, Bernie? You can't trust second-hand accounts.'

'We all need our fantasies, I suppose.'

'How did it go last night? When you saw him at the hospital?'

'That's what I'm working up to, Jack.'

'What do you mean?'

'Sit down, Jack. I can't talk when you're jumping around like that.'

'Okay. Is this better?'

'Yes.'

'Go ahead.'

'This is very difficult for me.'

'Shoot.'

'I've done something fairly rash. And stupid. I don't know how it happened, to tell the truth. I guess the whole disruption of this week sort of got to me.'

185

'Come on, Bernie. What are you trying to say?'

'I got – I guess you could say – carried away. If you know what I mean.'

'I think so, yes.'

'I'd do anything to undo this thing. But I can't think of a way. And it's you I really feel bad about, Jack.'

'Me?'

'I feel I've sold out on you.'

'What in hell do I have to do with it?'

'I'm trying to tell you – '

'Well, tell me then.'

'Me and my big mouth.'

'Come on, Bernie, spill it.'

'When I was talking to Larry last night – in the hospital room? Janey was sitting right there, of course.'

'Of course.'

'She was so anxious just for him to have a little company. She's been wonderful, really. She just wanted him to have some conversation. That's what she said earlier when we were driving over there. She wanted me to try and get his mind on something interesting.'

'Go on.'

'It was a little awkward at first. Until we started talking about you. I mean, you're our common link. If it hadn't been for you I never would have met this guy and been sitting there in a hospital room on a Tuesday night – '

'Get to the point.'

'So I told him I'd known you since we were kids.'

'Yes?'

'And that we'd gone to school together, all that, right through college. And that now we have lunch together every Friday.'

'And so?'

'Well, I told him what we talk about, some of the topics we've covered over the years. I could tell it was really getting his mind off his problems, listening to some of the things. He was really interested in entropy, he said, at one time. And he's read all of Kierkegaard.'

'What happened then?'

'Well, he was really responding. Asking questions and looking lively and so on. He kept saying how he thought it was really remarkable that we've kept this up all these years. Twenty years. Actually, Jack, you know, it is rather remarkable.'

'I know.'

'The thing was, he *kept saying* how remarkable it was. And how important it was to have that kind of – well, I forget the term he used – that kind of bond. Or something like that.'

'And?'

'And the next thing that happened was I opened my mouth and said maybe he'd like to join us this Friday.'

'Larry? You asked Larry Carpenter to come for lunch?'

'Don't ask me why. I did it, I just did it. Maybe it's a little more complicated than that but – '

'And he's coming?'

'I hate to say it, but yes. He was – I can only say he was elated at the idea.'

'Of going to Roberto's? Christ, wait until he gets there and sees the place.'

'Jack, I could cut my throat. One minute after I suggested it, I could cheerfully have cut my tongue out.'

'But it was too late.'

'But, look, it's only for one Friday. I mean, we're not committed to this guy forever, you know. I didn't say to come and join the club or anything like that.'

'We can sort of try him out, then?'

'It was just that – I'm not making excuses – but if you'd been there – '

'I would have done the same thing?'

'I don't know. Maybe not. I know you're not all that crazy about the guy. Anyway, I did it and I'm really sorry. I feel first cousin to Benedict Arnold, to tell the truth.'

'It's okay, Bernie. Maybe we need a little fresh blood after all this time. Maybe we're into a new era or something – '

'It was an act of charity. Well, maybe that's not quite the word.'

'Expiation?'

'That's closer.'

'You're sure you don't want a drink?'

'No.' Bernie stood up, stretched. 'I'm going home. You've probably got some work to do on the book.'

'I'm thinking of maybe bowing out to Harriet.'

'Why?'

'Oh, I don't know.' Jack tried for a light tone. 'I'd like to say it was an act of charity.'

'Charity?'

'Or maybe I just want out.'

'Well, if that's what you want – '

'I think it is. I think – '

'Sleep on it.'

'That's the first advice you've ever given me, Bernie, you know that?'

'Really? Is it really?'

'Good night, Bernie.'

'Good night, old friend. See you – Friday I guess.'

'Right. See you then.'

Chapter Twenty-Nine

A T ONE MINUTE AFTER ELEVEN JACK PHONED ROCHESTER. The call went straight through. No cozy chats with Bell operators tonight; the world was back to normal.

'Go ahead,' the operator said.

'Harriet?' Was that his voice, that craven squeak?

'You wanted to speak to Harriet?' A man's voice, solid, educated, wonderfully baritone; Jack pictured a cask of a chest, plentiful hair.

'Yes. May I speak to Harriet please?' Ah, that was better.

'I'm afraid Harriet's out of town.'

'Out of town?'

'She won't be back for another three days, I'm afraid. She's out of the country actually. Is this long distance?'

'Yes. Chicago.'

'Perhaps' – the voice was polite, warm, solicitous, something British about it – 'perhaps if you left your number Harriet could ring you back when she gets in.'

'Three days, you said?'

'Yes. She's in Calcutta, but she's flying to Bombay tomorrow and directly home from there.'

'Calcutta?'

'May I tell her who called?' Yes, definitely British.

'A colleague of hers.' An old colleague – the word colleague came as an inspiration. Much better than old friend or fellow student or –

'I see. Well, Harriet dashed off to check a few sources and so on for her new book – '

'The book on Indian trade practices?'

'Yes.' A rising tone of wonderment. 'You know about the book, then?'

'Yes, well, I saw the announcement. In the *Historical Journal*.'

'Good lord, has it been announced already? Her publishers don't miss a trick.'

189

'Calcutta, you said? Bombay?'

'New Delhi, too, but that was just a bit of a holiday.'

'I see.'

'You in the same general field, then?'

'Not exactly. No. Not at all, in fact. I just phoned to offer my congratulations.'

'I'll have her ring you back.'

'Perhaps you could just convey my heartfelt – '

'Certainly, I'd be delighted to. Harriet will be pleased you thought of her.'

'If you could just tell her – '

'I'm afraid I missed your name.'

'Jack Bowman.'

'Wonderful, Jack. So thoughtful of you to call.'

'Not at all.' Not at all.

Chapter Thirty

BRENDA'S PLANE GOT IN EARLY THURSDAY EVENING. JACK drove to O'Hare straight from the Institute and arrived half an hour early.

Much of the snow in the city had melted. Brenda would never believe how bad it had been. How could such a weight of snow melt and run so quickly into the earth? The downtown streets were almost bare, returned overnight to their state of dry grittiness. The roofs of houses and factories under the warm, humid-looking moon were losing their loads of whiteness. All flights from the east, he was told, were on schedule.

When he had phoned home, Laurie had answered in a voice that was close to hysteria. 'I'm trying to get the living room cleaned up,' she shrilled. 'Can you hear that vacuuming in the background? That's Rob.'

'Don't worry too much about cleaning up.'

'But it's such a mess.'

'No one expects perfection.'

'I cut out my skirt today Dad. In Home Ec.'

'Good.'

'Mrs. Frost likes the material you picked out. It suits me, she says.'

'That's great, sweetie.'

He waited for the plane, thinking how, early this morning, he had pushed open the door to Brenda's workroom. The air in the room had been settled and chilly; the door must have been shut since Brenda had left. This morning this room had seemed to him to be the only orderly place left in the house. The frame, the box of quilts, the flash and splutter of sun through the plants at the window, the confused cleanliness of tangled thread and cut cloth; a kind of slow-moving music rose from the stillness, each note spoon-shaped and perfect. Laid out on two chairs was Brenda's newest quilt-in-progress.

It was a whirl of colour, mostly yellows with a few slashes of violent green. The yellows churned from a boiling centre. He had never realized that there were so many shades of yellow. The shapes meant nothing to him. There was no recognizable image here, as there had been in Brenda's earlier quilts. This was a simple – no, not simple – a strange and complex explosion of light. Brenda is so *open*, everyone was always telling Jack, but this whirlpool had been laid down in cipher. What, he wondered, did Brenda think about as she sat in this room, hour after hour, sewing? Those hours existed and must mean something. He ran his fingers over the stitching. A thought slipped into his head, a silverfish, in and out, too quick to grasp. This kind of quilting, Brenda had told him, was called meandering, the meander stitch. It wandered across the fabric, following and reflecting the pattern, a dancing adhesive, plucking and gathering at the coloured shapes. But meander seemed the wrong word for it, for this stitching was purposeful and relentless, suggesting something contradictory and ironic that interested him; he would like to ask her about it. But he wouldn't. She wouldn't know what his question meant; he wouldn't understand what she said in reply.

He jumped as a light flashed on the ARRIVALS board overhead. Brenda's plane was down. She would be coming through the gate in a few minutes.

She had often met him at this same gate. From here it was a half-hour drive home; it always took longer than they thought because of the traffic. 'What's the best thing that happened to you when you were away?' she always asked. And then, 'What was the worst?'

It was a formula she had, a way of defusing the strangeness of reunion. First the good news and then the bad news. Or was it the other way round? He couldn't remember.

He had often noticed that these revelations in the car only skated toward truth, that the real best and worst news was inevitably saved until they got safely home. What they settled for on the way was something in between, some mild and humorous representation, the kind of anecdote that told well in the car, that eased them back on their first step toward familiarity.

The best news, he would tell her, was that Laurie might be on her way to thinness. She had told him over the phone tonight that she had decided to fast for a week. She planned to start on

Saturday, as soon as Rob finished. 'I can't wait,' she'd shrilled in his ear.

The worst news, he would tell Brenda, was that Dr. Middleton, in conference with him this morning, had suggested, in view of their long relationship, that Jack drop this formal Dr. Middleton business and call him Gerald.

Gerald! He had spent the rest of the day avoiding him, ducking out late for lunch, slipping back early afterwards. He'd skipped the afternoon coffee break. Gerald! It would take getting used to. He had yet to test it, the fulsome, plunging sound of it, good morning, Gerald. Well, yes, Gerald, Chapter Seven should be ready by early March. Or April at the latest. Yes, Gerald, we had a pleasant weekend. How about you, Gerald?

The best and worst – and the rest could wait, some of it, possibly, forever. Or at least until he had time to absorb what had happened; he had lost faith; but had undergone a gradual and incomprehensible mending of spirit. It could happen again, he saw. And again.

There she was now. He could see her red raincoat, but not her face. Someone was standing in the way, waving a bag. He stepped sideways. Yes, there she was. But she didn't see him; she was looking around, bewildered. He wanted suddenly to rescue her from bewilderment, to rush at her with love and exhortation.

He moved closer to the gate, and felt, as he moved, a sudden buckling of his heart, for already he was sealing this moment in the clean preserving gel of history. He couldn't, it seemed, help himself. He felt failing light, physical weakness. He loved her. But feared that something in his greeting might fall short. Some connection between perception and the moment itself would fail, would always fail. He must, whatever else happened in his life, keep her from ever knowing.

There! She had seen him. She was waving, calling his name, coming toward him now.

The Wife's Story

Chapter One

EVERY MORNING BRENDA WAKES UP, SLIPS INTO HER BELTED robe, and glides – *glides* – down the wide oak stairs to make breakfast for her husband and children. The descent down the broad, uncarpeted stairs has something of ceremony about it, it has gone on so long. She and Jack have lived in the Elm Park house for thirteen years now; Rob was a baby when they moved in; Laurie, twelve last October, has never lived anywhere else.

In the kitchen she reaches for the wall switch. It's seven-thirty, a January morning, and the overhead fixture blinks once, twice, then pours steady, lurid light down onto the blue countertops, causing her to reel slightly. Her hands set out plates, reach into the refrigerator for frozen orange juice and milk, into the cupboards for Raisin Bran and coffee beans. Her husband, Jack, has given her a new coffee-grinder for Christmas, a small Swedish toy of a machine which is still a little unfamiliar to the touch. A button on its smooth side sets a tiny motor whirring, a brief zzzz which releases a pleasing instantaneous cloud of coffee smells. 'Philadelphia,' Brenda murmurs into the coffee-softened air of the kitchen.

She boils water, pours it carefully. 'Philadelphia.' Her voice is low and so secretive she might be addressing a priest or a lover.

For a month now, ever since she decided to go to Philadelphia, she has had her flight schedule thumbtacked in the lower right-hand corner of the kitchen bulletin board. Departure time, arrival time, flight number – all printed in her own hand on one of Jack's three-by-five index cards.

Above where the card is pinned there are a number of other items. It seems to Brenda, yawning and retying the belt of her robe, that some of them have been there for weeks. Months. She tells herself she could get busy and weed out a few, but the confusion of notices and messages mainly pleases her. She likes to think of herself as a busy person. *Brenda Bowman – what a busy person!*

1

The clutter on the brown corkboard speaks to her, a font of possibility, firmly securing her, for the moment at least, against inactivity. On the other hand, she sometimes feels when she glances at it a stab of impatience; is there no end to the nagging of details? Appointments. Bills. Lists. Announcements. Furthermore, these small reminders of events past and present carry with them a suggestion of disappointment or risk. That old theatre programme, for instance, the one from the Little Theatre production they'd gone to – when was that? last November? *The Duchess of Malfi*. She had hated *The Duchess of Malfi*. So, surprisingly, had Jack.

Someone – Jack, of course, who else? – had pinned up a newspaper cartoon about the School Board scandal, two pear-shaped men balancing on penny-farthing bicycles and grappling over a sack labelled $$$. The point of the bicycles, though Brenda has been following the scandal with some interest, escapes her.

And there, snugged cleanly in the corner – she has cleared a small area around it – is her flight schedule. It looks purposeful and bright, winning from the welter of other items its small claim to priority. Brenda glances at it every morning when she comes downstairs to make breakfast. It is the first thing to catch her eye, and even before she plugs in the coffee-grinder and starts the eggs, she examines and is reassured by her own meticulous printing, Flight 452, United Airlines, departing Chicago at 8:35. Tomorrow morning, Saturday. Arrival at Philadelphia at 1:33.

There are two short stops, Fort Wayne and Cleveland. The round-trip ticket – she will be gone only five days and so cannot qualify for the one-week excursion rate – comes to $218. Her tickets lie in an envelope on the hall table under a piece of pink quartz someone once brought them from Greece. The thought of the tickets touches her with a wingbeat of happiness which is both absurd and childish and which makes her for a moment the object of her own pity. Ridiculous. As though her life at forty was so impoverished that the thought of spending five days in Philadelphia could stir her to exaltation. Pathetic!

Not only pathetic, but unrealistic. She and Jack have been to New York a number of times. Once, when she was a child, she went for a trip to the Smoky Mountains with her mother. Later there was her honeymoon in Williamsburg; to Denver and to

San Francisco with Jack for a meeting of the National Historical Society; twice to Bermuda; and four years ago to France. Philadelphia wasn't even supposed to be a particularly attractive city. Someone – she's forgotten who, someone at a party recently – referred to Philadelphia as the anus of the east coast, one of those cities that suffers from being too close to New York, nothing but highways and hotels and factories and an inferiority complex. Nevertheless, when she murmurs the word 'Philadelphia' into the rising coffee fumes, she feels engorged with anticipation, a rich, pink strangeness jiggling round her heart that interferes with her concentration.

In recent days she has felt impelled to disguise her excitement, to affect calm. A hand on her shoulder seems to warn her to be careful, to practise sanity and steadiness. (A false steadiness that has nevertheless yielded a real calm, for she *has* succeeded in making lists, she *has* been orderly.) She even managed a shrug of nonchalance when the printed programme from the Philadelphia Exhibition arrived in the mail a week ago with her name listed on the back: Brenda Bowman, Quilter, Chicago Craft Guild.

Admittedly she was one of hundreds listed; the print was the size of telephone-book type, all the quilters crowded together with the spinners, the weavers, even the tapestry-makers and macramé people. Yes, Brenda has told Hap Lewis, herself a macramé person, yes, she's glad she decided to go. Why not? It would be interesting (and here she had shrugged, lightly, dismissively) to see what quilters from other parts of the country were doing. It might even be (another shrug) inspiring. She had held herself in check, even with Hap, whom she regarded as one of her closest friends, projecting a half-grimace over the cost of domestic flights, passing off the trip to Philadelphia as a mere whim – though a whim which required a certain amount of preparation. Jack and the children weren't used to having her gone. There were the meals. There was the laundry. 'Fuck the meals, fuck the damn laundry,' Hap had encouraged her.

Leaving 8:35, arriving 1:33. Brenda has taken this information over the phone asking the United reservation clerk to repeat the times and the flight number. She loves the busyness of facts, but distrusts them, and today, after breakfast, after everyone has left for the day, she plans to phone United again for a confirmation.

3

In the frying pan she melts a minute quantity of butter and cracks in four eggs, two for Jack, one for each of the children, none for herself. She is watching her weight, not dieting, just watching. Maintaining. And keeping a restive eye on her daughter Laurie, who in the last year has gone from a child's size twelve to a fourteen Chubette. Laurie's brand-new Big Sister jeans hardly fit as it is, but when she finishes her egg this morning she will be sure to reach for a second piece of toast. Only the stuffing of carbohydrates keeps her civil these days. Puberty is the worst of diseases, worse in its way than diseases of withering appetites and painful restrictions. Brenda stares at the shiny side of the percolator and sees beyond it the tender beginnings of Laurie's breasts, melting and disappearing under new layers of fat. She imagines returning home in a week's time and finding her daughter obscenely bloated with food and maddened by sugary cravings. Poor Laurie. 'It looks like we're going to have a baby elephant on our hands,' Jack had remarked to Brenda only a week earlier. Brenda had reacted with fury. 'It's only baby fat. All girls go through a period of baby fat.'

She should, though, sit down with Laurie today; have a little talk, just the two of them.

But there is so much still to do, and she hasn't started packing. Two of her blouses need pressing: the green one, the one that goes with her suit and with the pants outfit as well, and the printed one, which she plans to wear to the final banquet. At 3:15 she is having her hair cut, tinted, and blown dry at a new place over on Lake Street which has wicker baskets and geraniums in the window and scarlet and silver wallpaper inside. And if there's time, she wants to make a casserole or two to leave for Jack and the children – lasagna maybe, they love lasagna. Not that they aren't capable of looking after themselves; even Rob can cook easy things – scrambled eggs, hamburgers – and Laurie's learned to make a fairly good Caesar salad. They're not babies any more, Brenda says to herself, either of them.

Tomorrow morning. Saturday. Jack will drive her to the airport. They should plan to leave the house by seven; no, earlier, the car's been acting up lately, the rear brakes. She'll have to take it in herself when she gets back from Philadelphia and have it checked over. Jack tends to be vague and overly trusting (or overly distrusting) about mechanical things. What if

4

they get a flat tyre on the way to the airport? Unlikely, but still . . . She should set the alarm for six, have her shower, get dressed, and then wake Jack. She will say goodbye to the children tonight. No point hauling them out of their beds on a weekend morning.

Besides, there's always the danger that Laurie might cling to her. She should be past clinging, but she's not. Even going off to school in the morning she sometimes stands in the open doorway, letting the heat escape, clinging to Brenda. These embraces are wordless and pressing, and Laurie's breath seems imprisoned inside her heaving chest. Brenda can feel, or imagines she feels, the desperate, irregular thud of her daughter's heart through the material of her ski jacket.

And Rob has been so bad-tempered in the morning lately. Loutish, Jack calls it, though Brenda rises to his defence; Rob, or Robbie as she still sometimes thinks of him, is, after all, her first-born child, and his lowered eyes (sulkiness) and dark, curling hair still make her heart seize with love. 'It's only adolescence,' she tells Jack. 'It's hormones. Fourteen's the worst age. We should be thankful he isn't on drugs. Or skipping school. Look at Benny Wallberg. Even Billy Lewis . . . '

She puts forks and knives on the table, checks the eggs. She will have to stock up on eggs today. They could always fall back on eggs. Eggs, the compleat food; where had she read that? And she should buy some canned soup. Jack likes chicken and rice, but Rob only likes tomato, and Laurie . . . and what else?

From upstairs come noises, the familiar early-morning noises coming from different corners, but weaving together into a kind of coarsely made filament of sound from which the house at this hour seems suspended. A radio (Rob's) playing behind a closed door, and the uneven clumping of Laurie's Swedish clogs across the bedroom floor. And the endless running of the shower; don't they realize – even Jack – what hot water costs per month!

In another two minutes they will all be down, hungry, frowning, slouching in their chairs, demanding, accepting, preoccupied, still bound up in sleep and resistant to smiles or greetings. Rob will have sprouted a colony of new pimples on his chin, and last week's batch, the old ones, will be tipped with scabs – 'never scratch, never squeeze' the doctor has advised. Poor Rob. Laurie's blouse will be pulling out of her skirt already,

5

and there will be a dribble of egg, round as a tear, next to her mouth. Jack will come down smelling of talcum, smelling of a male sort of privacy, as though his body has already completed half its daily rituals. He will reach out blindly for the *Trib*.

Should she perhaps resent the fact that he always helps himself to the front section of the *Trib* and, like a potentate, hands round to the others the lesser sections, the fashion page, the sports, the business pages. Brenda herself tends to get stuck most mornings with the business section, which she has found over the years to be surprisingly interesting. Not that she studies the graphs or reads the articles about Gross National Products or falling cocoa prices in west Africa; what she likes is to look at the photographs, the column-wide pictures of men – an occasional woman too, of course, times are changing – who have achieved some sort of recent executive splendour, who are freshly appointed to some distinguished board of directors, or who have been transformed into vice-presidents of silverware companies or management-consulting firms or fire-and-casualty companies. Or else they are rising through the hierarchies of curious firms which manufacture mysterious products like vacufiles or turfspinners or gyrograters. Their success seems to Brenda to be dazzling but contained; they are poised for action, about to leap off the page, but something restrains them. There's a withheld muscularity in the pleasant, truncated necks and knotted ties, a darkness at the hairline which gives an air of brisk loyalty and purpose and probably good health. No perilous sodium nitrates or cholesterol-loaded eggs for these chosen stars. So-and-So, a graduate of Northwestern (A.B.), master's degree in Business Administration from Harvard, long record of service with firm since joining as trainee in 1960. (1960? – that was the year Jack had been taken on part-time at the Institute.)

This public recognition, Brenda supposes, is deserved, richly deserved. And where do these rising executives live, she cannot help asking herself. Wilmette? Clarendon Hills? The Near North Side? Here in Elm Park perhaps? – of course; she has several times seen people she and Jack know featured in the business pages. But for the most part these men are strangers, mere names attached to faces. Are they married? Divorced? Are there children? Children grown difficult and morose? Never

6

mind, they are the climbers of ladders. Their faces are fleshed out, made smooth and calm and American by success.

It is amazing, Brenda thinks, that every day there can be a new batch of these success stories; it is a wonder that there is room in the world for so much success and money. These photographs and announcements aren't cheap, she's been told. Space in the *Trib* costs money. The Great Lakes Institute where Jack works considers these announcements an unnecessary extravagance.

Otherwise he might have had *his* picture in the paper when he was made Acting Curator of Explorations. And though he's never expressed any disappointment about this lack of public recognition, Brenda knows that he would probably like to have had his picture in the paper. He is surprisingly photogenic. That picture of him at the lake last summer in his gold-striped golf shirt – he could pass for thirty-eight, not forty-three. He has a useful, temperate face, and he's been lucky with his teeth, which are both straight and white. In the summer he tans more easily than many men, and his sandy-coloured hair doesn't show up baldness the way dark hair does. Poor Jack. He would have liked his picture in the paper. He would have bought extra copies: one for his parents, one for his Aunt Ruth in the retirement village near Indianapolis. When he went to Elm Park wine-and-cheese parties or barbecues at the weekend he would have been happy thinking that his friends knew of his promotion, that they had seen his picture alongside those of stockbrokers and equipment salesmen. 'Well, yes,' he would have said, 'there will be a little more responsibility, maybe a little more travelling, but more headaches, too.'

But the Institute where he works is funded by trust money and has a board which examines finances and which has recently suggested that air conditioning be cut back except during July and August. The library budget is under review too, and the decision to upgrade the office equipment has been postponed. Furthermore, Dr. Middleton, who heads the Institute, is attached to the scholarly ideal of anonymity, and so staff promotions are soft-pedalled rather than celebrated and announced in the newspapers for the entertainment of women in the suburbs who sit idling over their black coffee and dry toast.

But tomorrow, Brenda thinks, tomorrow at this time she will

be gone. The newspaper, the coffee-grinder, the window over the sink with its red curtain, the morning skin of frost on the backyard grass – all this will remain, but she will be gone. Like the reassembled atoms in Rob's science-fiction stories, her bones will rise from this room and soar brightly over the city of Chicago. She will give a small salute to the coloured roofs below, to the plumes of smoke, neat as a painting. Around the tip of the lake, then Gary with its evil fumes dissolving in blueness, then Fort Wayne – she has never been to Fort Wayne, nor to Cleveland either for that matter. Lunch on the plane, followed by coffee, and then Philadelphia. (She and Jack had talked once about taking the children to visit Independence Hall and to see the Liberty Bell, but they had wanted to go to Washington too, and at that time Jack had only two weeks' vacation.)

So much to do: the packing, her hair, then the groceries. The backs of her legs ache too; she's expecting her period. What timing! She will be running furiously all day, a thought that floods her with happiness so that she wants to weep. And tomorrow someone else will be jiggling the coffee-maker; someone else will be slapping the side of the toaster to make it pop. Her eyes won't be here to seek out the specks of dust on the dining-room rug or light upon the breadcrumbs around the toaster. Tomorrow she will not be standing here in this room chanting into the mild early-morning silence this irrational and unasked-for prayer, her ritual lament of pity and helplessness: *poor Laurie, poor Rob, poor Jack.*

It is an incantation which she knows is addressed to no one in particular, but which returns often to scrape along the edge of her vision like a piece of pumice. *Poor Laurie, poor Rob, poor Jack.* She supposes it is a blessing of sorts, but one from which caring has lately been subtracted.

Ah well, she brightens, turning over the eggs and pouring herself some coffee. Ah well. And then she begins to hum, as she often does in the morning: *Amazing grace! how sweet the sound that saved a wretch like me.*

Chapter Two

ELEVEN O'CLOCK IN THE MORNING, AND HAP LEWIS STOOD at Brenda's back door, her arms clutched in a fit of shivering and a smile breaking across her long face.

'Come on in,' Brenda cried through the storm door.

It was cold outside, less than twenty degrees according to the radio, and getting colder. Snow was forecast. Brenda, wearing an old brown sweater and a new pair of jeans, could feel the damp outside air reaching her ankles.

Hap's voice came buzzing through the glass. 'You sure you've got a sec, Brenda? Jesus, you must be up to your neck.'

'Sure I've got a sec. Come on in. It's freezing out there and you don't even have a coat.'

'But, God, you must have a million and a half things – '

'I'm getting there,' Brenda said, waving one hand over her shoulder and shutting the door with the other. Already she'd made the beds, done a load of laundry, and put together a casserole of Spanish rice with cheese topping which she'd covered with foil and placed in the refrigerator ready to be heated up. Her suitcase – a good thing she owned one decent suitcase – lay open on the bed; her blouses, carefully pressed, were on hangers waiting to be folded; she could put them in at the last minute.

'Look Bren, the reason I dashed over – I wanted to pop in to see if I could give you a hand or anything.'

'I don't think there's a thing, Hap. But thanks anyway. I appreciate it. For once, everything's more or less organized.'

'Honest? You sure?'

'I think so. Really. Unless you're going out to the A & P – '

'The A & P? Oh, Jesus, of all days. The trouble is the car isn't here. Bud took it downtown, he had a special meeting or something. A sales meeting. I hate those lousy sales meetings. Otherwise – '

'It doesn't matter – '

'Look, just tell me what it is you need. Maybe I've got – '

'No, really, Hap. I've got to go out anyway. My hair. I'll just stop at Vogel's and pick up a few things when I'm out.'

'Look, you know how I've always got the goddamned freezer full of food, if it's food you need. Corn, zucchini, gobs of hamburgers, just let me know – '

'No, really – '

'If there's anything else. Christ, what are neighbours for? Anything at all – '

She was a good-hearted woman; even Jack admitted she was good-hearted. At times she seemed to Brenda to be almost lopsided with good will, as though an excess of kindness had somehow deformed her. And her energy was prodigious. It made Brenda feel weak looking out the back window at the Lewes' house and seeing Hap scramble up ladders, scraping off chipped paint with a wire brush, getting ready to paint the house in the spring. She and Bud and the boys were going to tackle it themselves. Last year they'd put on a new roof; Hap had seemed right at home perched over the gables, her hammer flying. She also made lemon layer-cakes to present to new neighbours on the block, a gesture which Brenda could only think sprang from Hap's Danville, Illinois, upbringing. (Brenda had never been to Danville, Illinois; she had rarely been down-state at all, in fact, and imagined it as a simple oblong, pleasantly populated by neighbourly-minded souls waving to one another from porches of trim wooden houses.) She and Jack, thirteen years ago, moving into the house in Elm Park, had been recipients of one of Hap Lewis's lemon layer-cakes. It had come on a pale blue Fostoria plate, accompanied by a breezy note: 'Hi folks. Welcome to the ol' neighbourhood.'

Brenda had been amazed, she who had grown up in Cicero in a three-room apartment over a dry cleaner's; such a gesture had seemed a leftover from another age. It made her think of Broadway musicals like *Oklahoma!* or *The Music Man*. Returning the plate a day or two later, she had brimmed with gratitude. This stranger, this Hap Lewis, was happy to have her as a neighbour; this wonderful warm-hearted woman wanted to be her friend.

Hap Lewis did other things besides bake cakes. She played tournament bridge, good, consistent tournament bridge; she and a woman called Ruby Bellamy twice won the West Suburban Champion Playoff. Hap was chairperson of a book group that was presently tackling Solzhenitsyn and thinking about Flaubert for spring. She ran a Girl Scout troop, old Troop Twelve, the oldest troop in Elm Park, and still found time to knit sweaters for her husband Bud and for her two teen-aged sons – beautiful sweaters, with raglan sleeves and intricate animal patterns worked into the backs. She froze vegetables from her own yard – string beans artfully concealed behind the peonies, a border of cauliflower running inside the petunias – and made pickled zucchini from a secret family recipe, a recipe which she had nevertheless passed on to Brenda – and to Leah Wallberg and Ruby Bellamy and one or two others in the neighbourhood.

And in the last few years she had started to make, and occasionally sell, large wall-hangings composed of unbleached wool and tree bark and other natural materials. These wall-hangings, with their swags and knots, reminded Jack of certain dark portions of the human digestive tract which had been flayed open with a knife and left to rot. 'They're considered very good,' Brenda told him. 'Would you want one on your wall?' Jack demanded. 'You have to think of them as a form of sculpture,' Brenda told him. 'I'd rather not think of them at all,' Jack said.

She was Brenda's age, but taller and heavier. Her hips swelled downward in a savage double roll, and to conceal these haunches she wore over her jeans long, loose-fitting tunics which she designed and made herself. Her face, poking through the tops of these tunics, was surprisingly angular, and seemed to contain more than the usual amount of bone. It was a long, nervous, mobile face; behind her glasses her eyes shone bright, inquiring, naive, and hopeful. A large, homely woman with a lumbering body. She had been, Brenda imagined, an even homelier girl; a long history of homeliness could be read in all those wild, random acts of kindness.

'Will you look at you, Brenda,' she raved, grinning. 'You're all organized, for crissake. If it were me going away tomorrow, there'd be bedlam, pure unadulterated bedlam.'

'Believe me, it has been – '

'And will you look at this goddamned kitchen. Floor wax! My God, I haven't had a whiff of floor wax for years – '

'It isn't really – '

'Listen Brenda, I promise you, on my word of honour, my Girl Scout honour – ha – that I'm not staying. I know you've got a million and one things to do, but I just thought, I got to thinking – have you packed the quilts yet? Or not?'

'Jack said he'd give me a hand tonight when – '

'I just had to come over and say bon voyage to *The Second Coming*. Did you get it finished?'

'Just about. All but a little handwork on one corner. And the quilting part's done.'

'That's terrific. I never thought you'd – '

'I took it off the frame yesterday. At, let's see, four- thirty-five, I think it was.'

'Bren, you're fabulous. You should have called me up. We could have celebrated. I don't know how you do it.'

'Come on upstairs. I was just getting started on it. You can give it your good-luck pat.'

Brenda's quilt room – sometimes she called it her workroom – was in the southeast corner of the house. Only four years ago it had been the guest room, containing not much more than a chintz-covered studio couch, which they opened up for the occasional overnight guest. The studio couch was still there, but Brenda had moved it into a corner and upholstered it with one of her early quilts, a staggered-circle design in several shades of blue; the three back cushions were covered with a reduced version of the same pattern. She liked to sit here late in the afternoon, sipping coffee and running her fingers over the raised squares, testing the springiness between the rows of stitching, thinking: I made this.

Her quilting frame filled all of one wall. It was so large that it had to be angled slightly at one end to make it fit, an arrangement which made the room look cheerful and slightly off-balance, reminding Brenda of the matted print they once had of Van Gogh's bedroom, a golden cube of a room which tilted and swayed under the weight of thick, straw-coloured fairytale furniture. It may have been with this particular print in mind that Brenda decided on the colours for the quilt room. She had painted the walls herself – three of them white, the fourth a brilliant yellow.

With its paint, with its hooked rug on the polished floor-boards, it was the brightest room in the house. It seemed to have sprung of its own accord out of the cluster of duller rooms: the living room with its pale-green walls and toneless carpet (stick with neutral, the decorating magazines had advised); the dining room with the gold Bigelow (not bad) and the Italian provincial table and chairs and buffet (a mistake, all of it); and their bedroom – beige walls, a scatter rug that was too small, a chest of drawers that had seen better days. The quilt room, on the other hand, though it was the most recently decorated room in the house, seemed to Brenda to be the room of a much younger family, belonging to more cheerful, more energetic people, people who knew the kind of thing they liked. There was a white cutting-table of shiny plastic, picked up at Sears sale, but looking smartly Scandinavian. Across from it was a pine dresser, where Brenda stored her patterns and sewing things. Above it, Rob, newly competent after a single semester of woodworking, had installed a shelf that held wicker baskets in which Brenda stored her material. (She had started with blues, then gone into greens. Now she was working into the yellow family.) 'Brenda Bowman, local quiltmaker, is not afraid to confront the simplicities of primary colour,' said a September article in the *Elm Leaves Weekly*. In a corner of the room stood a low table made of bricks and boards, rather like the brick-and-board table of their long-ago student apartment, only somehow more stylish, where Brenda kept a small electric coffee-maker and a tray of earthenware mugs. Lately she had taken to bringing her friends up here when they dropped in.

There was only one window, but it was large and square and on good days filled with sun. She had decided, finally, against curtains. Instead there were hanging plants: a spider plant, an asparagus fern, and a new one in a plastic pot called string-of-pearls. There were elm trees outside in the backyard, and Japanese cherries, and a small scrub oak which was gnarled and scabrous but healthy – when the children were younger they used to spend hours perched in its branches. There was, in addition, a view of the new cedar deck next door, which Larry and Janey Carpenter had put in. Across the alley was Bud and Hap Lewis's house, a large Victorian three-storey clapboard which, now that it was winter, could be seen through the bare branches. In summer it was almost completely obscured by foliage.

Brenda loved her house, a two-storey red brick dating from the twenties; she had loved it on sight. Most of all she loved the oak hall and stairs, which for some reason had been built on a grander scale than the rest of the house. The broad stairs had a kind of power over her; to descend them each morning was to launch her day with calmness. It was the stairs that commanded her to *glide*. The wall panelling was solid and heavy; the banister had a satiny coolness that imparted serenity.

After the hall, Brenda like the backyard best, especially the trees. Some of the elms had died, of course, and the three that remained were undergoing a radical new treatment which involved injections of serum. Expensive, but worth it in the long run, Jack had decided. And she loved the Japanese cherry trees that they had planted in front of the garage the summer they moved in.

Jack had been nervous; he had never planted a tree in his life, and the occasion had seemed to him, and to Brenda too, to be serious, almost a test that they were forced to undergo. They had both grown up in city apartments and feared they might harbour certain city-bred deficiencies. They had bought – recklessly, Jack's father maintained – a house in one of the oldest, most established suburbs. Perhaps they overreached themselves, acquiring, along with this solid brick structure, a garage, a toolshed, soil and grass, flower beds and shrubbery. Mysteries.

They bought the two young Japanese cherries at the nearby Westgate Nursery, where the manager was happy to dispense advice. Jack, listening politely, wrote the instructions down on a small pad of paper: the depth of the holes to be dug, the distance the trees should be planted from the garage; tree roots can interfere with foundations, they were told. And they were also told that late fall was the best time for planting trees. It was only July; it might be risky putting in trees in the middle of the summer. 'Well . . . ' Jack said, rubbing his chin with the back of his hand.

Together he and Brenda regarded the tree roots, bundled blindly in sacking; how would a tree know which month it was, they seemed to ask each other. They decided to take a chance. 'Don't say I didn't warn you,' the man from Westgate Nursery threatened.

At first one of the trees showed signs of withering, and Jack went back to the nursery and bought a recommended brand of insect spray. Every evening, arriving home from the Institute and setting his briefcase down on the grass, he checked the undersides of the leaves for mites. Brenda, often carrying Rob in her arms, came out of the house to watch. 'It looks okay to me,' she always told him.

'I should have bought a hardier strain,' Jack grieved. They both recalled that Bud and Hap Lewis across the alley had suggested a certain kind of flowering plum, which was just as decorative but stood up better to the cold winds. They dreaded the first frost.

But the fall had been unexpectedly moderate that year, and that winter one of the mildest on record. By mid-March the two fledgling trees were in bud. The second summer they grew a spectacular two feet, and the stucco garage behind the rosy branches seemed softened by their presence. Jack talked about planting asparagus. He still mentioned it, twelve years later, from time to time, how it might be a good idea to try asparagus.

'I'm sure this view from your studio is an inspiration in your work,' the reporter from the *Elm Leaves Weekly* said. She was a young girl wearing an embroidered blouse, a journalism student hired for the summer, and she had come to the house one afternoon to interview Brenda.

'Well, yes,' Brenda replied in a voice weighted with doubt. 'I suppose you could say that.'

Perhaps it was even true. Certainly her first real quilt – the first one she actually sold – had contained the natural green harmonies of shadow and light. She had called it *Spruce Forest*. 'Why *Spruce Forest*?' Jack had asked. 'Why not oak or something?'

'Because I had to call it something,' she said. 'I was filling out the entry form, and *Spruce Forest* just popped into my head.'

'You'd have to go up to Wisconsin to see a spruce forest,' Jack said in a nagging tone, unusual for him.

In fact, the quilt had looked more like an expanse of grass cooling off late in the day, a suburban lawn overlaid with the darkened, simplified shapes of spirea and mock orange and grape leaf. She had cut long spears of dark linen (grass? spruce boughs? waves perhaps? knives?) and had arranged them so that they swept and curved the length of the quilt. The forms advanced and overlapped, and the green, drenching effect of colour was carried right to the borders, and even beyond, for Brenda, in a sudden awakening of inspiration, decided to make the border of the quilt irregular. (Later the use of the irregular border became something of a trademark for her.)

15

Spruce Forest: it won first prize in the Chicago Craft Show four years ago. There was a ceremony; the mayor was in attendance; there was a medal and a bouquet of roses. 'How did you feel at that moment, Mrs Bowman?' the girl reporter from the *Elm Leaves Weekly* asked. 'Did you feel you were standing at the gateway to a new career?'

She hadn't. She'd felt only that she had had an extraordinary piece of beginner's luck. Someone had paid money for something she had dreamed into existence. It was days before she could bring herself to deposit the cheque in the bank.

The quilt had been bought by a flamboyant-looking middle-aged couple, Sy Adelman and his wife, Slim Morgan. They came to the craft-show reception, saw *Spruce Forest*, and on the spot wrote Brenda a cheque for six hundred dollars. 'It'll be incredible in our living room,' Sy Adelman said. 'We live down in Oldtown, a little gem of a house, high ceilings, skylight, you know the type.'

'Your living room?'

'He means on the wall,' Slim Morgan said in a red-plum voice. 'Over the piano. It's just what we've been looking high and low for.'

'High and low,' Sy Adelman said.

'Who's Sy Adelman?' Brenda asked Jack later. 'Who's Slim Morgan?'

'You remember Sy Adelman. That nightclub act? The old Chicago Review group. And Slim Morgan's practically a classic now. Someone was telling me the other day that her early records are almost priceless.'

'Imagine that,' Brenda said.

When she was working on a quilt, she seldom looked out of the window, or anywhere else for that matter. Occasionally she made a small sketch, very rough, just a few lines on a sheet of paper, but the patterns seemed to come from some more simplified root of memory; sometimes they arrived as a pulsating rush when she was pulling weeds in the yard or shovelling snow off the front walk, but more often they appeared to her early in the morning before she opened her eyes, an entire design projected on the interior screen of her eyelids. She could see the smallest details, the individual stitches. All the pieces were there, the colours and shapes and proportions selected and arranged. When she opened her eyes to the light, she always expected the image to dissolve, but it remained intact, printed on an imaginary wall or beating slowly at the back of her head. She had no idea where the ideas came from.

There must be, she assumed, some interior reservoir, and she wondered what this might be. She imagined a vibrating organ, half-heart, half-placenta. She thought of patterns stacked up like china plates on a neat shelf, and it puzzled her to think that she could extract these complicated images from the same section of her head where she stored simple recipes and kept track of the birthdays of friends. She had never considered herself introspective or original. ('Brenda is such an open person,' Hap Lewis has said several times in Brenda's hearing.)

'I think there's a Byzantine or Turkish influence in Brenda's work,' said Leah Wallberg, who had studied art history. Brenda, who had been a secretary-typist before she married Jack, knew little – nothing really – about art history. Nevertheless, despite this, it seemed that she did indeed possess an inner pool of colour and pattern which was oddly accessible and easily drawn upon. It pumped naturally and steadily and in a form which she was able to translate without serious difficulty. It seemed at times almost ridiculously easy, in fact, and Brenda guarded a belief that this was something anyone could do, anyone at all.

At the same time she recognized the fact that her quilts were changing. The birds and flowers and boats and houses of her early designs – what Leah Wallberg called her folky thing – were giving way to something more abstract. The shapes interlocked in different, more complex, ways. A year ago she wouldn't have risked her new feather-shadowed borders. She was thankful no one asked her anymore what such-and-such a quilt was 'about'. She wouldn't have known. And she was thankful, too, that she was seldom pressed about the reasons behind the naming of her quilts. Even Jack no longer cocked an eyebrow and asked: Why *Spruce Forest*? Why *Buddha's Chant*? Why *Rock Splinter*? It was assumed that she must have her reasons, that along with her gift for stitchery went a body of belief, an artist's right to interpret and name.

She might, of course, have called them after colours or numbers – *Study in Green, Burnt Yellow #2* – but she preferred real names, which tied the design to her, even though she knew the quilts themselves would pass into other hands. She remembered that Rob and Laurie, when they were younger, gave names to the tiny islands near the summer cottage they rented each August. Naming was a form of possession. It was a privilege; there were lots of people who never had a chance to bestow names.

The name of *The Second Coming* had come to her less than a month ago. She and Jack were driving downtown one night for a reception at the Institute and happened to pass a small, blackened Baptist church on a weedy corner off Madison. The lit-up message on its roof proclaimed: 'The Second Coming Is at Hand.' The Second Coming. She said it aloud.

'What?' Jack said, braking at a red light.

'Nothing.'

She said it again, this time to herself. The Second Coming. It sounded important. It sounded lucky.

'It's a great name,' Hap Lewis was saying, following Brenda upstairs and into the quilt room. 'I mean, it's got all kinds of overtones. If you know what I mean.'

Brenda unfolded the quilt briskly, spread it on the cutting-table, and announced with a shaky flourish, 'Well, here she is.'

'Jesus!' Hap's gravel voice dropped.

'Well?' Brenda held her breath. 'What's your honest-to-goodness opinion?'

'My honest opinion, my gut reaction' – Hap paused – 'is that this is the best thing you've done. Terrific, in fact, A plus. Better than the Buddha thing. Je – suss! Here, let's hold it up.'

'You don't think that purple is too purple – ?'

'God, no, it's fucking sensational, that purple. Sort of unexpected, but just right at the same time.'

They lifted the quilt, each taking two corners, and together carried it toward the window. The grey January light fell inward onto a blocked bed of colour – greens and yellows mostly – with a kind of frenetic heat rising from one end. And, like a footnote or an inscription, dark-purple stains printed the edges with shapes that resembled mouths.

'If you don't come back from Philly with a ribbon or two, I'll eat my chicken feathers.'

'I'm not counting on – '

'Now you're doing your modesty thing, Bren. Wait'll the judges see this. You've seen the junk some of these gals churn out. I mean, Brenda, you've done it. You know what I mean. There's something so contained about this, not quiet exactly, but you know, slow-moving, like someone trying to say something, but they can't get the words out. Know what I mean?

'Well – '

'I mean, it's got the sensual thing all sewn up – pardon the lousy pun – but it's also got, you know, sex.'

'Sex?' Brenda was laughing.

'Like you want to reach out and touch it. Or hop out of your clothes and roll around in it. I don't mean just plain old intercourse sex, ugh, not that there's anything wrong with intercourse. I mean, well, energy. But the kind of energy you keep the lid on. Energy contained – you know what I mean? About to jump out at you if you let it.'

Over the slanting expanse of the quilt, Brenda regarded Hap fondly, gratefully. She felt her throat grow warm with tears.

Hap Lewis is a babbler, Jack always said. And it was true. She did have a tendency to go on and on. Verbal overdrive, Jack called it. She got on his nerves, and he wondered, sometimes aloud, how Brenda could stand her. His heart bled, he said, for Bud Lewis, the poor sap; what kind of sex life could you have with a woman who never shuts up for ten seconds!

'But she means it,' Brenda always said. 'That's the thing about Hap. She means every word.'

They stood for a minute longer, holding the quilt up to the window. Brenda had the dizzying sensation of something biblical happening: two women at the well, gathering light in a net. Neither of them spoke, and the silence seemed to Brenda to be unbreakable and dipped into earlier memories of happiness. 'I wish you were coming, Hap,' she said impulsively. 'I wish you had decided to come after all.'

Hap, still gripping the quilt, shrugged. 'How could I? Bud, the boys – '

'Aha! Remember what you told me when I said I didn't think I could get away?'

'What did I say?'

'You said, and I quote, fuck them all.'

'Hey,' Hap shrieked. 'Hey Brenda. You did it. You said it. The big F. You finally said it. Do you know what I think that means?'

'What?' Moving together they began refolding the quilt, first in halves, then in quarters.

'I think,' Hap said, 'that it's some kind of omen. That something good is going to happen to you.'

Chapter Three

'J ACK?'
    No answer.
    She tried again, a little louder. 'Jack.'
    'Yes.' The voice, husky and toneless, cracked from a deep sleep.
    'It's six-fifteen.'
    He turned over, buried his face in the pillow.
    'It's time to get up, Jack.'
    'Ten more minutes. It's still night-time.'
    'I've brought you some coffee. Here on the table.'
    'Bribing me,' he groaned into the feathers.
    She sat on the edge of the bed. 'How'd you sleep?'
    'Fine. While it lasted.'
    'Ask me how I slept.'
    'How'd you sleep?'
    'Terrible.' She began rubbing his back through the striped pyjamas. 'Terrible.'
    'Don't stop. That feels good. Ahhhh.'
    'I kept thinking of all the things I'd forgotten. Like the man coming to fix the valve on the furnace. I think he said it was Monday he was going to come.'
    'Hmmmmm.'
    'I just lay there, it seemed like hours. I could hear the clock ticking downstairs, that was how quiet it was. Then I got to worrying how I was going to get the quilts out of air-freight when I get to Philadelphia. Do they bring the package to the luggage place or do you have to pick it up at the air-freight place?'
    'I think – '
    'I decided I could get my suitcase first, and if the quilt box wasn't there, I'd get a cab and then get the cab-driver to stop at the air-freight place.'
    'Hmmmm.'
    'What did you say?'

'I said that sounds like a very solid and well-thought-out plan.'

'You're falling back to sleep again.'

'I was having the best dream.'

'Your coffee's getting cold.'

'Oh, that feels good. A little lower.'

'Here?'

'We ought to get a new mattress. How about it? A waterbed.'

'What's wrong with this mattress? It isn't even worn out.'

'After twenty years we deserve a new mattress. They say it does wonders for – '

'What was the dream about?'

'I don't know. I think it was about bouncing on a waterbed. It all disappeared when someone with a loud voice bellowed six-fifteen in my ear.'

'I don't want to be late.'

'Take my word for it, you'll be early.'

'Jack?'

'What?'

'I forgot to buy the material for Laurie.'

'What material?'

'For school, her Home Ec class. They're making skirts or something, and she was supposed to have her material last week.'

Silence.

'Do you think,' Brenda said, 'you could take her out to get it? This afternoon maybe? Zimmermans or Mary Ann's or some place like that?'

'Okay.'

'And she needs a pattern too. She knows which one. I asked her yesterday.'

'Okay.'

'You won't forget, will you?'

'On my honour.'

'And another thing, I was thinking about Rob.'

'What about him?'

'I was just thinking about him. Last night when I couldn't sleep. I mean, maybe you should have a talk with him.'

'I think he's fairly well informed – '

'I think you, or maybe both of us, should have a talk with him about his attitude.'

21

'Brenda.'

'What?'

'Why don't you just crawl under the covers for a minute and we could discuss it.'

'You're stalling. You just don't want to get up.'

'Not true.'

'Anyway, I'm all dressed. I've been up for an hour. Didn't you hear the shower running?'

'No. I was having this beautiful dream – '

'Was it raunchy?'

'Raunchy?' He turned over, smiled at her lazily. 'Now that's a word I haven't heard in – what? – twenty years.'

'Horny then. Was it one of your horny dreams?'

'You sure you wouldn't like to crawl under the covers for just two minutes?'

'I'm sure. It's six-thirty, almost – '

'One minute then. I promise to be quick.'

'Jack – '

'You smell like toothpaste. I love a woman who reeks of toothpaste. Eau de Crest.'

'It's Infini. It's that perfume your aunt sent. Smell my wrist.'

'Hmmmm.'

'Nice?'

'I won't ask what I smell like,' Jack said.

'It would be better if you didn't.' He smelled of sheets, unbrushed teeth, and something vaguely fecal. His body was warm and relaxed under the electric blanket – bonded with the heat of the blanket, in fact – and for an instant she considered slipping off her skirt and getting in beside him. No, there wasn't time. And she would have to shower again, maybe press her blouse . . .

'Spurned,' Jack said. 'Spurned and abandoned. That would make a good title for a movie.

She touched his cheek. 'Your coffee – '

'You career women are all alike.'

'You don't say.'

'Always rushing off to catch planes.'

'How cruel.'

'You could bring a little joy.'

'And why didn't you think of this last night, bringing a little joy?'

22

'Because you made me watch that Barbra Streisand thing on TV, you and your children.'

'I thought you liked Barbra Streisand. You used to love – '

'Fatigue is what Barbra Streisand gives me. A wracking case of fatigue.'

'Anyway, you never answered my question, Jack.'

'What question?'

'About the man coming to adjust the furnace valve.'

'He'll come, Brenda. He'll ring the bell. No one will answer. So he'll go away, quietly.'

'They might charge for making the call.'

'I doubt it.'

'But it seems to me I said I'd be here. They phoned last week and asked if the lady of the house would be home on – '

'The lady of the house?'

'And I said – '

He squinted at her and said again in a tone of wonderment, 'The Lady of the House.'

'What's so funny about that?'

'Like the Lady of the Lake. Are you really,' he paused, 'the Lady of the House?'

'If you aren't going to drink this coffee, I am.'

'No, you don't.' He propped himself on one elbow and reached for the cup.

'Maybe you should drink it while you're getting dressed.'

He took a swallow. 'Strong.'

'On purpose. To get you awake.'

'I always did love cold coffee. It goes with cold toothpaste.'

'You won't forget about the material. It's supposed to be part polyester, she said.'

'What?'

'The material for Laurie. I just told you. She – '

'Oh, *that* material.'

'And, Jack, maybe you could let the furnace people know I won't be here. The number's in that little book of mine. Under O for oil. Or else it's under – '

'Brenda, lovey.'

'Yes.'

'Let me ask you a question. If it's not too early in the morning that is.'

'What question?'

'What is the population of Chicago?'

'The population of Chicago? How on earth would I know the population of Chicago?'

'You've lived here all your life. You must have some vague idea of – '

'Three million. It just came to me.'

'When you were in school it was three million. Or thereabouts. Now it's more like six.'

'And?'

'Well, if you figure four to a household, that makes, let's see, one and a half million – *million* – households that manage to get along on a day-to-day basis without that famous lady of the house, Brenda Bowman, steering the ship.'

'Up!' she ordered, standing abruptly and with one move stripping the covers down.

'My God, it's freezing.' He made a grab for the blanket and missed.

'It's cold because of the valve on the furnace. It cuts the heat back. When the man came to clean the filter he explained – '

'What a job! I wouldn't mind having a job like that. Going around all day talking to women about how valves work.'

'He was really nice. Young and – '

'Do you know, you look really beautiful this morning.'

'Do you know what time it is, Jack?'

'Sort of Olivia de Havillandish.' He caught her hand. 'Thank you, Brenda.'

'For what?' She sat down on the edge of the bed.

'For not looking like Barbra Streisand.'

'If only I did.'

'And for not sounding like Barbra Streisand. And for not opening your mouth wide wide wide like Barbra Streisand – '

She put her arms around him. The hair at the back of his head stood up in tufts, and she smoothed it with her hand. Soon there would be a completely bare patch; the thought of this vulnerable spot made her throat contract, and she bent over and kissed him on the forehead, where she detected the faint taste of salt.

'Ah, lovey,' he murmured and closed his eyes.

'We really should be getting going,' she said after a minute.

He opened his eyes. 'Is this new?'

'What?'

24

'That blouse.'

'This? I got it last week. At Field's. I showed it to you, remember?'

'Oh, yes.'

'Don't you like it?'

'I love it.'

He was undoing the buttons. She, half-protesting, uttered a girlish meow, and he reached around and unhooked her bra.

It was an old game of theirs: he the pursuer, the flatterer, the one with all the lines, some of which were both true and untrue. And she: silent, sly, pretending reluctance, pretending to be preoccupied, and then, finally, allowing herself to be won. There were other games, other scenes, some sharper and more savage, but this was the one they returned to again and again. It was a way of invoking youth, it seemed to Brenda, a kind of play they put on for the entertainment of their younger selves. He murmured into the long cavity between her breasts the words *beautiful beautiful*, and she felt herself grow opaque and speechless, making small gasping sounds as his tongue circled her nipples. Slowly.

Her blouse lay under them, and her skirt – wool tweed, black and emerald – was hiked up in a roll around her waist. Far away at a green and more level distance she found herself thinking that the wrinkles would probably fall out. And that the blouse would be under her jacket anyway; who would see it? She might even have minute to touch up the collar while Jack shaved.

Philadelphia, Philadelphia, she chanted to herself, pushing up against him, and like a mantra the word opened the door into a space wider and warmer than usual. She was assailed by familiarity, cotton, skin, the pressure of Jack's legs, and her eyes sealed shut to a large, dark corridor lit by small sconces of light, reddish in colour and vaguely Victorian in design.

'I love you,' she said, as she always did when the lights flared, and then – this morning, because she was going away – she added, 'I really do.'

'My lovey,' he said into her collapsing hair. 'My Brenda-Bear, my only only.'

Chapter Four

IT WAS BRENDA'S MOTHER, ELSA PULASKI, WHO TAUGHT HER
to sew in the first place. All the time Brenda was growing up
in Cicero, Illinois, her mother's black sewing machine had
stood in a corner of the crowded living room, squeezed in
between the radiator and the saggy couch. The machine was a
Singer Standard, made of shiny black metal, always a little
dusty, with gold scrollwork about its base and a lever which
was operated by pressure from the knee. A busy, oily fragrance
rose from the region of the motor. Its sound was sweet and
rhythmic, almost human. Elsa like to boast about how little she
had paid for it; with only a little bit of finagling she had got it for
thirty dollars wholesale, which was almost half-price. It was a
cabinet-style machine and could be folded away into a little
walnut-veneer table – though, in fact, it seldom was.

For what was the use of putting it away, she used to say, with
a rising intonation she had; what was the sense of it when she
was always working away on something – in the evenings, at
weekends, whenever she had a minute. Elsa's knee resting on
the pedal, so delicate for a heavy woman, had constituted for
Brenda an education in lightheartedness. She made all her own
clothes, the size twenty-two dresses – long sleeves for winter,
short for summer – that she needed for work. (For thirty years,
until she died, she sold men's socks and underpants at Wards –
five days a week, nine to five, and on alternate Saturday
mornings until the unions came in and a put a stop to that.) She
made her skirts and blouses and even her own winter coats:
'Just try and find decent ready-to-wear for a gal my size.' She
made herself nightgowns out of remnants – some of them were
of strange non-nightgown materials, moire or taffeta, that were
more suitable for evening wear – and she would have made her
own underwear, too, if Wards hadn't allowed their saleswomen
fifteen per cent off. She sewed nylon curtains for the front
windows of the apartment on 26th Street and the stretch slip-
covers for the two armchairs and for the couch which she

opened up at night for her bed. She hemmed her own dish towels and sheets. 'Better goods,' she explained to Brenda. 'One hundred per cent better, and they don't ravel out their first time in the wash.'

Brenda can remember the tone of her mother's voice when she said this, but can't recall whether she spoke in English or Polish. Elsa alternated easily between the two, and Brenda, in childhood, was accustomed to the rapid movement between the two languages; not just the shifting vocabularies but the towering structures of consciousness and mood. When Elsa was happiest she spouted a loud, comic, Cicero-flavoured English.

Brenda grew up wearing beautiful clothes. At Wilmot Public Grammar School in Cicero, when other girls wore dresses of faded rayon passed on to them by their older sisters, Brenda Pulaski wore fresh cotton dresses – Egyptian cotton; 'Irons like a hanky,' Elsa said – made from the latest back-to-school Butterick and Simplicity patterns. There was hand-embroidery or white piqué trim on the sleeves and the collars. In fourth grade Brenda was the first in school to have a New Look ballerina skirt, the first to have a blouse with a Barrymore collar. Never once in all the years she was growing up did she reach into her closet in the jumbled back bedroom and find she had nothing to wear; never once did she wear a dress or a jumper or a blouse that had not been finished with French seams and bound buttonholes; never was she embarrassed to find her hem coming down or a button missing or a blouse opening up under the arm when she raised her hand in class. At the age of nine or ten she went to neighbourhood birthday parties wearing royal blue or wine-coloured velvet dresses with bows at the back and lace at the yoke; when she twirled around, the skirts of these dresses spread out in a full circle. At Morton High School, where she was Senior Class Secretary, she had a wardrobe of coordinated corduroy skirts and weskits and wool dresses with the plaids matching at the back and the sides as well, and white, handmade Peter Pan collars to pin to the necks of her sweaters. For her first school dance when she was fifteen, Elsa made her a 'formal' of nylon net, boned and strapless, with a matching circle of tulle for her ponytail. There is a picture of her wearing this dress in one of her old yearbooks. She is standing beneath a basketball hoop which is draped with paper streamers, looking popeyed and happy on the arm of a slim boy, Randy Saroka, with short, curly hair and a striped necktie, and at the waist of her full-skirted dress is a corsage of two gardenias.

When it came to Brenda's clothes, Elsa had done most of the actual sewing, and she had done all the cutting. 'Cutting tells,' she liked to say, emphatically and mysteriously. She had insisted, too, on putting in the zippers and setting the sleeves. 'When you're older you can set a sleeve,' she promised Brenda. 'Plenty of time for that later on.' (Brenda at age thirteen or fourteen ran up side seams, basted, and did hems.) In the evenings while Brenda did her homework, or later, when she was in bed, Elsa sat under the lamp with the radio playing and worked on inverted pleats or handmade eyelets. 'Sewing's damn hard work,' she used to say with just a hint of Slavic inflection, 'so it's just plain stupid to use cheap yard goods.' Thus, for her daughter, Brenda, there were no bargain blends and no remnants; even during the war, Elsa managed to find one hundred per cent virgin wool for Brenda's school clothes. For a yard of real English jersey she once paid six-fifty. 'Just look at the way it hangs,' she exclaimed, holding the material up to the light, stretching it between her fingers and giving it a sharp sideways tug. 'I always say, don't skimp when you sew. Quality shows; it shows every time.' (The wool jersey, Brenda still remembered years later, had been made into something called a tube dress. She had been one of the first to have a tube dress.)

She felt certain that, had her mother been alive, she would have admired the new red raincoat she'd bought for the trip to Philadelphia. Elsa would have turned it inside out and laid it flat on a table; she would have examined the seams and the lining and pronounced it, at last, a well-made garment, a quality garment. She would have read the label, nodding, approving, blowing through her teeth: 'Cheap at the price.'

The thought of her mother's posthumous approval – Elsa died four years ago at age fifty-six from complications following a routine gall-bladder operation – comforted Brenda, sitting in the car, wearing her new coat over her suit. Jack was silent now, driving to the airport, his teeth set in an attitude of grim dutifulness.

'Damn window-washers.' He leaned forward, peering through the smeared windshield. 'Cheap window-washers they put in these cars.'

His earlier good humour had evaporated, dispelled by the small mechanical failings of the car, and possibly by the cold wind blowing across the highway and the early-morning darkness, purplish with arc lights. A truck-driver passed them, swerving suddenly, causing Jack to curse violently. 'Fuck.' All these things seemed to Brenda to be inexplicably her fault, tied up in some way with her decision to go to Philadelphia.

No, that was absurd. Ridiculous. She recalled that it had been Jack's idea in the first place that she go. He had been the one to suggest it, and it was he who finally persuaded her that it would be a valuable experience. He had used those very words: 'A valuable experience.' She was about to mention this to him when he braked suddenly, pitching the two of them forward. 'Did you see that? Christ! He didn't even signal. We could have ploughed right into him.'

Brenda said nothing, concentrating instead on her hands, which rested on the smooth fabric of her new raincoat. She had bought it a week ago at Carsons for $250.

Peering at the price tag under the subdued store lights, she had felt panic. It was unbelievable. Two hundred and fifty dollars! And tax on top of that! She had been aghast. ('I was aghast,' she imagined herself saying to someone – anyone – later.) She had no idea coats had gone up so much. When did it happen? Inflation? It seemed not all that long ago that she had paid eighty dollars for a warm winter coat with a chamois lining and a real fur collar on it – no, that had been ages ago, the year Jack got his first promotion at the Institute – her blue tweed coat; she had worn it for eight years.

The red raincoat at Carsons had been reduced from $315. What a laugh, Brenda heard herself saying in some future conversation, her voice rising. A mere raincoat, and they had the nerve to ask $315.

On the other hand, it was a good make, she could say. She had seen those ads in the *New Yorker*: that long-haired girl standing out there on the rock; that grey-haired man, strongly muscular, finely featured, a few steps behind her, turned to half-profile, his gaze sternly directed at the surf. And it did have a zip-in lining, which meant she would be able to wear it almost year round. She would get all kinds of wear from it. If it faded – reds sometimes did – she could return it. She would put the sales slip away carefully in her dresser drawer. . . .

The tag said size twelve. Perfect. It wasn't that easy finding size twelves, you had to look and look. (Already she was going to buy it; of course she was; it would be idiotic not to.)

She slipped it off the hanger and tried it on. It fit smoothly across the shoulders – it *better* fit for that price, she muttered to herself, making a face. She was feeling cheerful now. It made her hips look almost slim – something ingenious about the way it was cut. ('Cutting tells . . . ') There was a gathered yoke at the back, and top-stitching on the collar and pockets, the kind of detailing that costs money, that has to be done by hand. ('You can tell quality by the detailing.') Still, $250 was an incredible amount of money. Two and a half weeks' groceries at least. You could buy a man's suit for $250, a three-piece suit. She could get a new glass-topped coffee table for the living room for $250. They needed a new coffee table; the old one, that scratched, phony Duncan Phyfe, was looking tackier by the day. Two hundred and fifty dollars was a sizeable chunk of money.

On the other hand, she had been shopping all morning – Field's, Stevens, Saks – and was beginning to feel discouraged and hot. She pictured herself putting on this coat and walking down a street in Philadelphia, a neutral sky overhead – a narrow street, medieval-looking and chilly, with small shops; a bakeshop flashed into view, fresh buns lined up in a window. She would be warm and courageous, marching past it, swinging her leather shoulder-bag as she went.

She wrote a cheque for the coat instead of putting it on her charge account. When she got home she carried it upstairs to the bedroom, lifted it from its box, and removed the tags. She tried it on again, examining herself in the full-length mirror on the back of the closet door. The material felt silky to the touch. Even the hem was perfect, just meeting the top of her boots – at least she wouldn't need new boots this year. It was worth every penny of two hundred and fifty dollars; her mother's lightly accented voice reached her through the silvery bevelled edge of the mirror – 'Cheap at the price.' 'Quality shows.' Brenda curled her hands under the lapels and smiled.

She and Jack no longer had to watch every penny, she reminded herself. Jack earned a comfortable salary at the Institute; eventually he would move up to Senior Administrator. Dr. Middleton was due to retire in five years. Anything could happen. And there was her quilt money. She was close to being a regular earner now. For the last two years she had even filed her own tax form. ('Now that's a milestone and a half, you lucky duck,' Hap Lewis had raved, 'when you get your own tax form. You've made it, kiddo.')

She had been lucky. Her first quilt selling for six hundred dollars. A fluke, she'd thought at the time; it was only because it had won the prize and been written up in *Chicago Today*. 'Elm Park Housewife Turns Hobby to Profit.' At the time she'd thought it could never happen again. But it had. People seemed willing to spend exorbitant sums for original handworked articles. The last quilt she'd sold, *Michigan Blue*, had gone for $800. Some people from Evanston had bought it, a dentist and his wife. They'd paid the price cheerfully, no dickering, no suggestion that she knock off fifty dollars or forgo the sales tax. They had heard about her work from an acquaintance; they had driven down from Evanston one evening, phoning ahead for an appointment. Her signature was embroidered in the right-hand corner, and they had fingered it with satisfaction. ('I love it,' the wife had whispered. 'We'll take it,' her husband said.)

She now had printed business cards of her own, Jack's idea.

Brenda Bowman

HANDMADE QUILTS
ORIGINAL AND ADAPTED

576 North Franklin Blvd. Elm Park, Ill.

She had a receipt book and a ledger where she kept track of expenses and sales. And this week – today – she was going to the National Handicraft Exhibition, where the top quilters in the country would be showing. Eleanor Parkins, *the* Eleanor Parkins. Sandra French. Dorothea Thomas. W.B. Marx. Verna of Virginia. These quilters asked a thousand dollars, even fifteen hundred dollars, for a commissioned piece. Verna of Virginia had recently sold a quilt to the Metropolitan Museum of Modern Art; there had been a write-up in *Quilting and Stitchery* and a suggestion that the price had been in excess of $4000.

And *she* was stewing about paying $250 for a coat! A few days' work – that was all; the thought gave her a glimpse of a dazzling new kind of power.

And Jack had liked the coat too. She modelled it for him when he got home, parading the length of the living room, showing how it looked with her boots and shoulder-bag, pointing out the zip-in lining and the buttonholes which had been worked by hand so that each one looked like a perfect, satiny tear. 'Nice,' he had told her. 'Really nice.'

He appreciated good clothes. And was not above impulsive extravagance himself. Just weeks before he'd bought himself a suede vest, he who had never worn a suede vest before in his life and probably, Brenda suspected, never would. (He had not told her how much it cost; she had resisted asking; meanwhile it hung in their closet, smelling expensive and new.)

'You really do like it?' She turned so that the hem of the coat swirled out girlishly. Her hands smoothed the material over her hips and, impulsively, she gave a short, sharp, forward kick – a cancan kick, neatly executed.

'You'll be the smash hit of Philly,' he told her, smiling.

She gave him a long, level look. He was sitting back, relaxed on the brown sofa, sipping a gin and tonic from his favourite frosted glass. One leg was crossed over the other; a year ago he had started wearing executive-length socks at Brenda's suggestion. In his eyes stood approval. And he was nodding, *beautiful, beautiful* – but he was reaching sideways for the newspaper; the smile was slipping already from his face. She longed suddenly to restore it, to hold it there an instant longer, and so she announced with a final swirl: 'And guess what, Jack? It was on sale.'

His eyebrows went up. The smile seemed on the point of resurrection.

'A special sale. Marked down to a hundred and fifty dollars.'

She had said this, freezing in front of the coffee table, her hands caught voguishly in the side pockets of the red coat.

There was an instant's pause; then Jack made a gesture of celebration, lifting his glass in her direction. 'A steal,' he said.

'A steal?' She smiled icily. 'You call a hundred and fifty dollars a steal?' Her voice, she knew, sounded shrill. And she felt a shameful expression of foxiness resting on the bones of her face.

'Well, these days . . . ' Jack swirled his drink in his glass. 'Inflation . . . '

He was a man too easily deceived; there was no resistance in him; she had felt obscurely cheated. And furious with self-loathing. Why, why, why? Later she had torn up the sales slip. What if it did fade? What did it matter? She would never return it now.

This small deception was coupled with another – though in a way that owned nothing to logic; the $218 air fare to Philadelphia.

When she first decided to go to Philadelphia, the air fare had seemed the least of her worries. The real worry was how she could get away for a week.

'It's not a week, it's five days,' Jack had reminded her.

'Still . . . '

It would be different if her mother were still alive and could come and look after things. Jack's parents, though they lived close by, were too old, too nervous, away from home, even overnight; the children got on their nerves after a few hours.

Jack assured her he could manage. The children were old enough now anyway. They didn't need looking after. All they needed was food in their stomachs and someone to boot them off to bed at night. He was certainly capable of doing that.

Two days later she got around to phoning United Airlines. The fare was $218. 'What about an excursion rate?' she'd asked. Jack had suggested that she inquire about special fares.

'There's our night flight,' the sweet-voiced United girl told her. 'That's only $176.'

'What time does that get into Philadelphia?' she asked.

'Three-fifteen. A.M.'

'Three-fifteen?'

'It's very popular with businessmen.'

Brenda hesitated. Three-fifteen in the morning. In the dark. Gary, Fort Wayne, Cleveland would all be traversed in dark-ness. And in January, when the year seemed at its weakest point. She imagined the plane burrowing through black Appalachian air, eastern air. And over Philadelphia there would be the steepness of descent, and then stepping off into blindness and confusion and the garish lights of an unknown airport. There would be gateways and ramps leading off in unfamiliar directions. The thought made her feel uneasy and faintly sick.

Where could she possibly go at that hour? How? She would require sleep, a bed, a pillow.

$218 take away $176. That was $42 difference; Brenda had always been good at arithmetic, better than Jack at tabulating prices and figuring percentages. It was she who handled their bills and worked over their tax forms in the spring.

$42. It wasn't even worth considering. She gave her head a violent shake. What was $42 these days? A small price to pay for safety; she had the children to think of, and Jack too. Flying at night was riskier, everyone knew that, although Jack, who flew often, professed that it was safer than driving down the expressway at five o'clock.

Furthermore, in the few days since Jack had suggested she go, she had had time to envision the trip to Philadelphia, and part of the vision had included a morning departure – drinking coffee out of a Styrofoam cup at the airport while the sun struggled up through the streaky Chicago dawn, and finally, minutes before the actual takeoff, a burst of broad daylight.

'I think I'll just stick with the morning flight,' she said into the phone.

'Fine. I'll put you down for Flight 452 then. Bowman, you said. Is that Miss or Mrs.?'

'Mrs.' She was brisk now, all business.

'Thank you, Mrs. Bowman. And thank you for phoning United.'

A few days later the tickets arrived in the mail. She showed them to Jack.

'Seems reasonable,' he said. Then, 'I guess they didn't have a special fare?'

'No,' Brenda said. 'Not for five days.'

'Oh well . . . ' He was preoccupied, busy at the Institute and frustrated because he never seemed to find time to work on his book.

Brenda put the tickets on the hall table under the chunk of pink quartz.

Chapter Five

'EXCUSE ME,' A VERY YOUNG MAN IN A BRIGHT-BROWN SUIT was saying. He stood in the aisle, addressing Brenda, his head ducked down like a diver about to plunge. 'Excuse me, ma'am?'

Brenda looked up from her magazine. 'Yes?'

'I'm afraid you're in my seat.'

'Your seat?'

'14 A.' He opened his mouth – a pink cushion of a mouth in an eager face – revealing a surprising amount of lower gum. 'I'm supposed to be in 14 A.'

'I think it said on my boarding pass – '

'There's gotta be some mistake,' he said firmly.

Brenda, rattled, reached for her bag. 'I'm sure I've got my boarding pass here somewhere.'

'You're probably supposed to be in 14 B. The middle seat here. There isn't anyone in 14 B. Or in 14 C either. And practically everyone's on. They're shutting the doors.'

'I don't know what I did with it, my boarding pass. I had it in my hand just a minute ago.'

'Isn't that it there? That pink card. Under your coat there?

'Oh, yes, here it is.'

'Well?'

'It says 14 A. At least it looks like an A to me. Isn't that funny. And you said you had 14 A too.'

'Here.' He thrust it at her. 'You can see for yourself.'

'Isn't that strange.'

He shook his head, knocked it back fiercely, showing his lower gums again. They were as pink as a child's. 'It never fails. Every single time I get on an airplane, something gets botched up. Last time – '

'Look, why don't we just ask the stewardess if – '

'Last time,' he perched on the edge of 14 B and spoke confidentially, 'last time they put me in the smoking section. All the way from Chicago to Cleveland in the smoking section. Not

35

that I object to smokers per se, but it triggers off my allergies. And that triggers off my motion-sickness.'

'Oh,' Brenda said, unable to think of anything else.

'When I was a kid, even, I used to get sick in the car. Car sickness. We had only to go around the block and I'd be upchucking. That's why I always ask for the window seat. If you got problems with motion-sickness, they say you're better off if you sit by the window. Something psychological about – '

'I'll be happy to move over – '

'Somebody at the desk must have made a mistake or why would they give us both 14 A.'

'The computers,' Brenda suggested frailly.

'Computers. I'd like to tell them what they can do with their computers.'

'You sit here,' Brenda said, suddenly resolute, gathering her things together – her magazine, her bag, her red coat – 'and I'll sit in the middle seat.'

'You sure you don't mind?'

'Not at all.'

'You don't get motion-sickness?'

'Never,' she said, stirred by the affirmative ring in her voice, the plump, healthy strength of it.

'Someone ought to write a letter to the airline,' he said, rising, 'and tell them what they think of their service. Their so-called service, I should have said. Maybe when I get back to Chicago I'll – '

'Actually, I'd just as soon – ' Brenda stood up and squeezed past him into the aisle.

'Hey, at least let me put your coat up there for you.'

'Thank you.' Brenda handed him her raincoat and, with sorrow, watched as he wadded it into a tight ball and stuffed it into an overhead compartment.

'Whew, that's better.' He sank into the window seat and reached up to adjust the oxygen vent, a bony wrist shooting out past the shiny edge of brown sleeve. 'That too draughty on you ?'

'No, it's fine.' She sighed, feeling suddenly elderly and sex-less and accommodating; a kind of gummy pleasantness adhered to her like plaque; she could feel it coating her teeth and tongue. Her awful niceness.

'I always like to grab a good lungful of oxygen before takeoff. They say it helps fight down that queasiness you sometimes get . . . '

Brenda opened her magazine. *The Quilter's Quarterly*. Jack had given her a subscription for her birthday. The latest issue contained, among other things, diagrams for three-dimensional animal quilts for children. At one time these kinds of quilts would have interested her; now they struck her as gimmicky, especially a bright-hued elephant quilt which had large button eyes and a three-foot-long stuffed trunk. Only four years ago, she would have looked at that and thought –

'Hey, that's really something!' The young man was peering over her shoulder. She could feel his breath on her neck.

'Pardon?'

'That elephant thing there. Cute idea. For a little kid, I mean.'

'Hmmmm.' A strand of hair fell over her eyes and she brushed it aside. She had never worn her hair in quite this way before, blown loose like this, rising from a centre parting. Hairspray was a thing of the past, she'd been told by the hairdresser the day before. Nowadays the look was strong and healthy. Perms – forget them. Everyone wanted the natural glossy look. Let it flow, let it find its own shape.

When she emerged from the He/She Salon on Lake Street yesterday, her body had seemed exceptionally buoyant; the air around her head had felt tender, and, looking about, she had experienced an acute longing for – what? – spring. Almost a belief that it was spring.

But today sections of her hair kept falling over her eyes. ('You should try one of the new ornamental combs,' the hairdresser had urged her. 'Or a flower.' The thought of herself with a flower pinned in her hair made her want to laugh out loud. She had meant to tell Jack about that – couldn't he just see her, cooking dinner with a flower over one ear.)

'Hey, it looks like we're taking off,' the young man shrilled. He glanced excitedly at his watch. Bony wrist, Brenda noticed, an absence of calcium. And freckles, hundreds of freckles; the kind of skin that was hopelessly vulnerable. 'Five minutes late. We'll make up for it once we're up there.'

'Probably,' Brenda said pleasantly. Pleasant, pleasant, always pleasant. Aside from quiltmaking, pleasantness was her one talent. (She said this to herself with sour pleasure, not for a minute believing it.)

'Oh, boy. This is the part I don't like. Going up. Once you're up there it's not so bad, you can relax.'

'Yes,' Brenda agreed,

'And coming down. That's bad news too.'

'Uh-huh.' She watched him grope for his seatbelt, his hands flapping pinkly at his sides.

'Here,' she said, coming to his rescue. 'Here's the buckle.'

'Thanks. Tricky things these belts.'

'Yes.' She turned the page to an article on intaglio quilting. It was a European technique; she'd heard about it at the Craft Guild; it was difficult to do well, but offered some interesting effects. She would have to try it some time, she decided.

'You off to Cleveland too?' came the voice at her side.

'No. Philadelphia.'

A short silence. Then, 'I've never been to Philadelphia.'

This time the silence was longer. Brenda decided to give up on her article.

'We don't have a branch in Philly,' he confided. 'Only Cleveland. And Syracuse, New York.'

'Oh.'

'And Chicago, of course. As a matter of fact, Chicago happens to be our head office.'

'Hmmmm.'

'As a matter of fact, I just might be in line for a transfer to the Cleveland office next year. Permanent. Not that I'm all that hot about Cleveland as a city. It's a dying city. Practically dead. That's what they say, anyhow.

'Is it?'

'I don't really want to get transferred all that much, but the thing is, the supervisor in the office, he and I don't always see eye to eye.'

'That's too bad.'

'It's not policy. On policy we see eye to eye. It's more what you might call a kind of personality conflict.'

'Uh-huh.'

'Most of the time it's not so bad, him and me. But then, for no reason at all that I can put my finger on, some little thing will trigger him off. This guy gets just violent. A real temper like you've never seen. Irish, but they say that doesn't hold any more. Still, he's Irish by descent, for what it's worth. We were having this discussion one day and all of a sudden he called me a dumb bastard.'

'Oh?'

'Excuse my French. But that's what he called me. Just came right out and called me a bastard. Right in the office there, with everyone standing around listening. Oh, boy.'

'Terrible.'

'You can imagine how that made me feel.'

'Yes, I certainly can.'

'Imagine how you'd feel if someone called you a . . . ' he paused.

'Someone did once.'

'Did what?'

'Someone called me a bastard once,' Brenda said.

'You? Really?'

'Yes.'

'I . . . I didn't think that word was, well, was ever used with ladies. Only men.'

'This was when I was very young. A little girl in school.'

'So what did you do?'

'Well, not much. I mean, I'd never heard the word before. I must have been only about six.'

'Six! But you still remember, huh?' His mouth fell open. Yellow teeth, plump pink gums, a soft, nursery look. 'That must have been really awful.'

'The funny thing is, I found out later that I really was a bastard.'

'Huh?'

'In the real sense of the word, yes, I was a bastard.'

'You – '

'Meaning,' Brenda said, 'I didn't have a father.'

'Everyone has a father.' He giggled slightly at this and reached up to readjust the oxygen vent.

'What I mean is, my mother never got married. So that makes me, technically speaking anyway, a bastard.'

'And this kid at your school, I guess he knew it, huh? About your mother.'

'He must have.'

'Kids can be cruel, you know that.'

'The funny thing is, I didn't mind. At least not very much.

39

Not when I found out what it meant, that it was a real word. I remember I looked it up in the dictionary at school. I must have been older than six, maybe about eight or nine. Anyway, it was right there in the big school dictionary we had at the back of the room. So it seemed all right.'

'It must have been tough, not having a father.'

'Oh, I don't know . . .'

'I mean, no dad coming home at night.'

'The only thing was that my mother had to work. And this was in the days when most of the mothers stayed home and just kept house. But that was the only thing. Otherwise I don't think I missed much.'

'My old man was a pretty good guy. I'll say that much for him.'

'That's nice.'

'But, gee, I'll bet it was sort of rough at times. I mean the stigma, carrying the stigma. Like, nowadays it isn't anything. Look at Vanessa Redgrave. But back then – '

'Actually,' Brenda cleared her throat, making her voice clear and firm – several of her friends had commented over the years on the clarity of her voice – 'actually I don't remember being particularly conscious of any stigma. Maybe it was the neighbourhood I lived in. Or maybe it was just my mother, the kind of person she was.'

'You must have had a lot of self-confidence then. They say if you're born with a lot of self-confidence you can rise above just about anything.'

'You may be right.' She smoothed the cover of her magazine with the palm of her hand, regarded the ring on her finger, a small sapphire; Jack had given it to her two years ago. A sentimental occasion.

'Me, I never had much self-confidence. I'm taking this course now at the Y. Wednesday nights. How to be more assertive, push yourself forward. I figure it will help me in business.'

'How's it going?'

'I don't know. I just don't know. Either you've got it or you don't, that's what some experts think. That's another reason I'm thinking seriously of transferring to the Cleveland area next year. It would be kind of a new start, if you see what I mean.'

'I think I do.'

'You can't run away from your problems though, I know that.'

'No, that's true.'

'Of course, I'm young.' He shot her a glance which seemed to Brenda to be partly apologetic, partly sly. 'I've got lots of time to develop my, you know, my potential.'

'Oh, yes,' Brenda said. 'That's true.'

'Hey, look out there.'

'Clouds.'

'Pretty, huh?'

'Yes.'

The clouds rolled by the window, white as steam. Brenda brightened, feeling suddenly at peace. The relief of not being young! The pleasure of being bored, of deserving that pleasure, of being able to admit to it. This poor, freckled creature beside her, working his jaw, struggling against airsickness, gasping for oxygen and courage. She should feel pity for him; he had all his life to cope with, all of it. She should reach out and give his knee a consoling pat. Consolation – that was what he most needed, though he didn't know it. She smiled past his lap, sending her soft look of pity out across the clouds. Poor boy, poor young man.

Nevertheless, when he opened his mouth a minute later to inquire again where it was she was going, she replied with uncharacteristic sharpness, 'Philadelphia.'

She said it curtly, a sting of vinegar on her tongue, not at all the way she had pronounced it at home, not the way she had whispered it over the morning coffee: Philadelphia.

Stupid. Foolish. What had she expected? What on earth had she expected?

Not this. She glanced at her travelling companion, who with his little finger was attempting to dislodge something from a back tooth. He had already forgotten what she had told him – or rather he had disregarded it. What had she expected? Not this, not this.

Chapter Six

THE WORLD WAS NOT FILLED WITH BEAUTIFUL PEOPLE, NO, certainly it was not; and Brenda was not such a fool as to believe it was.

Fashion models, TV stars – they had nothing to do with the way people really were. Real people, even the strongest of them, were sadly perforated by weakness and inconsistency. Failure was everywhere, also selfishness, cowardice, disharmony, and physical imperfection – gross physical imperfection. People did not live for great ideals or for noble visions; they lived for their divorces, their promotions, the instant gratifications of sex and food. They told lies, they smiled slyly at themselves in mirrors as they passed. Brenda knew this only too well. 'Brenda is a realist,' Jack used to say, back in the days when he made such statements. 'Brenda sees things the way they are.'

Did she? In their early married days, when her husband Jack made these claims for her sense of reality, he was, she suspected, stating something else as well: that *he* was *not* a realist. That his vision of things was romantic, withheld, speculative. There was such a thing as allegory, there was such a thing as metaphor, there were the rewarding riches of symbol and myth. There were layers and layers – infinite layers – of meaning.

Perspective altered events, Jack liked to say; he was working then on his thesis, a new view of the explorer LaSalle and his voyages of discovery. Brenda, who was doing the typing in the evening and helping him with the index, thought at the time that he would never get it finished. The research and writing took all of one year and part of a second summer. That second summer was the worst. Their student apartment near Lincoln Park was hot and airless, especially at night when the heat had been piling up all day – ninety degrees, ninety-five.

Brenda remembered how the two of them, hot and irritable, had gone for a walk late one night in the park, and had come unexpectedly, upon a genuine sixties phenomenon, a love-in.

She had been reading about flower children in *Time* magazine and had heard the slogan, 'Make Love Not War.' And now, here was a demonstration right in the middle of Lincoln Park, not six blocks away from where she and Jack lived.

Bodies were everywhere, stretched on the cool grass; guitars, long hair, some singing, low voices calling, strewn flowers, a smell of sweet smoke rising in the air – she knew what *that* was. There were swaying shadows from large trees, and overhead, a blown nursery-rhyme globe of a moon. A TV camera, WGTV, whirred away, making its own circle of light.

Brenda had been amazed and excited by the spectacle, but Jack had watched from a distance, standing back under a tree, observing, commenting, and composing, it seemed to Brenda, instant documentation. This bizarre scene might be viewed as a morsel of history. Already, a fraction of hindsight could be attached to it. Events, said Jack, even while they were unfolding, could be softened and explained by context, suspended on thin strands of reason and analogy. And – most difficult of all for Brenda to grasp – they could be undercut by a disturbing existential edge: is this real? is this really happening?

Brenda's view of the world was simpler, Jack seemed to believe. Things were a certain way, and that was all there was to it. It was what he loved about her. He had fallen in love with her level glance, with her quick way of nodding and absorbing and calling a spade a spade, and especially, oh especially, with the way she held up her hands and, with a gesture of ripe female acceptance – lucky, lucky Brenda – shrugged.

The simple act of shrugging. It was so exotic, so European, but at the same time so primitive; he saw it romantically as a chunk of ancestral heritage which had luckily come his way.

Shrugging, in truth, was almost the only visible characteristic Brenda had inherited from her Polish mother: an atavistic raising of the shoulders, elbows levitated, hands opened up to the sky, a gesture which proclaimed with wonderful helpless Slavic silence – let it be, so be it, God's will be done. Jack always maintained, fondly, that Brenda had given one of her famous shrugs the first day they had met, eating lunch at Roberto's. She had been halfway through her bowl of vegetable soup when it happened. Up went her hands. Up went her eyebrows. Something about it, the simplicity, the grace; it had done him in, he liked to say, done him in on the spot.

43

He was not a shrugger himself. (It was a joke of theirs, in the early days, that he was equipped instead with all the good lower-middle-class gestures: chin-stroking, lip-biting, finger-drumming, foot-tapping.) Nor were their children, Rob and Laurie, given to shrugging; they were nail-biters, shin-scratchers; Rob sometimes wrinkled his forehead in a peculiarly lopsided way; Laurie kicked at table legs and ground her teeth at night. Only Brenda shrugged. She was, she supposed, the last of the line.

But even she seemed to be shrugging less frequently these days – though Jack liked to claim she had a way of shrugging with her voice. Something had happened, she wasn't sure what, but nothing seemed as simple as it once had. She had children who were growing up. Her mother was dead. She herself was forty years old. There was a reluctance, now, to say: well, that's the way it is. When she looked at something these days – a face, a house, an expanse of scenery – she was more likely to think, is this all there is?

At times she found herself longing for that other self, the Brenda of old, smiling and matter-of-fact. (Her organization of the LaSalle index had been a model of logic; Dr. Middleton at the Institute said he had never seen anything to equal it.) Whatever it was that had come into her life during the last year or so had brought frustration with it. A restless anger and a sense of undelivered messages. Early in the fall, soon after they got back from the lake, she had begun work on a new quilt. It was still unfinished, lying there on a chair in a corner of her workroom. She had set it aside temporarily in order to work on *The Second Coming*, which, while experimental in workmanship, was more traditional in design, less risky for an exhibition (judges could be quirky; it was better to strike a balance in these things.) The unfinished quilt – that was how she thought of it, *The Unfinished Quilt* – had no real pattern to it, only a cauldron of colour, yellow mostly. There was a bounty and a vigour to it which magnetized her. Yet it represented a worrying departure, almost a violation of the order and equanimity of her early quilt. 'There is a satisfying orderliness in Brenda Bowman's work,' the article in the *Elm Leaves Weekly* had declared.

Sometimes at night she dreamed about it. Only three-quarters finished, it already contained hundreds of pieces. There were particles of colour as small as the tips of her fingers, a pulse of life travelling atop a torrent of private energy. She had felt a wish to trap this torrent in stitches, but had put off the moment of completion. The quilting frame seemed altogether too rigid to contain what she wanted. Instead, she had begun the process of quilting on a lap frame – and before the actual piecing was finished. She was, in fact, uncertain about how to finish it, and feared that the weight of her hand might be overly heavy. She wanted a pattern that was severe but lyrical; she would have to be careful or she might rush it toward something finite and explanatory, when all the while she wanted more. Perhaps, she admitted to herself, staring out the window late one afternoon at the weak sunlight striping the garage roof, perhaps she wanted more than mere cloth and stitching could accomplish. Nevertheless, more was suddenly what she wanted. What she spent her time thinking about. *More*.

'You've got terrific cheekbones,' Leah Wallberg once told Brenda.

When Leah Wallberg was younger, before she and Irv were married, she had worked as a stage-designer for the Goodman Theatre. She still dabbled in this and that, working in what she liked to call a semiprofessional capacity. It had been Leah Wallberg who designed the set for the recent Elm Park Little Theatre production of *Hamlet*. (White and yellow drapery and an arrangement of stairs, all very stark and pure, it was reported to Brenda, who had missed the play.) It was said that Leah had a good eye for line; cheekbones were the kind of thing she took note of. 'It's not like Hepburn bones. What you've got, Brenda, is wide bones. Which is really more interesting-looking in the long run.'

Where had these cheekbones of hers come from? From her mother? Elsa had been a heavy woman all her life – or at least as far back as Brenda could remember. At one point, shortly before she died, she had weighed over two hundred and thirty pounds. She was a big-boned woman, she said, big all over. Large breasts under print-jersey dresses – she favoured blues and whites – spoke of bulk, and also of a perfumed looseness. Girdles and brassieres gave her cramps, and so she dispensed with them after work and at week-ends, allowing her flesh to flow as it wished. 'Wait'll I get this girdle off and have a cup of coffee.' For years that had been her greeting to her daughter,

Brenda, when she came in from work at night. Her hips, almost sighing with release, spread wide; her escaped thighs were baggy and blotched where the elastic had cut in. (Brenda, growing up and sharing with her the dimly lit bathroom, had observed these lacerations calmly – clearly this was to be her future too.) Elsa's upper arms were round and as thick as the waist of a smaller woman. After a big meal she slapped her hips in a friendly conspiratorial way. Fat, if not prized, was at least accommodated. Elsa's face had melted into something wide and florid, and imbedded in that face had been a pair of small, lively eyes and a mouth that went into a crimped, lipsticked H when she laughed. If Elsa Maria Pulaski had even been known for her wide cheekbones, Brenda had not heard of it; her face was a circle of smiling fat. Where in that circle was there a need for cheekbones?

Brenda's cheekbones, on the other hand, had a sleek, pulled-back look of cleanliness. Her eyes were slightly creased, faintly Oriental – what Jack called Magyar eyes. In her high-school graduation picture she had looked healthy and winsome; some of her friends had seen a strong resemblance to June Allyson. She had been voted 'Miss Friendly Personality' of her class, and that title was printed in shaded script beneath her picture. In those days her hair had been lighter – dishwater blonde – though in her daydreams she liked to think of herself as a honey blonde. ('I absolutely adore your honey-coloured hair,' he whispered softly.) The light hair, the Magyar eyes, and the sleek, flat bones of her cheeks had given her a look of amiability.

The image was a true one. She had a certain natural ease, which, as she grew older, earned her the reputation for great reasonableness. 'How come you don't have any hang-ups like the rest of us slobs?' Hap Lewis had once asked her. She didn't know. Her own reflection stared back at her, pleasant, serene, a little sly. Behind that face lay acceptance and good nature. Perhaps Jack was right. She was a realist. She took things as they came.

Why was it then that during the last few years certain things had begun to annoy her. Enrage her. She found it hard to account for the contempt she sometimes felt, this new secret fastidiousness. Who was she anyway to make judgments? Brenda Pulaski Bowman (fatherless) of Cicero, Illinois, now a resident of Elm Park – though not the best end of Elm Park.

Graduate of Katherine Gibbs School of Secretarial Science. She had taken the two-year course instead of the twelve-month one, but even so, that wasn't the same as going to college, not even teachers' college. Who did she think she was, she asked herself roughly, who the hell did she think she was? Why should it suddenly start to bother her that Jack stuck business cards and Chargex receipts in the frame of their bedroom mirror? He had been doing this ever since she'd known him. Sometimes he left them there for weeks. He also had a habit of putting old rubber bands around doorknobs. Why did he do this? Frugality? Tidiness? She didn't know. But suddenly she minded. She broke them off with a snap and threw then away. She yanked the cards out of the mirror, tossing them into Jack's dresser drawer on top of his rolled socks.

Other annoyances: the name Farrah Fawcett-Majors made her go numb. 'You should see her on *Charlie's Angels*,' her son Rob said in one of their pally moments. She watched one night. Disbelievingly. She felt herself twitch with boredom and contempt. 'It's only supposed to be entertainment,' Rob had said stiffly. 'Hmmmm,' she said in a condemning way – she who had grown up on *Fibber McGee and Molly* and *Duffy's Tavern*. Who was she to harp about Farrah Fawcett-Majors?

When she went to a party not long ago at Larry and Janey Carpenter's she noticed, with inexplicable fury, that there was a copy of the *New Yorker* in their bathroom. The bathroom itself was the showpiece of the Carpenter house, with its tinted skylight, its suspended sculpture carved from the backbone of a whale, its antique bathtub painted purple. Aubergine, Larry called it. Aubergine! Most of the things in the bathroom she admired; only the presence of the *New Yorker* seemed intolerable, positioned as it was on a neat white shelf over the toilet. *New Yorker* whimsy combined with private gruntings and strainings; it seemed to her to be obscene. She sneered at herself for this new delicacy. Who was she anyway to look down on the Carpenters? Larry Carpenter had gone to Princeton. Or one of those places.

She had had a note from Laurie's teacher which began with the words: 'As you know, we feel that Laurie is one of the most unique kids in the seventh grade.' 'Unique is unique,' Brenda had stormed to Jack. 'You can't be one of the most unique anything.' ('You're overreacting,' Jack replied with a puzzled look.)

She cringed when Rob left the house on the way to school in the morning and called out a loud, hoarse 'Ciao.' Ciao yourself, she wanted to yell at him. Anything would be better than ciao; nothing at all would be better than ciao.

She had been irked with Jack's best friend, Bernie Koltz, for sending her a floral arrangement for Christmas. 'Does he think I'm ready for the geriatric ward?' she complained to Jack. 'Look at these. Gladiolas!' ('Gladioli,' Jack had corrected her absently. 'Go to hell,' she told him, which immediately cheered her up.)

She went one day to buy a new blouse in a store called The Cockeyed Cat. It was on Michigan Boulevard. There was a deep café-au-lait carpet, a mirrored ceiling, and soft, Lucite lighting fixtures. The blouses were encased in transparent bags and cost between eighty and a hundred and eighty dollars. Tweed skirts cost two hundred dollars. There were matching tweed blazers, and she was inspecting the label on one of these when she heard in the background the soft sounds of Simon and Garfunkel singing 'Scarborough Fair'.

> Are you going to Scarborough Fair
> Parsley, Sage, Rosemary and Thyme.
> Remember me to one who lives there.
> She once was a true love of mine.

It was a song she had loved once. It reminded her of lying on the pier at the lake or cutting the grass in the backyard. But in this store, issuing from louvered openings in the wall, it sounded sweet and sappy. The lyrics were shallow, meaningless. Why hadn't she ever noticed that before?

Just before Christmas she and Jack had been invited to dinner at Milton and Shirley McInnis's in Evanston. Milt was the new head of restoration at the Institute, and Shirley, tall, brisk, brunette, was a social-worker in the Evanston school system; the family had spent two years in Zurich, and the children, when they came into the dining room one by one to be introduced, had shaken hands gravely. 'She's quite bright,' Shirley McInnis had murmured of Daphne. 'He's awfully bright,' she said of Roger. 'We think she's going to be bright,' she had confided about little Stephanie, four years old. Brenda, with a forkful of risotto halfway to her mouth, had felt indignant, then put upon, finally angry.

Last week they had gone, as usual, to have Sunday breakfast at Jack's parents'. Ma and Dad Bowman lived in a dark, old six-room apartment in Austin. Breakfast was always the same. Sara Lee coffee cake, cinnamon or cherry. Perked coffee. Plates set out at the kitchen table. Jack's mother humming, wearing bedroom slippers, pouring coffee into striped mugs. Brenda loved them both; they loved her and thought of her as a daughter. But last Sunday, sitting at the table, they had handed her an envelope. It was a bon voyage card with sparkles on it and a picture of bluebirds winging through a blue sky. Inside the card was a ten-dollar bill folded in half. 'For your vacation trip,' Ma Bowman had smiled, suddenly shy. 'To have yourself a real good meal on us,' Dad Bowman had winked.

Brenda had felt wounded, indignant. She was going to a national exhibit; she was one of the exhibitors; she had been *invited* to participate. Ma and Dad Bowman didn't present Jack with ten-dollar bills when he went off to Milwaukee or Detroit to present papers at the other branches of the Institute. Further-more, the card seemed a reminder that she was, perhaps, abandoning her family, that the trip she was taking was not one of necessity, but merely an indulgence. She thanked them profusely – they meant well, they meant only to be kind – but she had barely managed to restrain her tears.

What did this mean, this new impatience, this seething reaction to petty irritations? It could get worse, she saw. You could become crippled by this kind of rage. It was all so wasteful in the long run. And what, she wondered, was the name of this new anger, this seismic sensitivity to the cheap-ness of things?

Part of it, she sensed, was regret, for lately she had been assailed by a sense of opportunities missed. Events from the past reached out and inspired fruitless feelings of resentment. She recalled that long-ago summer night in Lincoln Park – the love-in, the long-haired flower children lying on the grass. She had watched, excitedly at first, but then, too soon, had suc-cumbed to Jack's watchful detachment. Now she wanted the scene replayed. She wanted to set down her handbag by the shadowy roots of a tree and take off her shoes. She would step forward, a little hesitantly. She imagined the moon touching her smooth cheeks; she imagined how the ground would feel, cool, a little gritty where the grass was worn down. In no time at all she would be submerged in the sweetness of music and the proximity of those other bodies. Brothers and sisters, all so young. Someone would call out her name in a low voice . . .

Two problems faced her, it seemed, and both involved an inability to make distinctions. *The Unfinished Quilt* lying on a chair in her workroom; it was either the best thing she had ever done or it was the worst. She did not know which. And this new anger she felt; it might mean no more than that she needed a few days away from home. A vacation. A change of pace.

Or it might mean – and a new wave of anger overtook her at the thought – it might mean that all her life had been a mistake.

Chapter Seven

'Name?'
   'Brenda Bowman.'
'Spelled like it sounds?'
'Yes.'
'You're one of the last ones to register.'
'Am I?' Brenda set down her suitcase.

The woman at the desk ran a ballpoint pen down a list of names. Her greying hair, the colour of roofing paper, was caught in a careless roll and anchored with a slice of tortoise comb. She had a look of intelligence and frenzy, and an extreme accuracy about her make-up. 'And you're from?' she asked.

'Chicago.'

'Chicago?' She looked up and gave Brenda a smile which was wide and bright and which seemed to take in all of the hotel lobby. Then, 'I'm afraid I can't find you listed here. Did you go through our preregistration procedure?'

'I sent in a form – '

'Hmmmm, funny, you're not listed here under Chicago.'

'Elm Park, maybe?' Brenda had to speak forcefully because of an ornamental fountain bubbling noisily behind her. 'I'm a member of the Chicago Craft Guild, but I live in Elm Park, Illinois. That's a suburb of Chicago.'

'Oh!' A look of lively interest. 'I've heard of Elm Park. Isn't that the place where Hemingway – ?'

'That's Oak Park. It's right next – '

'Here we go. I knew I'd find it. Brenda Bowman, Mrs. From 576 North Franklin Boulevard?'

'That's it.'

'All the way from Franklin Boulevard to the Franklin Court Arms.' She gave a dry little laugh and threw back her head in an animated way.

'I hadn't thought of that,' Brenda said.

'I'll tell you what I'll do. I'm going to make a little note here that you're really part of the Chicago delegation.'

'Fine,' Brenda said, feeling happier and liking the sound of the word delegation. 'Thank you.'

'Everything looks A-OK, Mrs. Bowman. You're all registered now. And we received your cheque for the fee. Just a min and I'll type you out a receipt on the spot.'

'Oh, you don't need to bother with – '

'You'll need it when tax time rolls round.' Her bright eyes rolled upwards. 'You can deduct it on your form. It's a valid deduction.'

'I keep forgetting about things like that,' Brenda said. 'I've only been paying taxes for the last two years.' She gave a laugh, more girlish than she'd intended.

'Every penny counts these days.'

'That's right,' Brenda said with enthusiasm.

'And your exhibit? It's quilts, right?'

'I've got them with me,' Brenda pointed to the large carton beside her suitcase. 'Right here.'

'If you want to leave it with me, I'll make sure it gets looked after.'

'Oh, that would be wonderful. I'd really appreciate it. It's so bulky – '

'And here's your name tag. We've got this new kind with adhesive backing this year. You just peel off the strip and stick it on your coat. They won't poke holes in your clothes like last year. We had I don't know how many complaints. So we switched to these – '

'I didn't come last year. In fact, this is my first time – '

'And here's your kit, all ready for you. As you can see, it's got your name on it already.'

'That's beautiful. The kit, I mean.'

'Isn't it gorgeous? It was designed for us in New York. Sort of captures the craft theme, we all thought – '

'With that textured look – '

'And the earth tones. We asked for earth tones.'

'I like earth tones,' Brenda heard herself saying.

'Now here, inside, you have your map of Philadelphia. Courtesy of the Tourist Board, bless their hearts. You been to Philly before? It doesn't matter, it's easy to get around here. And here's your bumper-sticker.'

'Bumper-sticker?'

'It says "I'm a Quilter." We've got versions for the weavers too, and the spinners. That's the one I like – "I'm a Spinner."'

'Are you a spinner?'

'Oh no, not me. I'm the PR person for the Association. Betty Vetter. I should have introduced myself before now. I got the idea for the bumper-stickers last year, and they were a real hit.'

'Oh,' Brenda said, smiling across the welcome desk at Betty Vetter.

'Besides the map and the bumper-sticker you'll find a card listing the inner-city churches and synagogues, the service of your choice, courtesy of the Interfaith Council of Phil – '

'I don't think I'll need – '

'And, in case you've got some time on your hands, which I very much doubt – we've got a great programme this year – but, just in case, there's some touristy info. They've got one of those Ye Olde Walking Tours. Which is supposed to be excellent. All run by volunteers. Women who really know their stuff.'

'That sounds – '

'And a little sewing kit, thread, needles. And here's one of those disposable raincoats. Donated by one of the yarn companies. You never know, it might come in handy. Although I see you brought a raincoat.'

'Yes. At least it's supposed to be showerproof – '

'And here's a make-up kit, sample lipstick, sample blush, what have you. Donated by New Women Industries of Houston – '

'Thank you,' Brenda said, hearing her thank-you drowned by the hotel fountain, which seemed to be pumping and splashing more furiously now. For an instant she imagined she felt a fine spray reaching the back of her neck.

'And here's the brochure on theatres in town. *Mame* is playing; that's always good entertainment. And some new thing about a man dying. If you want tickets to anything, just talk to them at the desk. And here's your directory. You've got the name of everyone taking part in the Exhibition, plus their spouses or whatever. You don't have any accompanying person with you, do you?'

'No,' Brenda said, resting her eyes on Betty Vetter's tiny brown earrings. 'No,' she said more loudly. 'I'm here on my own.'

'Wonderful, wonderful,' Betty Vetter said. Besides the earrings she wore a man's antique pocket-watch on a chain around her neck, and when she leaned forward to write, it bumped softly against the desk. Her hands were reddish, thin, without rings, and under her eyes there were small, scaly pouches, which were oddly attractive. 'Since you're alone,' she said to Brenda, leaning forward on her elbows, 'could I ask you one great big favour?'

'Of course,' Brenda said, wanting to be helpful.

'Well, it seems we've got a' – Betty Vetter paused and pursed her lips – 'a leetle bit of a problem on our cotton-pickin' hands.'

'Oh?'

'What happened is, we're the victims of our own crazy success. Everyone had such a great time last year that, well, all of a sudden we've got more people registering than we thought we'd get in a million years. I mean, they're literally coming out of the woodwork. And with the spouses and accompanying persons, well, it looks like everyone wanted to come to Philadelphia, Pennsylvania all of a sudden. Anyway, to make a long story short, the Franklin is seriously over-booked.'

'Oh?' Brenda said again.

'We had to get some extra rooms at the Holiday Inn and even at the Travelodge. The problem is really because of the metallurgists.'

'The metallurgists?'

'Metallurgists. International Society of. They're overlapping with us, wouldn't you know it. Hundreds of them. What I'd like to ask you, Mrs. Bowman – or is it okay if I just call you Brenda?'

'Brenda's fine,' Brenda said quickly.

'And you call me Betty. Everyone does. Crazy Betty, the wild woman. I know it's sort of inconvenient, Brenda, and I hate like hell to even suggest it, but, well, would you mind very much if you had to share a room?'

'Share a room? Well, I . . . ' Brenda's voice stopped working. She could feel the dryness of her lips.

'Like, we've got quite a few women here on their own who're doubling up. And it isn't as if they're really strangers. I mean, we're all part of the craft movement, right? So it's not like they're, you know, untrustworthy. We feel sure that – '

'It's not that.'

'And,' Betty Vetter's voice hurried on, 'it's not for long. Only five nights. And you know how much time you spend in a hotel

54

room when you're at a conference. Hardly any at all – just to sleep, really, and take your shower. Furthermore,' she took a breath and tugged at her watch,' it goes without saying that the room rate would be way down. Let's see, you were originally booked at $41 per day. If you share a room it would be $32. I've had the absolute assurance of the management here that we could get it for $32. That's a net saving of, let's see, $41 take away – '

'Nine dollars.'

'Nine dollars.'

'It's not the money, ' Brenda said.

'Well, then? The ballpoint pen paused, hooked in air.

'It's just – '

Damn it, damn it. Brenda felt tired. She *was* tired. She was expecting her period; that always made the backs of her legs ache. And the Philadelphia airport had been enormous and oddly organized, so different from O'Hare, and the air-freight man had been abrupt, almost, in fact, impolite. Her red raincoat was wrinkled down the front, and there was a tiny spot on the collar which just might be grease. Yes, she was tired. She wanted to lie down on a bed and close her eyes. And she had visualized – for a month she had visualized – a small room of her own, a single bed, severely made up with hotel linen, almost a nun's bed. A chair in one corner, and a table where she might, if she liked, have coffee and muffins in the morning. Bran muffins. There would be a long, narrow window which overlooked a street; this street would be faintly historical and there would be a wall of pinkish brick opposite; and a street lamp probably, one of those ornate old iron –

It was not to be. A wave of disappointment struck her. She looked at Betty Vetter, who sat waiting. She tried to smile at her, and did. Betty Vetter smiled back. Suddenly all that was left of her disappointment was a mild pang of regret – and even that began almost immediately to recede. The plate of muffins spun off into space. The fountain behind her bubbled cheerfully.

'I can't tell you, Brenda, how much we do appreciate this. I mean – the fact is, I don't know what else we can do at this moment in time.'

'It really isn't that important – '

'That's great. That's terrific. Frankly, that's the spirit we were hoping for. But you'd be surprised how many people don't adjust to the idea of – '

'It's only for five nights after all.'

'And we all of us believe in the same thing.'

'Uh-huh,' Brenda said inadequately.

'They'll give you your key at the desk. It's room 2424.' She gave Brenda a twinkly look and said, 'Hope you're not scared of heights.'

'Oh, no. Heights never – '

'And your roommate will be, let's see, Verna Glanville. Another quilter.'

'Did you say Verna Glanville?'

'She's a great girl. You're going to get along like a house – '

'From Norfolk, Virginia?'

'I think so.'

'Verna of Virginia. That's the name she goes by. Professionally.'

'Is that right? She checked in a couple of hours ago, and she was a really good sport. About the balls-up with the rooms. "The more the merrier," she said. That was when I asked her if she'd mind sharing a room –'

'It's really funny,' Brenda said, 'but you know I was just reading an article about her the other day. Verna of Virginia. About a quilt she's just sold to the Metropolitan Museum in New York – '

'She's pretty well known in her field – '

'Oh, she's one of the best, the very best – '

' – and a smile for everyone, that's how she struck me.'

'I was hoping I'd get a chance to meet her. And now, here I'm going to be – '

'One more thing, Mrs. Bowman. Brenda. They asked us to have everyone meet in the Constitution Room at four sharp for the rundown on the programme. That's just one floor up. The Mezzanine. It's just going on four now, so if you want to go there directly, I'll send your baggage up to your room.'

'Thank you so much' – Brenda paused – 'Betty.'

'It's nothing.'

'I really appreciate – '

'No trouble at all. Glad to help out. That's what we're here for.

56

Chapter Eight

THE LOBBY OF THE FRANKLIN COURT ARMS, WITH ITS BITTER-green carpeting and its natural-wood walls, reminds Brenda of the out-of-doors, in particular of a corner of Columbus Park in Chicago where she and Jack and the children used to go for walks on summer evenings. There are large potted plants – trees really – and near the Welcome desk, the big noisy fountain made of stainless steel sheets and glass tubes. Everywhere the lighting falls with a soft-tinted focus that seems to emit, along with its invisibility, a kind of purring sound. The stairs that rise to the mezzanine level – the convention floor – are made of light-coloured wood. Oak perhaps, Brenda thinks. The steps are exceptionally thick, with open risers; she almost floats on her way up. Baskets of greenery hang overhead, most of them of a variety Brenda doesn't recognize, pale-green, feathery, threaded with light. Some kind of fern almost certainly.

The Constitution Room is rapidly filling up with people; most of them, Brenda notices, are women. Well, that was to be expected. There are two or three men sitting together on one side, and there is a handsome man with a grey beard standing at the front, gesticulating largely. At the far end of the room is a platform draped with beige-and-brown burlap panels – the same burlap used on the kitbag which she carries in her hand. Folding chairs have been lined up in curved rows, hundreds of them, most of them occupied, and hotel attendants are struggling to fit one more row in at the back. The room echoes with voices, a friendly-sounding hubbub bouncing off the smooth walls and rising to the wood-arched ceiling, where three chandeliers twinkle and glitter. Brenda touches her name card with the tip of her finger and looks for a place to sit down.

'Shhhh,' a woman is saying. 'Shhh.'

'They're trying to get started up there.'

'Ladies and gentleman – '

'What man?' A raucous laugh.

'Excuse me,' Brenda whispers. 'Is this seat taken?'

'I'm saving it for someone. She's coming in a minute or two.'

'Sorry.'

'Shhh.'

'Ladies and gentlemen, can we please come to order.'

'Excuse me, is anyone sitting here?'

''Fraid so.'

'Can you hear me in the back of the room? If you can't hear, would you mind putting up your hand. Testing, one, two, three.'

'Sounds okay,' a hoarse voice calls out, 'but what about some more chairs back here.'

'They're coming,' a man's voice says. 'They should be here in a few minutes.'

'If I could have your attention – '

'Excuse me, Madam Chairman, Madam Chair*person*, rather.' It is the same hoarse voice, booming from a back corner of the room.

Brenda feels a tug on her sleeve and hears a sweet voice saying, 'There's an empty place over here.'

'Oh, thank you.'

'I'm Lenora Knox. From Sante Fe.' She wears glasses with pale blue frames, and her hair is brown and slightly wavy.

'Oh, you've come a long way.' Brenda says this in a social way.

'And you're . . . ?' Lenora smiles pressingly. Her features are tiny.

'Brenda Bowman. From Chicago. Well, the Chicago area – '

'I've never been to Chicago. But someday we hope – I mean with the Art Institute and everything – '

'Will the Fourth Annual National Handicrafts Exhibition please come to order. '

'What are you in?' Lenora Knox whispers in her girlish voice.

'Quilts.'

'Me too!'

'Really?'

'Isn't that a coincidence. We'll have to get together and have coffee and really talk quilts.'

'Madam Chairperson, may I pose a question?' It is the voice again.

'Out of order.'

'Not on the agenda.'

'It so happens,' the voice persists, 'that this is a matter of the greatest urgency. Which I am sure the Chair will recognize if she will just give me a chance to speak.'

'I'm afraid – ' The chairperson is a stout blonde woman of about forty. She has a soft, pretty face and an air of calm.

'May I assure the Chair that this is a question that concerns each and every one of us here.'

'Who's that?' Brenda whispers.

'I don't know.' Lenora Knox has a way of speaking that is sweet and small and clean. 'This is my first time at one of these things.'

'Mine too.'

'I had no idea there'd be this many people.'

Brenda looks around. One of these women must be Verna Glanville, Verna of Virginia. If only she knew what she looked like. Too bad there hadn't been a picture –

'Order, order.'

'I humbly request – '

'The Chair recognizes Charlotte Dance.'

'Madam Chairperson. I thank you for your cooperation, and I think that when you hear – '

'But can you make it brief, Char. And non-political. This is supposed to be an orientation session.'

For some reason, which Brenda doesn't understand, there is loud laughter at this. Even Charlotte Dance laughs in a deep New England-sounding way. 'All I ask is for a mere two minutes.'

'Go ahead. You've got the floor.'

'Whew! The problem I want to raise is not exactly political but it does concern us because it concerns the violation of our rights as women – '

Cheering. One or two groans.

'It seems that the hotel, the hotel which we have *favoured* with our exhibition – I speak of the Franklin Court Arms – it seems this hotel has proven itself no different from any other male-dominated commercial institution – '

'Do you think you could get to the point, Charlotte.' The chairperson is smiling broadly. 'We've only got this room for one hour and it's already – '

'Perhaps some of you here are aware that there is a serious problem with accommodation.'

A scattering of applause at this.

'It seems we are being told by the management of this hotel that there are not enough hotel rooms for all of us. And this in spite of the fact that our organization has had bookings, *confirmed bookings*,' she pauses, 'for several months.'

'What room are you in?' Lenora whispers.

'2424,' Brenda whispers back.

'Were you asked to share with someone?'

'Yes, I – '

'Me too.'

'I wish to direct the Chair's attention to the fact that quite a number of us have been asked to double up, and let me say that this in itself is fine. I have no objection to doubling up. But quite a lot of our membership is also being asked to stay at the Ramada Inn, which just happens to be two miles from here. Two miles! Naturally, I inquired the reason for this. And it appears we have been – I believe the word is bumped – by the International Society of Metallurgists. Does the Chair agree that this is what has, in fact, occurred?'

'There does seem to be a problem with overbooking. I was told an hour or so ago that some of our members will be bussed free of charge – '

'In spite of the fact that we had the prior bookings, we are now being asked to give way to another body – '

'I think it was only those with accompanying persons – '

'Excuse me, Madam Chairperson, but what I wish to point out, loudly and clearly, is the fact that we are an organization which is made up almost entirely of women – '

'Not entirely, Charlotte my duck,' came a good-natured male voice – the grey beard – from the front row.

'Pardon me. An organization, *mainly* made up of women, is being asked to give way to an organization which just happens – just happens – to be almost entirely made up of men.'

There is loud cheering. Foot-stamping. Applause. Brenda and Lenora exchange looks. Lenora looks frightened. The Chair raps for order.

'I know I've been asked to be as brief as possible,' Charlotte Dance continues, 'and I think, having said what I've just said, that there's no need to say any more. The very fact that this has

been allowed to happen says it all. The circumstances themselves are enough to point to a blatant lack of moral responsibility on the part of the management of this hotel, and I would
like to propose setting up a committee to look into the matter at
once – this evening if possible.'

'Count me in.'

'We're with you, Charlotte.'

'And to those of you from the press – I presume that the press
is in attendance – I would be happy to get together with you
after this meeting and discuss further manifestations – '

'Thank you, Char, for bringing this to our attention. I think
we'd better get to the programme now. We have a number of
items to deal with – '

'Question.'

'I'm, afraid we just can't allow any further – '

'One question. That's all, I promise.' The speaker is a woman
in front of Brenda who has risen and is holding up her arms.
She is young – at least she looks young from the back – and has
long, black hair falling to her waist. She is wearing a knitted
shawl in tones of purple and mauve. Could this possibly be
Verna of Virginia?

'Let her talk. Give her a minute.'

'All right.' A sigh comes whistling through the microphone.
'One question only, and one minute only, too. Then, I'm afraid
– '

'I want to protest, on behalf of every woman in this room – '

'Will you kindly state your name, please, for the record.'

'Margaret Malone, Atlanta Craft Guild.'

'The Chair recognizes Margaret Malone.'

'She's gorgeous,' Lenora Knox breathes.

Brenda nods. 'Yes.'

'I wish to protest the so-called gift we have all received today
from a group calling itself New Women Industries. I speak' –
and she holds up the make-up kit – 'of this, this gratuitous
tribute to traditional female vanity.'

'You tell 'em.' Charlotte Dance is on her feet again.

'I wish to inquire,' Margaret Malone continues, 'whether the
International Society of Metallurgists has also been given little
bundles of . . . of goodies like this. Like aftershave lotion, for
instance. Or some good, manly, seductive cologne.'

'You know, she's got a point,' Lenora Knox says quietly.

'You've raised a valid point,' the chairperson says, 'but we really have to – '

'I just happen to have here in my hand a large green garbage bag, which I propose, with the permission of the Chair, to put in the back of the room. If anyone would like to part with this unasked-for gift from' – she pauses – 'New Women Industries, perhaps you will join me in – '

'Thank you very much. I'm sure we all appreciate what it is you're saying – '

Suddenly everyone in the room is talking. Some of them are getting up and walking to the back of the room where the garbage bag has been placed. Brenda thinks of joining them but worries about losing her seat. The chairperson's gavel is going up and down, but the microphone system appears to have broken down. On one side of the room a woman is climbing up on a chair. Someone else is helping her up; and now she has started talking. Brenda strains to hear what she is saying, but with all the noise she can scarcely make it out. Something about abortion legislation. Something about basic rights in the states of Mississippi and Alabama. Someone else in the room seems to be crying; or perhaps she is only shouting to be heard. There is an electronic squawk from the sound system; the room seems to Brenda to be tilting. Two or three women are singing in the back of the room. 'The Battle Hymn of the Republic'? *Glory, glory, Hallelujah*. Someone is laughing hysterically. The man with the grey beard is whispering into Charlotte Dance's ear. Charlotte Dance has placed her hands on her hips. Her mouth has gone slack; her head is rocking back and forth.

'Heavens,' Lenora Knox says in her sweet voice.

Chapter Nine

THE MAN IN THE ELEVATOR WITH BRENDA, RIDING UP TO the twenty-fourth floor, was wearing a pinstriped suit. She regarded it appraisingly out of the corner of her eye; she had recently talked Jack into buying a pinstriped suit, and this one was really quite similar in cut, only a dark blue instead of brown.

As it happened, the man in the suit was getting off at the twenty-fourth floor too, and as though this coincidence were some sort of joke they shared, he sent Brenda a fleeting, absentminded smile. On his breast pocket she saw a small plasticized card: International Metallurgical Society. One of those, she thought, and eyed him more sharply. His name in smaller print was on the card as well, but Brenda, stepping out of the elevator, didn't catch it, and felt it would be impossible to stare too closely. And what did it matter anyway? He moved off down the hall in one direction, and she, more hesitantly, in the other. The twenty-fourth floor; she thought of Betty Vetter asking if she were afraid of heights, and then, with a shade of triumph, she remembered the young man on the plane, the one with the pink gums. How would he, with his whining fears, like being put on the twenty-fourth floor?

Once, when the Historical Society met in New York, she and Jack had stayed on the thirty-third floor of a downtown hotel, and lying in bed they had imagined they could feel the building sway slightly in the wind. She had not felt at all afraid; she had liked the idea of the slim steel tower bending a lean quarter-inch in the gale, of feeling herself part of that minute technical surrender. Heights could actually make you feel safe – everything was left behind, the lobby and coffee shops and bars were all miles away. Up here the rooms were unmoored and loosened into their own sweep of darkness. It was utterly quiet in the corridor.

Brenda pulled the heavy key out of her raincoat pocket to check the number. Room 2424 must be at the end of the hall;

yes, there it was, the room next to the ice machine. She was anxious to open the door, to get her shoes off – the right shoe especially, which was too tight across the toes; she should remember never to buy Italian shoes, even when they were on sale. It wasn't worth it.

Would Verna of Virginia have arrived? Brenda hoped not. She was looking forward to meeting her, but at the same time she wanted, needed, a few minutes to herself. She would take off her shoes, and perhaps her skirt as well. There was an hour and a half before the reception. Time to slide between the sheets, enough time, if she wanted, to shut her eyes and allow herself the luxury of a few minutes' sleep. A short nap could be amazingly revitalizing; ten minutes of what Jack's father always referred to as 'shut-eye' could do wonders. (Occasionally, if they were going out in the evening, Jack would stretch out for a few minutes first.) It was a good thing she had brought along her little travel clock; if she set the alarm for six she would still have time for a shower before the reception. That is, if Verna wasn't in the room.

But Verna *was* in the room. She was lying on her back on one of the twin beds.

At least Brenda assumed it must be Verna. There was a woman, at any rate, without any clothes on, lying on the bed next to the window. The lights were turned on – a lamp on the dresser, a floor lamp in one corner – but it was altogether impossible for Brenda to see Verna's face – or much of her body, for that matter – since there was a man lying on top of her. He was unclothed as well. He had smooth, muscled shoulders, Brenda noted, and a broad, oval back. She perceived moderate hairiness and white skin beneath. And a pair of buttocks which were reddish in colour and rather small. It always came as a surprise to her to realize how small male buttocks were.

From the bed came the sound of music. No, it wasn't music, it was moaning – his or hers Brenda was unable to tell for sure. The curtains were partly open. It was five o'clock in the afternoon, dark outside, wintery. The man's buttocks rose and fell in a strenuous, fitful way. Verna's (Verna's?) long legs kicked outward, then closed over the hairy back, the feet locking together. Brenda thought of statuary, something mounted on a heavy pedestal in the middle of a park, a Henry Moore, all angles and openings. There was another low moan, almost a

64

whisper, then the drier sound of panting and thrashing, and a woman's muffled cry: 'Almost, almost.'

Brenda regarded them for perhaps two or three seconds. The word *humping*, a word she had never used, struck her with a wallop; nevertheless, she felt extraordinarily clam. Her suitcase had been brought up, she noticed. There it was, standing primly between the two beds. Over the beds was a framed picture, a still life, fruit, what looked like apricots, and –

An instant later she was in the corridor again. She had managed to close the door behind her without making a sound. Nearby, just around the corner, someone was rattling the ice machine. She glanced down the length of the hall, which seemed endlessly and unnaturally serene. Every door was closed – a series of smooth slabs, proclaiming privacy, decency. And behind those false doors: she had a dazzling multiple vision of fierce couplings, strange wet limbs coming together, muffled cries, inhuman late-afternoon murmurings. Peaks of ecstasy. Randomness. Accident. Risk. She had a glimpse down a deep historical hole containing millions of couplings – it was bottomless. She dropped the room key back into her pocket and leaned, swaying slightly, against the wall; her teeth for some reason were chattering.

'Locked out?' someone was asking her. It was the man in the pinstriped suit, carrying a plastic ice-bucket in his hand. He spoke in a merry voice, a neighbourly voice. 'No,' she told him.

He came to a halt in front of her and peered at her rather closely. 'Well, then, can I . . . Is there something the matter?'

He was looking into her eyes. Intently. Perhaps he thought she was drunk. Or sick. The size of her pupils? And there was the matter of her teeth chattering. She was, in fact, shaking all over.

'Perhaps you should sit down,' he advised kindly. The pinstripes danced before her, hurting her eyes. She observed that the knot of his blue-and-maroon tie was luxurious and silky.

'Yes,' she nodded, and waved a vague hand. Where?

'Or maybe you'd like me to call someone for you?'

'Call someone?'

'They must have a hotel doctor. Or a nurse. Or someone like that on call.'

'I don't need a doctor,' Brenda said, dazed by this suggestion.

'I just thought, well, that perhaps you weren't feeling well
. . .'

'I'm just . . . a little dizzy, I think.'

'Look, why don't you let me see you to your room. Make sure you're all right.'

'This is my room. Right here.' As proof, Brenda patted the smooth wood of the door.

'I see.' He waited.

'I'm really feeling better now.' Why didn't he go away, just take his ice-bucket and go away? 'I mean, I'm not feeling dizzy at all now.'

'Good, that's good.' He was a slightly built man, not much taller than she was. His brown eyes were alert, lively, worried, and his hair – Brenda always noticed hair, just as Leah Wallberg noticed cheekbones – was a mixture of brown and grey, exceptionally thick, the hair of a healthy man. A man in his late forties, Brenda imagined.

'I'll be just fine.' She did feel better, and for some reason was now on the verge of laughter. Nerves probably. Don't laugh, she instructed herself.

'Look,' he said after a pause. 'I was just going to make myself a drink. Would you like to come along – I'm just down the hall a little way – and join me?'

'Oh, thank you but – '

'You could sit down for a few minutes, pull yourself together – '

'Really, I'm fine.' She shook her head hard to prove it.

'If you're concerned about me, I promise I'm not a rapist or a murderer or anything.' As though to confirm this, he touched the card which announced him a member of the metallurgical profession. 'If you sit down a minute or two, maybe have a drink, you'll be fine.'

'But I am fine – '

'To tell the truth, if you don't mind my saying so, you still look a bit on the shaky side.'

'Really.'

'Sometimes these damn elevators bother people, these heights . . . ' He smiled in his merry way, and Brenda thought, what a kind man, what a thoughtful man, to have thought of the elevators.

'Actually,' she started to explain – she owed him some sort of explanation – 'it's such a funny thing. The thing that just happened.'

'Funny peculiar or – '

'Both.'

'Well . . . ' He waited, smiling quizzically. The way in which his front teeth overlapped made Brenda feel friendly toward him.

'Not exactly funny.' She stopped; smiled. 'Sort of – '

'Bizarre?'

'Bizarre, yes, that's the word for it. Surreal too. And,' now she was starting to laugh, she couldn't help herself, 'and I guess just plain, well, funny.'

She recalled the red buttocks, firm as apples, cheerful, though oddly menacing. She began to laugh even harder. She leaned against the wall, her head rolling back and forth, her mouth open. She must sound crazy; this man in the striped suit, hanging on to his bucket of ice cubes, must think she was insane.

But he didn't appear to. He began to laugh along with her, in a manner which was easy and companionable. Brenda couldn't imagine why. She could hear his ice cubes rattle, a nice social sound, restorative and normal. She took a breath.

'It *would* be nice,' she said. 'Having a drink, I mean.'

'Good. Great. I'm just down this way. Next to the elevator.'

'This is very nice of you. I mean, when I don't even know – '

'It's my pleasure.' He took her elbow, a gesture she felt she should find alarming, but for some reason didn't. His voice sounded faintly English, the way he pronounced elevator – elevatah.

He had a double room. Over the beds were more pictures of fruit, wobbly-looking and bruised and lost in the bottoms of deep pottery bowls. There was a suitcase on a rack, the lid up, a necktie dragging out, rumpled underwear. In one corner a swag lamp hung over a smooth brown armchair of padded vinyl. 'Why don't you sit there,' he suggested, helping her off with her coat and folding it neatly across one of the beds. He did not say, what a lovely coat, or, did you know you have beautiful cheekbones. He said, 'Please. Make yourself at home.'

'Isn't it strange!' Brenda sat down and immediately felt sharp pains piercing the back of her knees. It had been a long day. She leaned forward and with one hand rubbed the instep of her right foot. Would it be impolite to take off her shoe? Probably.

'Strange?' He was standing by a table, slipping glasses out of their paper wrappers.

'Being here, I mean. Having a drink. When I don't even know your – '

'Barry Ollershaw. I should have said earlier. Sorry.'

Barry. It was a name she had never particularly liked. As a name it lacked seriousness; something about it that was fetching and coy. 'And you're from – ' she asked politely.

'From Vancouver, B.C. That's Canada.'

'That's supposed to be beautiful,' Brenda said, not entirely sure where Vancouver, B.C., was. Mountains . . . ? She wondered suddenly what she was doing in this man's room, and involuntarily her eyes went to the door.

'Would you like me to leave the door open?' Barry Ollershaw asked her.

'It's not that – '

'We used to have to do that back at university. In the fraternity house. When we entertained girls in our rooms – that was the word we used, entertain – we were supposed to leave the door ajar.' (He pronounced it ajah.) 'House rules. Of course, that was back in the fifties. Almost the dark ages.'

'Really?' Her nervous laugh again.

'I wouldn't blame you for being uneasy. Good God, when you read the newspapers – so if you'd rather have the door open . . . '

'It's fine the way it is.' Rapists and murderers didn't look like this: relaxed, intelligent, wearing name tags. What did they look like? She felt sure she could tell.

'Is gin okay? I'm afraid it's all I've got. And tonic water and a little bitter lemon, that's about it.'

'Tonic is fine. I like tonic.' She was babbling, as bad as Hap Lewis. 'With not too much gin.'

'How's this?'

'Perfect. I'm glad you came along when you did. I really was feeling dizzy.'

'Cheers.' He lifted his glass.

'Pardon? Oh, cheers.'

'And you are,' he peered down at her name card, 'Brenda Bowman. Of the Chicago Craft Guild.'

'Yes.' She was beginning to relax. 'How do you do.'

He perched on the side of the bed and faced her, his drink cradled in his hands. 'And now I hope to hear about this strange and bizarre and surreal thing that made you dizzy.'

'It's going to be an awful letdown, I'm afraid. To tell the truth, it seems sort of silly now.'

'I could use some light entertainment. I've been in meetings all afternoon.'

'You're not' – she looked him in the eye, brown eyes, reddish eyebrows – 'you're not prudish by any chance?'

'Prudish? I've never been accused of it. Do I look as though I might be prudish?'

'Well I've never met any Canadians.'

Why had she said a ridiculous thing like that? What was the matter with her? And it wasn't even true – there was Bill Lawless at the Institute. He came from Winnipeg, and he certainly wasn't prudish. In fact –

'Well?' Barry Ollershaw said, and gave his glass an encouraging swirl.

'Well,' Brenda began, 'I should explain first that I'm here with the National Handicrafts Exhibition.'

'So I gathered. Your name tag.'

'And I was supposed to have a room of my own. But for some reason there weren't enough rooms to go around. As a matter of fact, there's a rumour going around that we've been bumped by the International Society of – '

'Say no more. I know all about it. I've just come from a committee meeting, and it seems we're really in the shit.'

'So they asked me at the Welcome Desk if I'd mind sharing a room. With another quiltmaker. That's what I do. Quilts.'

'I'm nuts about quilts. My mother used to make quilts. And my aunt. Patchwork. Of course they wouldn't be in the same class. Anyway, go on.'

'I didn't know this other quilter, except by reputation. I mean, we'd never met. But when I went up to the room, well, there she was.'

'Yes?'

'When I walked in the door just now, there she was – but she wasn't . . . alone.' Brenda was having trouble with her mouth, which felt oddly loose and moist. And she wasn't sure where to look.

'She wasn't alone.' Barry Ollershaw repeated this as though it were a mere statement.

'As a matter of fact, she didn't even see me come in. She was . . . well . . . with a man. Making . . . you know . . . love.'

'Aha!' Barry's head went back. 'Yes, I do see.'

'You do?'

'Even we Canadians – '

'It was just, I don't know how to explain it, just sort of surprising. But only for a minute or two. I guess I was a little overwhelmed. I mean, it was the last thing I expected. When I opened that door. The lights were all on. Only now – ' Brenda had started laughing again. A drop of gin spilled on her suit skirt and she brushed at it with her hand.

'Only now?'

'Now, well, it just seems funny. Absurd. Crazy when you stop to think about it.'

Barry smiled broadly and shook his head appreciatively.

'Position one?' he asked abruptly.

'Pardon?'

'Missionary position? Is that how they were – missionary position?'

'Actually,' Brenda paused and took a gulp of gin, 'yes.' She drained her glass quickly and stared past Barry Ollershaw's head at the fruit on the wall.

'I can imagine it must have been something of a surprise.'

'And when you think about it in the abstract – '

'Think about what?'

'Sex. In the abstract it really is a little bit, I don't know, ludicrous.'

'The beast with two backs.' Another statement.

'What? Oh yes, that's right. So you know what I mean then?'

'I do. It's a sort of joke on the human race. To keep us humble. But who knows, maybe in ten million years, if we last that long, we'll evolve toward something a little more . . . graceful.'

'Like fish,' Brenda heard herself saying. 'I was just reading an article about fish – I think it was in *Newsweek*, maybe you saw it. About fish eggs just sort of . . . expelled . . . and spreading out like fans in the water.'

'Would you like another drink?'

'Maybe some tonic water, if you've got enough. I don't know why I'm so thirsty. Nerves probably. But I don't want to keep you. You've probably got something – ' She held her breath. The last thing she wanted to do was to get up out of this chair.

'Nothing until eight. So please have another. To keep me company. Here, let me get it for you.'

Perhaps she could take her shoes off. At least the right one. On second thought –

'Are you married?' she said to Barry Ollershaw's back. He was busily shaking more ice into her glass, somewhat awkwardly trying to avoid using his fingers.

'Yes,' he told her.

'So am I. And it's funny. I've been married for twenty years, a long time. But I've never seen, never actually seen, anyone – anyone else that is – making love. Isn't that odd when you think about it.'

'A little, I suppose, considering what a common activity it is. But probably not all that strange.'

'I'm glad to hear you say that. Because it suddenly seems very strange to me.'

'Well,' he said, turning around, 'of course some people go in for mirrors on the ceiling and that sort of thing.' He said this in a slow, speculative way which made Brenda wonder if he might be one of those people.

'I suppose.'

'And there are always movies. Blue movies, I mean. Sometimes at stag parties – but I don't imagine you go to stag parties.'

'But that's not quite the same thing as . . . as actually being in the room where two people – '

'I suppose not. But then, most kids, growing up, come across their parents once or twice, by accident – '

'Did you ever?' She thought of the mother who made quilts.

'Once, as a matter of fact. My brother and I. Of course it was dark, so we didn't see much. Just bedclothes moving around, that sort of thing. I can remember how it affected my brother and me. I think we were half hysterical, laughing like crazy, but at the same time deeply shocked.

'I think that's how I felt today.'

'And *your* parents? Didn't you ever – ?'

'The thing was, I never really had a father.'

'Oh?' His face showed interest. Halfway through his second gin and tonic, his look of merriment sparkled even more brightly, and Brenda wondered if this might be some social trick

71

of his, professional and perfected – always respond, always radiate energy. What was it a metallurgist did, anyway? Something with metal – testing it probably.

'That is,' she said carefully, 'my mother never really got married.'

'I see.' An emphatic nod, brown eyes held still.

'Of course, there must have been someone once. Not that my mother ever talked about it. But there was never anyone else – not that I know of anyway.'

'Hmmm.'

Why lately, was she making such a point of telling people, especially strangers, about this, her lack of a father? This was the second time today; she would have to watch that. Was this the only interesting thing she had to confide, the only thing about her that set her apart: her fatherless state? She couldn't, having read a number of magazine articles on psychology, entirely dismiss the idea of exhibitionism, and what lay just beneath it. The desire to shock? Or maybe she just wanted to impress people with how easily she had absorbed this supposed psychic trauma. People went into therapy over things like this. Endless years with shrinks, nightmares, neuroses. People placed ads in the newspapers, hoping to find their lost fathers, hoping to complete themselves somehow. They hired detectives. And they tormented their mothers with questions and accusations. But not she, no, not she. She preened herself on the robustness of her mental health – just as she flaunted her lack of fear of heights.

Barry Ollershaw gave a little cough. 'So there was no one – no man anyway – in the picture?'

'Never. So, needless to say, I never came across – and, of course, now at home – '

'Yes?'

'Well, we have a lock on our bedroom door.'

'Oh?' His bright look. 'A good idea.'

'Well,' she felt she had to explain, 'the lock was there when we moved into our house, just one of those little hooks. We thought it was funny at first, my husband and I, but later, when the children got older – '

'Of course.'

'Well, anyway, nothing like this has happened to me before, walking into a room like that. I'm just glad they didn't see me.

72

At least, I'm fairly sure they didn't notice me coming in. I mean, what do you say in a situation like that?'

'Maybe, "Please don't let me disturb you."'

'Carry on folks.'

'Even if they had seen you,' Barry said, 'it would hardly have been your fault. They could have double-bolted the door if they really wanted privacy. That's what people usually do.'

Did they? Brenda supposed they did. 'Maybe it was just, you know, unpremeditated.'

'Maybe. Human nature being what it is.'

'That's an expression my husband Jack uses – human nature being what it is.'

'Are you hungry by any chance? I could have some food sent up, sandwiches, some coffee.'

Brenda almost leapt out of her chair. The reception. It was almost six-thirty. 'I've got to go,' she told Barry. Her feet, oh, her feet! 'Would you mind, would it be all right, if I used your bathroom, just to clean up a bit?' She touched her hair, pushed it back, reached for her coat on the bed.

'Of course not.' He stepped aside and indicated the way. His face seemed to Brenda to be innocent, to be scoured with trustworthiness. She felt she should say something, anything. 'I really appreciate your not raping or murdering me.'

In response he gave her a mock bow, and she noticed again the thickness of his hair. It was remarkable hair. Coarse as grass, with its own energy. She would like to have placed her hand on it for a minute to test its resilience. Then she remembered her desire, earlier, to reach out and touch the knee of the man on the plane. But she would never have done either of these things, she realized. Never.

Chapter Ten

A T THE RECEPTION THERE IS A FREE BAR, TABLES OF FOOD, and hundreds of people standing about eating and drinking, and talking. The blended sound of human voices is brain-numbing but pleasurable, and Brenda, arriving late and helping herself to a small, square sandwich, feels a surge of anticipation. Anything could happen.

There is something rubbery in the sandwich, herring probably. (She loves herring; at home she keeps a jar of it in the refrigerator and sometimes in the middle of the afternoon she dips her fingers in and helps herself to a slice.) There are pastries the size of her thumbnail, which ooze with orangey cheese. And something hot on toothpicks – what is it? – some kind of meatball thing with a slice of mushroom on top. Delicious. A waiter in a white uniform offers her a drink from a tray. 'Punch, madam?'

Brenda looks around the Republic Room for someone she knows, anyone at all. Lottie Hart should be here from the Chicago Craft Guild. At least she said she was coming, but that was two weeks ago. And Susan Hammerman – Susan Hammerman was on the national executive – she would be here for sure. Of course Brenda hardly knows Susan Hammerman; she has only met her once, and that was last spring at a reception in Chicago which had been large and noisy, rather like this reception in fact. Still it would be nice if – then Brenda catches sight of Betty Vetter standing only a few feet away. A familiar face; she tries to catch her eye, but Betty is talking to a waiter with a tray of punch cups. She is waving her arms – not exactly waving them, but taking little chops at the air in front of her – and Brenda hears the fervent rising end of a sentence which is: 'keeping in mind the contingency plan and allowing for possible cancellations.' It sounds like a serious and urgent conversation.

Behind Brenda two women are talking. One of them is saying: 'At least the programme looks better than last year. Meat-

74

ier, if you know what I mean.' The other woman replies, half peevish, half nostalgic, 'Yes, but when these meetings first started, we knew everyone. Remember? Remember that first year in St. Louis? I'll just never forget it, the spirit there was . . . We knew absolutely everyone. And now – '

There was Susan Hammerman now, standing on the other side of the room. Beautiful – she looks beautiful, Brenda thinks. The swing of grey hair, expensively cut. That yellow silk dress. Not everyone can wear yellow, not after a certain age, it does something to the skin, but not Susan Hammerman's skin. Brenda sees that Susan Hammerman is deep in conversation with a group of women, and for a moment she considers joining them. She could interrupt with, 'I don't know if you remember me, but we met at the Craft Fair last spring.'

It is not very likely that Susan Hammerman *will* remember her, but she was from the same city and –

'Another drink? More punch, madam?'

'Not just yet, thanks.'

Brenda wonders if Verna of Virginia has come down to the reception. She might be here now, glowing, freshly showered, drinking a cool cup of punch; and *he* might be here too, standing at her side, looking ruddy and pleased with himself.

'Hi there, Brenda.' It's Lenora Knox from Santa Fe, appearing out of nowhere, smiling sweetly and wearing a long pink cotton skirt which is faintly wrinkled. The scent of musty flowers rises from her combed hair. Brenda comes close to embracing her. 'I don't know a soul here,' she tells Lenora, and the words settle on her own ears like a confession of inadequacy.

'Did you find your room all right, Brenda?' Lenora inquires.

'Yes,' Brenda pauses. 'How about you?'

'Well,' Lenora begins – and already Brenda knows it will be a long story – 'well, my roomie is from Texas, Fort Worth, real sweet, she designs needlepoint patterns. I guess they thought with both of us coming from the Southwest . . . but she's the shyest thing. I don't know what to do. She hardly says two words, just seems lost, you know. When I said, are you coming on down to the reception, she said, no, she didn't know anyone, so what was the use. I said, well that's how you meet people, that's the purpose behind these receptions, just to mix us all up and get us acquainted.'

'Brenda Bowman!' a powerful voice cries. It's Susan Hammerman's voice; and there she is, striding like an opera-singer
across the room, dodging the waiter, dodging Betty Vetter, the
yellow dress shining over her hips. 'I didn't know you were
coming, Brenda. You should have let me know. I must say, the
Chicago contingent isn't exactly out in force this year, is it?
Lottie Hart had to cancel. Isn't this fabulous though, people
from all over the country. I've just been talking to this marvellous woman from St. Paul, Minnesota, who started weaving at
the age of sixty-five. Can you picture it, sixty-five? My God, if I
can just keep going that long without the old fingers seizing up.
It's really an inspiration, isn't it?'

'Yes,' Brenda says, 'it is.'

'It certainly is,' says Lenora Knox in her small, straight, oboe
of a voice.

'It was my grandmother who got me started,' someone is telling
Brenda. 'My grandmother on the maternal side. I used to think,
poor old Nana and those poor old cronies of hers with their
Tuesday sewing circle. I'd rather curl up and die than spend my
life doing that kind of thing. I majored in biology, Missouri
State. But my grandmother got me going on this. I was married
at that time and had the kids. I just started with little things,
time-filler sort of thing. I can honestly say that I had no idea in
the beginning of the kind of satisfaction that comes from
making something with your own hands, just making something out of nothing. Well, practically nothing. What's in this
punch anyway? Rum? Sort of sneaks up on you, doesn't it? But
now I think I really understand those women better, the sew-
ing-circle women. All those afghans and aprons and pot-
holders. Who's to say those women weren't artists? Folk artists,
anyway. You're from Chicago, I see.'

'Yes,' Brenda says.

'I've got a brother in Chicago. Well, Riverside to be precise . . .'

'What I don't understand is how he got asked to be the Keynote
Speaker. I mean, what does he know about anything?'

'I think he's going to talk about the new international trends
in the craft market – '

'But what does he *know* about it. Sure, he may know about marketing, but there's selling and there's making.'

'Someone told me he was very amusing – '

'Amusing! Who needs amusing!'

Brenda helps herself to a small pickled artichoke heart and bites down into something hard at the centre. An almond. Who would have thought of that! She will have to remember to tell Bev Coulson about that. Bev will write it down on one of her cards and file it away with her other appetizer ideas. The last time she and Jack were at the Coulsons', Bev served curried soya balls, a vegetarian recipe she had adapted herself from something she and Roger had been served in Japan.

Is cooking an art? Brenda and Jack had discussed this after-wards, driving home. Jack said no, because it lacked perma-nence, even the pretence of permanence. Brenda said yes, cooking was an art because it appealed directly to the aesthetic sense and it involved aesthetic deliberations. (Lately she has grown more skilled at this kind of discussion.) Jack was doubt-ful, but agreed she might have a point. Brenda reminded him of origami, how impermanent origami was. She mentioned the string sculptures made by Eskimos. She reminded Jack how far Bev Coulson was from the days when she used to invite them to post-football suppers and serve them something called Crowd-pleasers, which were wet ground beef and beans on Toastmas-ter buns. 'True,' Jack said.

'So you're a quilter?' someone says to Brenda. 'Or should that be quiltmaker?'

'Either one,' Brenda says, feeling happy. 'Once at a party one of our neighbours introduced me to someone as "a quilter in her own right".'

'I just heard that Verna of Virginia was going to be here. Have you ever met her?'

'Well, no, but as a matter of fact – '

A man in a business suit tells Brenda, 'I'm what you call an accompanying person. Husband, that is. That's my wife over there in the white outfit. She's the crafty person in the family. Macramé. She was into macramé before it even started to take off. Now she teaches a class at the Y. It keeps her busy. Out of trouble. I'm in hydraulics. Just a small firm, two partners, secretarial staff. And we're doing our darnedest to keep it small. Things get so big and then they collapse on you. What's the joy in that? I was just reading this pocketbook, *Small is Beautiful*, and all the time I was reading it I was saying, right on, right on. Philadelphia's got a lot to recommend it, but who'd want to live here, right? Can I get you some more of this punch? I was just on my way over for a refill. Nice talking to you. Quite an affair, this.'

'No, it's true. Capricorns are more artistic than Geminis.'
  'Really?'

'I've been in crafts for eight years now,' a woman says. 'I learned when I was in the hospital. A therapist used to come in every day and give us instructions. Basic stuff, but I'd never learned to use my hands, so it was all new to me. I had had several electric-shock treatments and half the time I couldn't think straight, but my fingers at least could move. It was just like a dream when I look back on it. The yarn was just there in my hands, and this woman was helping my fingers to hang on to it. Some of the women hated it. They used to cry. One of them sat down in the middle of the floor and took off her shoes and wound the yarn around and around her legs. It was funny in a way. It took me about a month to finish my first piece. I kept falling asleep. But the second piece went faster, and the actual workmanship was a hundred per cent better; even I could tell the difference. They moved me to another unit and let me work as long as I wanted to on any one day. That was how I got started.'

' – the Crossland variation.'
  'But is it convincing?'
  'Yes and no.'

One woman asks, 'Say, do any of you know if they sorted out the mess with the rooms?'
  'I don't know,' Brenda replies. 'I haven't heard any more about it.'
  'Well,' someone volunteers, 'I heard the committee is going

to meet with the metallurgists in the morning. Of course, it's really the hotel management that's at fault.'

'But someone said the metallurgists were given the extra rooms because we got this room for the reception. It was some kind of deal they worked out.'

'Apparently *they* had to hold their reception downstairs in the Bavarian Cellar.'

'Really? Heavens, that's way down in the bowels of – '

'Nice atmosphere though. Informal. Conducive to conversation. This is really sort of overly formal.'

'That's for sure.'

Brenda's eyes sweep upwards, taking in the white scrollwork on the ceiling, the chandeliers, the Georgian moulding, the heavy blue velvet curtains caught back with curious gnarled hardware. An immense portrait of Benjamin Franklin hangs on one wall.

'Just look at the way he's peering down at us,' one of the women says.

'Those pink cheeks.'

'A great old man really. But that portrait makes him look like a country judge, not a man of genius.'

'Is it a true likeness,' Brenda wonders, 'or just a sort of idealized version . . . '

'He looks positively condemning, looking down at us guzzling up punch when we should be doing the early-to-bed early-to-rise deal.'

'A penny saved – '

'Was that one of Franklin's?'

'I think so. I get him mixed up with Proverbs.'

'Versatility. A real Renaissance man.'

'You know something, you never hear about Renaissance women, do you?'

'Versatility takes time. Who has time?'

'The whole picture is changing. I was reading this article in *Ms.* – '

'What I mean is, how much time does the average woman get to spend pursuing anything? She can't afford to make a false start and begin over again. If she's an artist of any kind, and I include crafts people in that – '

'Amen.'

' – then she's expected to do her stuff between loads of wash.

Jumping through hoops just to find herself an hour or two a day.'

'That's changing now, don't you think?'

'I finally laid down the law and got myself a studio. What about you Brenda?'

'Well – '

'A room of one's own. Good old Virginia. She had her head screwed on right.'

'But – '

'We really owe a lot to those early – '

'I sit down at that loom and catch myself thinking, maybe I should bake the kids some cookies. Or a pie. Some dumb thing like that. Ha.'

'I haven't made a pie in five years.'

'I've never made a pie.'

'Who needs pie!'

'Not me, that's for sure.'

'I sometimes think of that book *The Greening of America*, remember that? How he said something about handicrafts being a sign of spiritual resurgence in America.

'I love it. That's fabulous. I'm going to write that down.'

'Well, it's only a paraphrase. But it was something along those lines.'

'This punch is getting to me. I think I'll call it a day.'

'Me too. We've got the Keynote Address at nine sharp.'

'Early to bed, early to – '

'It's after one o'clock. I don't believe it.'

'And I was going to phone home. Check up on the family.'

'It's pretty late.'

'I suppose.'

'Have you got children, Brenda?'

'Yes,' Brenda says, 'two.'

'Me too. How old are yours?'

'A boy fourteen. And a girl twelve.'

'I'll bet you miss them already.' The woman who says this has a soft, faintly Southern voice, but the words hit Brenda like an electric shock. She hasn't thought of her children all day. Not once all day.

Room 2424. Brenda puts the key in the lock, turns it slowly, feels her heart contract. This is ridiculous, she lectures herself, she can't camp in the corridor all night. This is her room; she was assigned to it.

The room is empty. Verna's bed is empty, the sheets and blankets pulled up in a semblance of order and propriety. The table lamp has been left on; it projects a circle of yellow welcoming light onto the ceiling, almost as though it has been specially lit for her.

She is tired, exhausted; the rum punch has made her giddy, and so has the number of people she's met and talked to. Names, all those names, she'll never remember them all. She can wash her hair in the morning, she decides. Tomorrow she can borrow an iron from the chambermaid and press her other skirt. She can't wait to get into bed, to close her eyes.

And sleep comes with ease. Small, puffed clouds blow soundlessly past her. She thinks of Jack – not his face, but the density and smell of his body. She thinks of her children, asleep at home, not as they are now, but as they were when they were little – warm, sweet-smelling after their bath. She thinks of her quilts; somewhere in the darkness of this hotel her three quilts wait. *The Second Coming, The Second Coming.* She can move an imaginary finger along the raised centre piece, remembering the accuracy of edges and corners. She thinks of her red coat (small, worrying stain on collar), which is hanging down the hall in Barry Ollershaw's room. He will bring it to her tomorrow, he promised, and she has no doubt but that he will. The promise brings a flare of happiness. Faith presses; it has the weight of gravity; all is safe, all is well. She dreams of the pale-green artichoke heart, its leaves pushed apart, the sharpened oval of an almond embedded in its centre.

Chapter Eleven

SHE LOVED HER CHILDREN, OF COURSE SHE LOVED HER CHILD-ren, her babies, Rob and Laurie. (Robert John Bowman, born 1964, seven pounds, four ounces. Laura Jane Bowman, born 1966, one minute past midnight, eight pounds, two ounces.) Brenda's first thought when she woke up on Sunday morning in an empty hotel room was of her children.

Six-thirty by the travel clock, but only five-thirty back home in Elm Park; Rob and Laurie would be sound asleep; they loved to sleep in on Sunday mornings, especially Rob, who would lie in bed until noon if they let him – and more and more they did let him. These marathon Sunday-morning sleeping bouts left his bedroom filled with evil smells – dust, sour breath, chilled, comfortless air. This and the clutter of dirty socks, and coins on the bureau, and record albums, and old Sprite cans – all of this depressed Brenda. He always punched in the sides of his Sprite cans when he'd emptied them, an act which seemed to her to be compulsive and vaguely worrying, though she knew other people did the same thing.

As recently as a year ago the walls in Rob's bedroom had been covered with triangular felt souvenir pennants. The Chicago Bears. The Wisconsin Dells. Cave of the Mounds. Dearborn, Mich. Delavan, Wisc. Crystal Lake, Ill. They were made of cheap flimsy felt, cracked at the edges, crudely stamped in uneven ink, but they had brightened the room with boyishness and innocence, reminding Brenda of family trips in the car, and of days which now seemed less troubled.

Rob had taken the pennants down one Saturday morning last January, rolling them up and stowing them on his closet shelf. And he had hung up in their place a small, framed Escher print, which he had bought with his own money – his Christmas money, he told Brenda when she questioned him. He had seen it in the window in the Westgate shopping mall and immediately wanted it. It had cost $35, reduced from $50, at a post-Christmas sale.

Brenda couldn't remember now why she had been so alarmed by the purchase of this print. Was it the amount of money – $35 was a considerable amount for Rob, who received only $5 a week for allowance – or was it the secrecy with which he had spent it? (He hadn't consulted them; he had simply gone out and bought it.) Now, a year later, whenever she went into his room to change his sheets – she seldom went into his room for any other reason these days – she paused and examined the print.

At first glance it looked like an abstract done in blacks and whites, but on close examination it revealed a flock of stately birds, seagulls, their wings outstretched, flying across the paper from right to left, veering upwards slightly. The spaces between the birds were white, and these spaces became progressively smaller as the birds approached the left margin, taking on, finally, the exact shapes of the birds themselves. It was a puzzle, a spatial question mark. There was a balance, she sensed, some mystery, precision, and something ironic too about the relationship between those birds and the small, airy, but distinct distances that separated them. Brenda could feel the suspended movement of their wings pressing like a weight on her eyes. The angle of ascent, not more than ten degrees, filled her with a curious, sweet melancholy. 'What does "covet" mean?' Rob had asked her not long ago, sitting at the dining-room table, writing a composition on mythology for school. She told him it meant wanting something that someone else had. 'For instance,' she told him, 'I covet your Escher print.' He had looked up, pleased. It had been almost painful for her to see how pleased and unguarded he had looked.

Laurie's room was larger, brighter, and tidier than Rob's, but a mistake. All that dotted Swiss, those ruffles; it was neat enough, but never quite clean-looking. That maple dresser, fake Ethan Allen, from their student apartment at DePaul, red and garish and covered with tiny scratches. Laurie had discovered the rolled up pennants in Rob's closet and had begged to have them; now they were thumbtacked on her rose-garlanded wallpaper. The arrangement was hectic and unbalanced. An old perfume bottle of Brenda's sat on Laurie's bedside table, stuffed with paper flowers, another cast-off. (Laurie was always rescuing things from wastebaskets, always spending her allowance at church bazaars or garage sales.) There were piles of comics on her shelves and sets of old Bobbsey Twin books with warped streaky covers. Miniature china animals in rows, miniature china jugs. Plastic pinwheels and whistles from cereal boxes. Bedroom slippers in dusty pink plush, a size too small. A pair of rag dolls propped on her pillow. ('I believe in dolls' – Laurie had whispered this solemn truth in Brenda's ear long ago when she was being put to bed.) There was a small rug on the floor which had been in the upstairs hall before they got the good beige carpeting. The radiator under Laurie's window needed painting; it oozed rust. Brenda promised herself she would get around to it in the spring. There was nothing in her daughter's room she coveted, nothing. No, that wasn't true. She coveted the view, which looked out onto the quiet width of North Franklin Boulevard. Despite the trees at the back of the house, electric wires and board fences and glimpses of alley disturbed the view. On the east side they were only feet away from Larry and Janey Carpenter's smooth grey stucco, and on the west their mock-orange bushes rubbed up against Herb and Ginger Morrison's hedge. Lucky Laurie at the front of the house had a wide, softly curtained view of elm trees (leafless at the moment), lawns, shrubbery, the street lamp across the street with its frosted glass, the dark, beseeching front doors of the neighbouring houses, one or two still silvery with Christmas arrangements. Lucky Laurie.

Brenda couldn't help wondering if Verna of Virginia had any children. She doubted it. There sat Verna's suitcase, a blue-and-red canvas carryall, zippered and jaunty, so different from her own. 'I am not the kind of person who looks in other people's suitcases,' Brenda said this to herself, feeling warmed by her virtue, but surprised at the same time that the thought had come to her.

Where was Verna anyway? Brenda could tell from the arrangement of sheets and blankets that Verna had not returned to the room. Where exactly *had* she spent the night? Perhaps there had been some change. She might have asked for another room. (An image of red buttocks flickered in her mind, brief as the light of a flashbulb.) But the suitcase was still here. It was a puzzle, even in an obscure way a rebuke. No, that was ridiculous.

She decided to have breakfast sent up. When she and Jack were on vacation and staying in a hotel, they always had breakfast sent up; it was one of the pleasures of travelling, they claimed. But it was always Jack who phoned room service. Which was strange, now that she thought of it, since she was the one who organized breakfast at home.

'Orange juice, bran muffins, and coffee,' she said into the phone, forcing her voice into briskness. (Ah, a no-nonsense woman, ordering herself a nourishing breakfast. A woman, alert and active, a woman who had certain expectations, who was accustomed to giving commands.) Brenda put down the receiver thinking: I am forty years old and have just phoned room service for the first time in my life.

Brenda knew, of course – she had known for years – that her life was out of joint with the times. Her richly simulated, commanding voice on the phone told her so, and so did the articles she read in magazines. Articles about women who set up their own law firms, women who conducted symphony orchestras, did photographic essays on Cambodia. Articles about women who lived alone in wilderness cabins and loved it, thrived on it, wrote books about surviving it. Articles about women who understood and provided for the needs of their bodies, who took as their due a satisfying schedule of 'screwing' – yes, that was the word for it now; only sweet Mrs. Brenda Bowman from Elm Park, Illinois, still referred to the act of love as the act of love. What a dumb sap she was, detained too long in girlhood, an abstainer from the adult life.

Only a week ago she had read a whole article on pubic hair, its importance, its differing types, how to look after it, how to augment it if necessary. There were women in the world, it seemed, who cared deeply about their pubic hair, and the thought of these women reinforced her feelings of estrangement. She had come to this awkward age, forty, at an awkward time in history – too soon to be one of the new women, whatever that meant, and too late to be an old-style woman. It was funny, she sometimes thought, or it was heartbreaking. She knew, on one hand, that it was idiotic to go out and buy a special cream rinse (a natural product made of pureed strawberries) to add lustre to her pubic hair, but perhaps, who knows, she was missing out on something. And she couldn't say fuck out loud; did that mean what she suspected it meant? (Probably not?) She loved her children, she loved her husband, but had seized, frantically seized, this chance to escape them.

And for this: a silent room, a solitary breakfast – cold muffins, bitter coffee, orange juice made from crystals. What a chump she was.

She thought of Jack's father, whose lament ever since she'd known him was that he had been too young to fight in the First World War and too old for the Second. (Though he *had* been made an air-raid warden during the second war and equipped with a prized flashlight and gas mask.) He had been 'cheated by time', he said, and she too had been cheated. Jack would call it historical accident, happenstance. There she had been, diapering babies, buying groceries at the A & P, wallpapering bathrooms, while other women – who were these women? – fought for equal rights, while a terrible war raged, while the country teetered on the brink of revolution. She had seen it all – but all of it on television and in the pages of *Newsweek*. A cheat. But probably she had chosen to be cheated. The coward's way out. Brenda could never make up her mind if she was the only one on the planet to suffer this particular species of dislocation or if the condition was so common it went unvoiced.

Frequently in the last year or so she has been struck with a sudden wish to freeze herself in time and announce to herself her exact location in the universe. Here I am, Brenda Bowman, boarding an aircraft for Philadelphia. Here I am, Brenda Bowman, sitting at a pine kitchen-table, filling out my tax form. Here I am, forty years old, the mother of two children, the wife of a historian, sitting on the edge of my bed applying Tawny Silk nail polish at three o'clock in the afternoon. My name is Brenda Mary Pulaski Bowman, I am forty years old, it is eleven-thirty at night, and I am engaged in the act of sexual intercourse, the act of love, with a man call Jack Bowman. Here I stand, a woman of forty, staring out of an upstairs bedroom window at a small patch of lawn (my own) in the state of Illinois in the United States of America in the . . .

Her pronouncements, rising out of moments that seemed to demand them, came as a comfort to her. They had the effect of running water, cooling and powerful. She could, with these utterances, draw precise circles around herself, observe the outlines of her body, the rhythms of daily acts which had previously been invisible. (Here I am sweeping my kitchen floor.) And she could cordon off, with remarkable clarity, certain areas of experience which had thus far eluded her. I have never been to Majorca; I have never owned any diamond jewellery except for my engagement ring; I have never been hospitalized for an illness; I have never been abandoned or down to my last cent; I have never been accused of a crime; I have never been told that someone hated me; I have never slept with a man other than my husband; I have never kissed another man since I was married, except Bernie Koltz, once, when he was drunk; I have never been really drunk; I have never until this moment picked up a phone in a hotel and ordered myself muffins and coffee.

Ah, but she had done it. And it had been easy, easy. Here sat the breakfast tray for proof. She could reach for a pencil, make a checkmark; she could say: I have just ordered myself a breakfast.

It was too quiet in the room, and for company she put on the television. Sunday morning. Nothing but cartoons and rosy-voiced evangelists. 'Ma Brethren – '

She turned the knob and found an educational programme for children, a farm broadcast sponsored by the National Dairy Association. 'Good morning, my young friends.' A farmer, looking more like a businessman in his coat and tie, was shown in close-up, his face tanned and nicely seamed as befitted a farmer. He was saying in a friendly, flinty way, 'Boys and girls, all over America cows are being milked.'

If Jack were here, Brenda thought, he would have laughed at this. It was the kind of statement he found funny. 'All over America women are hitching up their pantyhose,' he would say. 'All over America men are whistling Dixie and stepping into their jockey shorts.'

What was Jack doing now? Only seven-thirty. He would be asleep. Probably he had gone to the Carpenters' party last night. He had few close friends, but found it almost impossible to resist a party. He might wake up this morning with a hangover. If it was a bad enough hangover, he might be awake already, stumbling into the bathroom to look for the aspirin. He might even be downstairs, making himself a cup of instant coffee, rubbing the back of his neck, thinking he should put in a little work on the book he was writing about Indian trading practices. He might push that thought aside and switch on the television, instead, in an idle way and hear this same farmer saying, 'All over America cows are being milked.'

Would he laugh out loud in the empty living room? She doubted it. She couldn't imagine what it would sound like if he did. Twenty-four hours away from home and already she had forgotten what his laugh sounded like; amazing. It might be a good idea to phone home later in the day, just to see how they were getting along without her. On the other hand, a long-distance call presented certain small vexations. Should she phone person-to-person? What time would they be back from Dad and Ma Bowman's? And wasn't it a little neurotic anyway to phone home when she'd only been gone for twenty-four hours – a little bit flakey, as Rob would say. Flakey. She cringed when he said it.

A week ago Brenda had read a humour piece in the *Tribune* about the changing dialogue of the seventies. Certain expressions were out, it seemed, and others – new jargon words – were in. It was no longer fashionable to talk about one's identity; if you did you declared yourself a leftover from the sixties. It was no longer okay to talk about getting in touch with your anger or in touch with your feelings, and certainly not in touch with yourself. It was corny (oddly this was still an okay word) to talk about having a relationship, and especially corny it you were *working* at a relationship. The word 'trendy' was passé, and so was the word 'passé'. Only twelve-year-olds talked about having their own space. Both 'kitsch' and 'seminal' had had their season. If you went about shouting to the world that you had been deprived of certain 'life choices', then you were, without a doubt, mired in the hackneyed old early seventies and might never get out. You might run the risk, with your anger and your insistence on validity, of hitching yourself to a nostalgic chunk of time, like those old folksy sorts who still said 'neat' and 'terrif' and 'boy-oh-boy'.

Reading this article had made Brenda furious. It was shallow and coy, and, in a way, a betrayal. She had felt anger when she read it – real anger, not the kind you used or shared. But she had also felt a heartbreaking sense of exclusion. She had missed another decade, first the sixties, now this. For things *had* happened. Enormous shifts of perspective had taken place. Ideas had lived and died without touching the heart and mind of Brenda Bowman in Elm Park, Illinois, U.S.A., Continent of North America, *et cetera, et cetera*. She might never catch up now; she would spend her life in this perplexing cul-de-sac which time and circumstance had prepared for her. Brenda Bowman, forty years old, mother of Rob and Laurie Bowman, drifting, coping – should she grieve or rejoice? – responding, waiting, escaping occasionally (how pathetic!) to hotel rooms in secondary cities, ordering muffins and then regretting them, thinking of phoning home, wishing Hap Lewis had come, wondering if her husband Jack had heard that farmer on TV saying, 'All over America – '

A knock on the door. Brenda jumped. Surely not the chambermaid already. She brushed the crumbs from her robe. It might be Verna returning for her suitcase. She reached up and patted her hair.

No. She opened the door to find Barry Ollershaw, smiling nervously, smelling of aftershave, saying good morning (good mahning), and handing her a bouquet of flowers.

Chapter Twelve

'R OSES!' SHE SAID BY WAY OF GREETING.
Yellow roses. About half a dozen tiny blooms still tightly
closed and looking to Brenda more like onions than flowers.
How extraordinary! (And how expensive; the thought came to
her unbidden.) 'These can't be for me,' she managed.

'Happy Sunday.' He smiled an eager, edgy smile.

'But –' Her hands reached out and felt the dampness of green
florist paper. She became flustered, girlish; something was
warning her, watch out. 'But why – ?'

He spread his hands. 'A girl was selling them down in the
lobby. She was wearing a long dress and had one of those carts.'
His eyes smiled. 'I couldn't resist.'

'Lovely.' Brenda poked a finger into the nested centre. There
were soft-looking sprays of pale fern tucked in with the roses,
giving off a humid, hothouse smell.

'Actually, ah, Brenda' – he seemed to be testing her name for
accuracy – 'is it all right' – he glanced past her into the room – 'if
I come in for a minute?'

'Well, yes, I mean come in.' She stepped aside, feeling not so
much alarm as confusion. Flowers, expensive flowers, and so
early – not even eight o'clock – and that racket coming from the
television. 'I'm afraid I'm not dressed yet.' She backed into the
room, clutching her robe, apologizing, 'I was being lazy –'

'Why not when you have a chance.' He was being kind. And
careful.

'Just let me turn off the TV.' How had she managed to get
muffin crumbs all over the table. She was as bad as Laurie. And
coffee sloshed in her saucer too. And a wet bath towel on the
chair; she never did that at home. 'Come in, sit down.'

She made a grab for the towel and twisted it awkwardly in
her hands; what should she do with it? Then, regarding the
flowers, she said, 'I should put these in water right away.'

'Here,' he jumped. 'What about this coffee flask? That should
do the trick.'

'Oh, do you think – '

'It's just about empty. I could dump out the rest – unless you want it – and get some water.'

'It's terrible coffee anyway.'

'Oh?'

'Bitter.'

'Oh.' The word bitter hung between them. He nodded slowly. 'Hotels – '

Brenda reached for the coffee flask, bumping against his arm.

'I'll get it,' he said, and went whistling off into her bathroom.

She was left alone, listening to the water running, regarding herself in the mirror. This is crazy, she mouthed, and made a face at herself. She remembered she had left the bathroom in a mess, littered with – what? Stockings on the shower rail, talcum powder. Shampoo. Ban Roll-on. Her Second Debut in the large economy size. All the intimate equipment for her travel case dumped out on the counter, including, oh God, her new box of Tampax (always be prepared). What was that he was whistling in there? Something tuneless, whatever it was. 'Yankee Doodle'. She was reminded sharply of Jack's bathtub singing, which was modest, almost a mumble.

'There we go.' Barry Ollershaw settled the flowers on the writing table.

'They're really lovely,' she said again.

'I was wondering, ah, Brenda, if you were planning to go out this morning.' His voice had taken on a measure of shrewdness.

'Out?'

'Outside of the hotel.' He perched on the arm of the chair, waiting.

Brenda thought for a minute. 'Well, I don't know,' she said. 'We've got a talk at nine, the Keynote Address. And then a workshop at eleven. So I guess I won't be going out this morning. Why?'

He gave a sharp sigh. 'It's about your coat, the coat you left in my room last night.'

'My new coat?' The word 'new' came out involuntarily.

'Was it new? Oh, God.'

'What happened?'

'I was going to bring it back this morning. If you remember.'

'I remember.' What was the matter with him?

'Well' – he paused, and his hands curled into fists – 'I might as well just tell you outright. It seems to have disappeared.'

'What has? My coat?'

'I'm sure it will come back. What I mean is, nobody stole it, nothing like that. It's just that I don't know where it is. At this moment. You haven't,' he asked brightening, 'brought another coat with you by any chance?'

'No,' Brenda said slowly. 'Just the one coat.'

'Oh.'

There seemed nothing to add.

'You mean,' Brenda said, taking a breath, 'that it was hanging there in your room last night, and this morning it's not there?'

'More or less, yes, that's what happened.'

'But the maid probably knows. Maybe she thought it needed pressing or cleaning or – '

'I've already asked her.'

'But,' and Brenda laughed more loudly then she meant to, a near cackle, 'a coat doesn't just walk away.'

'I think I do have an idea about what might have happened to it. The circumstances.'

'What?'

'I think it was just, well, borrowed.'

'But who – ?'

'It's awkward to explain . . . ' His eyes seemed to wander toward the arrangement of yellow roses, scowling, scrutinizing, questioning their presence.

Brenda waited. 'How awkward?' she said at last.

'Actually not all that awkward. I mean, there is a logical explanation. The thing is, well, the management asked me if I would mind sharing my room, since I had a double. You know all about the trouble with the overbookings – '

'Yes?'

'This was last night, when they asked me. Around midnight.'

'Midnight?

'So I said, sure, why not, it didn't matter to me.'

'And then what?'

'They told me another metallurgist, from, New York I think, would be coming. But I didn't realize he would be bringing . . . well . . . a friend for the night.'

'A woman friend, you mean.'

'Exactly. You've got it.'

'Did you meet her?'

'To tell the truth I haven't met either of them.' (Brenda liked the way he said 'eye-there'.) 'I was asleep when they came in. That must have been around two or so. I guess I woke up briefly when I heard them, but they didn't even put the light on, just stumbled around in the dark. I think they were fairly drunk. At least it sounded like it. And in a fairly amorous mood. So I kept discreetly turned toward the wall.'

'I can imagine.' Brenda was smiling and shaking her head.

'It was a fairly long and noisy performance. It made me think of you and what you ran into yesterday. God! And when I woke up this morning – I slept like the proverbial log in spite of everything – they had already left. And your coat – '

' – was gone too.'

'What I figure is, they must have gone for a walk or something. And just sort of borrowed your coat. I'm sure they'll bring it back. It could be back there now for all I know. I went downstairs and asked at the desk, but they – '

'Was that why you brought the flowers?'

'Well . . . '

'It wasn't your fault. About the coat.'

'I can't help feeling somewhat responsible – '

'I'm sure it will come back . . . Barry.' She tried out his name.

'I hope so.'

What an Irish-looking face he had – small, compact, with clear eyes and a mouth that closed with quickness. She wondered if he *was* Irish.

'I was afraid,' he was saying, 'that you'd be stuck inside the hotel all morning without a coat. Especially now with all the snow.'

'Snow?'

'You haven't seen the snow? It's been snowing all night according to the news.'

'I haven't even looked outside.'

She pulled the curtains, and there it was, everywhere. It was still falling; the sky was filled with heavy wet flakes. They drifted slowly past the window, reminding Brenda of bars of music, densely harmonic. Long rectangles of snow clung even to the blank glass office-building across the street (who would have thought there were places on that smooth face that could catch and hold these slim shapes). The smaller brick building next to

93

it (a bank?) was softened by its white covering, the flat roof transformed to an untouched field, rural-looking, a farmer's pasture. The sky was surprisingly radiant, a sheet of photographic film, whitish-grey with a backing of silver, and far below Brenda could see the narrow street choked with drifts. This was a village lane. What had happened to the traffic, the flow of cars and buses and cabs? It had vanished, leaving this simple, bright river of white. A swarm of discs, human figures, moved toward what must be the front door of the hotel. Brenda, watching them, was reminded of iron filings, of an electromagnet, of Mr. Sloan at Morton High School, earnest and theatrical and prone to puns, giving a demonstration in the school basement. Brenda had been drawn to him, the herringbone of his jacket and the way his pack of Pall Malls stuck out of his pocket. He had only stayed a year; later another girl told her he was a 'homo' and so had been asked to leave. She hadn't believed it at the time; her innocence was stalwart and denying in those days, but probably, thinking about it now –

'Peaceful, isn't it?' Barry Ollershaw said.

'I should get dressed.'

'We were in Japan a couple of years ago.' (We? – his wife probably.) 'For another conference. There was snow falling right in Tokyo. Like this, these big flakes. And everyone just stopped and watched it. People sat all afternoon in restaurants, drinking tea and looking out of the windows. Someone told us it was a regular Japanese pastime. In the spring they sit and watch cherry blossoms, just watch them. And in winter – '

'It must be hypnotizing.'

'Sort of an art form, they say – '

'Meditation. A background to meditation.'

'Tranquillity.'

'It's the silence you feel. This thick glass – '

'With everything muffled and far away.'

'Chicago snow doesn't look like this.'

'Doesn't it?'

'Maybe it does, but I never really look at it. Not while it's coming down like this.'

'We're all too busy, I guess.'

'Rushing around.'

'I think children do.'

'What?'

94

'Stop. And really see things.'

'I think you're right.'

'You have children?'

'Two, a boy and a girl. You?'

'No.'

'Oh.'

'But I remember how when I was a kid I noticed things. I was telling you yesterday about how my mother made quilts, and even now, after all these years, I can remember exactly what the quilt on my bed looked like. Especially one jagged patch in the middle, sort of eight-sided.'

'Imagine.'

'It was some kind of scratchy wool, dark blue. I remember falling asleep with my fingers on it. When I think of all the things I've forgotten about. But I remember that patch, the exact shape and feel of it.'

'My husband's like that.'

'Jack?'

A pause. 'How did you know his name?'

'You said it yesterday.'

'Did I? I guess I did. Well, when he was young he used to have one of those wooden tops. Just an ordinary wooden top with a string. When Rob and Laurie were small he kept looking in stores for one just like it, but he never found one that felt exactly the same. He says he remembers just how it felt in his hand.'

'We don't have much snow in Vancouver. Maybe once or twice a year.'

'I didn't know that. I thought in Canada – '

'I suppose that's why I love snow.'

'Look at it. It's coming down even faster.'

'You can hardly see across – '

'I wonder how deep it is. From up here you really can't tell.'

'Strange isn't it, looking at the world from this height. What I mean is, weather hardly matters when you're up this high. It's sort of, well . . . '

'Abstract.'

'That's it. Abstract.'

'Maybe that's a bad thing in a way. Not feeling a part of the weather. Not needing weather.'

'The way farmers need it, you mean?'

'Something like that. One more thing taken away from us.'

'Peaceful though.'

'Watching it like this.'

'What else do you need when you come right down to it? Entertainment, television, who needs things like that?'

'We forget how to stop now and then and just look.'

'Popping pills. Running to shrinks. When all you have to do is stop and –'

'We're afraid of silence. A friend of mine says that. We feel we've failed if there's even a little pause in the conversation.'

'That's contemporary society. We feel we have to be communicating from morning to night.'

'Sometimes I think there's too much communication in the world.'

'And not enough time.'

'What we need is time to just . . . be.'

'Like this.'

'Just sitting. Looking at the snow coming down. '

'It's restorative.'

'It's so strange.'

'Yes.'

Brenda has never been unfaithful to Jack. In twenty years of marriage she has never once been unfaithful. When Bernie Koltz, a few months ago at a picnic, drunk on wine, cornered her and told her he adored her, had always adored her, she had not for a minute considered having an affair with him. She had taken his hand, patted it, offered to get him coffee from the thermos, told him he was sweet – which he was. For a week or two she recalled herself, at odd moments, especially at bedtime, the exact way he had looked at her that day in the Forest Preserve and said, 'I adore you, Brenda.' But that was all.

Once, years ago, Dr. Middleton, Director of the Great Lakes Institute, said a strange thing to her. 'You have beautiful eyes, Brenda. They are eyes that could melt a man's heart. You'll think I'm being foolish, but sometimes I dream about your eyes.' Brenda had been astonished, puzzled, embarrassed. She tried to make a joke of it. 'Ah, Dr. Middleton,' she teased him in a daughterly way. 'I won't be fit to live with if you go on saying nice things like that.'

Another time she ran into Hap Lewis's husband, Bud, at Marshall Field's in the middle of the afternoon . She was on the main floor, buying socks for Laurie. He invited her out for a drink at a bar on State Street. After a bourbon and water he groped for her hand and told her she was a 'marvel'. He thought it was a marvel the way she had kept her figure. That she was a marvel of a mother to her children. He urged her to have another drink. He was sometimes subject to depression, he told her. He and Hap seemed to have little in common but the boys and the house. Brenda had some difficulty getting rid of him, and in the end invented a doctor's appointment.

Only a few weeks ago, at a party, she had met a travel photographer. He specialized in beaches he told her, going all over the world photographing beaches for hotel brochures. He suggested she drop into his studio one afternoon and see some of his work. He told her he was turned on by women who are intelligent and good listeners.

Brenda never considered having an affair with either Dr. Middleton or Bud Lewis or Bernie Koltz. Or the travel photographer – whose name she never did discover. She loved Jack, she trusted him. She knew all the creases and odours of his body. She was grateful and a little awed by his fidelity; many of the couples she and Jack knew were unfaithful to each other. But not them.

Now for the first time she felt she had stepped into faithlessness. So this was it! Not sex at all, but novelty, risk, possibility. She was sitting in a hotel room in Philadelphia, watching the snow coming down and keeping an elaborate silence – minute after minute passed in silence. The silence seemed to her to be pure, composed, and possibly dangerous. The longer it lasted, minute by minute, the more rarefied it became. (Later she would see it as miniaturized but undiminished.) This person sitting beside her – this man with his vivid Irish face and nervous hands – had surrendered to her, without caution or hesitation, his early memory of a particular eight-sided patch centred in his childhood quilt. Out of all his life, he had chosen that. There were things she would like to tell him in exchange. But not yet.

She thought of Jack at home in Elm Park, waking in the empty bed, reaching sleepily for the clock, already – though he didn't know it – betrayed.

Chapter Thirteen

MORTON HOLMAN IS WINDING UP THE KEYNOTE ADDRESS. His eyes glitter and pierce, sweep to the domed ceiling, dart downward to his wristwatch; he fixes his audience with a pleading high-pitched cry, begging them for just five more minutes.

'The history of craft is a history of renunciation,' he croons into the microphone. 'The pride of doing without. All of you here know the truth of that historic declaration: Less is More. But ladies, and I should say gentlemen, too, look around you and what do you see in the world today? We see the artifice of art, brought into being by a tasteless elite who' – he pauses, shakes his head with sadness, opening his mouth for air – 'an elite who, for all their philanthropy and their trusts and their endless advisory councils, are the greatest enemy of the true art. I speak, of course, of that art which grows from necessity. What a word that is – *necessity! Need*. I ask you, did we *need* paintings of Greek battles done by languid Englishmen idling in Italy? Porcelain *objets d'art* for the bedchambers of invalid kings? The odious fringes and tassels of novelty, and the equally odious insanity of vain pretension which fills this world of ours with non-objects – the unspeakable, untouchable horror of museum sculpture, for example. Ladies and gentlemen, the objects I've shown you today – and they will be displayed in the foyer this afternoon – the Shaker hayrake, the china doorknob, the New England weathervane – these objects demonstrate what the human imagination, tempered by stern utility and need, can produce. Sense and sensibility, to borrow a phrase. The human hand reaching out and touching what another human hand has fashioned. The subtlety of this doorknob, the way it fits the hand, its ability to rotate and create a secondary movement, a functional movement! I know I'm running out of time, but bear with me another minute please. These things must be said, ladies. And gentlemen. We can find, through this kind of tactility – I'm speaking of the doorknob – find what I

98

believe to be a new spirituality. A sense of needful community. We must first know the maker, the craftsperson, and be able to trust his or her nearness, seeing him or her not as effete or ethereal – but I see I am getting a signal from your chairman and so must draw these words to a conclusion. In closing, then, I ask you to bear in mind, to carry away with you, the words of William Morris: sweetness, simplicity, and soul. A trinity for the honest artist, the man or woman not afraid of the label – dare I say it – the label of artisan. One who, in fact, rejoices in this acknowledgement of his or her utility in a world so badly in need of refreshment. I'm afraid I haven't had time to fine-tune these thoughts as I'd like, but I realize I am speaking to the converted, the very practitioners of these concepts, the men and women who carry their tools openly, unashamedly, and who leave the imprint of their own humanness on whatever they touch. I see I really must stop. Thank you for your kind attention. I am honoured, in my small way, to march beside you.'

'The old bore,' Susan Hammerman murmurs to Brenda over the noise of the applause.

'They say he's nothing but a pimp for the Gallery Naif in New York,' says Lottie Hart, who has arrived unexpectedly on the morning plane. 'How he wangled his way onto the programme I'd give my eyeteeth to know.'

' – nothing to say I didn't already know.'

' – still – '

'I thought he'd fine-tune me right to sleep for a minute there.'

'He's awfully inspiring though,' Lenora Knox whispers. 'About art and the sense of community and everything.'

'I didn't hear one word about needlepoint. I suppose he thinks needlepoint is too damned effete.'

'He does have a point,' Susan Hammerman admits, 'about us not taking a back seat to the so-called true and pure artists of the world.'

'Why the hell should we go around apologizing just because our stuff has a degree of usefulness.'

'He really does know his primitive Americana backwards and forwards. I read a write-up on him somewhere. In *Time*, I think it was.

'Shhh.'

'Now what?'

'God, not more speeches.'

Betty Vetter, trim in a blue wool pantsuit and with a flower in her lapel, is at the lectern, pounding for attention. 'Ladies and gentlemen, I've just come from the meeting of the ad hoc committee to look into the grievance about the hotel arrangements, and I'm happy to report to you that a tentative solution has been reached with the International Society of Metallurgists – '

'Boo – '

' – a tentative solution regarding space.'

There are cheers. Charlotte Dance, sitting in front of Brenda, raises a fist and looks around, grinning a toothy look of triumph.

Betty holds up her hand for silence. 'Forty of their delegates have agreed to double up, freeing twenty rooms for our members which' – she holds up her hand again – 'which just happens to be the exact number we need.'

More cheers. Brenda finds she is clapping furiously.

'Furthermore, they have agreed to hold their final banquet at six-thirty on Wednesday evening, if – no, wait – *if* we are willing to put ours off until nine o'clock. Can I have a vote on that?'

'Compromise!' a condemning voice calls out.

'Some of us have planes to catch.' Another voice.

But the vote is carried, and Brenda, raising her right hand, feels a swelling exhilaration. How quickly, how almost magically, solutions are found. What a remarkable thing agreement is. The world needs people like Charlotte Dance and Betty Vetter, people who know how to solve problems.

She says this later to Lenora as they make their way across the convention floor to the room where the first workshop is being held.

Lenora agrees. 'Of course, I myself am not political.'

Brenda is about to say that she is not political either, but she is interrupted by a man's voice calling her name. 'Mrs. Bowman. Are you Mrs. Bowman?'

'Yes,' Brenda says, and feels a wave of panic. Something has happened at home. The children. Jack.

'Excuse me, Mrs. Bowman.' The voice is smooth and practiced. 'Let me introduce myself. I'm Hal Rago from the Philadelphia *Examiner* and we're doing some coverage of the exhibition. Features kind of thing. Interviews. We'd like something real personal and down to earth, and I was just talking to a Mrs.' – he pulls out a card, turns it over – 'a Mrs. Hammerman. Who said you might be agreeable to an interview.'

'Me?'

'Sort of Midwest perspective, something along that line. We've already cased the East and the Northeast. They're in the can.'

'I don't know. I mean, I don't know what I could say, but I'd be happy – '

'Great. Terrific. Look, what about we meet at the Emerald Room – say this aft some time. Around three.'

'Emerald Room?'

'St. Christopher Hotel. Just a few blocks away. Nice atmosphere, the press sort of hangs out there, you know what I mean.'

'A few blocks away?' Brenda is thinking of the snow outside and the fact that she has no coat. Surely, though, she will have it back by three. But maybe – 'Could we maybe make it a little later? Say four?'

'You've got yourself a date, Mrs. Bowman. See ya, four p.m. Emerald Room. Just ask for Hal Rago.'

'What do you know,' Lenora says. 'You're going to be in the newspaper.'

Brenda thinks of telling her about the articles in *Chicago Today* and the *Elm Leaves Weekly*, and the radio interview on WOPA, but she resists, and says instead. 'I wonder what they mean by Midwest perspective.'

'The kind of regional-motif thing maybe. Like in the Southwest we've got this strong tie with the outdoors, and then the whole Navaho-Mexican influence. It shows up. You must have noticed that.'

Brenda shakes her head; she can't remember having had any thoughts which encompassed both quilting and the Midwest. Of course there was that one quilt, *Michigan Blue*; she could always talk about that. How does she feel about the Midwest anyway? Space. Cornfields. Rivers. Fertility. That was it, she could mention fertility. Or something like that.

A hand-printed sign on a door says 'Quilting Seminar'. More than twenty women – Brenda does a quick count – are gathered around a long table. A woman wearing the name card 'Reddie Grogan: Concord, N.H.' kicks off the discussion with a question about the place of nostalgia in the quilting tradition – how the sight of patchwork and appliqué free-associates with thoughts of home, hearth, warmth, the whole yesteryear sort of thing – and how this process enters into the basic aesthetic response of the public.

'But isn't this an enrichment?' someone suggests. 'A time-dimension thing, kind of a bonus, which gives a sort of creative head start – '

'But interferes, you have to agree, with the statement a particular piece is trying to make. Muddies the water, blurs the edges, dims the message – '

'A nostalgic quilt is a throwback,' a young woman calls out. 'Hacking out new forms is what it's all about.'

'I'm not talking about immersion, I'm talking about retrospective – '

'Listen,' a brave-looking woman in a tight sweater says, 'Do we as quiltmakers have to "aspire to cosmology"?' – she makes quotation marks with her fingers – 'I mean, *do* we? Can't we get back to making warm, attractive bed coverings?'

Laughter flows. Smiles all around. A sense of release. Brenda sits back, happy now, exchanging looks with Lenora Knox, who has put on a pair of rimless spectacles that pick up the light from the overhead fixture, making her look, for an instant, about a hundred years old.

'What sets quilting apart from other crafts is the built-in shiver of history.' Has she actually said this? She? Brenda Bowman? Yes. Amazingly enough, Brenda from Elm Park, Illinois, has spoken, and all around her women are listening and nodding. (It is Jack's phrase, 'the shiver of history' – borrowed from Flaubert, always scrupulously acknowledged. He uses it fairly often.)

'But is it holding us back? That's what I want to know. I don't mean consciously, I mean unconsciously.'

'Is that supposed to mean – ?'

'A hand reaching from the past, a restraint in the end. Unless, that is, we recognize it for what it is.'

'The Mexican tradition – ' Even Lenora is jumping in now.

'But do we actually know where our patterns come from?' someone is asking. 'Is it possible to say that some forms are legacies from the past and others are original and innovative?'

'You mean like some are just kind of made up?'

'They're all made up, aren't they? When I'm cutting something out with a pair of shears, I'm making a new form.'

'I don't think so,' Brenda is saying. She is thinking now of *The Unfinished Quilt* at home. 'Certain forms are basic. I mean, take the circle.'

'The mandala,' someone contributes knowingly.

'The what ?'

'How can you get away from a circle? It's not just a traditional form, it's more basic than that even.

'Mythic.'

'The shape of the world, a boiling pot.'

'A baby's mouth.'

'Or a . . . what do you call it . . . you know what I mean . . . '

'Yes.'

'But do these things ask for definition? I mean, do we have to put a name to them?'

'No,' Brenda says. 'We don't even have to think of them. They come out of our fingers.' What has she said? Does she know what she's talking about? Does she believe it? Yes, she does.

'You mean you're saying that art is anti-intellectual. The old instinct thing working it all out?'

'Well' – she feels trapped now – 'what I meant was more of a – '

'I think I know what you mean. I think you're saying we have to trust our hands. That sometimes our hands are a move or two ahead of our brains.'

'Yes,' Brenda says. 'Like typing. The fingers just know where the keys are.'

'I see what you're getting at.'

'Interesting. I never thought of it like that. Comparing it to typing. I always make these elaborate patterns first – '

'Always worrying about what it means. Does it make a statement or does it not make a statement.'

'Me too.'

'Instinct and spontaneity, they're like flip sides of a coin.'

'Whereas the deliberate suppression of memory or nostalgia – '

'I like Brenda's phrase better, the shiver of history.'

Brenda looks around the table. What intelligent women these are! She feels a surge of love for each of them. One of them is jabbing at the air now, saying something about the juxtaposition of time and matter.

Time and matter. In her mind Brenda sets these works carefully aside. She will have to tell Jack . . .

Chapter Fourteen

BRENDA WAS NINETEEN WHEN SHE MET JACK BOWMAN. IT happened during a cold Chicago winter. She can remember that at the end of March that year there were snow flurries; the wind off the lake carried with it particles of ice and dirt and shook the coats of the young secretaries and office clerks, lifting them unexpectedly as these young women descended from their buses in the early mornings.

Somehow Brenda had found a typing and filing job at the Great Lakes Institute on Keeley Avenue in the Loop. There had been an ad in the paper: Experienced Typist Needed. Dr. Middleton himself interviewed her. He offered her tea. A window in his office looked down into the small, green chilliness of a park, sparely symmetrical with stone benches and shrubs and statuary. On one wall of his office Dr. Middleton had a number of dark, oily landscapes, and on another an arrangement of wooden figures. 'Iroquois,' he said to Brenda in a cold, lonely voice. On his desk was a photograph of a woman with smooth blonde hair pulled back from a lean face. That must be his wife, Brenda said to herself. 'My wife, Anne,' Dr. Middleton said in a voice suddenly thawed into warmth. Brenda was amazed at the way he said, 'My wife, Anne'. She had never heard anyone, except perhaps Cary Grant, speak so delicately about a woman.

'Do you mind, Miss Pulaski, if I inquire as to why you are considering leaving Commonwealth Edison after only four months?'

Brenda hesitated. One hand went to her mouth. What should she say? That she wanted to find more interesting work? Something more challenging? Or the truth: that she was suffering unspeakable and undreamt of loneliness in her first job, sitting all day in a long, shadowless room with thirty other girls, all of them typing away, under the savage overhead lights, clack-clacking all the day long. A week earlier, riding the bus to work, her coat gathered tightly around her, tears had sprung into her eyes. Why? And in Dr. Middleton's office it was happening to her again; her throat was suddenly tight with tears, her eyes filling. She lifted the teacup and held it hard against her lips.

'Perhaps you just wanted a change,' Dr. Middleton said after a moment, and at that Brenda managed to nod.

There were only four of them – Brenda, Glenda, Rosemary, and Gussie – in the Great Lakes typing pool; it was one of Dr. Middleton's jokes that they constituted not a pool at all, but a pond. Glenda was red-headed, big-busted, wide-hipped. She powdered her broad nose with Charles-of-the-Ritz loose powder in a shade especially blended for redheads. Her sweaters and blouses were in tones of pink and copper. 'Arlene Dahl says we' – *we* meant all the redheads in the world – 'should stick with the pinks and the coppers.' She wore a girdle which had been specially made for her in the corset department at Field's, and she was saving her money for a pair of custom-made shoes. 'Face it,' she said, 'every foot is different, right?' At Billings the doctor swore he'd never seen an arch like this.

Rosemary. Rosemary was thirty and had speckled skin and watery eyes. She was given to dim, helpless, endearing confessions of mortification. 'There I stood, blushing like a *beet*' or 'Well, I just about dropped dead on the *spot*.' She had been engaged for two years and wore a zircon. When would her wedding take place? It was discussed endlessly. But there were problems. Art wasn't ready to settle down; he lived with his mother and father in Skokie; it was hard to find a decent apartment; besides, he was Jewish and expected her to convert.

Gussie Sears was twenty-two and had a brace on one leg. Polio. Her face was dark, skeletal, and ugly, but despite this she was married. She had been married for almost a year to a shy, ugly youth named Franklin Sears, who worked for an insurance company on LaSalle Street. Brenda and Glenda and Rosemary saw Franklin Sears every day, for at five o'clock sharp he would arrive at the Great Lakes Institute, red-faced and winded from his walk, to take Gussie home on the El. At lunchtime he phoned Gussie or else she phoned him. 'It's hard,' Gussie told Brenda one day in the washroom, 'for us to be away from each other all day.'

The words, shyly uttered, had fallen on Brenda's ears like revelation. That love could be like this, so strong that it brought pain. And was it really possible that love came even to those who fell short of physical beauty, whose bodies, untaught by Arlene Dahl and Charles of the Ritz, were simple, shallow vessels of hair and bones and skin? How could passion rise from so much flatness? But it did, it did! Gussie *longed* for Franklin; by mid-afternoon she was tapping her pencil and watching the clock. And Franklin's slack and reddened flesh clearly longed for Gussie. His long legs hurried into the typing room at five o'clock, and his awkward hands shook as he helped Gussie into her woollen coat. This sensual excitement seemed to Brenda grotesque, a little laughable, but also dazzling.

From the first day she loved working at the Great Lakes Institute. She relaxed. She felt at home. The terrors of Commonwealth Edison faded fast. She loved her partitioned desk drawers, with their paperclips and pencils and extra typewriter ribbons. And she loved Rosemary and Gussie and Glenda. Hours spent together in the typing pool knit them together within days into a tough, jokey sisterhood. They lent each other nail polish and Kleenex, they discussed their mothers, they conspired tenderly against Dr. Middleton. They covered for each other; they trusted each other. On payday they went to Roberto's around the corner and ordered platters of spaghetti or lasagna. They were the four fish in Dr. Middleton's pool and felt themselves to be worthy and cherished.

Only Gussie stood slightly apart, and this, Brenda perceived, was because she, alone of the four, was married.

Married! It was another state of being, a state that was sealed like an envelope in its inviolability. The state of marriage was secret and safe, a circle of charmed light beyond the horizon of the easily capsized now.

Glenda and Brenda and Rosemary probed for details. What did Gussie fix for dinner? Had she tried doing pork chops the new way with condensed cream-of-mushroom soup? Had she tried her hand at making cloverleaf rolls? What about a budget? Did she and Franklin have a budget? Of course they must; so much for entertainment, so much for groceries. Did Gussie think spray wax was as good as paste wax? What did Gussie and Franklin do in the evenings? Did they watch TV? In the furniture line, did they like Early American better than French Provincial? What about goals and ideals? Were they hoping to get their own automatic washing-machine eventually? Saving

107

for a house? Was a Hide-a-Bed a sound investment for a young couple? When they had children, would Gussie quit work and stay at home with the kids? Sterling or silverplate?

Brenda and Glenda and Rosemary hungered for these details. (It was 1957.) Even more, they longed to know, but didn't ask, whether or not Gussie had a supply of pastel nylon nightgowns and if she took the brace off her leg when she went to bed – of course she must! And how it had felt when . . . well . . . the first time? Did it hurt? How often did they do it and did they turn the lights off and did Gussie use a douche after?

Gussie, poor Gussie, smiled at the questions about cloverleaf rolls and paste wax; her pale, uneven lips parted; it seemed a miracle that her teeth weren't broken. 'Well,' she would say, puzzled, letting the 'well' drift off like cigarette smoke, 'well, I don't exactly know.' She was clearly baffled by their interest. These domesticities seemed not to have occurred to her. Franklin was planning to finish off his accounting course at night school, that much she volunteered. On Sundays they drove out to Sycamore to visit his family. They saved Green Stamps – but in a haphazard way, half the time forgetting. And occasionally, in the summer, they had attended the concerts at Grant Park. (At the mention of the Grant Park concerts, Brenda and Glenda and Rosemary had beamed and nodded. It seemed the right thing for a young couple to do, educational and romantic, and was free besides.)

But about the colour of her kitchen cupboards, Gussie was oddly unforthcoming. ('They're just painted, sort of yellowish.') She seemed not to know much about the new spray wax or very much about shelf paper or bleaching agents. At work she was quietly industrious, an excellent typist with a tidy desk top. If Dr. Middleton had a special job, something he wanted done quickly, he always gave it to Gussie. Her small, wiry body, straining forward, pressed the typewriter keys with energy and knowing; there were days when she typed right through the coffee break, leaving Brenda and Glenda and Rosemary to go off on their own to the cafeteria and speculate, endlessly speculate, about the intricacies, the mysteries, of married life.

Brenda herself could not understand her new mania for domestic details. Certainly it was not the domesticity of her own life that had ripened her for this; she and her mother still lived in the same old apartment in Cicero, over the dry cleaner's, where they had always lived. Dust continued to settle in a friendly way on her mother's sewing machine and on the living-room radiator; the refrigerator in the kitchen still whined its old tune, and its stale, metallic-smelling shelves held salami, herring, a carton of milk, a net bag of navel oranges. The wiped oilcloth on the kitchen table was weighted down, as it had always been, by the pink-and-white sugar bowl and the salt shakers in the form of twin squirrels. All of this comforted Brenda in a vague way; none of it interested her.

It was the domesticity of the newly married that enchanted her, its crisp, glazed magazine aura, rising out of the whiteness of weddings and opening like a play onto rooms paved with Armstrong flooring. Basket chairs with corduroy cushions. Café curtains on brass rods; Brenda, in those days, sometimes dreamed about café curtains. And what else? A Duncan Phyfe coffee table in front of the couch; a white padded wedding-album brought out for visitors to see. Carpeting on the stairs, and a staggering of small, framed flower prints. In the bedroom: coloured sheets, a dust-ruffle, perhaps a canopy. Brightly toned towels in the bathroom, stacked on open shelves – such riches – and little cakes of scented soap in a glass apothecary jar. She wanted an organized linen cupboard. She wanted to plunge with a brave face into low-budget entertaining, to put the whole of her heart into steaming casseroles of beef Stroganoff and, for desert, frozen lemon pie with graham-cracker crust. She wanted it all, all of it: a vacuum cleaner with a set of attachments, a spice rack of carved red maple, a doorbell that chimed – all of it.

Years later at a party given in her honour – she had just won her first award – someone asked her why she had married so young. She replied with a truthfulness that surprised even her. 'I wanted to have a pink kitchen,' she said. 'I was *dying* to have a pink kitchen.'

In those days, Jack, a history major, was in his senior year at DePaul, and was doing his Special Project on the French explorer LaSalle. One morning in late March he turned up at the Great Lakes Institute to look at an old survey map. Dr. Middleton greeted him warmly enough, shaking his hand and expressing interest in the project – 'We need young men like you in the field' – but was clearly anxious to have him off his hands. 'Miss Pulaski here, Brenda that is, will look after you,' he assured Jack.

Brenda led Jack down the hall and around the corner to the map room. It was kept locked, and she struggled for a moment with the key.

'Here, let me.' He stepped forward. He had lean hands, rather hairy (but in a nice way), and a plaid shirt. The door opened at once, making a creaking noise that encouraged them to turn and smile at each other.

He told Brenda about the Special Project. 'It's a sort of thesis, you might say, only they don't call it that except in grad school.'

At that time Brenda didn't know what a thesis was, and she had never been in the map room before. It felt dry, and was filled with air which seemed too thin for health. The walls were entirely lined with locked drawers and cupboards, all painted an unglinting metallic green. She examined the keyring Dr. Middleton had given her; she regarded the cupboards. 'Eenie, meenie, miney, mo,' she said inanely.

She unlocked a drawer and stepped aside. Jack began to extract maps, one at a time, taking care to hold them at the edges, not to bend them. She noticed that his plaid shirt was made of the kind of cotton flannel no one wore any more. The cuffs were soft with wear, almost colourless, and the sight of them touched her deeply.

'Here it is,' he said, holding up a map.

'Are your sure?' It seemed impossible that he could have found it so readily, and in the first drawer she'd opened.

'Absolutely. Here, you can tell by the markings at the bottom.'

She looked and saw a wavering line of unreadable script. 'Oh.'

'I really appreciate you helping me like this.'

She felt she should explain. It was pure luck, she said, that she had opened the right drawer. She'd only been at the Institute for a month and had never been in the map room before. It was another girl, she explained, Rosemary, who usually looked after visitors. Before coming to work at the Institute she had worked at Commonwealth Ed. But it was so big. There were so many girls.

She was babbling. She could hear herself babbling, and was acutely aware of a small, red coldsore on her upper lip. He was staring at her oddly, as though she might be crazy.

A bad beginning.

Nevertheless, he asked her to lunch. 'There's a place around the corner. Italian. Do you like Italian food?'

'You mean Roberto's? I love Italian food. Last week, on payday, we – '

She stopped herself in time.

She loved his face, even though it struck her as being overly wide and rather blank. This effect of blankness was false; he was, at twenty-one, waiting only to be unlocked. (Brenda thought of the shut drawers in the map room.)

At Roberto's, remembering his worn shirt-cuffs, she ordered vegetable soup, thirty-five cents, the cheapest thing on the menu – and a grilled-cheese sandwich and told him about how she had found the job at the Institute, how nervous she'd been during the interview, how she had almost spilled her tea in her lap. 'Oh, it was so funny,' she said, almost believing it.

His glance, which at first seemed withheld, opened an inch. He had wide, sleepy-looking eyes. She saw him taking in the blue curves of her angora sweater and saw something which might have been surprise break over his face. How had she done this – surprised him like this?

He told her about the explorer LaSalle, and, in a slow, thoughtful voice, he admitted that he had chosen the topic because a professor had suggested it. Not much work had been done on LaSalle's last journey; it was open territory, so to speak.

His words had the quality of being chosen rather than spilled, and Brenda sensed a consciousness as carefully mapped as a coastline. Nevertheless, she felt she could say anything to him, even something shocking. His hands on his fork and knife carried the peculiar density of someone who was waiting to be shocked.

'This is delicious,' Brenda said, finishing her soup and starting on her grilled cheese.

He wanted to order a bottle of wine.

She looked at her watch; she was worried, she said, about being late getting back to the Institute. 'And besides,' she added, 'wine for lunch isn't my cup of tea.'

Or at least this is what Jack, when he reminisces about their first meeting, claims she said.

She cannot imagine saying anything as witless as this. But she is not absolutely sure, and doesn't like to spoil what is one of Jack's favourite stories – a story which reflects badly on her, she thinks, but hints at an innocence she would like to claim.

She would marry him. The thought came like a streak of lightning cutting swift stripes on sleepy darkness. She would tell Jimmy Soderstrom, who had been taking her out all winter, that she had met someone else. She wouldn't have to go into details. She could be gentle and vague; it would be easier on the telephone. She would miss him, his shyness, his difficult courtesies, and especially his eager hands groping under her winter coat, searching over the softness of her sweater front. Oh, she would miss that eagerness, that quick snuffle of breath against her neck, that powerful moment when she would, safely, gently, push him away.

Years later she saw Jimmy Soderstrom on Roosevelt Road when she was going to visit her mother. He was stepping out of a small sportscar, slamming the little door in an energetic and familiar way. They stood talking for a few minutes, and she had been astonished at how easily he had talked – he was a car salesman, Chrysler – he who had been so tonguetied in the old days.

Everything changes, or at least everything seems changed. Looking back, Brenda finds it difficult to believe that, when she first went to work at the Institute, Dr. Middleton had been only forty years old, younger than Jack is now. Incredible. And she knows now that when this younger Dr. Middleton pronounced the words 'my dear wife, Anne', he spoke not with affection but with grievous exhaustion. She had no idea then how much people had to pay simply to endure.

Once a year now she has lunch with Gussie and Glenda and Rosemary. They have these annual lunches during the week or two preceding Christmas, always meeting at a table in the Fountain Room at Field's and always ordering something light like tuna-fish salad or the fruit plate.

None of them works at the Institute now. They are all married. Glenda, in fact, has been married twice; her first

112

husband was an alcoholic. Once he socked her in the jaw; once he broke two of her ribs. And even so, she had gone back to him.

Rosemary, at last, had converted to Judaism and, at last, married Art, and now they live with their young daughter in a tiny, stone-faced house in Berwyn. Art, an industrial engineer, is prey to bouts of unemployment; once he was without a job for two years and four months.

And Gussie? Gussie and Franklin Sears live in a rambling old house in Sycamore, Illinois, fifty miles from Chicago. Franklin has had rheumatoid arthritis for years, and despite occasional remissions, he is more or less bedridden. (Yes, Gussie confesses, there are bedpans.) To keep the family going, Gussie has a bookkeeping job with a local lumberyard and, in addition, she serves as secretary to the Sycamore School Board. When she takes the bus in for the Christmas lunches, she brings snapshots of the two children, a boy with dark hair and glasses, and a little girl, blonde as an angel and strikingly beautiful. Gussie is always the last to arrive, and she comes in, exuberant at having a day off, slipping out of her coat, and saying in a single rising breath, 'Franklin sends all of you his love.'

When Brenda thinks back to her typing-pool days at the Institute and to the time when she first met Jack, she cannot believe in her own luck. How confidently, but how blindly, she had allowed herself to drift along, a lazy swimmer adrift in a dangerous sea. What was it she had wanted then? What, besides the pink kitchen, had she asked for? Nothing much, it seemed, only something glimpsed from the corner of an eye, an image of shelter and its scanty furnishings. What did she know then of ecstasy? Nothing.

But anything can break the fragile arc of fortune, anything. There are casualties everywhere; Brenda is always running into them or hearing about them. She has been one of the lucky ones, and in her leather handbag she carries charms to protect her: snapshots, a tarnished French coin, her mother's old thimble, a newspaper clipping announcing Jack's appointment to the Elm Park Heritage Committee. Even her keyring jingles with good fortune, promising provision, enclosure, safety.

Chapter Fifteen

'A RE THERE ANY MESSAGES?'
'For?'

Brenda, standing at the hotel desk after lunch, finds her breath stuck dry as as nut in her throat, although she couldn't have said why. 'Room 2424.'

The harried desk clerk scowls, turns, then hands her a single folded slip. 'Just this.'

It's from Barry Ollershaw, a scribbled message on hotel notepaper. 'Brenda (dash dash) No coat yet, but I'm getting warm. Will keep in touch. Regards (dash dash) Barry O.'

Brenda holds the note in her hand and feels herself lifted by an unexpected sensation of buoyancy, a sudden lightening of the air in her lungs. Her throat relaxes, breathes. Getting warm, Barry Ollershaw has written – as though the two of them, she and Barry, were cheerful conspirators let loose in the Franklin Court Arms, a couple of children off on a scavenger hunt. (Brenda shuts her eyes for an instant; a film-strip, softly coloured, shunts into view; she and Barry composed in their chairs on the twenty-fourth floor of this hotel, watching the silent snow drift past the window to land somewhere out of sight.)

'I hope it's not bad news,' Lenora Knox whispers. Brenda has forgotten about Lenora.

'No, not really.' She can't bring herself to meet Lenora's anxious, probing eyes.

'Not your kiddies, I hope,' Lenora inquires.

Her children. Rob and Laurie. 'No.' Brenda shakes her head. Why is she smiling like this? Like a crazy woman. She feels her face pulling back, ready to split in two. She looks at the floor and bites down on her lower lip.

'When I'm away I always worry about the craziest darned things,' Lenora is saying, folding her granny glasses and stowing them in the depths of her felt bag. 'Like maybe the kids locking themselves out of the house or forgetting their lunches or something. Once – '

Brenda refolds the note, creasing the length of it with her thumbnail and tucking it in the side section of her bag. Hmmm. She gives the bag a pat, appreciating anew the silkiness of the soft bulging leather. Should *she* leave a note for Barry? Tell him not to worry? Tell him *she* will be in touch?

'You know,' Lenora says, 'we really should keep in touch, you and I, Brenda. When this is over, I mean. Like, who knows, maybe you'll get to New Mexico one of these days, for a visit. Like on a trip to the Grand Canyon or Mexico or something like that. Of course, the Grand Canyon's in Arizona, but that's only one state over from us. Have you ever been out there, to the Grand Canyon? They have these packhorses you can rent by the day – '

'Pardon?' Brenda says, pushing her hair out of her eyes. Why is Lenora talking about the Grand Canyon?

'Or at least we should exchange Christmas cards once a year. That's one good thing about Christmas cards. It may be commercial and all, but it's the only way to keep in touch.'

'Yes,' Brenda says enthusiastically. The fountain in the middle of the lobby sucks and gurgles as though someone is tinkering with its pump. Yes, there is a workman, bending over it, reaching an arm into its stainless-steel innards. It spouts suddenly at his touch – a whooshing sound that makes her feel lighthearted and generous. She *will* leave Barry a message. Why not? It is only common courtesy to reply to a note. (Years ago Brenda served as Corresponding Secretary to the Woodrow Wilson P.T.A.; recently she was asked if she would consider filling the same office for the Chicago Craft Guild.) It wasn't fair to have Barry Ollershaw worrying about the loss of her coat; he didn't come all the way from Vancouver, Canada, to worry about her red raincoat, did he? It wasn't his fault it vanished.

'Heavens, Brenda, I just hope I haven't put my foot in it.'

'Your foot?'

'I mean, mentioning Christmas cards just then. I mean, you could be Jewish for all I know. Or – '

'No, I'm not, we're not. Jewish that is.'

'Last year I quilted my Christmas cards. You just use cotton percale and tissue paper and just a little snitch of rickrack. My husband said I was just plain out of my head, just plain up a tree, but I found this pattern in *Quilter's Quarterly*. I could send it to you if you're interested, or maybe – '

Brenda is thinking; why not suggest to Barry Ollershaw that the two of them get together for a drink? She calculates quickly: the newspaper interview with Hal Rago is at four; it would have to be later, maybe after the President's Dinner, she couldn't miss that; or would that be too late? It might be after eleven, but the bars would still be open and there wasn't a law that said she couldn't –

"Course the silly things took me ages to do. Ages. Allen and I usually send out seventy-five cards in all, so you can imagine. But the postage was the same, that was a good thing – '

Yes, she would leave a note. The curious, peaceful levity she was feeling would stabilize the pen in her hand, enable her to slash at the paper like a schoolgirl. Greetings, she would write in a jaunty, jabbing backhand. She would be cheerful, buoyant, splashing the page with large loopy letters, and she would sign her name simply 'Brenda' – so that it rose at the end like a banner or a silk scarf floating – 'Brenda'. She would dash a line or two beneath it – make it firm, joyful, unhesitating, girlish – 'Brenda'.

'The thing is, they're kind of a keepsake in a way, if you know what I mean. At least that's what everyone kept telling me.'

'Lenora?'

'Yes, Brenda?' Lenora's eyes swim blue. Pure blue. Innocent blue.

'Lenora, do you have a piece of paper by any chance? Any old thing will do. I have to leave a message for someone.'

The main exhibition hall can be reached directly from the hotel by way of a lengthy underground concourse lined with gift shops and travel agencies and lingerie boutiques. (One of these, The Underneath Shop, catches Brenda's eye as she and Lenora pass.) Today, since it is Sunday, most of these stores are locked up and darkened by iron grills. Here and there along the way there are narrow underground avenues darting off in other directions, and these are signposted: Parking Garage, Theatre Complex, Museum Entrance. This, Brenda observes, is a complete underground city, all of it sealed off from the weather, and all of it as brilliantly lit as the out-of-doors. It would be possible to stay a week or a month in Philadelphia and never have to set a foot outside. Philadelphia backyards and fences and houses – where were they? They must exist. They had to exist. But outside this central underground trunk everything seemed reduced to supposition. It was even possible to imagine that there were no people above ground, no noisy population with fixed habits of restaurants or buses or jobs or favourite grocery stores. Only the visitors really exist, convention- goers, herds of metallurgical engineers and thronging needlewomen. The only people are *us*, Brenda thinks. She looks at Lenora and smiles.

Chatting, peering into windows, they walk for what seems a mile or more down the bright terrazzo-floored tunnels. Arrows in primary colours point all along the way to the Exhibition Hall. And there it is at last, a polished space opening before them, acres of unencumbered space, reminding Brenda of a gymnasium constructed for giants. The trusswork is exposed, and skylights high overhead let in natural light – though it is light that seems filtered and carried from a great distance, varnishy yellow light spreading a haze of seriousness over the vast,settled indoor air. The whole space hums with light, or is that the distant electric buzzing of ventilators? Probably.

'Hey, we're not open yet, ladies.' A uniformed guard, arms folded on navy-blue chest, blocks their way.

'We just wanted to look around.' Lenora says this in her high, sweet, reasonable voice. 'Would that be all right?'

'It says seven o'clock. Look in the paper. Didn't you see the paper? The show opens at seven.'

Lenora persists. Her little mouth goes straight as a coin slot. 'But you see, we're the exhibitioners. My friend here and I just want to check on our own displays.'

'The orders I got – '

'I've come all the way from New Mexico in the southwest United States.' Brenda recognizes the timbre of Lenora's voice – she has friends (Leah Wallberg, Sharon Olsen) with similar voices, voices that carry the sweetness of implacability.

The guard moves aside. 'They told us not to let anyone in here. How'm I supposed to know – '

'Thank you,' Lenora says pleasantly, and breezes past him.

There is the needlepoint section. There is the macramé section. There is a section devoted to Leather Arts, a subsection for Beadwork. But the largest section is set aside for quilts; the quilts, in fact, fill all of the east end of the hall. Brenda has never seen so many displayed at once. Even in the Chicago Craft Fair, which is the biggest fair in the Midwest, there are never more than thirty or forty in any one year. Here there are hundreds, perhaps even a thousand. To save space, each one has been suspended on a large, swinging frame that reminds Brenda of the display racks for Oriental rugs she has seen at Marshall Field's. It is necessary to view the quilts one at a time, turning the hinged frames as though they were pages in a book. Some of the quilts are still being hung by a team of young workmen in clean white overalls.

'Isn't this just . . . the most thrilling . . . ' Lenora bangs the side of her head with her fist. 'I can't believe it.'

'Yes,' Brenda says, awed.

'I mean to be shown. Here. With,' she jerks her arm in the direction of the quilts, 'with all these. The thrill.'

'I know what you mean,' Brenda says.

The quilts, they discover, are hung alphabetically by the quilter's last name, and Brenda and Lenora start at the far right in order to stay out of the way of the workmen's ladders. 'Look,' Brenda cries. 'These are Verna's. Verna of Virginia.'

'Your mysterious roommate.'

'Yes.'

'My heavens, Brenda, just look at this.' Lenora's hand plucks at the binding of Verna's quilt. Her voice has shrunk to a despairing whimper.

'I know,' Brenda actually wails.

'How does she do it?'

'Those colours.'

'Nerve, I guess. Just plain old nerve.'

'And workmanship.'

'Workpersonship,' Lenora giggles.

'The trapunto work! Those leaves!'

'Are those leaves?'

'The curve of them. And what's she used in the corner there? I don't believe it. It looks like denim.'

'It is denim. Old denim. Faded.'

'Marvellous.'

'Incredible.'

'The whole thing just sort of floats off, doesn't it?'

'Like the sky, like in the Southwest – '

'Or water – cool like water.'

'I guess you probably heard the Metropolitan Museum in New York City – '

'I *know.*'

They move along.

Lenora has bought two of her prize quilts for competition, *Fiesta* and *Terracotta*. The orange radiance of *Terracotta* wrings from Brenda an involuntary cry of delight. 'Why this is really wonderful, Lenora.'

'I sort of like *Terracotta* too, but my husband says, when it comes right down to it, that he really prefers *Fiesta*. Allen has this weakness for – '

'*Terracotta* leaps right out at you. You could put your arms around that central panel. Really, Lenora, I mean it, it's absolutely wonderful.'

And it is wonderful. In the centre stand a stalkless flower frazzled by its own heat and a ring of brittle birds with snapping jewelled eyes and cruel beaks. Wonderful. Brenda has to restrain her incredulity. On the other hand, why shouldn't Lenora Knox of Santa Fe, New Mexico, be able to create a work of art that shimmers with originality; and no doubt about it, it *was* original to sew a wide band of velvet, black velvet, around the edge of the hot, kindled centre panel like that. (Brenda thinks of a plain casket filled with dazzling primitive treasures.)

'It did get the ribbon at the State last year.' Lenora confides this in her soft, forthcoming voice. 'I was just so surprised, well, just bowled over really.'

Brenda's quilts *Clairvoyant* and *Lakeside* have been hung in place, and one of the workmen, standing on a stepladder, is easing *The Second Coming* onto the metal frame.

'My goodness,' Lenora says, 'my goodness, Brenda, you've really got talent.'

Lenora's lozenge eyes open wide, but Brenda detects something vacant in the words, as though she and Lenora are locked now into a kind of ritual of too-generous praise. She thinks of telling Lenora about *The Unfinished Quilt* at home, but stops herself. Lenora doesn't want to hear about *The Unfinished Quilt*. Brenda knows this. She knows because of the bright little sparrow of cynicism that sits on her shoulder now. It's been there for a while now, this sparrow. One year? Two years? It's hard to pin such things down. And equally hard to accuse the little fellow of specific damage. But he (he?) does chirp in her ear now, a fracturing peep-peep, posing cocky questions('But what is this for?') or throwing into doubt such steady, accustomed things as praise, condolence, sympathy – even, at times, truthtelling.

Lenora rattles on and on. 'I mean, Brenda, they are just absolutely gorgeous, all three of them. I'll just bet a dollar you're going to take home a prize. And especially with that one. *The Second Coming* did you say it was called?'

Brenda is watching the workman struggling with the top corner of the quilt. The irregular border makes it hard to attach it to the frame. ('Shit,' he is muttering into the cloth.) She is remembering how she and Hap Lewis had lifted this same quilt just two days before and carried it to the window in her workroom.

A sharp longing for home strikes her, and she yearns for her backyard with the stillness of elm and oak and leafless hedge, for Hap Lewis with her rich, nutritious laughter, for the hanging plants leafing out, even for the children's voices below, arguing, yelling, but making the walls vibrate and breath. *The Second Coming* seems lost in this enormous exhibition hall. Brenda would like to carry it away, off to her hotel room, put it on her narrow bed, lie down on its bracing squares of yellow. (Infantile, she upbraids herself.) Why *is* she so tired?

But she can't allow herself to be tired; she has an appointment at four o'clock at the St. Christopher Hotel, and it is after three now.

'Excuse me,' she says suddenly to the man on the ladder. 'Excuse me, but that's my quilt. I'm Brenda Bowman.'

'Yeah?' He looks down at her blankly.

'Well, look, I need it for a little while, okay?' (At home Laurie annoys Brenda by ending her sentences this way: okay?)

'I dunno – '

'I need to do a little more handwork on it, a few stitches. I'll bring it right back.'

'Do you think that's wise, Brenda?' Lenora worries.

'Yes.' Firmly.

'You gotta have it back before seven,' the man on the ladder says. 'Doors open at seven and we got to be done and outa here.'

'Oh, I'll have it back way before seven,' Brenda promises. 'I just thought I'd – '

'Suit yourself,' he shrugs. 'It's your blanket – you can do what you want with it.' And he lets it go, dropping it light as a parachute into her outstretched arms.

Chapter Sixteen

THE AIR OUTSIDE THE HOTEL WAS MOIST AND BRILLIANT, and the snow, which had stopped falling at last, lay melting on the sidewalks. Brenda, stepping through the wide bronze doors, congratulated herself for having brought along her winter boots.

The Second Coming was fastened beneath her chin, held in place by a large safety pin. Worn on the bias, with one corner tucked under, it fell warmly around her, reaching as far down as her knees. Lucky for her she'd decided to use light dacron batting – never mind what the purists said – and lucky, too, that she'd designed it off-centre, so that the bright elongated blocks showered in a circle from her shoulder; it might have been designed for this very purpose. Of course, it was awkward having to clutch it closed from the inside, but once she got used to it –

Only four blocks to the St. Christopher, but they were long city blocks. The doorman at the Franklin had pointed the way. He offered to get a cab for her, at the same time gesturing at the hopelessness of this, but Brenda had waved the idea aside. She needed fresh air, she needed time to herself, she felt feverish, and her eyes smarted with excitement. The doorman's glance lit on her cloak; the glance turned into a slow-tracking look of surprise, then open admiration, then a plump, courtly stepping aside to let her pass. 'Madam,' he crooned, and released into her face a puff of cologne and whiskey.

Outside the wind was brisk and reviving, and Brenda's hair, blowing straight across her face, seemed restored to richness, a richness lost to twenty-four hours of dry indoor air and to private metabolic eruptions (her approaching period, now three days late). Overhead the narrow sky fitted between the intricate roofs of buildings, topping them with blue and gold. I am not walking, Brenda said to herself; I am striding along. I am a forty-year-old woman, temporarily away from home, striding along a Philadelphia street wearing a quilt on my back. I am on my way to –

Two women at the corner, bundled in scarves, heads bent against the wind, looked up as she passed. Brenda floated a smile over their heads, and heard, as a reward, the drifting word 'gorgeous . . .'

Ah, *gorgeous* Brenda Bowman, striding along, or rather, being borne forward on rails of blue oxygen, her boots kicking out from the brilliant folds, punching sharp prints in the wafery layer of snow. Ms. Brenda Bowman of Elm Park and Chicago, gliding along, leaving a streak of indelible colour on the whitened street and trailing behind her the still more vivid colours of – what? Strength, purpose, certainty. And a piercing apprehension of what she might have been or might still become. Her shadow, which she could not help but admire, preceded her down the sun-struck street. She was, for once, splendidly detached from shop windows, posters, scrawled graffiti, the eaten snow around fire hydrants and lamp posts. Forty years of creeping, of tiptoeing, of learning to walk down a street like this. Forty years of preparing – a waste, a waste, but one that could be rectified, if only she could imagine how.

There was something epic in her wide step, a matriarchal zest, impossibly old. She was reminded suddenly of The Winged Victory of Samothrace.

When they were in France four years ago, she and Jack had made a point of going to the Louvre to see The Winged Victory. ('You can't go all the way to Paris and not see The Winged Victory,' Leah Wallberg had instructed them at the surprise bon-voyage dinner she and Irving had given for them.)

But a few days later, across the Atlantic and standing on the grand staircase in the Louvre directly before the statue, she and Jack had felt bewildered. Was this all there was?

'Well,' Jack said at last, 'considering it doesn't have a head or any arms – '

'Leah said to look at the drapery,' Brenda reminded him. 'And the way the figure is striding through the stone.'

'Hmmm.'

'She said to look at the legs. The legs seem to know just where they want to go.'

'I suppose so,' Jack said. He was a man with a gift for resisting disappointment.

'She said to concentrate on the wings and legs,' Brenda persevered, 'and sort of try to fill the rest of it in mentally.'

'I suppose it does have a *kind* of power,' Jack decided, and, in fact, he carried back to Elm Park and to Leah and Irv Wallberg the message that he and Brenda had glimpsed a very real power in The Winged Victory. ('Didn't I tell you!' Leah cried, eyes aglow, fingers pointed skyward.)

Brenda clutched at her cloak; the wind was colder than she'd thought, especially at the intersection, where it whirled and swept unpredictably, slapping at the skin of her neck and cheeks and lifting her hair straight up; the granite foundations of office-buildings wailed as the wind struck their sharp corners. In an hour or less the sun would be down and the air would be even colder. Why should she stand waiting, shivering, for the light to turn green? There was hardly a car to be seen. She stepped off the kerb. Bravely. With stateliness. The cape swirled around her knees. Inside her head she was smiling.

Years ago she had made her son, Rob, a Superman suit for Halloween. He must have been eight or nine at the time, a more excitable and passionate child than he was now. He had put it on and immediately run out into the backyard with the red cotton cape flying behind him. Brenda remembered that he was also wearing a pair of old blue tights, hers, and that they sagged ludicrously at the crotch and knees and ankles. But he seemed purely unaware of any imperfection. 'You know,' Brenda had marvelled, watching him through the kitchen window, 'he really thinks he *is* Superman. Just look at him.' Jack, coming to the window to look, had smiled. 'Clothes make the man.'

Together they watched as their son tore back and forth across the grass, leapt over the flower bed with its brown tangle of dead chrysanthemum heads, his arms outstretched. 'Up, up, and away,' they heard through the storm window, a wild cry, surprisingly high-pitched. He whirled and soared and in a minute was over the bushes into Miss Anderson's yard, grabbing for a branch of her oak tree, swinging widely, and dropping with an inspired pounce into her leaf pile. Brenda watched him, shaking her head. 'Now he'll catch it,' she said, unable out of pride to tear herself from the window. She saw Jack's mouth go slack with love. 'Superman himself,' he said tenderly, and his eyes filled.

Miss Anderson next door was a witch, a fact well known to Brenda's children and to the other children in the neighbourhood. Miss Anderson's was the only house that they approached on Halloween night with thrilling terror, though year after year she met them, amicably enough, on her front porch, wearing her soiled robe and dropping wrapped caramels into their open sacks. He reputation for witchcraft derived chiefly, Brenda supposed, from one of her eyes, which sagged shut, yellowed with chronic ulcers, and from the long black coat she liked to wear, a coat from the late forties or early fifties, absurdly, flowing, out of style, and made of a shiny, elegant material like taffeta. She wore this old coat year round, even when stalking up and down the back alleys of south Elm Park on her annual spring mission.

This mission was to plant hollyhocks in the small waste spaces that lay between neighbourhood garages and board fences and garbage cans. Here, in packed earth already captured by tough stands of dandelion and plantain, she scattered the seeds early on May mornings. Everyone knew about these expeditions – it was common knowledge – and once Brenda, up early and carrying out the garbage, had actually seen her with her own eyes. The sight had formed a lasting impression, like a moment frozen in an old newsreel. There came Miss Anderson, striding lankily down the alley in her rustling coat, a cotton scarf tied on her head and a cloth bag of seeds hung round her neck. There was no laborious bending, no meticulous placing of the seed – of course her eyes had been failing for years – just a willful, arrogant, almost random sowing of them. Her black-sleeved arm reached into the bag, withdrew, and hurled handfuls of seeds into the thin dirt.

A surprising number of these hollyhock seeds took root, and though Miss Anderson died two years ago, the long fuzzed stalks and delicate, frilled blooms persisted remarkably. The same could not be said of Miss Anderson's memory, for after her death, which occurred so swiftly and cleanly that Brenda cannot remember the exact cause, the house was sold to Larry and Janey Carpenter, who gutted it from top to bottom, dug up the garden, and built a handsome cedar deck, the first of its kind on Franklin Boulevard. Brenda found it hard to believe, and somewhat unfair, too, that a human personality, especially Miss Anderson's, could be so quickly and thoroughly obliterated. Occasionally Hap Lewis, out of cheerful sentimentality, reminisced about 'Old Cactus Cunt', but the younger couples on the block have hardly heard of her. To Brenda it is surprising that no mythology has grown up around her, given the peculiar coloration of her habits; even Rob and Laurie seem to have forgotten her name, referring to her, as they still do from time to time, as that old lady in the coat, or simply, The Coat Lady.

But this afternoon the thought of Miss Anderson and her vigorous, purposeful back-alley striding spoke to that part of Brenda she kept unexamined. Shouldn't she have tried to get to know her a little better when she was alive? The black coat and the eccentric preoccupation with hollyhock propagation had seemed, then, to make her impenetrable and unknowable, and her age had made her seem, to a younger Brenda, not worth bothering about.

But it might have been interesting, and perhaps even profitable, to discover what mysterious childhood shaping had determined that Miss Anderson would be old, relentless, and, in some strange way, content. Something historical had predetermined that straightforward gait. Something historical, too, had touched her mildly with madness. Everyone had a history, after all, everyone – even Miss Anderson, even Brenda's son, Rob, even that nameless classical beauty (complete with head and arms) who posed thousands of years ago as the model for The Winged Victory of Samothrace.

It was one of Jack's beliefs that she, Brenda, had no sense of history. What he meant, of course, was that she lacked his own vivid pictorial sense of a world in which he had never lived; she lacked even an interest in it. It was true enough, she had to agree. She knew, furthermore, that Jack pitied her for this disability, though he had never said so in so many words. He pitied her in much the same way that she pitied him for his seeming inability to learn foreign languages.

For her it had been different; she grew up speaking and understanding Polish, and was even said by an old friend of her mother's to have a cultivated, rather aristocratic, accent – though she could never account for that. And her old high-school French had stayed with her; four years with Mlle Wilson at Morton High School and she, even today, could pluck out a verb whenever she wanted to – which was seldom, she admitted, but it did happen. Coming down the stairs in the morning to make breakfast, the word *descendre* sometimes dropped, pale as an opal, into her consciousness. When she shopped for groceries at the A & P, the old vocabulary lists – *betterave, haricot vert, laitue* – popped up in her head, alphabetized, the irregular plurals carefully indicated, *pruneaux*.

Ah, poor Jack. When they were in France it was she who ordered their meals and arranged for their sightseeing buses, while he, hands behind his back, stood numbly locked into the everydayness of English. She had made, for his sake, careful, patient translations, which he received gratefully and with equal patience, but even so she felt he was being cheated and unfairly humbled. The flatness of the English words broke her heart, and particularly since Jack seemed innocent of any loss.

But he did possess that which she didn't: an historical sense, a sense of the past, or, more accurately, a sense of personal connection with the past. Jack, in Paris, had walked the old revolutionary quarter – he loved the French Revolution – dazed with happiness and so shut into meditation that he went for minutes without speaking, except to stop, consult the Michelin Guide – the English version – and ask Brenda, 'Do you realize that on these very cobblestones – ' or to exclaim, 'It was right here, under this arch – '

She tried to see a portion of what he saw, but couldn't. No, she could not imagine the brutal romance of peasants approaching in their rags. The eighteenth century was shut to her, and so was the nineteenth. No, she couldn't even picture Simone de Beauvoir sitting in a particular café with her note-book open on a table; no, she could not visualize the Allied armies marching up the Champs. It was her nature to resist the images of the past. But what Jack perceived as failure on her part was only the other side of her talent for calling a spade a spade, her bondage to facts and to the present moment.

Still, she felt it was not entirely true that she lacked a historical sense. In a way, her ability to perceive history whole was greater than Jack's, more detailed and more securely fastened to the springs of cause and effect. Jack was a romantic, and condemned to the broad stroke; his historical happenings were purpled with a flood of anonymous blood. History was a monster machine, a John Deere harvester, gathering everything into a hopper.

What he didn't seem to grasp (as Brenda did) was that history was no more than a chain of stories, the stories that happened to everyone and that, in time, came to form the patterns of entire lives, her own included. That some of these stories were dark (her mother's terrible and sudden death) and others drenched with light (the random inexactitude of her love for Jack and the children) – this made little difference in the end. These stories rose out of mystery, took shapes of their own, and gave way in good time to newer and different stories. It was all so simple, it seemed to Brenda; at other times it seemed not simple at all.

For some of these stories were as tentacled as the most exotic vegetation, reaching back impossibly far. Mlle Wilson at Morton High had encouraged Brenda to go to DeKalb State (where she herself had gone) to study to be a French teacher, but Brenda's mother Elsa wanted her to be a secretary so she wouldn't have to be on her feet all day (as she had to be). And so Brenda *had* become a secretary, going to work at the Great Lakes Institute, where she met Jack Bowman (out of the blue) and began the longest story of her life.

Some of Brenda's stories – more than she liked to admit – found their spaces in the improbable future. And one of these came to her now, on her way to the St. Christopher Hotel. It went like this: she and Jack might find themselves in Vancouver, Canada, for a historical conference perhaps – not really so unlikely – and she might be doing a little shopping in one of the department stores and suddenly see a familiar face. Why it was Barry Ollershaw, of all people! She would go up to him, touch his arm, surprise him with her voice. 'Do you remember . . .'

Or she might be sitting at a table with a man (face blurred) and he might place his fingertips on the inside of her wrist, the softest part of her body, and trace the faint cording of veins all the way up to her elbow. He might reach out and run those same fingertips across her lips and eyelids and then – the little table whisked from view and replaced with a width of soft grass – then he might lie down beside her, leading her out of this story and into the next one.

This kind of story, which seemed to her denser than a mere fantasy, might be told with differing annotation, depending on the imagined listener. 'How could I refuse?' to her mother's large eyebrows. 'Why not?' to Hap Lewis's open mouth. 'Life is short,' to her children's puzzled gaze.

One thing was certain. These imagined stories never ended as stories in books did, with telling declarations of arrival: ' – and then she realized – ' or 'It came to him suddenly that – ' Instead they ended somewhere on their own descending curvatures, simply run out of fuel or deprived of interest, or, as frequently happened, interrupted by the exigencies of real life and the return to the true and ongoing story that pressed as tightly as clothing against the skin. The street, the hardness of the pavement, the snow turning blue in the fading light.

And there it was, the St. Christopher. Old, ornate, with dark, wet stonework and leaded-glass doors and lights like rubies burning inside. Four o'clock exactly; the sun almost sunk, and Brenda stamping snow from her boots and beating out a poem on the brass grating of the vestibule. O snow, O Love, O Victory.

Chapter Seventeen

TWO HOURS LATER BRENDA WAS DRUNK. DRUNK AS A SKUNK, as Hap Lewis would say. Or zonked, as her husband Jack would say. Larry Carpenter next door would say, in his pompous, fake-British way, that she was ripped. She was blotto, her son Rob would say, also fried and frittered (or did that refer only to drugs?). She was stewed, sauced, pie-eyed, blitzed, and potted. She was lushed out, pissed to the eyeballs, Oh good God, Oh Christ, son of Mary.

It had happened so fast. She couldn't account for it. (Atmospheric pressure? Coursing hormones?) She had entered the St. Christopher Hotel, found the Emerald Room, and there, at the dark table in the corner, saw Hal Rago of the Philadelphia *Examiner* with a cigarette burning in his fingers. 'Hi there, Mrs. B.,' he greeted her.

Mrs. B.? The off-hand familiarity was wrenching, and seemed to certify her terrible ordinariness. Her housewifeliness.

She sat down and eased the quilt from her shoulders, *The Second Coming*, her transforming cape, now re-transformed into ridiculous improvisation. Kitsch.

'Hey, you dropped something,' Hal said loudly, and dived under the table for the safety pin. 'This yours?'

The ceiling of the Emerald Room was a depthless black, starred with hard little lights. The speciality of the house was something in a tall green glass called Irish Squint, and Hal Rago had clearly downed several before Brenda arrived. 'Try one,' he leered.

'I'll have a brandy,' Brenda said. She had a sudden, seething desire to be unaccommodating.

'Brandy it is.' He stuck a finger in the air to summon a waiter, and lewdly licked the butt end of a felt-tip pen. 'Then shall we get down to business?'

'Why not?' Brenda returned, heartened by the glassy minerals in her new voice. Gone was the full-spirited woman striding through the snow. Poof. The weight of twenty years had fallen in on her, along with the spectre of middle age, with its faked allegiances, its betrayals, its bodily leakages, and its secret pods of flesh and sour smells. Winged Victory – Ha! She shook her hair roughly back and downed her brandy.

'Atta girl. Just the thing for a lousy day like this.'

She glared at him, and he immediately signalled the waiter for another.

With grief and without the aid of mirrors, she saw herself: a woman with a flimsy comic-strip name – Brenda. She had never mastered her cuticles. She was missing two back teeth. She had stretch marks on her stomach and her neck was wrinkled, *wrinkled*. She would never again be able to command ardour; she was a fool.

Hal pulled out his notes; stared at them lengthily, as though trying to draw some restorative sobriety from what he had written earlier. 'Maybe you could tell me how you got your foot into the craft business,' he suggested.

'I can hardly remember,' Brenda said. The brandy was working its magic. She smiled at Hal Rago, her Princess Look as Jack called it.

'You're from Chi-Town, right?

'Right.'

He made a note. 'Midwest perspective, they want. Jesus, who thinks up these crazy angles? So what have you got pithy to say about the Midwest?'

'I don't really know.' She drank deeply.

'You grow up on a farm or something like that?'

'Cicero, Illinois. Over a dry cleaner's.'

'Cicero, Christ! Isn't that where the one and only Al Capone – ?'

She nodded.

'Jesus, that's a tough place, Cicero, a real tough place.'

She was beginning to like him. 'Where'd you grow up?' she asked sociably.

'In Pennsylvania. On a farm.'

They roared with laughter.

He told her a long, pointless joke about a Pennsylvania farmer going to New York for the opera season, and followed it up with a rambling anecdote about the young John O'Hara.

She told him why she was wearing a quilt instead of a coat.

He asked why it was called *The Second Coming*, and she told

131

him how she'd seen the neon sign on a West side Chicago church. '"The Second Coming Is at Hand." It sounded pithy,' she said with a burst of wit.

He told her about his Italian grandmother and how she'd wanted him to be a priest.

She told him about Mlle Wilson wanting her to be a French teacher. She even spoke a few words of French for him. And then a little Polish.

He had told her how he'd got fired from his first newspaper job (an involved story about interviewing a corpse).

She told him about how she'd met her husband in the map room of the Great Lakes Institute.

He told her about his divorce from a girl named JoAnne. This story, which had many chapters, took a long time to tell. It was a tragic story – JoAnne turned out to be a nymphomaniac – but it must have had some funny parts too, for later Brenda remembered downing several fierce little glasses of brandy and wiping away tears of laughter.

He took her elbow at last and put her in a cab. 'This has been beautiful, Mrs. B.' He said this through misted eyes. 'And you are one beautiful lady.'

She said goodbye to his large, hard, red face and managed to pronounce for the taxi-driver the words 'Franklin Court Arms.'

About the ride to the hotel she remembered nothing, but she did dimly recall passing through the lobby, where crowds of people passed like waves across the wide carpet and where the splashing of the fountain affected her with extreme nausea – which she managed to contain until she got up to the room.

She woke several times. Once the phone was ringing and ringing; the sound seemed to radiate from the dark walls, a bright fluorescent electric blue circling each separate ring. Her eyes and ears burned. At least twice she stumbled to the bathroom to pour glassfuls of water down her parched throat. Later, toward morning, she opened one eye and observed a woman lying back against the pillow on the next bed. She was smoking a cigarette. For a minute Brenda, hypnotized, watched the glowing red tip and the long, strenuous releasing of smoke.

Then she fell into a deep sleep which lasted until the fierce buzz of her travel clock announced eight o'clock.

Chapter Eighteen

'I DISGUST MYSELF,' BRENDA WAS SAYING, LEANING BACK on the pillow.

'Shhhh. Drink this.'

'I'm going to float away if I do.'

'It'll do you good. What time did you say you took an aspirin?'

'Three aspirins. Eight o'clock, I think. When the alarm went off.'

'You could probably have another one now. It's after eleven.'

'Eleven o'clock! I've missed the theory session on appliqué. *And* the English Quilting Workshop. Or maybe that's this afternoon. And the worst thing was missing the President's Dinner last night.'

'What you need is rest.' Barry took the orange-juice glass from her and handed her a wet facecloth.

'I can't tell you how embarrassed I am. I must look awful. This room must smell like – '

'Why don't you go back to sleep. I'll give you a call at two or so. You should be ready for some solid food by then.'

'Never.' A shade dramatic.

'You'll be surprised.'

'Barry.'

'What?' His hand rested on the bedspread like a weight placed just so.

'I really want you to know something. That this has never happened to me before. I don't know why, but I want to assure you that I've never thrown up all over a bathroom and passed out and made a complete fool of myself – '

'Don't – '

'It really is important to me – I don't know why – that you don't go home to Vancouver thinking – '

'Shhhh.'

'This is my first real . . . disgrace.' She pressed the cloth to her forehead. The word disgrace had a puzzling richness to it. She felt dismayingly theatrical, but didn't know how to stop.

'Is it really? Your first disgrace?'

'You sound amazed.'

'I am.'

'Why?'

'Why? Well, must of us have disgraced ourselves fairly often by – ' He paused.

'By this age? Say it.'

'By this age then.'

'Well . . . ' She was thinking.

'Well, what?'

'Well, once when Jack and I – Jack's my husband – '

'I know.'

'We were invited out to Highland Park, to Dr. Middleton's for dinner. He's the head of the place where Jack works – '

'And?'

'This was years ago. Back in the days before I didn't know enough to be nervous about going to dinner there. I remember they had endive, which I'd never seen before.' Brenda smiles faintly, starting to enjoy herself. 'And English trifle, which I'd never even heard of. But I managed to take all this in my stride. And when we were finally saying goodnight, I was feeling so cheerful and lively and happy to be at the end of that evening that I sort of swung my coat on. And in the process knocked over this little figurine they had in the hall. Which turned out to be some kind of ancient pottery.'

'Irreplaceable, I suppose.' Barry's eyes smiled.

'Not quite pre-Columbian, but almost. I found that out later. It was awful. Jack almost died. Dr. Middleton had tears in his eyes – real tears – picking up the pieces. Of course they were all very polite. Jack said that naturally we'd pay for it, and they said they wouldn't hear of it, it was their fault for having it there by the front door. Which it was in a way. But you can imagine how I felt.'

'Yes.'

'There was just no way to compensate for something like that. For years I kept inviting them to our house and hoping they'd break something of mine, but of course they never did.'

'Do you want the curtains left open? The sun's right in your eyes.'

'I know. But that's what I need. To suffer.'

'Sackcloth and ashes.' He smiled down at her.

'I suppose.'

'You're not the first person in the world to have too much to drink, you know.'

'I just thought of something else. Another awful disgrace.'

'Tell me.' He perched on the air-conditioning unit, his hands grasped around his knee.

'It was just after we'd moved to Elm Park. Before that we'd been living in a student apartment downtown and this was sort of our introduction into the middle class, you might say. I guess all my disgraces are social disgraces.'

'Go on.'

'Some people in the neighbourhood gave a little party so we'd meet everyone. It's that kind of neighbourhood – very friendly, without being chummy. Robin and Betty Fairweather – they're divorced now, as a matter of fact, just last year – they were the ones who gave the party for us. It was on a Sunday afternoon, just drinks and cheese and olives and so on. And they had hired a man to serve the drinks and pass things. And I'd never been to a party where someone had been hired to help. So what did I do but introduce myself to this man. He was wearing a white jacket and everything, but I never even thought he might be a waiter. "Hi, I'm Brenda Bowman." I actually said that – and stuck my hand out to shake hands with him.'

'And that was your worst disgrace?' Barry shook his head.

'Well, in a way, but I suppose it doesn't really count as a disgrace. Because, by some kind of miracle, there was no one else standing there at that moment. No witnesses, I mean. So no one ever found out about it except for this waiter and me. As a matter of fact, this is the first time I've told anyone else about it.'

'Not even – ?'

'Not even Jack.'

'Why not, I wonder.'

'I don't know. Jack would probably just laugh. Now, that is. But then – well, we were younger then. And I don't know, sometimes we don't always laugh at the same kind of things.'

'I know what you mean.'

'What was your worst disgrace?'

He was sitting leaning against the wall with one knee drawn up. This posture seemed in some way to invite intimacy. He considered the question gravely, and then said, 'I suppose it would be the same as for most men. A sexual failure of some kind.'

'Oh.' She shut her eyes. 'I shouldn't have asked. It's none of my business. I'm terribly sorry.'

'Why be sorry?'

'I must still be a little drunk. Rattling on like this.'

'You're looking, well, not so pale. As before.'

'Thank you. I mean thank you for looking after me like this. The orange juice and aspirin and everything. And taking the quilt over to the Exhibition Hall for me this morning. I was probably sick all over that, too.'

'Just a little.'

'Ooooohhhhh.' She groaned into her hands.

'I sprayed something on it. You had something in the bathroom – '

'Spray-Net.'

'I think so.'

'I deserve this.'

'Anyway, they said it was in plenty of time. The judging isn't until this afternoon some time. Three o'clock I think they said.'

'You know, I can't believe this.'

'What?'

'Here you are, all the way from the West Coast, attending a professional conference, and you spend your whole morning running around with a filthy quilt smelling of someone's vomit you hardly even know – '

'I've known you forever.' He said this lightly, with a twist of a smile, only slightly mocking.

'You don't believe in former lives, do you?' Brenda asked.

'No.' Apologetically.

'Good. I don't either.'

'My wife says I haven't got an occult bone in my body.'

'Neither have I. I don't even read the Horoscope in the *Trib*.

'I don't even open fortune cookies.'

'You're purer than I am. I open them but I don't believe them.'

'I've often wondered how people get like this. Like us.'

'So have I. I think we're born this way. A special race of people. The race that calls a spade a spade.'

'A deprived race maybe.'

'Why deprived?'

'Think of all we miss. All the excitement. An extra dimension.'

'Probably. But would you have it any other way?'

'No.'

'She was here last night.'

'Who?'

Brenda nodded at the other bed. 'Verna. My roommate.'

'Ah, Verna the post-virginal.'

'At least I think she was here. I woke up and saw a woman lying in bed smoking a cigarette. I think it was about five o'clock.'

'You could have been dreaming. Or – '

'I don't think so. And the bedspread does look a little bit rumpled, don't you think?'

'A little.'

'I shouldn't be keeping you,' Brenda said. 'I know you probably have something or other to do.'

'I should let you get some sleep. But, look, is there anything you'd like before I go?'

'I can't thank you enough – '

'Don't.' He stood up and closed the curtains. The cessation of sunlight came like an absolution.

'I feel like a child being taken care of,' Brenda said.

He stood in the dark for a moment, not saying anything.

'Is it really the worst thing?' Brenda said. 'Sexual failure?'

'I think so.'

'Worse than the failure of love?'

He considered. Brenda waited with her eyes shut.

'I'll have to think about that,' he said.

Chapter Nineteen

BRENDA CAN HARDLY BELIEVE WHAT SHE'S HEARING. IS THIS woman serious? Yes, she is.

Dr. Mary O'Leary, Guest Speaker: creamy high forehead, bluish highlights in thick auburn hair, a suit of heavy wool cloth, a voice springy with authority. And she appears to have the right credentials. Brenda reads about her in the programme: Radcliffe (Major in psychology), the Sorbonne, then a Ph.D. in Art History from Stanford. Her topic for today is Quilting Through the Freudian Looking-Glass: A New Interpretation.

Can it be true what she's saying? Is it possible? All around her, Brenda sees women, and one man, nodding agreement, nodding approval, listening. Dr. O'Leary, a stack of note cards in hand, touches on the best known of traditional quilting patterns, naming them lightly, as though they were as familiar to her as the names of her children or her oldest friends. The lecture is accompanied by slides projected on an overhead screen. Slide one: the Star of Bethlehem clearly representing an orgasmic explosion, though it has also been viewed as an immense, quivering vulva. 'Women in pioneer America suppressed their sexuality as society demanded, but ecstasy found a channel through circumscribed needlework.'

Slide two: the well-loved Wedding Ring quilt, symbolizing the enclosed nature of femaleness. Next: the Double Ring quilt, which, instead of breaking through that enclosure, merely amplified it. Then the traditional Fan quilt, quietly mocking male ontology – Brenda is not sure of the word ontology – with its dull, unrelenting repetitions; Dr. O'Leary sees this mockery as being subtle, punitive, and filled with pain. The Log Cabin quilt, the most telling, the most incriminating of quilting patterns, presents a seamless field of phallic symbols, so tightly bound together that there is no room at all for female genitalia. The multiple phallic images suggest penis envy on one hand and fantasies of gang rape on the other.

And finally, the ironically named Crazy Quilt, offering early

American women a sanctioned release from social and sexual stereotyping, and, in the hands of the most daring, an expression of savage and primitive longings. Dr. O'Leary has made a detailed study of the shapes in these so-called crazy quilts; the presence of many triangles suggests irresolution, perhaps even androgyny. Breast shapes, interestingly, outnumber phalli, but Dr. O'Leary and her assistant are hesitant about drawing premature conclusions. It may be that women were defending and proclaiming their femininity; or, and this seems more likely, they may have been expressing infantile needs which had not been satisfied. As for the present-day revival in quiltmaking, Dr. O'Leary interprets it partly as apologia, partly as retreat from responsibility, and partly a continuum of what it has always been, a means of exercising control over a disorganized and hostile universe. End of lecture.

From the audience there is scattered applause at first, which then grows; there are even a few cheers. But Brenda, who knows herself to be capable of serious acts of capitulation, does not clap at all. She is caught, silent, between stunned bewilderment and boiling laughter.

'Claptrap,' Dorothea Thomas from Lexington, Kentucky, says. 'Poppycock, every word of it.'

Brenda smiles, thinking of how she will relate these comments to Hap Lewis and Leah Wallberg and Andrea Lord when she gets home. ('And she actually said poppycock, just like Ma Perkins used to.')

Dorothea Thomas, who is considered to be the Grandma Moses of the quilt world, continues. 'Sometimes I wonder why the devil I bother coming to these things when all there is is talking, talking, talking, and about the craziest farfetched things. The Star of Bethlehem is the Star of Bethlehem for Pete's sake. That's what it *is*.'

'You don't think that, on an unconscious level, it symbolizes – '

'Fiddlesticks.' ('And she actually said fiddlesticks!')

'But the Log Cabin quilt – ?'

'One of the prettiest quilts around. My own mother – and this was way back in 1902 or 1903 – had a Log Cabin quilt, made it with her own hands, and if you'd have known my mother – of course she died in 1919 – you'd know better than to think she had thoughts like that in her head. Rape and so on. She was too darned busy raising kids and washing and sewing and keeping chickens and ducks and I don't know what all else to sit around worrying about rape. She was always sewing – the way that woman could sew. Made all our clothes, even for the boys, their pants and shirts, and she ended up with all these itty-bitty scraps, so what did she do but sit herself down and did like women in the country did then. She made this beautiful Log Cabin quilt; I still have it in my possession. No electricity, not back in those days, just the kerosene and the lights from the fireplace, and that's how she put all those pieces together. Then, for the quilting part, she had her friends. The friends that woman had! Not my father, a good man but he didn't hardly have a friend to his name, sort of kept to himself, quiet man, hardly talked. But my mother, what a difference, the house was always full, relatives, sisters, friends just stopping by, there was always coffee, I can't remember a day when there wasn't coffee hot on the stove, and there they'd sit. They had sewing baskets they'd take around with them when they visited, always had a little handwork on the go, darning, mending, embroidery, crotchet work, you name it. And the way they'd laugh, they'd laugh about anything, old times, old memories, gossip I suppose you'd call it, but nothing bad that I can remember, by that I mean nothing unkind. I was always there, at least that's how I remember it, just a little thing, seven or eight years of age, no one ever said run along and get lost. They'd hand me their basting threads to straighten out, and then they'd use them over again, imagine! Oh, I used to love it, just being in that front room when they sewed and laughed, it was wonderful. I'd stop and think of my father out there in the barn, doing chores all by his lonesome – it got freezing out there – and think how lucky I was to be inside with my mother and my mother's friends, just sewing away and laughing and telling each other stories.'

Dorothea Thomas's speciality was story quilts. She was famous for them. Some of her story quilts were on permanent exhibition in public galleries, and others had been sold to movie stars; Paul Newman and Joanne Woodward were said to own several. Last year she was written up, with photographs, in the Lifestyle section of *Time*, where she was quoted as saying: 'I like a pretty design as well as the next person, but it's got to tell a story.'

Brenda met Dorothea Thomas at the afternoon workshop on Narrative Quiltmaking. Thirty women (and two men) crowded into the Freedom Room at the end of the convention floor and listened to Mrs. Thomas, seventy-eight years old, chin sunk between the roughened roundness of cheeks, talking about her craft. By a story, she told them, she didn't mean anything long and complicated with lots of turnings like TV soap operas or *Gone With The Wind*. Just something with a beginning and a middle and an end. She'd done fairytale quilts and folktale quilts, but the ones she liked to do best were based on plain old everyday family stories.

As a demonstration, she showed her quilt *Prize Squash*, asking Brenda and Lenora Knox, who were sitting in the front row, to hold it up so everyone could see. It was rather small, a child's crib-cover, divided into four sections. Sometimes, she explained, she divides her quilts into eight or twelve sections, depending on how long the story is. The top left-hand square of *Prize Squash* showed the simplified outline of a boy on his knees, dropping a seed into the ground. The picture was composed of primitive colours and shapes, half patchwork, half appliqué, and all of it was tracked with whimsical stitchery – the young boy's overalls were held up with cross-stitched suspenders, and the seed held in his hand was a glowing triple French knot worked in silky thread. In the second square the boy was standing measuring with sunburned hands the height of a young green plant. The third square – Mrs. Thomas leaned over and pointed a bony finger at the bottom left-hand corner – was entirely filled with the swelling yellowness of squash, and the fourth panel showed the boy facing forward, a blue ribbon on his chest and an upturned hand holding a clutch of glistening seeds.

The story, Dorothea Thomas said, was a true one, based on her son Billy, now a man of fifty-five and the owner of a doughnut franchise in eastern Kentucky. When he was a boy, they had lived in the country, and he had raised, one summer, a prize Hubbard squash. 'One thing I know, for sure,' Mrs. Thomas told the roomful of listeners, 'is that if I live to be a hundred and ten, I'm never going to run out of stories. All I do is dig out the old picture album, and something jumps up for me every time.'

She has done birthday quilts and wedding quilts and even quite a few funeral quilts; the funeral quilts for some reason are the most sought after of all. One of her first designs – she began quilting seriously at sixty – was the life story in eight panels of a family pet, a she-goat named Ruthie-Sue. 'I just loved telling folks about that crazy old Ruthie-Sue of ours, the way she used to knock her head up against the back porch when she wanted attention and eat my morning glories, and the way she'd roll over on her back like a puppy dog – it seemed like she thought she *was* a puppy dog – and on real hot days she'd go crazy and start nibbling on the tyres of the half-ton truck we had at that time. Everyone was always asking me how Ruthie-Sue was getting on, everyone I met. One day I just thought, why the heck don't I make a quilt about it all? So that's just what I did.'

Brenda listened, thinking of stories – her own stories, or rather the stories she shared with Jack – stories too trivial even for family albums; the time Rob locked himself in the bathroom and had to be rescued through the window; the time Laurie, seven years old, figured out how to put the lawnmower back together again. And the time Brenda's mother got mugged down on Wabash with only thirty-one cents in her purse. The time she and Jack were snubbed – or thought they were snubbed – by a waiter at Jacques's. The time in France when they saw a man on a bicycle carrying a bottle of wine under his arm; the bicycle hit a stone, throwing him over the handlebars, but he leapt up like a gymnast, nimbly saving the bottle in the nick of time, and making the sign of the cross in the air, a wonderful silent movie of a story.

When they tell these stories to friends (as they sometimes do) Brenda never says to Jack, 'Please don't tell that old story again,' and he never says to her, 'We've all heard that one.' They love their stories and tacitly think of them as their private hoard, their private stock, exquisitely flavoured by the retelling. The timing and phrasing have reached a state of near perfection; it's taken them years to get them right. It seems to Brenda that all couples of long standing must have just such a stock of stories to draw upon.

In fact, when Robin Fairweather divorced Betty Fairweather last year and married a twenty-four-year-old beautician named

Sandra, the first thing Brenda thought about was that she would never again hear that wonderfully funny tale about Robin and Betty's 1953 honeymoon spent next door to a pet shop in Akron, Ohio. Robin, aged fifty now, with a jiggling belly, would have to start all over again building up a fund of tellable stories (and somehow Sandra, with her contact lenses and flat rear-end, seemed an unlikely repository). What a loss it all was, Brenda thought, all that shared history down the drain.

How could people bear it?

After the workshop Brenda went up to Dorothea Thomas and said, 'I can't tell you how much I've enjoyed this. It's wonderful to meet someone who's so sure of what she's doing. I could sense, while you were talking, that you don't have any doubts. I think most of us do, from time to time anyway.'

'Well, an old bag like me' – Mrs. Thomas said this in a firm voice, her large teeth shining – 'I just do what I can do, and that's all there is to it, I guess.'

'I saw your *Corn-Planting Quilt*. At the Art Institute show last year in Chicago.'

'Oh, that one! Boy oh boy, I'd like to get my hands on that one again. It's all wrong, the last two squares anyways are all wrong. As soon as it got sold I figured out what it was that wasn't right, what I should have done. Then, well, it was too late. That's how it goes.'

'It seemed to work for me,' Brenda said in her awful voice, her phony voice.

'The thing is,' Dorothea Thomas went on, 'I used to think stories only had the one ending. But then, this last year or so, I got to thinking that that's not right. The fact is, most stories have three of four endings, maybe even more.'

'I don't think I – '

'You've got your real ending, plain and simple. You know, the way things really happened. That's the ending I've been putting in my quilts all along. And then there's the ending a person's hoping for, the one he's got his fingers crossed for. That's real, too, in a way of speaking. And then there's the ending he's scared to death is going to happen. And worst of all – and don't we all know it – there's the way it might have been if only – '

'You mean the road not taken?'

'Good heavens,' Mrs. Thomas cried, 'that just exactly what I mean, what you just said. I like the way you put that now. The road not taken.'

'Oh, that's not my phrase. I think it was Robert Frost who – '

'The road not taken, I'm going to remember that. Keep it in mind for the future. All my new quilts, the ones I've been doing this fall and winter, they've all got two or three endings to them. 'Course they're getting bigger and bigger, kind of superduper king-size now, and still growing and growing. Some folks don't like them so much as they did. Too big to put on a bed for one thing. And kind of confusing, I guess. They like them like a picture book, just one ending, nice and simple. The people in New York that look after the selling for me say these new ones I've made, they're not so popular. Harder to sell, you know. They say they're not really primitive art any more, not like they were. But what the heck, I say, I'm not going to start fussing at my age about what people say, I could be dead next year, I could be dead tomorrow.'

'We all could,' Brenda said.

'You're so young, you're like a girl still, a young girl with your life ahead of you. My what I'd give . . . ' She stopped, pressed the palms of her hands together, shook her head.

Moved, Brenda vowed to be sterner with herself. But kinder.

Chapter Twenty

THE ART SCENE by Hal Rago

CHICAGO WOMAN SEES
PIONEER CRAFT AS ART FORM

Attractive Brenda Bowman hails from the American Midwest, but she's a long long way from being your stereotype image of a rural, cornbelt quiltmaker. Ms. Bowman is an urbanite to the core, a Chicagoan by birth, a quilter by profession.

Even the coat she was wearing yesterday as she battled her way through a Philadelphia blizzard was a handsome example of her work, a rich, vibrant collage of purples and yellows.

'I got into quilting accidentally,' Ms. Bowman confessed in an interview yesterday. 'A few years ago I went out to buy my daughter a new bedspread, and I was so floored by the prices that I decided to make her one instead. I had a few odds and ends of material around the house – luckily I was brought up by a thrifty mother who taught me to sew – so I cut out some squares and stitched them together and – presto – there was my first quilt. Some friends encouraged me to sign up for a design course the next winter at the Art Institute, and that was the beginning of the whole thing.'

Brenda Bowman hasn't looked back since. In the last four years she's made and sold dozens of quilts, and this week she's in Philadelphia attending the National Handicrafts Exhibition. Examples of her work are on display at the Exhibition Centre which opened last night to record crowds. Quilters and other needlework artists from coast to coast have converged at the Franklin Court Arms for a few days to discuss their crafts and compare their wares.

Asked if she could define the particular invigorating essence of the American Midwest, Ms. Bowman replied succinctly, 'Fertility, a tradition of fertility.' The warm, empathetic Brenda Bowman, mother of two teenagers, went on to discuss the connection between art and craft. 'Art poses a moral question; craft responds to that question and in a sense provides the enabling energy society requires.'

(Tomorrow Hal Rago talks to tapestry-maker
Lily Sherman from Tallahassee, Florida)

* * *

'Cheer up,' Barry Ollershaw said over the potato-and-leek soup. 'It's really quite a nice write-up.'

'It's awful,' Brenda said, spooning up soup. She was ravenous.

'Attractive, warm, empathetic. Nothing wrong with any of that.'

'I can't believe I said all that pompous junk about art posing questions. And the fertility thing. I don't even know what I mean.'

'I followed you all the way to enabling energy and then – '

'It's all hogwash, as Dorothea Thomas would probably say.'

'Succinctly put.'

'I'm being kind to myself. It's really worse than that. It's pretentious hogwash.'

'I think you're being too severe.'

'Another funny thing, even though he didn't mean it literally, was the part about never looking back. Because it seems to me I spend half my time looking back.'

'Do you? That surprises me.'

'Poor Lily Sherman, whoever she is. I suppose she's going to get the Emerald Room treatment too. Maybe I should look her up and give her fair warning.'

'I imagine it's too late by now.'

'The one consolation is that I don't know a soul in Philadelphia. And no one in Chicago's going to read a word of this. The worst part, when you think about it, is that dumb "presto" stuck in the middle. Did I really say presto? I probably did, I vaguely remember. I should go stick my head in a bucket of water.'

'Have some soup instead. How are you feeling?'

Brenda, cheerful, hungry, sitting at a candlelit table in a corner of The Captain's Buffet, felt removed from the feebleness of human complaint. She folded Hal Rago's column in two and smiled at Barry. 'I'm feeling better than I deserve. Fine, in fact.'

'Who's Dorothea Thomas?'

She liked him for asking; and for getting the name right. 'Dorothea Thomas? She's a prize quiltmaker from Kentucky, almost eighty years old. I met her today for the first time. She makes me think it might not be too bad, growing old.'

'Do you really fear it?' Barry asked her. (He was good at questions.) He lifted the wine bottle, asked her with his eyes if she wanted some.

'I'd better not.' Brenda shook her head at the wine. 'I must be a little afraid of getting old, because every morning I get down on the floor and go through this exercise routine. The Air Force exercises. Which I hate. All the time I'm bending and stretching I think to myself, all this just so I'll be spry when I'm seventy.'

'So do I.'

'What?'

'Air Force exercises.'

'Oh.'

A silence dropped between them. It came without warning. The waiter came and took away the soup bowls and brought hot platters of paella. Brenda placed a fork into a piece of scallop. It tasted of parsley and browned garlic.

The silence obstinately refused to lift. Brenda felt suddenly overly large and clumsy. What was she doing sitting across from this man? His hands, slender and more agile that her own, held the knife and fork in a way that she recognized as being European. What was she doing eating an intimate dinner with this stranger, surrounded by the romantic claptrap (another Dorothea word) of candlelight, wine bottle, solicitous service, soft piped music; what did she think she was doing anyway?

Perhaps he was thinking the same thing; how had he let himself in for an evening like this? She watched him chase a shrimp to the rim of his plate. He sat looking intently at a piece of tomato, then divided it in two. A delicate man with precise gestures. Perhaps a little prissy. She remembered the way he had said, when they first met, that he was nuts about quilts. An odd thing to say, now that she thought about it. Why exactly had he invited her to dinner anyway?

What had joined them earlier, her reaction – overreaction – to finding Verna in bed with a man, her lost coat, the falling snow, now seemed insubstantial, used up. They were just two people adrift, nothing more. Barry had a lead on her coat; the metallurgist sharing his room was called Storton McCormick, he was from New York, and apparently he had been called back suddenly. But he was due to return to Philadelphia in the

147

morning. He was giving a paper, in fact, in the afternoon, and Barry hoped to speak to him afterwards about the missing coat.

'I really would appreciate that,' Brenda said. 'You're sure it won't be too awkward?'

'Not at all,' Barry said, and fell silent.

After a minute he cleared his throat and went after the shrimp once more.

She should have gone with Lenora Knox and Lenora's roommate on the Philadelphia-by-Night bus tour.

The rice was cold, microwaved. She swallowed and heard, self-consciously, the sound of her swallowing. ('An urbanite to the core' – the phrase rolled down her throat like a marble.)

There was an arrangement of wet roses on the table; her paralysed eye hung on a single petal beaded with water. Shouldn't she be better strung together at this age, able to cope with silence gracefully? But this wasn't like the silence she'd shared with Barry yesterday morning as they sat in her room watching the snow come down. This was silence wrenched into being by the weight of occasion (an invitation: Barry on the phone asking her to join him for dinner; a date for heaven's sake, ridiculous word). The schmaltz of candlelight and soft music put a burden of expectation on her – and on him too she supposed – asking the question What is this leading to?

The waiter hovered. 'Is everything all right?'

'Fine,' they chorused.

Brenda felt immobilized, as though eating and chewing and swallowing were all she was capable of doing. There must be social questions she could ask. What? He had mentioned Japan. Do you do much travelling? Any good restaurants in Vancouver? Sports? Hobbies? How were your meetings today? (Too wifey, that last one.)

The wine was a deep red, soft-looking, probably very dry. His eyes seemed locked to the level of his glass.

What was the matter with her? Did she really think this pleasant, civilized man was softening her up for seduction? She had friends – Betty Corning, Kay Wigg – who were always thinking so-and-so was after them, looking them up and down, undressing them with their eyes. It happened to women in their forties, this kind of self-delusion.

What a bore she was. She imagined Barry Ollershaw recalling this evening, how he'd hoped for a cheerful dinner out and instead got stuck with dullness and silence. Maybe she was still hung over. Or premenstrual. Or both.

Or maybe she was feeling guilty. Would he tell his wife he asked a woman to dinner? Would she tell Jack? The question struck her forcibly, and so did a vigorous protestation: why shouldn't a man and a woman, meeting by accident, share a meal? It happened all the time (but never before to her).

The waiter was back. 'Would you care for dessert?'

He thinks we're husband and wife, Brenda thought.

Barry ordered Dutch apple tart.

'I couldn't eat another thing, ' Brenda said in a pinched voice. (Warm, empathetic Brenda Bowman.)

The tart was a lean triangle covered with a trail of cream. 'You're sure you wouldn't like some?' Barry asked politely.

'I'm sure.'

'Really?'

'Yes.'

'Brenda.' He pronounced her name in a quiet, tired voice. And reached across the table to cover her hand with his. His own was trembling slightly; the sight of a raised vein on the back of his hand touched her, and, to her relief, she abruptly broke the silence.

She began to talk, rushing from one thing to the next, telling him finally about Dorothea Thomas's stories, how Dorothea had discovered that stories have more than one ending.

Barry, still covering her hand, listened, tipped his head to one side, said yes, it was true, he could see that plainly, but was it wise to overcomplicate that which was simple and straightforward?

'But what choice does she really have?' Brenda asked, comfortable with the feel of his dryish hand on hers. 'Even at her age she can't go on pretending. It's like a primitive painter who's discovered perspective and shading and all the rest.'

'She could shut her eyes; keep her life simple.'

'Do people do that? I'm not sure they do. Or that they can. I can't. And I'd like to, believe me. I used to be happier than I am now.'

'Of course no one can recover innocence. When it's gone, it's gone. But most of us, I suppose, pretend.'

'You too?'

'Sure.'

'Give me an example,' Brenda said happily.

'Coffee?' the waiter again.

'Coffee?' Barry asked Brenda.

'Please.'

'Where were we?' He turned to her.

'Pretending things are simple when they're really not.'

'You asked for an example.'

Brenda nodded.

'This isn't a very happy example.'

She felt reckless. 'Go on.'

'It's about children.'

'Children?'

'The other day you asked if I had any. Do you remember?'

'And you said no.'

'But I do – that is we do, my wife and I. One child. A daughter. She might be dead. She probably is dead. We don't know for sure.'

Brenda wasn't sure she'd heard right. But, yes, she had. 'What happened?' she said slowly.

'She went over to Europe when she was eighteen, when school was out. Hitchhiking we think, although she had a rail pass. She started with a friend, but that didn't last long.'

'And then what?' The pressure of his hand increased.

'No one knows. They started in England. We think she was in France for a few weeks. Someone remembered seeing her, or someone who looked like her anyway, near Notre Dame in Paris, and she was talking about going to Morocco. That's all. There's never been any trace – nothing, no postcard, nothing.'

'How could that happen? How could someone disappear like that?'

'It does happen. And not just to us. We keep a running ad in the Paris *Herald Tribune*, a come-home ad, once every two weeks. There're lots of them, a column of them. "Come home, all is forgiven," that sort of thing.'

'That's awful, awful.'

'When it happened – when we realized she was lost – I went to France and spent a month looking for her, talking to the embassies, to the French police. But where do you begin? It was hopeless.'

'When was this, when she disappeared?'

'Four years ago now. She was eighteen. She'd be almost twenty-two now, if she's alive.'

'What time of year was it, when you were in France?' It seemed important to know.

'Easter. I flew to Paris on Easter Sunday.'

She wanted to cry out, 'But that's when Jack and I were in Paris.' Instead she said, 'Oh Barry. I'm so sorry. About your daughter. Not to know, that must be the most terrible part.'

'I suppose that's what I meant about pretending. It may be an act of dishonesty on one's part, but it's simpler – less painful anyway – just to say, if someone asks, as you did, that there are no children. Simpler than explaining and thinking about what might really have happened. My wife and I, it's as though we're in training to learn how to be a childless couple. It's harder for Ruth than for me. She blames herself. She can't bear it. It's changed her utterly.'

'I would die,' Brenda said, meaning it.

'You probably wouldn't.'

'I would.'

The waiter arrived with more coffee and a plate of chocolate mints. 'Brandy?' he asked.

'Nothing for me,' Brenda said.

'Nothing more,' Barry said.

With solemn faces they regarded each other. Then Barry brought her hand to his lips, kissing her fingertips.

Chapter Twenty-One

THE NEW SEXUAL FREEDOM HAS NOT TOUCHED BRENDA, THOUGH it has touched almost everything and everyone around her. She and Jack know several couples who have made, after many years, new arrangements which accommodate each other's private longings and needs. Bernie Koltz's wife, Sue, goes away occasionally for weekends without Bernie. 'Sue's out of town this weekend,' Bernie will say to Jack, letting the phrase sit out in the open like a plum on a plate, daring Jack to knock it off. 'Does *he* go "out of town" too?' Brenda asked Jack once. Jack didn't know for sure, but suspected he did. He must. 'I certainly hope so,' Brenda said emphatically. She had never liked Sue Koltz much.

When Robin and Betty Fairweather split up a year ago, Betty went to Puerto Rico for a week to lick her wounds and had sex one night in her hotel room with a man whose name she never did discover. 'Robin's playing his little games, why shouldn't I?' She'd said this to Brenda on her return, without a trace of guilt or sorrow or self-reproach or shame. 'And this guy was more of a man in bed than his royal highness Robin Redbreast ever was.'

Bill and Sally Block's daughter Lucy, seventeen years old, is living in Wheaton with a thirty-six-year-old-man, and Sally has recently been out for a visit, helping Lucy make curtains and wallpaper a bathroom.

Brenda's oldest friend in the world lives the life of a high-priced hooker. Rita Simard, later Rita Kozack, still later Rita LaFollet, went through grammar school with Brenda, and then through high school. Before she was twelve she had the breasts of a woman. She now lives in a sparkling glassy North Shore apartment, paid for by a number of out-of-town businessmen.

Larry Carpenter next door tells stories at parties which involve acts of fellatio, sodomy, and copulation with geese. Brenda, listening to him, remembers her mother's idea of a rowdy party joke: look down your blouse front and spell attic.

The world has changed, she admits it. Her own son, barely

fourteen, has a stack of *Penthouse*s under his bed. A neighbourhood party, one she and Jack luckily missed, apparently degenerated – reports were garbled – into something of a free-for-all.

Janey Carpenter, sunbathing in her backyard last summer, remarked to Brenda how worn out she was – fucking all night long, it got to be too much.

Calvin White, who works at the Institute with Jack, has moved in with Brian Petrie, who also works at the Institute, and Brenda suspects they are living as lovers.

Last year Jack and Brenda stayed in a new hotel in San Francisco where there was a vibrating bed which ran on quarters, also soft-porn movies which could be had for $6.50, also a notice slipped under their door one morning which said 'Dianne, Expert massage, any hour.' 'It's too much,' Brenda had burst out. 'I feel like I'm drowning in sex.' Jack had given her his Groucho leer – 'How can there ever be too much sex?' Later, though, he said, 'But I know what you mean.'

Ease, openness, a tearing down of rules. It had all taken place, and it seemed to Brenda it had happened overnight. Marital fidelity had become a thing of the past, the word itself antique, and as embarrassing as certain companion words like husband and household.

Not long ago Brenda discovered a scrap of paper in Jack's shirt pocket on which he had written 'Fidelity 15'. Fifteen what? she'd wondered. The word fidelity gnawed away at her for days, and its curious attached number opened up several possibilities, none of which she wanted to dwell on. Several times she thought of asking Jack about it, but held back. The contents of pockets were private. (And Jack, to his credit, never went into her purse or dresser drawers.) The enigma was abruptly solved when he told her one morning he was thinking of buying a Fidelity Trust savings certificate at fifteen per cent instead of their usual government bond. She had felt a dismaying flood of relief – dismaying because she trusted Jack, she always has. And he trusted her.

Before they were married Brenda and Jack talked frankly about sex. It was the spring of 1958; the *Ladies' Home Journal* had recently done a series of interviews on the current state of sex in America.

Premarital sex. It was risky. Should they chance it? Yes, Brenda said, though she dreaded, feared, the act itself, the ballooning pain exploding inside her; she didn't believe in the mere tablespoon of semen, it must be more than that. And she dreaded the knell of finality, for once this act was accomplished, what was left in her life? But she was strongly tempted; she wanted to see what it was all about, all this fuss.

No, Jack said, they'd waited this long, they could wait another month or two. It was hard to explain, difficult to justify, but the old myth of respect for the virgin bride persisted beyond logic. *The girl that I marry will have to be / As soft and as pink as a nursery / The girl I call my own. Et cetera.* Besides, he knew what sex was. He had gone steady with a fellow student named Harriet Post for a year; Harriet had been reckless and sensual; she had owned a diaphragm since her eighteenth birthday. She was quick and passionate, according to Jack, and sometimes impatient with him. More than once, he confessed to Brenda, he had felt himself a mere instrument in her arms. She had badgered him, hurried him; 'Now,' she had cried, 'hurry up for the love of God.'

Jack and Brenda, one damp night before their marriage, sitting in Jack's father's car, had related to each other versions of their sexual histories. Kissing, yes, Brenda admitted; and a little feeling around. Above the waist though, and on top of clothes. Except once, with Jimmy Soderstrom out at the Forest Preserve. He had undone her bra and kissed the tips of her breasts; she had felt ridiculous, but faint with pleasure.

Jack, in turn, told Brenda about his relationship with Harriet Post. He had broken up with her, said goodbye, but a kind of gratitude lingered. She had taught him something about women.

Both Jack and Brenda had believed that marriage stood a better chance if the male had had some previous sexual experience. This was verified by a set of graphs in a book they read.

The name of the book was *The Open Door: A Marriage Guide for Moderns*. They bought it shortly before their wedding, a solemn purchase, and poured over its pages. There were chapters on foreplay, climax, afterplay, premature ejaculation, impotence, and frigidity. There were cross-sections on a penis and its attached testicles, of a vagina and its linkage with the womb

154

and the ovaries. Graceful swollen passages, these, imprisoned in the lower portions of human bodies.

The mystery of life was that a tentacle of rigid flesh could be inserted into an answering vessel. This was what all the songs, poems, and Bob Hope jokes were about. A mystery, a joy, which in a matter of weeks would be theirs.

It hurt terribly. He had been guilt-stricken at the pain he inflicted on her – but not guilt-stricken enough to stop. 'Bite my shoulder,' he whispered to her in the darkness that night. She hadn't wanted to; she shrank from pain. She didn't want to hurt him; but she felt it was only polite to do as he requested. The circle of teeth marks on his upper arm lasted the whole of their honeymoon.

She had married him for his face, its puzzled withdrawn look of readiness. She hadn't banked on his body, especially its darker, hidden areas where the skin was coarse, folded, reddened, covered with hairs. It took getting used to.

She had expected the act of love to be accompanied by the clear, piping tones of an alto clarinet, but she heard only something guttural popping in Jack's throat.

Everything was spoiled. If only they could go back to what they had had before; those delicious, endless hours of kissing in Jack's father's car, the clean, solicitous feel of his tongue nudging at hers, and his grateful sighs as she stroked him through his cotton chino pants.

She had read too many articles, many of them damaging. A man wants to experience the feeling of a woman surrendering to him. But how was she to *express* this message of surrender? The timing of the climax was crucial. Was she moving her hips too much or not enough? She was constantly thinking, evaluating, planning, counting, asking herself what was the next move? And the next?

She worried about – was tormented by – the thought of Harriet Post.

In the motel room in Williamsburg where they spent their honeymoon she woke in the mornings depressed and sticky, her embroidered batiste nightgown a dishonoured roll at the foot of the bed. The jelly in her diaphragm gave off a sweetish, unwholesome perfume. Her legs ached. She imagined years of aching and soreness ahead for her.

And there came Jack, again, approaching her after his morning shower, his eyes soft, never to be so tender again, bringing her, again, the anxious, trembling gift of his love.

They had been married for three years when she asked him abruptly one night if he was circumcised. He had collapsed with laughter on their bed. He couldn't stop.

'Well,' she said coldly, a little hurt, 'are you or aren't you?'

'You honestly don't know?'

'How would I know? What would I compare – ?'

'Yes, yes,' he managed to moan between gasps.

'Yes what?'

'Yes, I'm circumcised. Yes.'

She couldn't help laughing too. He was so grateful for her innocence, by now so diminished as to be scarcely visible.

While not literary, Brenda had an ear for a phrase. Once she read, 'For certain of us, the colour of passion burns brighter.'

Did it for her? No. The thought hacked at her heart. But by an enormous effort of concentration she had been able to imagine a flame of sorts. It swayed before her eyes, a blue-footed, gold-tipped flame, growing steadily more brilliant, rising out of the palpable, solemn stillness of flesh.

She had surprised Jack with her new-found energy. She felt him falling back, stunned.

So this was what all the fuss was about. This rich enjoyment.

On alternate Sunday nights when they go over to the Lewises' to play bridge with Hap and Bud, she and Jack come home and dive into bed like troupers – he out of gratitude, she suspects, for not being married to Hap Lewis, and she thankful for having been spared the dark, groping, large-knuckled hands of Bud Lewis. On these nights they are especially generous with each other, languorous, assured, creative – what a lot they owe to Bud and Hap really.

Brenda wonders at times if Jack is aware of this almost laughable connection between their Sunday-night bridge games and the sharpness of their sexual love. She herself noticed it first years ago, and now she waits for it. The nights when she and Jack win at bridge are especially bountiful. Several times she's been on the verge of mentioning this to Jack, but is afraid that by drawing attention to the phenomenon, they will be robbed of what they've accidentally been given or what, in a sense, they've earned.

During the days of the Vietnam war, Brenda once overheard a discussion between Jack and his friend Bernie Koltz. Jack made the observation that because the strictures of modern society had effectively removed most issues of right and wrong, the war presented to many Americans the first serious moral choice they were ever called upon to make.

Bernie had disagreed. What about loyalty, he asked. Loyalty constituted a moral issue, and loyalty in the form of marital fidelity was a fact confronted by almost every adult. (This discussion took place two or three years before Bernie's wife, Sue, began having lovers.)

Jack had conceded that Bernie might be right; but he sounded to Brenda doubtful.

Was Jack faithful to her? Yes, she was sure he was. Despite Harriet Post – how that name was incised on her brain – she felt he was monogamous by nature,

Once, though, about two or three years ago, he had gone to Milwaukee to give a paper at the Milwaukee branch of the Great Lakes Institute. He had been away a week, staying in a room at the Milwaukee Hyatt. He seemed to her, on his return, to be newly gifted. His hands and mouth, especially his mouth, had learned a new sureness. She thought of asking him if something had happened in Milwaukee – she could make a kind of joke of it – but resisted.

Brenda sometimes thinks: I had a mother who came out of nowhere. I came out of nowhere. Surely that's mystery enough for anyone.

But it wasn't. Her children were secretive and ultimately mysterious. And when it came to Jack, there were larger, deeper mysteries. There are areas of his life, she realizes, that will remain unknown to her, areas as large as football fields.

She has her secrets too. Once, years ago, when she was painting her bedroom, she stood on a stepladder and saw carved into the moulding over the door frame the words 'Jake Parker, builder, 1923'. She thought of telling Jack about it, but never did. He would overprize it, lead friends upstairs to see it. She kept it to herself: Jake Parker, young, muscular, audacious.

It seems an innocent secret and in no way a betrayal. She and

Jack, by luck, and by the sheer length of time they've been together – twenty years is not to be sneezed at these days – have come in silence to certain understandings. The distances between them are delicately gauged, close to being perfect.

How fortunate they are. Only a fool would throw away this kind of rare good fortune.

Chapter Twenty-Two

BRENDA HAD SIGNED UP FOR THE NINE O'CLOCK WORKSHOP on Ethnic Stitchery, but when morning came she decided instead to spend the hour shopping for a new nightgown. She remembered seeing a lingerie speciality place in the shopping mall. The Underneath Shop. She and Lenora Knox had walked by it the other day and remarked on its name. Lenora told Brenda that there was a similar boutique in Sante Fe called The Bottom Line, and Brenda said there was one in Chicago called Sky with Diamonds.

The thought of buying a new nightgown had come to her late last night after she had said goodnight to Barry. They had turned outside her door and unexpectedly embraced. They collided awkwardly, and held on to each other for a long, unmoving minute, Brenda's face pressed against the clean sharpness of Barry's shirt collar. Her arms tightened on his neck, holding not just him, but his lost daughter, too, and the whole void left by her absence, including the agony of guilt that gripped and 'utterly changed' that person he mentioned in passing, his wife, Ruth. What did it mean anyway to be 'utterly changed'? The thought was frightening, unthinkable. She could not imagine it.

She had run herself a long, hot bath and had lingered in it a good half-hour, her brain numbed in the slow steam. Then she got out, dried herself with particular care, under her arms, between the toes, and pulled her pink flannelette nightgown over her head. With the side of her thumb she touched the place on her cheek where Barry's dry shirt-collar had pressed.

Sleep was slow to come. Her old nightgown should have been softened by wear, but wasn't. It scratched around the wrists, and Brenda pushed impatiently at the sleeves. She had never liked this kind of granny gown, but the Elm Park house was draughty in winter; the furnace was outdated and the old storm windows fitted badly. She and Jack talked from time to time about putting extra insulation in the attic, but Jack kept postponing it. He protested the drifting away of his dollars into unseen corners of the old house, and resisted, too, the violation brought about by clumsy, scratchy batts of fibreglass or rock wool. (He loved poking his head up through the trapdoor in the bathroom and gazing at that spare dusty space, narrowly braced with lines of dim light and shadow.)

Brenda remembered that she had bought this pink nightgown on sale. She recalled exactly what she paid for it – twelve dollars. That was three years ago at a sidewalk bazaar in LaGrange. She didn't even like pink, especially not this ripe watermelon shade – what her mother used to refer to as Goldblatt's pink.

Her face, restless on the pillow, pulled into sharp, scolding relief; what was she doing wearing an itchy faded pink nightgown anyway? Unaccustomed anger nudged at her and kept her from falling asleep.

In the morning she climbed out of bed, still tired and still scolding herself. 'What do you think you're doing in that get-up sister?' (Hap Lewis's borrowed voice.) 'That lace has had it, for God's sake! That elastic's right out of the sleeves, no wonder it's itchy. Time to throw this rag away, kiddo.'

She yanked it over her head, rolled it into a ball, gave it a wicked twist, and dropped it in the wastebasket.

Verna's bed, calm, unslept in, seemed indifferent to her rage, and Verna's suitcase rested at peace on the floor where it had been since Saturday. Or had it been turned around? Possibly.

It came to Brenda that something serious might have happened to Verna – she had a fleeting image of a body jammed in an air shaft. Perhaps she should just mention to Betty Vetter – no, that was ridiculous. Verna, she imagined, was a woman capable of travelling lightly. No nightgown at all, not even a toothbrush. Verna of Virginia. Lucky, free, uncluttered, transparent, invisible, talented Verna.

At The Underneath Shop Brenda was the first customer of the day. A cheerful salesgirl – about twenty, Brenda estimated – her front teeth slightly parted, showed her where the size twelves were, and Brenda carried an armload into the fitting room.

First she tried on a white, double-nylon full-length gown with a pleated ruffle around the hem. No, white might be all right in summer with a tan, but not now. Also, there was something a touch too Elizabethan about it, reminding Brenda of *The Duchess of Malfi*.

Next she slid a black and silky sheath over her head. It fell down around her body with a sibilant swish, then pressed and clung like a licking of lips. A fragile fan of lace lay across the bosom, and a thin halter-strap held it up – but bit into her collar bone. Nice, but painful to wear, and a little short; it stopped awkwardly at the mid-calf – what they used to call ballerina length when she was in high school.

After that she tried a creamy Anne-of-Green-Gables concoction in a material that looked like lawn. It fell from a wide yolk, transparent, but without being tartish. The long, bell sleeves were edged with antique-looking cotton lace, lovely. Perfect, in fact. No, it was too wide across the shoulders. No wonder – she peered at the tag – a size sixteen. (Thank God she wasn't a size sixteen.) She removed it carefully, gratefully.

Then a spruce-green affair composed of long, intricately fitted gores. It was made in France, and was beautifully finished. Brenda, hissing through her teeth, thought: this is it. It was beautiful. She examined herself sideways in the mirror. No. Too tight across the bust.

A purple satin with shoulder ties looked falsely theatrical.

So did the orange chiffon: more *Duchess of Malfi* – a dress for a giver of curses.

There was a silky spiderweb of a gown in café au lait, which fit not too badly and made her shoulders look soft. But a brown nightgown was a brown nightgown. No.

Maybe something in a print. But the full, gathered nightie – this kind of gown could only be called a nightie – looked worse on her than the one she'd thrown away. (She wondered if the chambermaid had emptied the wastebasket yet.)

A slim lavender wisp, the colour of a winter sky, looked more like a slip than a nightgown. And she couldn't go around holding in her stomach all the time.

'What exactly did you have in mind?' the salesgirl asked, sticking her head in.

'I'm not really sure,' Brenda said. She was stepping into a yellow brushed-nylon. It dragged heavily from shoulder to hem. Awful. All she needed was a candlestick. It even had buttons.

What did she want?

In the fitting room next to her a woman was trying on a bra. Brenda could tell by her stern voice that she was a determined shopper. The salesgirl was helping her do up the hooks. 'Well,' came the woman's voice, broad and powerful over the partition, 'how's it fit in back?'

'A little tight,' the answer came. (Brenda imagined an immense, moulded bosom – a solid, fused front that pushed forward as though directed by a nervous system of its own.)

'What I want – ' the woman boomed, then paused. 'What I want – '

Brenda listened. The salesgirl listened. The nightgowns on their plastic hangers listened.

'What I want is better separation.'

'Ah,' came the soft, immediate, girlish reply. 'Well, if *that's* what you want . . . '

'That's what I want.' The voice came down like thunder.

Brenda left without buying anything. She told herself she had lost the habit of wanting. It was no one's fault but her own; through lack of practice she had simply forgotten how it was done, how to open her mouth and say: I want. Perhaps she had never really known how to say it. Wanting required more than the force of sentence parts; it needed a kind of dogged, deliberate stamina she had been spared. It grieved her to think of the time she had expended on wasteful errands. A passionate search for towels for the powder room, for the perfect recipe for spinach quiche. These tasks seemed devised to sound out her own authenticity; and almost always she walked away – like this – light as air, empty-handed.

Back in the room she rescued the nightgown from the wastebasket and hung it on a hanger, smoothing out the shoulders, running a finger down the disintegrating lace, giving it a tug, which might have said either: 'Who cares?' or 'Hello, old girl.'

She felt herself stretched with happiness. Something fortunate was happening to her.

Ten-thirty. Time to meet Barry in the lobby.

She sniffed; the room smelled of cigarette smoke. Verna's zippered case smiled up at her with grinning metal teeth.

Chapter Twenty-Three

BETWEEN ELEVEN AND ELEVEN-THIRTY IN THE CONSTITUTION Room, Barry Ollershaw presented a paper on *Chlorine-Assisted Leaching of Uranium Ores*. Brenda sat in the fourth row, listening, observing. Unfamiliar terms – radionuclide and thorium and radium 226 – sailed past her, words that seemed rectangular and solid, with syllables securely riveted and lightly rusted like ingots long stored in a vault. She wondered if he was in the middle of his talk or getting close to the end; there seem no recognizable signs, no foothold to keep her on course.

When the applause came she was taken by surprise. It was so vigorous, so generous. Barry, relaxed now and catching her eye over the lectern, shuffled his notes back into order and leaned forward comfortably on his elbows.

There were a number of questions from the floor. The men (and one woman) who asked the questions seemed filled with benign earnestness. 'Have you considered the effect of – ?' 'Should future research take the direction of – ?' 'In your opinion, Dr. Ollershaw – ?' *Dr.* Ollershaw!

An elderly man in the front row, lean, snowy-headed, with a beak of a nose, rose with the help of a pair of canes and commented at length in a sweet quavering scholarly voice. His remarks were greeted with roars of laughter and thumping applause. This gathering, Brenda saw, was a small world of its own, stocked with its private jokes and beloved personalities. Oddly, it satisfied her to know that Barry, whose existence had seemed contingent on her own – *her* rescuer, *her* confidant, *her* comrade from the twenty-fourth floor – was clearly a part of this specialized world, recognized and listened to and agreed with. An absurd flame of pride fluttered within her.

His replies were deferential, carefully worded. He was not unlike Jack, she saw, in that respect.

Last year in San Francisco she had gone to hear Jack deliver a talk on patterns of Indian settlement in the Middle West. He had spoken for an hour, glancing only occasionally at his notes.

Exactly when and from where had he acquired this relaxed fund of material? She hadn't realized he knew this much about settlement patterns. 'You never told me all that about family cohesiveness in tribal societies,' she accused him afterwards.

He'd countered mildly, reflecting a little of her look of surprise. 'It's not that interesting.'

The truth was she had never really understood Jack's profession, never quite comprehended how a historian spent his days. Jack's office at the Institute was a tidy cork-lined box, his chair a squeaky swivel model. There he sat, day after day, reading, turning over papers, making notes; and for this he was rewarded with a salary, plus medical benefits and a guaranteed pension plan.

How were all those hours filled? – she had often tried to imagine. They must contain something, some level of daily substance. But what? When Rob and Laurie were babies she had occasionally phoned him at lunchtime – in those days he took a sack lunch; they had just moved in to the Elm Park house and needed every penny to make the mortgage payments. 'What did you do this morning?' she would ask, picturing how he must look, relaxed at his desk, unwrapping his sandwich, polishing his apple on his knee, staring at the leaves of his single philodendron.

His answers were vague, at times even evasive. 'This and that' or 'just collating some new stuff' or 'checking a few references'. Her own tasks at that time were tedious but sharply defined; by noon she had done a load of laundry, swabbed a bathroom floor, made up the formula, baked a cake, and vacuumed the living room. Jack seemed to her to be almost romantically idle.

Later she realized this was because of the nature of what he did. Historians didn't solve existing problems. They set the problems themselves, plucking them out of the banked past like prize jewels, and then played with them for years on end.

Jack had been working for three years now on his book about the Indian concept of trade and property. From time to time she's helped him with the typing and the sorting of notes, and she understands in a general way what the scope of the book is to be. What she hasn't been able to say to Jack is that she finds the project bewildering in its purposelessness.

Of course she could be wrong. It might be that dozens of

scholars in the field were waiting for exactly this kind of comprehensive study. Perhaps it *was* destined to fill a serious gap. Perhaps it would shed new light on old, perplexing, unanswered questions.

She doubted it though.

There was a time when she might have questioned Jack about it; now, after three years, it seemed somehow too late – particularly since she suspected he shared some of the same doubts.

Three years, and he was still in the middle of Chapter Six. In the last year he'd hardly worked on it at all; there were other projects, he said, claiming his attention. Dr. Middleton, in his sixties now and only a few short years from retirement, was pushing more and more administrative work his way. Jack's outline and notes for the book sat in his old briefcase or lay scattered on his desk. It was difficult to work at home, he said. Laurie was always barging in. Rob played the radio so loud it carried to every corner or the house. The phone was constantly ringing at weekends. The downstairs den where he worked was chilly; he talked about getting a little electric heater and had even looked at a few models at Wards one Saturday morning. Brenda suggested that he move his desk to a corner of their bedroom where it was warmer and where the light was better. She felt, as she made this suggestion, a brief blush of guilt, having taken the guest room herself – easily the brightest room in the house – for her quilting. On the other hand, needlework required good lighting, natural light if possible; and she used the room far more than he ever would. She was, in addition, more serious that Jack about her work.

She found this last – the fact of her seriousness – astounding, for in the beginning Jack had been the serious one, the one whose work had taken precedence. She had, in those days, shushed the children so he could read; she had zipped them into their snowsuits and taken them out for long walks in Scoville Common on Saturdays so that Jack could work on his papers. Her husband was a historian; once she had loved the sound of that word. He required for this quaint pursuit an envelope of quiet protection, and this she could provide, could joyfully provide.

And now she wanted to provide something more. She wanted – had tried, but courage failed her – to release him, let him off the hook. She wanted to tell him to forget about writing this book if he honestly felt it was a waste of his time.

She had given some thought as to how she might broach the subject. A Sunday morning would be best, while they were still in bed. Their Sundays, a relic of student days, were relaxed and easy. Often they woke up and made love while the sun streamed in, striking the white of the walls, rebounding to the surface of the blue-and-green quilt, touching the soft sides of Jack's face and the curve of his closed eyelids.

'Listen, Jack,' she planned to say. 'Just because you've invested three years in this project doesn't mean you have to sweat it out to the end.'

Or 'Listen Jack, no one's jumping up and down and demanding that you finish this book. Why not quit and try something you've got some faith in?'

'Listen, Jack,' she could say, giving a little laugh so he wouldn't think she lacked faith in him, 'Listen, love, your heart obviously isn't in this thing.'

The trouble with saying this was that she didn't know what his heart *was* in. Perhaps there was nothing, nothing at all. And she was fearful of letting the light fall on what might be a width of emptiness.

Chapter Twenty-Four

THE NIGHT BEFORE, AT DINNER, BRENDA HAD ASKED BARRY Ollershaw exactly what it was that metallurgical engineers did.

'Why don't you sit through a session in the morning,' he'd suggested. He was giving a paper himself, he said, on uranium ores. 'It'll be deadly dull,' he warned 'but it might give you an idea of what it's about.'

Today, sitting across from Brenda in the hotel coffee shop, he bit into a club sandwich and said, 'Well, didn't I warn you?'

Brenda admitted she hadn't understood a word. 'But when I looked around at all those other people, they seemed absolutely . . . well . . . rapt.'

He chewed happily. 'It did go better than I thought it was going to.'

'You're positively basking,' Brenda accused.

'We all need a bask now and then.'

Brenda agreed, but said, 'I wonder why we do. Why we need to be rewarded, I mean. You'd think we'd outgrow it somehow. At least, I'd like to think so.'

'You'd think so,' Barry said. 'Especially once you've had a glimpse at how artificially the reward system usually works, how really false most honours are. How they cater to our weaknesses and – ' He stopped and shrugged.

'I dread the announcement of the quilting prizes this afternoon,' Brenda told him. 'I'm excited by it, but I dread it more. It doesn't make sense, does it? It's even degrading in a way to have to go through it.'

'Would you have worked as hard on your quilts if there hadn't been a competition?'

Brenda thought for a minute, then said, 'Maybe. Yes, I think so.'

'You're one of the lucky ones.'

'Would you have written the same paper if you hadn't been invited to read it in front of all those people this morning?'

'Probably not. That is, I'm always working on something, but there's a certain excitement about actually presenting it. I'm sure it's a vanity thing.'

'Deep down we're all shallow,' Brenda said. 'That's what a friend of mine, Hap Lewis, always says.'

'I suppose your husband, Jack, is into all this too.' He pronounced Jack's name slowly, as though it were a difficult word in a foreign language, letting it expand warily like a collapsible drinking cup.

'Into what?'

'Writing papers for conferences and so on.'

'Jack? Yes, he does. I was just thinking this morning about a paper I heard him give last year on Indian settlement patterns. It was strange, but all the time he was on the platform talking, I had the feeling he was someone I hardly knew. Here was this middle-aged man, this authority for heaven's sake. His voice, his gestures, his face looking out from behind the microphone, everything, it all seemed so different.'

'It probably made a difference to him, too. Having you there in the audience, I mean.'

'I doubt it,' Brenda said. 'I think he just slipped away. Into his other self, as it were. His working self, the history part of him.'

'It made a difference to me,' Barry said, 'when I looked up from my notes and saw you sitting out there. In that green blouse. A woman in a green blouse. I felt twenty-five years old, not fifty.'

'Really?' Brenda said, absurdly flattered.

'I'd like to buy you a present this afternoon.'

'A present!' She put down her sandwich and stared.

'Why not?'

'I can't let you buy me a present. Why should you anyway? Because I went to your lecture? I wanted to go to your lecture.'

'You saw that elderly gentleman sitting in the front row this morning?'

'With the white hair and the two canes?'

'That's Professor Denton. From Cornell. Emeritus now. He came up to me this morning and handed me an envelope with an honorarium in it. Completely unexpected, I might say, and extremely generous.'

'Found money,' Brenda smiles over her coffee. 'Part of the reward system we were just talking about.'

'What I'd like to do with it – now don't interrupt me – is to take you shopping and buy you a coat.'

'A coat?'

'Yes.'

'Barry, you're not still worrying about my coat?'

'I am, yes.'

'But it'll turn up. I'm sure it will turn up. Didn't you say what's-his-name, the man sharing your room, is going to be here this afternoon to – '

'Storton McCormick. He's cancelled. Professor Denton just told me. He's left word that he won't be able to speak this afternoon. And he hasn't been back to the room at all. Not that I know of.'

'But he's bound to turn up eventually. He hasn't checked out officially, has he?'

'No, but no one's seen him.'

'It's only Tuesday – '

'And meanwhile you're stuck in this hotel without a coat.'

'But everything I need is right here: the exhibition centre, all the meetings, everything.'

'You haven't seen a thing of Philadelphia. This is a remarkable city, full of – '

'I can always see Philadelphia some other time.'

'And how exactly do you think you're going to get home to Chicago without a coat. If it doesn't turn up by Thursday, Brenda, what in hell are you going to do? Wrap yourself in the shower curtain? It's cold out there. This is January.'

'*Listen* to me a minute.'

'What?'

'In the first place, I lost the coat, not you.'

'The point is – '

'The point is, I'm not worried about it, so why should you be. Thursday's a long way off and – '

'The point really isn't the coat at all. I'm just wanting to buy you a present.'

'The roses, you've already – '

'A real present.'

'But why on earth should you – ?'

'Because you came to my lecture in your green silk blouse – '

'Polyester.' She said this sternly, a matter of keeping the record straight.

169

'And listened to me ramble on last night; and you held my hand – '

'I'm forty years old,' Brenda said.

'You're also lovely – '

'And married.'

'And married.' He brought his fingers together. 'That's the rub, I suppose.'

She tried to laugh. 'I'm not sure what you mean by rub.'

'It's against the law to buy presents for married women, I suppose.'

'It's not that at all. As you perfectly well know. It's just that it would make me feel . . . ' She hesitated. 'Make me feel rather . . . '

'Obligated,' he supplied.

'Exactly, yes. Obligated.'

'Even if I assured you – I can't of course very well go down on my hands and knees here in the coffee shop, not without making a scene – but even if I assured you from my heart that no obligation is attached to this wish of mine – '

'I know that. I really do know that. But the uneasiness would be there, on my side. It's difficult to explain, but I wouldn't feel easy about your giving me a gift like that. In fact, you don't know this yet, but when lunch is over, I intend to wrestle you for the cheque.'

'I'm loving this, you know.'

'Arguing with me?' she smiled. 'About buying a coat?'

'Sitting here. Eating a club sandwich. Sitting across a table from a nice woman.'

'I'm loving it too,' she said, surprising herself. 'I really am.'

'Brenda Bowman. Quiltmaker. Urbanite to the core. You bring a tear to my eye.'

'Truly?' She looked; his eyes did look faintly misty. On impulse she touched his sleeve.

'I love sentimental scenes,' he confessed, taking her hand. 'I even cried in *Mary Poppins*.'

So did Jack, she was about to confide, but didn't. Instead she said, 'Can I ask you a question?'

'Anything. As long as it's not about metallurgical engineering.'

'It's about something you said last night. About your wife.'

'Ruth.'

'About her being . . . ' Brenda fumbled for the exact words. 'I think you said she was utterly changed.'

'Yes.' He let go of Brenda's hand.

'How did you mean? Changed how? In what way?'

'Every way there is to change. She's lost herself. You'd have to know how she was before – '

'How was she?'

'Lively. Active. She did research at the university; she's a botanist. Or was. She played tennis like a pro.' He spread his hands. 'Now she doesn't do anything.'

'Nothing at all?'

'Of course, she's heavily tranquillized most of the time. But even so – '

'Oh, Barry – '

'And, of course,' his voice changed key, 'of course we no longer love each other.'

At this Brenda felt no surprise; she'd expected this for some reason. 'Not at all?'

He bore down hard on each syllable. 'Not at all.'

'Not even – ?'

'Not spiritually, not psychologically, not physically. It happens sometimes. So we've been told. When a child dies, the parents, or one of them anyway, blames the other.'

'What do you do?'

His voice sounded, for the first time, harsh. 'What do you mean, what do I do?'

'How do you cope with it is what I mean.'

'If you mean what do I do with my time, I work hard. I work at weekends; I work nights. I do a fair amount of consulting, and that requires travelling. I've got three or four research projects on the go. I swim, sail a little; we have quite a number of old friends – '

'But what about . . . ?' She hesitated, not sure what she was asking.

'It you're asking me am I faithful – and I think you are – the answer is no. I was faithful though – don't stop me, I want to tell you this – I was faithful for the first year and a half. Which is a long time, I think you'll agree.'

'I do agree, yes.' Brenda nodded quickly, cringing to hear how facile she sounded.

'She's been hospitalized twice,' he went on. 'She can't be left

171

on her own. Right now her sister is staying with us. Which is why I was able to get away to this conference. Which is why I'm able to sit here, boring the hell out of you with all this depressing tale of mine.'

After a minute Brenda said, 'What are you going to do this afternoon?'

'I'd hoped to take you shopping. But that . . . seems to be out.'

'Why don't you come with me to the Awards Ceremony. It's at three o'clock, in the Exhibition Hall. There are hundreds of quilts. And all kinds of other things. You'll love it.'

'Will I, Brenda? Yes, I think I will.'

Chapter Twenty-Five

'BRENDA BOWMAN, I'VE BEEN LOOKING HIGH AND LOW FOR you.'

It was Susan Hammerman, waving her arms, making her way through the crowd. On her forehead shone a fine, glistening, happy mask of perspiration. 'At last I found you.'

'Susan, this is Barry Ollershaw. Susan Hammerman. Susan's from Chicago too. She's a weaver.'

'Hello, Barry. You did say Barry? You a quilter too?'

'Well, no, I – '

'Oh, sorry, I didn't notice your name card. So – you're one of *those*.'

'I'm afraid so.'

'Anyway, Brenda, I just wanted to congratulate you. When I saw your name up there with an honourable mention, I just about – '

'Thank you.'

'I think we can really be proud of good old Chicago today.'

'We just got here, I'm afraid. Did – '

'Lottie's got an honourable too, in macramé, and I guess you must have seen my name – '

'No. What happened?'

'Second prize. I nearly flipped. I mean, two years in a row, how lucky can you get.'

'Congratulations,' Barry said.

'Why, that's wonderful, Susan.'

'I'm feeling crazy. There goes Lottie now. I've got to catch her while I've got the chance. Nice to meet you, Barry. See you, Brenda. Isn't this the wildest?'

'Brenda Bowman, *there* you are.'

'Barry, this is Betty Vetter, the organizer of the whole thing. Betty, this is Barry Ollershaw.'

'Aha! One of the infamous – '

'Afraid so.'

173

'Brenda, can you tell me where Verna is? I've been looking all over the place. I've had her paged and everything.'

'I haven't seen her. In fact – '

'The first-prize winner and she's not even here to accept her ribbon.'

'Have you asked – '

'I thought of making another announcement over the loud-speaker, but there's so much noise in this place I don't know if it'd do any good.'

'I was going to ask *you* about Verna, Betty, because the truth is – '

'Look, would you be a pal and help me out? When they call out her name, if she doesn't respond, would you mind getting up there and accepting for her? Just say a word or two, you know the sort of thing. I know it's asking a lot – '

'Me?'

'You're her roommate. I mean, it's sort of appropriate, if you know what I mean.'

'But I don't even know – '

'You're a honey. Honestly, you're a honey. I'll see you later, okay?'

'Brenda, for goodness' sake, where've you been hiding yourself?'

'Lenora! I'd like you to meet Barry Ollershaw. Barry, this is Lenora Knox, another quilter.'

'How do you do, Lenora.'

'To tell the truth, I've got a splitting headache. With all this noise. What branch are you in?'

'I'm with the metallurgists – that other group – I'm afraid.'

'Oh. I don't have my glasses on or I'd have seen your name card. I was looking for you this morning, Brenda. I thought maybe we could have lunch together today, but – '

'What about tomorrow?'

'Well, I don't know. I'm giving my workshop tomorrow. On the Genre Quilt. It's about animism. That's when – '

'Oh. That sounds interesting.

'I almost forgot. Congratulations for your honourable mention.'

'Thank you. I really was surprised.'

'I guess you've probably heard the rumours going around about the judges.'

'No, what rumours?'

'Morton Holman. Someone pointed out – but it was too late – about the conflict-of-interest thing. Apparently it's going to be looked into. For next year.'

'I see.'

'And Dorothea Thomas. She's marvellous, just marvellous, as a craftsperson she's one of a kind, but when it comes right down to the nitty-gritty of judging – '

'Yes?'

'She's just . . . well . . . you know. As someone was pointing out, new blood is what we need. And better regional distribution – '

'I suppose so,' Brenda said.

'Hey, it's Mrs. B herself, isn't it? How's Mrs. B. feeling today?'

'Barry, I'd like you to meet Hal Rago. Hal, this is Barry Ollershaw.

'Great to meet you, Barry, just great.'

'Good to meet you, Hal. I read your piece on Brenda in the paper yesterday.'

'Terrific, terrific. Well, you're going to be reading more about her today.'

'Oh, no,' Brenda said.

'Yeah, I got the list of winners last night, and we've got a nice news piece in the afternoon paper, sort of zeroing in on the whole caboodle of winners. Say, you don't happen to know this Verna of Virginia, do you? Thought I'd take her out for a liquid supper; do a spotlight thing on her for tomorrow.'

'I'm afraid I can't help you with that, Hal.'

'No one seems to know where the hell she is. Probably one of your shy, retiring types. Too bad. When she finds out she's missed out on some free PR.'

'Yes,' Brenda said.

'Hey, what do you know, someone's got a newspaper over there now.'

'Today's?'

'Looks like it.'

'Let's ask – '

'Can I just have a look at that, do you mind?'

'What page is it on?'

'Well, what do you know! An art story on the front page.'

'Will wonders never cease.'

'About time.'

'Jesus.'

'Look at those pictures.'

'Not bad.'

'What are you laughing so hard about?' Brenda asked Barry. He was doubled over. 'I can't stop. I can't stop.'

'Let me see that again. I don't see what's so funny about that.'

'The headline,' he gasped. 'No, not there, the subheadline.'

'It's just a headline, that's all.'

' "Second Coming Gets Honourable Mention". '

'Well?'

'And you don't think that's funny?'

'Well,' Brenda said, 'not particularly.'

'It's wonderful. It's priceless.'

'I don't –'

'And the best part,' he wiped at his eyes, 'the best part is he probably didn't even intend it to be funny.'

'Hmmmm.'

'Wonderful, wonderful.' He was off again, hanging on to a post for support. 'Wonderful.'

'Hmmmm,' Brenda said again, smiling at him, feeling weak with happiness.

Chapter Twenty-Six

At seven o'clock, from barry's room, brenda phoned home to Elm Park and talked to her children. It was Laurie who answered.

'It's Mom, ' she shrieked. 'She's phoning long distance. Hey, Rob, get on the upstairs phone, it's Mom.'

'How are you, sweetie?' Brenda held the phone in both hands and saw in soft-focus her twelve-year-old daughter, Laurie, with her round face ashine, rosy with its own heat, and her soft mouth open and eager – heartbreakingly eager.

'Guess what, Mom, I made a Caesar salad. And Bernie – he was here for dinner – he said it was the best he ever tasted.'

'Bernie was there for dinner? That's nice. When was this?

'Hi, Mom.' It was Rob on the extension. He sounded sleepy, dazed, cool. 'How're things in Philly?'

'It's been really – '

'Did you hear about the snowstorm?'

'You mean – '

'It was in all the papers, on TV – '

'We got eleven inches last night, Mom.'

'Ten inches.'

'Eleven it said in the *Trib*. You should've been here. We had a real white-out. And no school today, they were all closed, and this huge big tree over at Scoville – '

'No one even went to work,' Laurie said. 'Hardly anyone – '

'Everything was closed, all the stores and everything. Even the gas stations – '

'No one could get their cars out, you couldn't even open the garage door, there was so much snow.'

'How's Philadelphia?' Rob asked in his adult voice. 'What's it like?'

'Well, it's – '

'How was the plane? Did you get airsick?'

'You know I never get – '

177

'The snowplough hasn't even been down Franklin yet. It's done Holmes and Mann, but not Franklin. That's because – '

'It's over my head,' Laurie squealed.

'How could it be over your head,' Rob said, 'if it's only ten inches?'

'Between the Carpenters and us, I mean. It's all piled up, you should see it. You should've seen us jumping off the garage roof today, the whole neighbourhood – '

'It's a record. Since 1942 this is the most snow ever. Not the most snow in total, but the most inches in the shortest period of time.'

'How's Dad? Is he – ?'

'They're going to have it on radio tonight, all the stations, if the schools are going to be closed again tomorrow. They haven't decided yet.'

'The grammar schools are closed,' Laurie said, 'but not the high schools.'

'Where'd you hear that? Not on the radio.'

'Someone told me.'

'I bet.'

'You're getting along okay though?' Brenda asked.

'Yeah, we had hamburgers last night. Dad got them somewhere. He got home late because of all the snow. The Eisenhower was closed. It's the first time in history it's ever been closed, that's how bad the snow was.'

'They showed this man on TV who got a heart attack shovelling out his car.'

'He's going to be okay, though, they took him to the hospital.'

'Who? Who had a heart attack?'

'This guy on TV. Nobody we know.'

'How're Grandma and Grandpa? Did you go over on Sunday?'

'Yeah.'

'They're fine.'

'Where's Dad? Can I talk to him a sec?'

'I think he's still at work.'

'Yeah, he is.'

'I thought you said everything was closed today, all the offices.'

'What?'

'Because of the snow. You said everything was closed and no one went to work.'

'Yeah, but I think Dad went to work. He went somewhere.'

'How's Philadelphia, Mom? Did you see the Liberty Bell yet?'

'No, but I got an honourable mention. For *The Second Coming*.'

'Hey, that's neat.'

'Is that the one with the flower thing on it?'

'No, that's one of the other ones.'

'Neat.'

'I'd better go, kids. I'll see you on Thursday, okay? You're sure everything's okay?'

'Did you say Thursday?'

'Dad knows. It's on the bulletin board. The flight number and everything.'

'We're going to try and borrow a snowblower tomorrow. Remember the Pattersons? Next to the McArthurs. They've got a snowblower.'

'Listen, kids, give Dad my love, okay?'

'What?'

'She said give Dad her love.'

'Oh, love, that's what I thought she said.'

'Okay, we will.'

'Don't forget.'

'Forget what? Oh, okay.'

'Goodbye, kids. See you Thursday.'

"Bye, Mom.'

'I really do miss you both.'

'We miss you too, Mom.'

'So long.'

Chapter Twenty-Seven

OH, SHE LOVED THEM, LOVED THEM. FOR A MINUTE SHE kept her hand on the receiver, unwilling to lose the connection of love between herself and her two children.

'Well,' Barry said from across the room where he was pouring gin into glasses. 'Is everything all right?'

'Everything's fine,' Brenda said, and, a little giddily, turned and reached for the glass he offered. 'It's just that it's humbling when you realize that your children cope perfectly well without you.'

'Deflating?' He sat down on the bed and took a sip of his drink.

'No.' She sat across from him. 'No, it's sort of amazing.'

What amazed her was that, in the four short days she'd been away, she had completely forgotten what they were like. How selfish they both were, Rob and Laurie. But how purely and transcendentally selfish. Their self-concern glowed like some primitive element, bright and more fiercely than radium. And the intensity of their attachment to the present moment – to the trivia of weather records, the drama of their unfolded stormy day – touched her to the heart. This simplicity, this openness to sensation – they wore it like an adornment. The contamination of boredom would come, no doubt, no doubt – but not yet.

Oh, she loved them. And only days ago she had found them unlovable and unloving. Why was that? she asked Barry.

He was in a philosophical mood. 'I suppose love comes in waves. Like sound waves and lightwaves and everything else in nature. Blowing hot or cold. On again, off again.'

'It shouldn't though,' Brenda said, determinedly righteous. 'What about steadfast love? You know,' she gave a short laugh, 'the sustaining flame.'

'You mean what we all want? And what we think we deserve?'

'Maybe we don't really want it all the time.'

'Maybe not. I suppose it's a fantasy to think we can love

anyone with that kind of consistency. It might even kill us, getting loved back like that. Like being bombarded with a ray gun.'

Brenda set her glass on the night table. 'It may be true, but I hate to believe it.'

'So do I. But put to the empirical test, I can't think of anyone who's loved someone else unceasingly, unstintingly, and at full force, day in and day out. Maybe in literature or pop songs – '

'My mother maybe. Of course, I was the only one she had. But aside from her – '

'Aside from her?'

'I suppose love does fail from time to time.'

'It lapses anyway,' Barry said. He finished off his gin.

'That's a better word, yes. A lapse of love.'

'And you and . . .' He avoided the word, making a circle with his empty glass instead, 'you and . . . ?'

'Jack,' she said, helping him out, anchoring his question with matter-of-factness.

'You and Jack then.' His tone was elaborately cynical, but a little shy. 'I suppose it's been all steady flame for you. No lapses or anything like that.'

'I don't know,' she said with great care. Her hand, flat and sensible on the bedspread, spread wide. 'I suppose we've been . . . fairly . . .'

'Lucky?'

'Well, yes. Mainly anyway.'

He asked if she wanted more gin. She shook her head.

'Lucky Brenda,' he said, letting the word float on the air between them.

It was almost true, about the steadiness of the flame. But not quite. Four years ago Brenda had wakened one morning in her blue-and-white bedroom and looked at her sleeping husband. Jack's face in repose had been blank and shuttered and unfamiliar; she said to herself, or rather to the white walls, 'I don't love him any more.'

Minutes later he woke up, turned off the alarm, and reached for her through her newly forming haze of sorrow. They performed the motions of love, and Brenda registered with awful chilliness: now he's going to do this, now he's going to do that. When he took his shower afterwards, she stayed in bed thinking: now he's washing his neck, now he's standing on one foot soaping his toes. Now he's stepping out and stealing secret, prideful looks in the mirror, patting his stomach, cocking his head intelligently to one side, mumbling under his breath.

He came damp and powdered into the bedroom and saw her still in bed. With unforgivable nonchalance he asked her, 'Aren't you getting up this morning?'

It had fled. Love was gone. The world was spoiled. For months she had no idea what to do. There was, in fact, nothing she could do. Trapped in her own reputation for sunniness, she had to carry on as though nothing had happened. She could only pretend.

Jack, though, seemed not entirely taken in by her pretence. She caught him looking at her oddly, searchingly. A penny for your thoughts, he said to her far too often. He took her out to dinner at Jacques's in the middle of the week for no reason at all. He urged her to sign up for an evening class. He took her to see a rerun of *Laura* at the Arts Theatre, where she endured the soft pressure of his hand on her thigh. He even – she found this out much later – had a long, confidential talk with Brian Petrie at work about the advisability of psychiatric counselling for her. (Brian, who had been through the mill himself, advised against it.)

In the evening, when they were alone, he urged her to talk about her mother, who had died in the fall.

Of course! Of course. How like him to think that that was the problem: her shock at her mother's sudden death and her anger at the doctor who might have prevented it. Her withdrawal, her dullness, her easy daily tears and compulsive shopping – all this he laid at the blameless door of her mother's death. His eyes, as he tried to draw out her feelings, were so sad and so injured that she longed to run from the room.

During that winter Brenda slept woodenly beside this shallow, presumptuous stranger and allowed him to believe. His patience, his solicitude, his stroking hands – especially his stroking hands – would drive her mad, but she let him believe anyway.

When he went to work she sat in the kitchen, trying to imagine why she had committed her life to this empty human being. She resurrected her nineteen-year-old self and marvelled at the temporary illness that she had mistaken for love. One morning she sat at the kitchen table for two hours without moving, and out of her mouth came a strange, loose, whimpering sound that refused to yield to tears.

In the spring they went to France. He surprised her with the plane tickets, bringing them home one night along with an itinerary. Was it for a conference, something he was researching? No, he said, it was a vacation, just the two of them. Her heart plunged at the thought – just the two of them. She loathed herself in the role of neurotic, grieving woman, and resented him for inventing that role, for making her into an invalid who had to be jollied out of thoughts of her dead mother by being taken on an expensive vacation to France.

The first week went badly. The fervent sightseeing dragged on her energy. Their day at Versailles lingers in memory as an ordeal, wordless and odourless; they had wandered for hours, dully, through dull rooms; the Hall of Mirrors was a blur of smudged surfaces, sending back to them uneven images of disappointment.

Jack's efforts to interest her in the Gobelin tapestries – he arranged to go on a day when the lecture was in French, not English – had seemed to her to be staged and sacrificial and pathetic, and she resented the doses of gratitude she expended on him for his small acts of thoughtfulness. At meals, sitting in Paris bistros, she dutifully laced her fingers with his and despised him for the readiness with which he responded.

Then they rented a car and drove to Brittany, which was a wild place, wet and reeking in the countryside, prim and dusty in the towns. Through the windshield of the little white Peugeot they watched clouds pile themselves above along rises of land – clouds sooty brown and curled at the edges like soufflés set out on platters of air. It was beautiful; she forced herself to admit it. The sun that fell on the slaty rooftops seemed an older, wiser cousin of the American sun. In the country its pale light fell through the green lace of branches onto narrow fields of mustard and clover, and the shadows brought to mind the blue, intricate pattern of a cloisonné vase in their bedroom at home, a wedding gift from Dr. and Mrs. Middleton; when Brenda mentioned this to Jack, he nodded, as though the same thought had occurred to him simultaneously.

The eiderdowns in the chilly hotels smelled of mildew; the beds were cold and tipped towards the centre, causing them to cling to their separate sides, divided by Jack's respect for her terrible grief and by her failure to admit to him that she no longer loved him.

The food was extraordinary. Brenda, who had never eaten kidneys in her life, couldn't get over the delicacy of veal kidney flamed in cognac and served with mustard sauce; she ordered it three nights in a row, and Jack sat across from her, watching this indulgence with hope.

One day, on a narrow back road solidly hedged with green, their Michelin guidebook directed them to a small humped country church made of moss-green stone. It had rounded windows, very small and high up, and a thick oak door which swung open to a damp cave of darkness. But when they dropped a one-franc piece into a metal box, an electric light snapped on, revealing for three ticking minutes an ancient painting on wood over the altar: a scene of villagers in medieval dress, their bodies healthy and rounded with thankfulness. These people were carrying baskets of fruit and vegetables into a church, and, astonishingly, the church in the picture was *this* church – the church they stood in, only when it was new. The roof was a painted square of clean, yellow thatch; the walls were built of newly quarried whitish stone; the sky was fresh and alert; and the slightly elevated ground around the church looked newly levelled and surrealistically aglow.

When the electric light clicked off, they were left again in darkness, but now the darkness pulsated with colours. Brenda could see the arched roof of the church with its graceful timber-beams, the smoky stone of the old walls, and, beside her, the framed whiteness of Jack's face. She dared to put her arms around him, and they both, as though given permission, began to cry, it seemed to Brenda that at that moment they were one person, one body.

Her long nightmare, the loss of love, had inexplicably dissolved. Love was restored, for whatever reason. Jack, perhaps, was persuaded that the grieving process had come to its natural end – and perhaps it had, for Brenda was never able to unwind completely the complicated strands of that winter's despair. Looking back, it seemed to her to be a time of illness; she had been assailed by a freak visitation, and preserved the knowledge that it could happen again.

She thought of sharing this revelation with Barry. It would in a sense help right the imbalance between them: his unfortunate life and her lucky one.

She decided against it, if for no other reason than that it seemed a betrayal to pronounce aloud what had been resolved in silence. 'We've been fairly lucky, yes,' she was able to tell Barry Ollershaw, gazing across at the crease in his trousers, transfixed by the polished toes of his black oxfords.

'Well then,' he said, a little shortly, 'you've been exceptionally fortunate.'

To be kind she added, 'Of course, there've been ups and downs.'

'Of course.' He touched her hair.

There was a short silence, and then she asked, 'What time does your plane go on Thursday?'

'You mean Wednesday. Tomorrow.'

'Wednesday? You're going to be here until Thursday, aren't you? Aren't you?'

'I'm going to Montreal from here. I thought I told you, Brenda. I'm sure I told you. Tomorrow afternoon, around two.'

She sat back, dazed. 'You did tell me, but – I just assumed – I mean, the banquet for the metallurgists is tomorrow night, isn't it? And I just assumed – '

Barry was talking, moving around the room, making himself another drink, saying something about meetings and a government contract, people to see in Ottawa, an appointment hastily arranged and with great difficulty.

She shook her head in disbelief. 'I'm just surprised,' she said. 'I just took it for granted; I just assumed.'

Chapter Twenty-Eight

THEY DECIDED TO GO FOR A WALK SINCE THE EVENING HAD turned mild. Barry wore his tweed sports-jacket with a turtleneck sweater underneath, and lent Brenda his fleece-lined overcoat, which, except for the slightly too-long sleeves, fit fairly well. She expressed surprise. 'It fits,' she said, turning in front of the mirror.

'I suppose . . . ' he paused for effect, 'I suppose that . . . what's his name . . . '

'Jack.' She smiled broadly.

'I suppose *Jack* is a mountain of a man.'

'Yes,' she said, though Jack was just a fraction over six feet. 'A veritable tower.' She indicated with her arms.

'A bull moose out of the Chicago suburbs. What luck!' And they both laughed.

We're laughing at Jack, Brenda thought, flicked by the injustice of it. Jack who was absent and innocent and who had done nothing to deserve ridicule – poor Jack, transformed into an oversized oaf. How could they do it to him? How could *she* do it?

They walked along gravely, arms linked, down the lit-up city streets, pacing themselves, peering into store windows at displays of perfume, jewellery, books, fresh fruit, bottles of wine, women's dresses, shoes, furniture.

They stopped at one window to look at an arrangement of living-room furniture that included an expensive checked sofa, a glass-topped end table with trim brass legs, a stone-ware lamp with a wide, pleated shade, and an imitation fire flaring in an imitation fireplace. 'Nice,' Barry said. 'Let's buy it.'

'Let's,' Brenda said. 'But can we afford it?'

'We'll buy it on time, dearest.'

'But we've never done that before.'

'It's time we joined the twentieth century then, don't you think?'

'In that case – ' Brenda said.

At a dimly lit place called The Cheesecake Café, they sat at a table by the window and ordered cups of coffee with whipped cream and ground ginger. 'Lovely,' Brenda said, glancing around in the darkness at the clean, cool, marble tables and the iron chairs. The cafe was filled mostly with young couples with quiet, oval faces, at peace with the reflected gleam of tiny hurricane lamps. At the table next to theirs, two young men played chess, and Brenda could hear a fragment of their conversation, which was, 'It may seem cruel but – '

Barry leaned toward her and asked a question, but his words were drowned out by the sudden sound of a siren in the street outside.

'Pardon?' she said, and picked up her coffee cup. A fire engine came clanging by.

Barry mouthed something back which might have been anything. A second fire engine rushed past; Brenda saw the long, red gleam of its sides flash across the length of the café window.

'It must be a big fire,' she said into the suddenly clamorous air. People were pushing back chairs, getting up from their tables and crowding at the window. From outside on the sidewalk there came the sound of people yelling and running on the pavement. The cashier at the front of the café, a pretty young woman in a long skirt, stepped outside a minute, then came back in hugging her sides against the cold. 'It's the Franklin Court,' she announced in a clear, carrying voice that seemed both shaken and relieved.

Brenda gasped and reached for her coat.

'Let's go,' Barry said.

'Yes.' She was doing up the large buttons.

It was only three blocks, and they ran most of the way, dodging crowds of people as they went. The loose, heavy overcoat swished against Brenda's boots, dragging her down.

'Watch out for the ice,' Barry called.

'We're almost there. Isn't it around the next corner?'

'I think so. There's the furniture store we were looking in.'

'I don't smell any smoke, do you?'

'There it is.'

'Look at them all.'

'Good God.'

'I don't believe it.'

The sidewalk and street outside the Franklin was entirely filled with people.

But how orderly they look, Brenda thought, hundreds of people breathing out balloons of frosty air, speaking to each other in quiet tones, calmly stamping their cold feet on the pavement. A chain of police kept the area in front of the main door clear.

'Probably a false alarm,' someone told Brenda and Barry.

'Maybe even a fire drill, though you'd think – '

'Well, you never know. It could be a bomb scare. Large Irish population in Philadelphia.'

'They've got everyone out anyway, at least they think so. You got to give them credit.'

'Someone just having a good time, had one too many probably, got carried away.'

'Conventions – '

'I was sure I smelled smoke. Didn't you say you smelled smoke? You said – '

'We had to use the stairs for crissake. They wouldn't let us use the goddam elevators. Fifteen floors, all on foot – '

'The cables in elevators – '

'That's right. I read something about that in – '

'Could be arson. Like in Vegas.'

'Yeah, but where's the smoke? You see any flames shooting out? It's a false alarm, I'd put my money on it.'

'I just heard the cop over there say it's a wastebasket fire. One of the top floors.'

'Twenty-eighth floor, that's what I heard. Is that what you heard?'

'Did I ever tell you about the time I was at Cub camp and our tent caught fire?'

'You were a Cub Scout? Now I find that hard to picture.'

'One of the counsellors crawled in for a smoke and set the groundsheet on fire. We never squealed on him, though; we loved that guy. I saw him about a year ago. He's a circuit judge in upstate New York. Still a good guy. And I couldn't help noticing he still smokes Winstons.'

'Are you sure? Just a wastebasket?'

'Sort of an anticlimax. Why is it that every time something exciting happens, it turns out to be a wastebasket on fire. Metaphorically speaking.'

'Jesus, you mean they got us all out here for – ?'

'Just be thankful – '

'Is it out? I mean really out?'

'It must be. They're coming out now, the firemen. Look over there, behind that policeman.'

'Boy, they must be teed off, three trucks out and just because some dodo set fire to his wastebasket.'

'Getting all these people out – '

'Lucky it wasn't in the middle of the night. What a panic if we'd had to get out in the middle of the night.'

'Remember that fire on Long Island that time – '

'That was a real fire.'

'People jumping – '

'A wastebasket. Jesus Christ.'

'That's it, folks.'

'Hey, they're letting them back in up there.'

'Hurry up, I'm freezing.'

'Here, take this coat, why didn't you say so, for Pete's sake. You just got over that crummy cold – '

'I'm all right. You worry too much, that's your trouble.'

'It's my prerogative to worry.'

'Take it easy, folks, take it easy.'

'Will you look at that line-up for the elevators.'

'We'll never get in. We'll be here till midnight.'

'Want to walk up?'

'Fifteen floors. You got to be kidding.'

'Probably do you good – burn off a few – '

'No thanks. And I mean no thanks.'

'Wait'll the kids hear we walked up fifteen floors.'

'Do you want to walk up?' Brenda asked Barry.

'Twenty-four floors? We might as well; we're never going to get up any other way.'

They found the stairwell filled with people, climbing, puffing, leaning on the railing, moaning obscenities, calling encouragement. The cinderblock walls rang with noise. Brenda was reminded of certain spontaneous Elm Park parties she'd attended – all this gaiety, all this celebratory good-nature and exertion.

She and Barry rested on the eleventh floor, sitting on the far edge of the steps while people thronged past them. They rested again on the twentieth. 'I'm not going to be able to walk tomorrow,' Brenda said, and rubbed the back of her legs.

They leaned on each other, laughing. They were still laughing when they opened the door to Brenda's room and discovered a man and a woman standing by the window still in their coats, their hands joined. The man looked heavy, startled, but motioned broadly at them like a genial host. The woman smiled a wide welcome. She had a lively face, a red mouth, long untidy blonde hair. 'So,' she cried, 'we meet at last.'

Where have I seen this face? Brenda asked herself. But no, the smiling face was the face of a stranger. It was the coat that was familiar.

'How do you do,' the woman said, coming forward, her arm out. 'I'm Verna.'

Brenda for a minute couldn't think of anything to say except, 'I think that's my coat you're wearing.'

Chapter Twenty-Nine

STORTON McCORMICK IS A MAN WITH GOOD EASTERN MANNERS and a well-fitted suit that is so dark it's almost black. He speaks resonantly, like a radio announcer: 'Barry Ollershaw, I know that name, of course. You're from Canada, right? And Mrs. Bowman, so nice to meet you, sit down, both of you.'

Verna is all apologies. She takes Brenda aside and says, 'You must think I'm a thief, walking off with your coat like that. But there it was, hanging there in Stort's room, and we had had such a fabulous night, a colossal night, and in the morning Stort said to me, let's go out there and roll around in the snow. Not literally, of course. Well! Then, on Monday morning he got a call from his office – some kind of emergency – so he said, come to New York. So I said, why not? I've spent my whole life saying no to things. A Catholic girlhood, Baltimore, nuns. We took the train. Wonderful. More than wonderful. I can't believe I've known this man for only, what? Three days, well, four if you count today. We met on the elevator, can you imagine? Awfully corny, but – '

'I've got your blue ribbon,' Brenda tells her. 'You won first prize, did you know?'

Verna gives a shriek, twirls like a gypsy, then unzips her blue-and-red case and takes out a bottle of bourbon. 'I travel equipped for celebrations. I never want to miss out on another celebration, never. I've missed too many of those.'

They find four glasses. 'Here's to the quiltmakers of the world,' says Storton McCormick.

'Here's to the International Society of whatever-they're-called,' says Verna, clinking her glass with Brenda's.

'Here's to us,' says Brenda.

'To us,' Barry says, rising to his feet. 'To this night.'

For most of the night the two of them stayed awake talking in Barry's room. (It was decided after a single round of bourbon

191

and water that Verna and Stort should remain where they were for the night.)

Should they share a bed? They discussed it, first lightly, then solemnly, then lightly again. They ordered a tray of sandwiches and coffee and got undressed.

'This ridiculous nightgown – ' Brenda said, and made a face.

'What about these?' Barry pulled at his pyjamas. Beige with brown piping. 'Christ!'

'I suppose that Verna must think we've been – '

'I'm sure she does.'

'The trouble is I can't disconnect,' Brenda said. 'I don't mean just marriage vows. I mean my whole life.'

Barry reached for another sandwich and said in a grave voice, 'You mean the philosophy of living for today isn't yours.'

'It's such a cliché. Someone goes away for a week, and what happens? It's so predictable. And I hate to think that just because a thing is possible, it has to be done.'

Barry smiling, asked if she was in the habit of resisting the possible.

'Not usually.' She had taken off her slippers and was lying flat on the bed. 'But when Verna said that about not wanting to miss any celebrations – '

'Yes?'

'When I heard her say that, that's when I realized I'd already decided – I don't know when, but a long time ago – that I *was* going to miss a few. That I was prepared to miss a few.'

'That sounds rather stoic,' Barry said after a minute. He too was stretched out on his back, but on the other bed. 'It also sounds a little resigned.'

'I'm glad you didn't say puritanical at least.'

'Not that. No, I wouldn't think that.'

'Of course it makes it easier that I got my period this morning.'

He was in a mood to talk. It was two o'clock; the room was in darkness; he was all candour. The fact was, he told Brenda, he wasn't much good as an adulterer. It didn't come easily; it would take time. At first there was a brief affair with a secretary in his office. Then with a divorced family friend. Then a woman who was quite a lot younger. He met her playing golf. He despises himself in the role of pursuer – the one who must telephone, make pleasing arrangements, bring tokens. He has been, in the last couple of years, through scenes of almost adolescent awkwardness, absurd fumblings. He is, he supposes, what is called today a lousy fuck. Probably he was married too long to one woman.

'I know,' Brenda said, not really knowing, but thinking of the privateness of sex.

Another thing, Barry went on, was discovering that there are just so many ways for human flesh to meet human flesh. And only so many degrees of loneliness that can be banished by an hour of ecstasy in a double bed.

Brenda decided, after all, to tell Barry about the year she stopped loving Jack, and about their trip to Brittany. He listened in silence, then said in a puzzled voice, 'I suppose it was one of those catalytic moments. Completely irrational, but difficult to deny.'

'Have you ever felt like that?' Brenda turned her head to see him. 'The world turned suddenly orderly and neat as a pin.'

'A transcendental moment? Yes, I think so, but not often.'

'I don't think it happens very often. At least not to two people at the same time.'

'No,' he agreed. 'It hardly every happens like that.'

They talked at length about Barry's wife, Ruth; would she recover? And what would happen to their marriage if she didn't? 'We've taken too many strips off each other,' he told Brenda. 'We're like a pair of cripples. But in an odd way we still depend on each other. That's the ultimate insanity, that we do.'

'You can't live with just that. It's not enough,' Brenda said.

But he surprised her by protesting, 'It's not that bad really. I've probably exaggerated. There are good days. We have breakfast together, and when it's clear we can see right down to the bay. It's just – '

'Just what?'

'Just that we were twenty-two when we were married. That's what we gave each other. Our whole lives. Bodies that were still young. You can't do that a second time.'

'No,' Brenda said, 'you can't.'

'Are you tired?' he asked after a long silence.

'Yes.' Then, 'Can you sleep?'

'I don't think so.' Another silence. 'I think I could if I could just hold you for a minute. Unless,' his tone was light, 'unless that would make you technically unfaithful.'

Such an easy thing to give, comfort. (It would have been an act of unfaithfulness to withhold comfort – that was what she always told herself later.) She moved between the beds and slipped in beside him. His arms, encircling the copious pink flannel, felt sinewy and warm; there was something familiar about this heat, even something familiar about the odour of his body. His legs fit against hers, and the denser flesh of his penis stirred for a moment against her thigh. She felt herself grow luminous, transparent.

Sleep came to both of them almost at once, but Brenda, half-conscious, had a momentary vision of the colours and passions of the world, steep streets leading out of old cities, the cool orbits of planets. Old age would come, but not, she hoped, regret.

They woke only once, when they moved apart in sleep and shifted into different positions. His lips brushed her ear, saying something which sounded like, 'I do love you.'

'I love you too,' Brenda murmured back, and from the spiralling shell of profound sleep, it seemed to her that what they were saying was at least partly true.

Chapter Thirty

Last year when Jack and Brenda went to San Francisco for the National Historical Society meeting, their plane circled over the bay area for several minutes in a holding pattern, then made a brief descent through sparkling air onto the baked runway. The landing was routine, smooth as glass after the first mild jolt, but for some reason the passengers broke into spontaneous applause the instant the wheels touched down.

Brenda looked sideways at Jack: why this applause? He made a gesture with his hand – a gesture that said, Who knows? Who can explain such things?

A single passenger perhaps, feeling euphoric after a good lunch, might have clapped his hands and started a chain reaction; the others would have joined in out of simple obedience and good nature. Why not? Weren't they thankful to be here in the white California daylight? The lipsticked stewardess, smiling in the aisle, seemed suddenly a gift from God, as worthy as the gift of providence, the gift of good health. Why not, in the burst of affection that binds fellow travellers at the end of a journey, give thanks for the solid earth?

In contrast, Brenda's landing at O'Hare on Thursday evening was brisk and without ceremony. The plane had not even reached a full stop when businessmen turned in their seats and began reaching down for their briefcases. The scent of leather and wet raincoats grew strong. Home. Safety. The seatbelts unbuckled. Brenda pulled on her coat. A slice of dark, industrial Chicago sky showed itself at the window, oily and dense and slashed by searchlights. Across the sheen of the runway, less than two hundred yards away, another jet was lifting off, and it seemed to Brenda that the twinkling taillights boasted of a more exotic destiny, Marrakesh, Bombay, God only knows where else.

She was home. She buttoned her coat and tied the belt. It would have to be sent to the cleaner's; besides the small stain on the collar there was a black smudge on the hem. Maybe Verna really had rolled in the snow.

Jack would be there to meet her. He would come alone, without the children, just as she always came alone to meet him after a short trip. This habit of theirs was like many of their habits, too firmly fixed to merit analysis or even thought. It must have begun out of a need to keep their reunions uncluttered, to give them time on the drive home to find their footing again.

Jack would have prepared two or three amusing stories to tell her. 'First the good news,' he would say. Separation seemed to arouse in him an obligation to be once again the amusing and diverting stranger.

The strangeness would last all the way to Elm Park. The drive, in spite of the traffic, always seemed shorter than she thought it would be. As they neared home, the streets and the houses would grow increasingly familiar, until finally they were there, turning off Euclid onto Horace Mann, which led directly to Franklin Boulevard. They would pull up in front of their house and see lights burning in every window. Rob and Laurie were careless about turning off lights, and Jack, who was also careless, would nevertheless utter a soft moan and say, 'Lit up like a Christmas tree, for Christ sake.'

She imagined opening the front door: first the vestibule, then the waxed oak trim of the front hall and the paleness of refined light filtering from the old brass ceiling fixture. In the kitchen the floor would be sticky underfoot, but someone would have attempted to sweep it. She would come quickly to the familiarity of lingering supper odours and the circle of crumbs around the toaster.

Laurie's soft body would annihilate her with love, pouncing, squeezing, clinging. Rob would hang back, the sleeves of his sweater pushed up, scrupulously clean, a comb sticking out of his back pocket. He would eye her warily for the first hour, then relax.

The four of them would have some mint tea. The box of tea-bags on the shelf, and the mugs too, would declare themselves objects with an existence of their own, both novel and familiar. The mail would be spread on the table: bills mostly, maybe a letter from Patsy Kleinhart, who had never married – she was in Hawaii now, teaching school. There might be an invitation to a post-Christmas cocktail party or to the annual Alumni dance at DePaul, which they have never attended but always mean to.

Jack would finish his supply of diverting anecdotes and have a look at the newspaper. They might watch the news if they remembered. And then go up to bed. 'Well,' Jack would say, his arms around her, 'tell me all about it.'

They might lie awake for an hour or more talking. She would tell him about Verna of Virginia, who was coming to Chicago in April for a one-woman show at the Calico Gallery on Dearborn. She would tell him she has been asked to be one of the judges of the Novelty Quilts Division for next year's exhibition. Next year the meeting will be in Charleston, South Carolina; the hotel has already been booked; a woman she met from New Mexico has been elected to the executive. Jack will be interested in all these things – though Brenda knows what he really means when he says to her, 'Tell me all about it.' He is like his father, who, every Sunday morning when they arrive for breakfast, says, 'Well, kids, what's new?'

What's new, Grandpa Bowman asks, as though he is frantic for news, when all the while he wants to be told that there is no news, that no calamity has overtaken them in the seven days since he's seen them last. He wants to hear of the things which are continuing and already tested, and Jack, his son, is adept at knowing what can and what can't be told. His father does not want revelations; he does not want them to open every last cell in their bodies for him.

'I've missed you,' Brenda will say to Jack in the dark, knowing he needs to hear this and knowing also that it's true. 'I missed you terribly,' he will say, and then ask her if she's remembered to lock the bedroom door. Yes, she will say, readying her body for tenderness.

At this hour she occasionally feels the return of her younger self, the Brenda of old – serene, unruffled, uncritical, untouched by darkness or death or complex angers – a self that is curiously, childishly brave. The visitation is usually short in duration, but cordial. Brenda, older, less happy, but unconquerably sane, greets her old ally and merges with her briefly. Then, in the minutes before true sleep comes, she lets go, and drifts away on her own.

197

All Fourth Estate books are available from your local bookshop.

For a monthly update on Fourth Estate's latest releases, with interviews, extracts, competitions and special offers visit **www.4thestate.com**

Or visit
www.4thestate.com/readingroom
for the very latest reading guides on our bestselling authors, including Michael Chabon, Annie Proulx, Lorna Sage, Carol Shields.

London · New York